Russ & Kathy,

THE TITLE "MANY A MOON"
IS APPROPRIATE, BECAUSE AS
YOU KNOW VERY WELL, IT TOOK
"MANY A MOON" TO WRITE IT!
THANKS FOR YOUR FRIENDSHIP!
UNDER HIS MERCY & GRACE,

Jeff Brooks

Many a Moon

Jennifer Brooks

WESTBOW
PRESS®
A DIVISION OF THOMAS NELSON
& ZONDERVAN

WestBow Press books may be ordered through booksellers or by contacting:

WestBow Press
A Division of Thomas Nelson & Zondervan
1663 Liberty Drive
Bloomington, IN 47403
www.westbowpress.com
1 (866) 928-1240

Scripture taken from the King James Version of the Bible.

ISBN: 978-1-9736-9813-5 (sc)
ISBN: 978-1-9736-9812-8 (e)

Print information available on the last page.

WestBow Press rev. date: 08/12/2020

To:
Those who came before and those to come after.

Special thanks to my husband, Gary, whose wisdom, love and patience I would be lost without.

Contents

Prologue

I remember, even as a young person, always enjoying stories of my family roots being told over the years. My mom, Beatrice (Beatie), would talk about how as a little girl she read her favorite book, *"A Girl of the Limberlost"*, by lantern light because they had no electricity. She used an outhouse, had no indoor running water and slept three or four to a bed with her sisters to stay warm on cold winter nights. I looked forward to family reunions in the Alanson Village Park and reminiscing with my many aunts, uncles and cousins. And of course, I loved it when we would gather around the piano and Gramma or Aunt Joie would pound out that lively ragtime music, and everyone would sing in loud harmony as we children danced around the room. We were tied by a common bond: we were family.

A few years ago my children gave me a DNA test kit for Christmas, and I was so excited to get the results to find out "who I was". As I began to pursue the deeper details of my ancestry, I found it all to be fascinating - names and dates of when and where people were born, who they married, where they lived, when they died. I could see them in my mind's eye. These were real people who walked the earth through the events of history surrounding them.

Sharing with my children the exciting news of ancient ancestors arriving from England or the historic significance of girdling trees proved to be a disappointment. Their eyes would glaze over, and their heads would nod in patronizing interest. And who could blame them?! Hearing about people who have been dead, in some cases for hundreds of years, is like... well, it's like being asked to get excited about skeletons. And who wants to spend much time contemplating skeletons? But what if you knew some of the details and circumstances pertaining to those skeletons? What if you knew their story? Who were they really? What was it like to live in that time? What historical events affected them? Did they live a good life? Did they have faith? What motivated them? And not just when they died, but how? Thus, my incentive to take my "family skeletons" and try and put some flesh on the bones and bring them to life.

So that is what you are holding in your hands. If you find it to be even half as interesting and intriguing as I have, I will consider my efforts a success!

Jennifer

Genealogical Timeline

1. Rev. John Greenwood, b. 1556, Heptonstall, England, d. 4-6-1593, Tyburn, England
   m. 1584 - Isabella Greenwood (b. Lea), b. 4-17-1555, Halifax, Yorkshire, d. ABT. 1595.

2. Abel Greenwood (*John*), b. 10-1585, Heptonstall, England, d. 1623, m. 1601- Reading, England - Elizabeth Greenwood (b. Mitchell), b. 1-1588, Halifax, England, d.1670.
   Elizabeth's Parents: John Mitchell 1562-? - Tryphenia Mitchell (b. Buckland) 1567-?

3. Thomas Greenwood (*John, Abel*), b. ABT. 1610 or 1617, Heptonstall, England, d.?
   Discrepancy as to dates and location of death, as well as marriage. Elizabeth Hurd 1613-1693 and/or Sarah Sutcliffe 1620-?

4. Thomas Greenwood (*John, Abel, Thomas*), b. 6-4-1643, Heptonstall, England,
   d. 9-1-1693, Newton, MA. Bay Colony, m. 6-8-1670, Newton, MA. Bay Colony - Hannah Greenwood (b. Ward), b. ABT 1650, Newton, MA. Bay Colony, d. 1686, Newton, MA. Bay Colony.
   Hannah's Parent's: John Ward,1626-1708 - Hannah Ward (b. Jackson) 1634-1704.

5. Rev. Thomas Greenwood (*John, Abel, Thomas, Thomas*), b. 7-15-1673, Newton, MA. Bay Colony, d. 9-8-1720, Rehoboth, * MA. Bay Colony, m. 12-28-1693 - Elizabeth Greenwood (b. Wiswall), b. 9-20-1668, Newton, MA. Bay, d. 1-24-1736, Norfolk, MA. Bay Colony.

Elizabeth's Parents: <u>Noah Wiswall Sr</u>, 1638-1690 - <u>Theodosia Wiswall</u> <u>(b. Jackson)</u> 1643-1725.

6. <u>Rev. John Greenwood</u> (*John, Abel, Thomas, Thomas, Thomas*), b. 5-20-1697, Rehoboth, MA. Bay Colony, d. 12-1-1766, Rehoboth, Province of MA. Bay, m. 4-22-1721- <u>Lydia Greenwood (b. Holmes)</u>, b. 11-19-1696, Boston, MA. Bay Colony, d. 9-8-1757, Rehoboth, Province of MA. Bay.
    Lydia's Parents: <u>Nathaniel Holmes</u>, 1664-1711 - <u>Sarah Holmes (b.</u> <u>Thaxter)</u>, 1671-1726.

7. <u>Sarah Sheldon (b. Greenwood)</u>, (*John, Abel, Thomas, Thomas, Thomas, John*),
    b. 3-26-1725, Rehoboth, Province of MA. Bay, d. 5-24-1763, m. 5-4-1745, Rehoboth, Province of MA. Bay, <u>Rev. Benjamin Sheldon</u>, b. 2-12-1720, Providence, Rhode Island, d. 12-31-1781, Tiverton, Rhode Island.
    Benjamin's Parents (b. Pawtuxet, R.I.): <u>Timothy Sheldon</u> 1689-1741 - <u>Rebecca Sheldon (b. Carr)</u>, 1692-1760.
    Timothy's Parents (b. Pawtuxet, R.I.): <u>Timothy Sheldon</u> 1661-1744 - <u>Sarah Sheldon</u> (b. <u>Balcom</u>), 1663-1744.
    Timothy's Parents: <u>John Sheldon</u> (of Providence), ABT. 1628-1708, m. 4-27-1660, Providence, <u>Joan Sheldon (b. Vincent)</u> b. 1632, Nettlecombe, Somerset, England, d. 1704, Pawtuxet, Providence, R.I.

8. <u>Jonathan Sheldon</u> (*John, Abel, Thomas, Thomas, Thomas, John, Sarah/ Benjamin Sheldon*) b. 2-16-1749, Rehoboth, MA. Bay, d. 8-8-1835, Trumbull County, OH, m. Mary Sheldon (b. Durfey), 1752-1790. m. <u>Priscilla Sheldon (b. Manchester)</u>, ABT 1791, b. 7-13-1760, Little Compton, R.I, d. 8-19-1847, Fowler, OH.
    Priscilla's Parents: <u>William Manchester</u>, 1734-1797 - <u>Mary Manchester</u> <u>(b. Irish)</u>, 1734-1790.

9. <u>Jonathan Sheldon</u> (*John, Abel, Thomas, Thomas, Thomas, John, Sarah/ Benjamin Sheldon, Jonathan*) b. 6-16-1797, Tolland, MA, d. 6-1-1871, Fowler, Trumbull Co, OH,

m. 4-4-1830, <u>Martha Patricia "Patty" Sheldon (b. Shipman)</u>, b. 4-23-1807, Hartford, CT, d. 11-4-1883, Fowler, OH.

Patty's Parents: <u>David Shipman</u> 1762-1835 - <u>Tabitha Shipman (b. Meacham)</u> 1765-1833.

10. <u>Chauncey Sheldon</u> (*John, Abel, Thomas, Thomas, Thomas, John, Sarah/Benjamin Sheldon, Jonathan, Jonathan*) b. 4-11-1831, Fowler, OH, d. 1882, Fowler, OH, m. 10-19-1854, Trumbull Co, <u>Harriet Sheldon (b. Trumbull)</u>, b. 7-6-1834, MA, d. 5-15-1884, Trumbull Co.

Harriet's Parents: Not Known.

11. <u>Charles Robinson Sheldon</u> (*John, Abel, Thomas, Thomas, Thomas, John, Sarah/Benjamin Sheldon, Jonathan, Jonathan, Chauncey*) b. 3-15-1861, Fowler, OH, d. 6-12-1924, Toledo, OH, m. <u>Ella Viola Sheldon (b.Boyd)</u>,12-12-1881, Trumbull Co, OH,, b. 4-1862, OH. d. ABT, Littlefield Twp. Emmet Co. MI.

Ella's Parents: <u>James Boyd</u> m. 4-24-1861 - <u>Jane Boyd (b. Howe)</u> 1840-?

12. <u>Leslie Lester Sheldon</u> (*John, Abel, Thomas, Thomas, Thomas, John, Sarah/Benjamin Sheldon, Jonathan, Jonathan, Chauncey, Charles*), b. 1-11-1898, Alanson, MI, d. 12-30-1967, Petoskey, MI, m. 6-27-1918, Petoskey, MI - <u>Gladys Louise Sheldon (b. Dodge)</u>, b. 6-28-1893, d. 7-28-1996, Petoskey, MI.

Gladys' Parents: <u>Melanchthon "Lank" Washington Dodge</u> 1871-1948, m. 10-29-1891 - <u>Julina Percilla Dodge</u> (b. Davis) b. 5-6-1873, Ada, OH, d. 5-10-1919, Toledo, OH.

Lank's Parents: <u>Reuben Dodge</u> 1832-1920, m. 7-1-1856 - <u>Lucy "Anna" Ann Davis (b. Shaffer)</u>.

Julina's Parents: <u>William Washington Davis</u> 1830-1911, m. 12-30-1852 - <u>Sarah Davis (b. Wingate)</u> 1832-1917.

*A boundary dispute between MA Bay Colony and Plymouth Colony persisted for many years concerning Rehoboth. A new charter was issued in 1691 joining the colonies as the Province of Massachusetts.

1

John Greenwood and Isabella Lea

1550's

Isabella sank to her knees when the news arrived. She never really believed that he would be hanged. Her prayers had been the faithful and fervent pleadings of a loving wife. Now, she was truly alone to raise their eight-year-old son. Her heart ached, yet somehow, she also felt a profound peace. Even in her loss, she knew God's comforting hand. Even as she contemplated how she would tell Abel that his father had died, she knew that her prayers did not fall on the deaf ears of a distant God.

Abel was still sleeping. Having had a fitful night with a slight fever and a raspy cough, she had decided to let him sleep for another few hours. A light snowfall from the night before was just beginning to melt in the Calder Valley and the promise of spring was in the crisp morning air. *"April, the month* of new beginnings. *God be with us," she* prayed aloud. Looking out the large front window, she watched the darkness fade and the cobblestone street below brighten with the sun, as the shadows of neighboring buildings crept away.

She was grateful for the glass. It was an inexpensive quality, with a muted opaqueness, including bubble tracks, which she knew by heart. It gave light to the room and relaxed her eyes from the strain of working the loom. Heptonstall, [1] a sleepy village built on a steep hill in West Yorkshire, far from London. Another world away.

Heptonstall would appear bleak to some. Quaint cottages and terraced houses lined the narrow streets. This was high country with a sense of wildness surrounding the civilized structures of this serene village and, of course, St. Thomas a Becket church. Rocky streams, secret waterfalls and the rise of lush green hills dipping into wide valleys meandered in every direction. The unsettled softness of deep silhouettes moving with the sun mesmerized Isabella as she watched the world awaken. Both she and John had been born here. It was home. Yet she knew that she was a stranger in a foreign land.

The Greenwood name was well known. All one had to do was visit the old cemetery to see the name ceremoniously enscripted hither and yon on stone markers. The cemetery set next to the church, built in 1260 and named for Thomas a Becket, the Archduke of Canterbury, a priest who was murdered in 1170 over a conflict regarding church rights with King Henry II. Thomas was later venerated as a saint by the Catholic Church and by the Church of England.

St. Thomas a Becket Church, as the Established Protestant Church of England, had been the center of life for both John and Isabella. The vestments, the signs of the cross, the Book of Common Prayer, priests and the sacraments were familiar and accepted. It was where they had been christened as babies and where Abel would have been christened [2], had time and circumstances permitted. Her mind once again pondered her sweet son and his future. He never really knew his father. John had been imprisoned less than a year after Abel was born, and thus, her son held an uncluttered love and admiration for his father. [3]

John Greenwood was a zealous and influential man. From the time they were children, Isabella remembered how his staunch convictions in all types of matters, but especially faith, would toss him into the throws of controversy and sometimes blows. Belief was the center of significant and violent conflict in most every realm of life, even among school age children. [4]

Queen Elizabeth I, a Protestant, had come to power in 1558, two years after John Greenwood was born. She inherited the intricacies created by the monarchy of her father Henry VIII, a Catholic, who had severed the link between the Church of England and Rome in 1533, but never permitted the renunciation of Catholic doctrine or ceremony. Religious and political ideals collided on many fronts.

The Reformation in Europe began in 1517, at the time Martin Luther published his Ninety-Five Theses. It had been the initial catalyst that sparked division and war in the determined efforts to purify the Catholic Church across Europe.[5] England remained staunchly in support of Rome until The Act of Supremacy was ultimately passed in 1540 by Parliament, allowing Henry VIII to divorce his Queen and marry Anne Boleyn, Elizabeth's mother.

In his prime, Henry VIII was regarded as a most attractive and accomplished king and was described as, *"one of the most charismatic rulers to sit on the English throne."* However, time changes a man, especially a man with unchecked passions. Although Henry VIII was indeed a Catholic, his own passionate and reprehensible desires led him to not only break his ties with the Pope, but eventually execute two of his six wives, and indulge himself into obscene obesity, which contributed to the death of this lustful, egotistical and insecure king in 1547.

Elizabeth's half-brother, Edward VI, succeeded their father, Henry VIII, to the throne at the age of nine. He was the son of King Henry's third wife, Jane Seymour. The transformation of the Protestant church in England became recognizable under King Edward's short rule, who took great interest in religious matters. He brought reforms that included the abolition of clerical celibacy and Mass. When Edward fell terminally ill at age fifteen, there was tremendous apprehension throughout the realm among Protestants. Unless succession was favorable to the Protestant cause, Catholicism could return.

And indeed, it came to pass. Mary I, whose mother, Catherine of Aragon, was the divorced first wife of Henry VIII, took the throne in 1553, after young Edward's death. Mary, a staunchly devoted Catholic, began her aggressive and violent pursuit to restore Roman Catholicism in England as an attempt to reverse the English Reformation, having over 280 religious dissenters burned at the stake. Protestants denounced her as *"Bloody Mary "*. When Mary fell ill in 1558, at age forty-two, with no children, she was forced to accept that Elizabeth, her Protestant half-sister, was the lawful successor.

As the Monarch of England and Ireland, Queen Elizabeth I solidified the establishment of the Protestant Church of England, of which she became *"Supreme Governor "*. She was viewed as relatively tolerant and avoided systematic executions. However, the more radical Puritans who were pushing for far reaching reforms, were becoming an increasing threat as their teachings and practices grew greater in popularity. On May 8, 1559, the Act of Uniformity Law was implemented, making attendance at church and the use of the Book of Common Prayer compulsory. Though the penalties were not extreme, one could be imprisoned and if continued disregard ensued, deported.

The Church of England was indeed Protestant, yet many Catholic elements continued to remain. Elizabeth held those elements tightly in place, including the crucifix, The Common Book of Prayer and vestments. Puritans, seeking to purify the church from anything that was not soundly based on Scripture alone, had a "fight" on many fronts, but most notably two. First, accurate Biblical interpretation was of the highest priority, which inevitably led them to oppose both papal teaching and church traditions, putting them at great odds with authorities. Secondly, there were false teachers among their own ranks. Puritan mindset always sought truth, specifically the truth of God's Holy Word and these wilder, more radical men were of paramount concern.

> "Always watch *for the false but do not stop at that. It does not lead anywhere. The demonstration of God's spirit at work, in our attitudes and practices are of the greatest value. Shall we simply live in pride with knowledge and understanding, but be of no help to anyone else?"* [6]

John's words always burned Conviction into Isabella's heart, as she now sat alone, watching the morning break and wondering what the future held for herself and for Abel.

Isabella suddenly caught herself in her memories. She could still hear John's voice, strong and sure.

> *"I shall not hear that voice again, this side of Heaven."* she sighed.

Sipping her morning tea, she smiled in the morning solitude to remember the story of John's short life and how God had allowed her to be a part of it.

2

Growing Discontent

John Greenwood found a love of the scriptures very early in life. Isabella knew that John loved God's Word even more than he loved her. Yet this man of deep conviction and nonconformity was her man of God's own choosing. She accepted and honored the fact that his devotion was first to God, as was hers. Her own devotion was, as John would often say, *"without peer."* And from the very first th*ey* acknowledged their common bond in Christ.

Their relationship began with a festival which Isabella had decided not to attend. Heptonstall was known for its *"Hill Running"* and many men, young and old, shepherds and farmers, weavers and tanners, competed in these community races. She was eighteen years old and had witnessed many competitions as well as other sports, such as wrestling and *"throwing the hamme*r". Speed and strength, each competitor trying to outdo the other. It was always exciting, but this year, she felt entirely uninterested. As much as she had enjoyed a festival day in years past; watching these men flex and work to impress the pretty girls seemed frivolous today. She could hear the music echoing through the street and chose to forego the festivities.

Isabella often sought solitude. She loved her family, yet there were so many siblings. It was crowded with four brothers and two sisters all in various stages of need. *"I need a clean nappy." "I need water." "I need turnips." "I need shoes." "I need a wife."* She cherished the chaos, energy

5

and laughter of her family, but with so many competing voices, at times it became overwhelming. Perhaps this was why she avoided the festival; with all the competition at home, a respite was welcome.

She searched the sky for rain. Faint wispy clouds were of no threat as she wrapped a woolen shawl around her shoulders and determined a direction. Finding her way down the steep cobbled street, shuffling her feet and randomly kicking stones along the roadway, she soon found herself far from the noise and bustle of the festival. Aimlessly, she slipped over a low stone wall and veered into a grassy field. Sheep lazily grazing dotted the hillsides.

"Thank you, Lord, for the beauty and the quiet", she prayed aloud.

The field was as green as she had ever seen, and large rocks were scattered about as if dropped from the sky. Spring had come early this year.

As she absentmindedly looked up and adjusted her eyes against the brightness of the sun, there sat a figure in the field, leaning against a large stone, reading a book. He was perfectly motionless and although it must have been obvious that she, an intruder, was so nearby, he did not lift his head or acknowledge her. She cleared her throat and still he did not move. Finally, she recognized him.

"Are you to pretend that you do not see me, John Greenwood?"

He gave a quiet, short laugh. She felt irritated.

"Do you mock me or simply find me to be so entertaining?"

Even she was surprised at her forwardness. He lifted his head.

"Isabella Lea, you walk with the stealth of a stampeding sheep herd. Of course, I see you, and I do not mock you, I'm simply surprised to find you wandering this field rather than enjoying the games in the village."

She was unsure of what to say next. One part of her wished to address the unveiled insult, although she knew it to be in jest. Her thought was to respond as to why she wasn't at the games like everyone else. Thinking better of the two, she replied,

> *"And you, John Greenwood, why do I find you slumped over, reading a book at mid-day, while competitions are going on down below?"*

The slight was clear. Was he not a man to be competing for accolades of strength and speed? He ignored the implication.

> *"Sometimes I seek solitude."*

She understood that. He was a kindred spirit. He invited her to sit, and when she did, she saw a manuscript of the New Testament. She marveled that he had it, yet it did not surprise her. She had heard that he was leaving for Corpus Christi College at Cambridge University, where he would enroll as a theology student. Everyone knew that he was intelligent, and of his passion for the Church. He was twenty-one years old, and he knew who he was and what he wanted to do with his life. That impressed Isabella so much more than a muscle-bound shepherd who could throw a hammer or win a wrestling match. But she kept her admiration for John Greenwood to herself, as John tentatively asked,

> *"Would you care if I read aloud?"*
> *"No, I mind not at all. Please."*

As John read to her from the Epistle of Romans, she closed her eyes and soaked in the warmth of words that outweighed the hot sun on the back of her neck. Never before had she realized the power in that book. God's book. In church it always felt so cold and impersonal. John's voice rang with emotion as he read,

> *"There is then no damnation to them which are in Christ Jesus, which walk not after the flesh, but after the spirit. For the law of the Spirit, which bringeth life through Jesus Christ, hath delivered me from the law of sin and death."* [1]

She looked down at the handwritten manuscript and again wondered how John had possession of such a beautiful thing.

> *"Who shall separate us from the love of God? Shall tribulation? Or persecution? Or hunger? Other peril? Other sword? As it is written: For Thy sake we are killed all day long and are counted as sheep appointed to be slain. Nevertheless, in all these things we overcome strongly through His help that loved us. Yea, and I am sure that neither death, nor life, neither angels, nor rule, neither power, neither things present, neither things to come, neither any other creature shall be able to depart us from the love of God, showed in Christ Jesus our Lord."*

John explained that William Tyndale had provided a translation in 1534, so that the common man could have the scriptures in their hands. She found herself grateful for William Tyndale. At the same time, she looked differently at John Greenwood. She had never noticed how truly pleasing he was.

3

Separatists

1577 -1586

John moved to Cambridge, entering Corpus Christi College on March 18, 1577. He and Isabella had quickly realized a love and mutual respect on that fateful spring afternoon. After much prayer and continued courtship, it became clear that marriage was soon to follow, although not a simple prospect. John had very little money and no income, other than his sizar position at the university [1], performing menial duties, acting as a servant to other more prominent students and receiving an allowance toward his college expenses. Even so, John's love for Isabella could not be thwarted and rather than risk losing her to another man by asking her to wait for him to graduate, he inquired for her hand.

Her father was amenable, trusting in John's character and prospects for his future as a priest, yet her father was also of great humor. With a twinkle in his eye, he responded,

> *"Thou may marry Isabella, but only after thou work seven years at the weaving loom. Then thou may have my precious daughter in marriage."*

Isabella burst with laughter at the deflated look on John's face.

A Future Together

John and Isabella married [2] on a warm summer morning in St. Thomas a Becket Church. Isabella loved getting to know John in all the ways that a wife has privilege. John was tall and sparse, his physique being very slender, greatly due to the fact that food was never of much concern to him. He would read and write throughout the day and never think to eat.

"Dinner be ready," Isabella would announce.

John would look up, with his hazel-brown eyes adjusting to the light, in confusion as if this were some strange and unforeseen interruption.

"In a few minutes," he would reply, always to Isabella's exasperation.

There was nothing imposing about John's physical appearance [3] and Isabella would often marvel at how he could hold people spellbound with his teaching while at the same time possess such an unassuming stature. His wavy, sandy-colored hair was already thinning, and by age thirty, grey strands were interspersed, although she doubted that anyone other than she would notice such a detail. His eyes were narrow, reflecting a forlorn intenseness that didn't truly reflect the truth about who he was, yet Isabella knew the twinkle behind those eyes.

For all of the discipline and studiousness of John Greenwood, he cherished the wife that God had given him. She was often unaware of how he would watch her busily cooking over the fire, her brown waistcoat, green woolen skirt and white linen apron spinning from the pot to the table as she stirred and mixed. He noticed her hair coming loose under her bonnet, those brown and golden strands. And when she did realize that he watched her, how he loved to see those brown eyes light up with pleasure as she teasingly scolded,

"John Greenwood, have ye nothing better to do?!"

After they married, Isabella could not return to Cambridge with John. [4] Finances simply would not allow it. She remained in Heptonstall with a distance of two hundred miles separating them. Loneliness kept her company for those three years, while his life was filled with academia and the camaraderie of other students. How she treasured those times when he could come back to her. Spending time together, walking and hearing him share all that he was learning was exciting, yet at the same time there was a foreboding dark cloud building in her heart.

While John studied with enthusiasm and poured himself into the scriptures, he was changing. Following the writings of men such as Robert Browne, [5] John was becoming more and more disillusioned with the established Church of England, which he had loved with such passion and which he had determined to serve as a priest. Spending long nights with fellow theology students debating the authority of the monarchy and the values of the ecclesiastical order, his faithful resolve to serve the Church of England began to ebb. He saw falsehoods and contradictions to the truth of scripture, especially after hearing a rousing sermon just before his graduation in 1580. [6]

With his bachelor's degree, he was ordained as a priest in The Church of England by John Almer, the Bishop of London and Thomas Cooper, the Bishop of Lincoln. He served for five years in Norfolk County where Isabella was finally able to join him. It was a trying time for her. She loved her husband, but his passionate drive to see reforms in the Church of England took him deeper and deeper into the dangerous waters of what could be considered sedition.

After five years, John was deprived of his pastoral/priestly duties. He had renounced his ordination as *"Wholly unlawful"* [7] and began holding secret religious services in the home of Lord Robert Rich [8] of Rochford, Essex County. Lord Rich was a leading political figure in the county and a powerful landlord, owning over seventy-five manors. Soon Lord Rich and a Puritan clergyman by the name of Robert Wright, who had been holding open services at Rochford Hall, were arrested and thrown into prison for insurrection. Isabella feared for her husband, and rightfully so.

By 1585, with tensions rising, Isabella and John found it best that she return to Heptonstall. [9] She was pregnant with their first child. Securing a room for herself near family and old friends, she settled back into the town she knew so well. By mid-summer Abel was born. John was not present for his son's birth, but upon hearing of his arrival he made the journey home to be with Isabella and to hold his newborn son in his arms. He could not stay but a few days before his duties required him to return.

His heart burned with anguish as he traveled back into what would be the lion's den - London.

John Greenwood's congregation was one of Puritan believers, like-minded godly people who simply sought to be taught the truth of God's Word in freedom from the strictures of the Church of England. They secretly met outside the laws of the land, and in doing so risked much. Puritans were problematic to the crown, and John Greenwood was much more than simply a Puritan. His ideas of Separatism were considered especially threatening and dangerous. He believed that the definition of "church" was a company of faithful believers separated from unbelievers and gathered in the name of Christ, whom they faithfully worship and readily obey as their only King, Priest and Prophet, and joined together as members of one body. This flew in the face of the Queen's ecclesiastical authority and was regarded as treasonous.

Independent-thinking Puritans believed that the Church of England was not altogether wrong. They did not oppose occasional attendance at services. Generally speaking, there was an ebb and flow of open thought among the Puritans with most men being willing to change their beliefs when they perceived new evidence from Scripture coming to light. However, John Greenwood was not like most men.

The failure of Protestant attempts to reshape the Church of England led Separatist Puritans to opt out altogether. Isabella was never clear as to exactly how John had been led to arrive at this most rigid conclusion, adopting the ideals of Separatism. He had become familiar with the Separatist teachings of Robert Browne who, like John, had matriculated from Corpus Christi College a few years earlier. She wondered if Browne's imprisonment (32 times) and ultimate exile from England in 1582 had fostered a deepening impact on John's passionate and unmoving convictions. Meanwhile, the London congregation continued in secret worship, meeting in the home of Henry Martin at St. Andrews.

In the winter of 1586, Isabella traveled to London with infant son Abel, hoping to finally be reunited permanently. The long journey was exhausting as they traveled the bumpy, potholed road. The final leg brought them into the thick of London. Stepping from the carriage with Abel in her arms, Isabella felt overwhelmed by the sights and sounds of the city, as people crowded the streets pushing, shoving and casting epithets of irritation and anger. Searching frantically, she finally caught the face she had longed to see. There was John with his wonderful smile, like sunshine through a shadow of darkness, emanating from his ever-gentle eyes.

London was a far cry from the serene hillsides of Heptonstall. Isabella was amazed at the sheer number of people. London was not her home, yet she was willing to make it so in order to be a family once again. She had determined that she would remain with John whatever the cost. But as the days passed into weeks, the cost was becoming all too apparent.

Upon getting settled, Isabella found an opportunity to share her heart with John. With tears streaming down her face, she confided,

> *"John, I fear your life be one of such singular devotion, there be no room for query."*

His eyes flashed and then softened, not sure at first how to respond. Choosing his words carefully, finally he spoke.

> *"My resolve is set, it is true. Every new duty God brings before me calls for more grace than I now possess. I pray that my desires be enlarged and my hopes emboldened that I may honor my beloved Lord with complete faithfulness. I ask not for man's wisdom of mind, but that my steps and desires be honoring to Christ and Christ alone. I love you, my Isabella, but my first duty is to my Savior."*

Isabella's voice choked,

> *"May God graciously expel the unbelief and despair from my heart."*

John wrapped her in his arms,

> *"May it be so, my love. May it be so."*

To her frustration, John had deemed it too unsafe, again, for her to remain with him in London. He made arrangements for her and Abel to return to Heptonstall. Isabella had grown to love sharing his life, meeting the devoted men and women of this remarkable secret church and coming to understand his heartfelt passion.

> *"I am so saddened to see these faithful people, who simply desire to worship the Lord in freedom and openness, yet hiding as common criminals,"* she commented to John.

She prepared herself and Abel for their long journey back to Heptonstall after only six short weeks of being together as a family.

The previous evening, she had attended a service. The people had greeted her with such love and acceptance, and as John prayed tears flowed down her face. His words rang out with power:

> *"Oh Lord, we come into thy holy presence to worship Thee. We come to praise thy name. Lord, thou knowest our desire for thy name to be magnified and that we be humbled before Thee. Oh God, authenticate thy Word, revive thy work in this city and beyond and lead us now by thy Spirit. In the mighty name of Jesus our Lord and Savior, Amen."* [10]

The Clink

It was 1586 and John Greenwood was now the recognized leader of the London Separatists, many of whom had been arrested numerous times. He too was soon arrested, while conducting a service in early October of that year and promptly lodged in the Clink Prison. [11]

Upon receiving the news Isabella's heart was overcome with anguish, yet at the same time flooded with relief. She shuddered to think of what would have happened to Abel had she not returned to Heptonstall and had she been arrested as well. Abel needed his mother and she knew that God's hand of grace had been on their tiny family, even as John suffered incarceration.

4

Sedition

1586-1592

Preceding John Greenwood by ten years at Cambridge was a man of marked ability by the name of Henry Barrowe. He was an ingenious and learned man, but with a much warmer spirit than that of John Greenwood. Henry was a lawyer and practiced in Her Majesty's courts. Having become interested in the teachings of John and hearing of his arrest, Henry visited him on the morning of Sunday, November 19, 1586, at the Clink. Suddenly, with no pretense of legal warrant, Henry himself was seized, arrested and thrown into the same prison cell as John.

A few days later, both were removed to Fleet Prison. [1] Their quarters were close which gave them opportunities to converse, giving each other encouragement and bolstering their faith. They were deprived of proper food, sufficient warmth and many necessities of life. [2] There they remained in confinement for seven years. But God had not abandoned them. Like the apostle Paul centuries before, they found ways to worship the Lord and spread the message of the gospel.

Many times John Greenwood and Henry Barrowe were taken before the authorities of the Established Church of England and questioned as to their beliefs. Such an examination took place almost immediately after being transferred to Fleet Prison. John Aylmer, the Bishop of London, began the questioning, [3]

"John Greenwood, do you believe in baptism?"

15

"Yes, I do believe in baptism."

John assumed that the bishop was seeking to lay a trap to condemn him even further. The bishop continued,

> *"Is it not true that you have a son, a son who is already past a year of age, and that he is unbaptized?"*

John weighed his words carefully.

> *"My son Abel is just over one year of age and is unbaptized. I have been in prison sir, and was unable to take him to a reformed church where he could be baptized according to God's ordinance."*

The bishop's face flushed with anger. John was not one to conform in the face of interrogation and threat of continued imprisonment or death.

> *"Do you consider The Church of England God's church?",* the bishop shouted with indignation and rage.

John felt God's loving hand on his shoulder as he stoically replied:

> *"No. I do not. Every congregation of Christ should be governed by a minister, teacher and elders. The authority over the church is Christ and no other. Indeed, I would excommunicate any member of the church who disobeyed the teachings of the Word of God. I would make no exception, even if it be the Prince or Queen herself."*

Then, as if that were not enough, he continued:

> *"The scriptures set down efficient laws for the worship of God and government of church which no man may add to or diminish. Her majesty is not the supreme head of the church - only Christ."* [4]

Sedition. There was no conformity, no effort on John's part to appease either the crown or the Church. John went back to prison, where he, along with Henry Barrow, continued to write controversial tracts. John was perhaps less militant than Henry, who in his 1587 treatise, *"Four Causes of Separation"*, identified four falsehoods in the Church of England as false worship, false ministry, false discipline and false membership. The hostilities of the Church toward both John and Henry burned even hotter. Both men stoutly defended Separatism, at times in an unduly belligerent manner, with rigidity and intolerance. Yet, to John Greenwood and Henry Barrowe, the scriptures were clear and defending them was paramount, no matter the cost.

Prison gave John time to continue ministry through his writing. He began his treatise against read prayers and devised liturgies, *"By John Greenwood, Christ's poor afflicted prisoner in the Fleet at London, for the truth of the gospel."* [5] As the years followed, he and Henry collaborated their writings. Denied proper writing material they were forced to use their own ingenuity, using any bits of scrap they could find to continue spreading the message for which they were willing to stake their lives. These conditions would have crushed the spirits of men of lesser fiber or inferior courage.

For seven years both John and Henry persisted in refusing to return to The Church of England. They both remained incarcerated, with only a few brief breaks for John granted to him by the prison. On one such rare occasion in 1592, John was released. Isabella and Abel travelled to London, [6] with John briefly residing with Robert Rippon in Southwark. Mr. Rippon's home was the current location at which members of the secret church held their meetings.

Abel was seven years old and had only known his father from his mother's accounts and was anxious to meet him.

"Mother, will father know who I am?"

he nervously asked as they bounced along in the carriage on the rutted road from Heptonstall to London.

"Oh, he will know you; of that you can be sure. You are the image of your father. There is no doubt you are John Greenwood's son. Yes my dear, he will know you!"

Abel giggled and snuggled closer to his mother as he continued to watch the autumn countryside roll by.

If John Greenwood's release from prison was a test, he failed. With Isabella and Abel by his side, John found great pleasure, yet he could not be content to settle into quiet conformity. The falsehoods that he saw in The Established Church of England were too egregious. He was appointed teacher and immediately the ecclesiastical bishops were alarmed and agitated at the continued spread of Separatism. Isabella begged John to pull back,

> *"There are others. Ye are faithful and have suffered so greatly, no one woul judge ye for waiting to teach and recover from such a long ordeal."*

Isabella feared what was coming if John did not set aside his teaching. She felt as though she was approaching a nightmare from which she could not escape. John would be arrested again; of this she had no doubt.

After a little more than two months in London with John, Isabella knew, once again, that she needed to return to Heptonstall with Abel. Trembling, she found it hard to breathe the cold December air as the carriage waited for her to board. John was quiet. There was a part of him that could not help but wonder if he would ever see his family again. His emotions were on edge. Isabella, smiling, finally spoke,

> *"Ye are stubborn as stone in your convictions, John Greenwood. And for that I admire ye so much, but I fear that I will one day lose ye."*

John's smile was tense and he understood the fear that was welling up inside her heart. With tenderness in his voice, he answered,

> *"Whatever shall happen, I shall bear it for the sake of Christ. I have no merit in myself. I can only allow the merit of Jesus to stand on my behalf. I can stand on nothing else, no matter the price."*

As he wrapped her in his arms, her knees buckled, and she began to sob. Holding her tightly, he tried to memorize the way her slender body felt in his arms, the smell of her hair, the sound of her soft crying. They did not know the future, but they both knew that it would be the most difficult chapter of their lives thus far.

5

Tyburn

1592-1593

Three days after Isabella's departure, on December 5, 1592, John was again arrested, this time at the home of Edward Boyse, and imprisoned at the Fleet with his friend and fellow combatant, Henry Barrowe. They were brought to trial on March 23, 1593 on charges of devising and circulating seditious books. The proof of the charges was found in the books themselves, which had been published by Holland printers while they were in prison. Sedition was founded on denying Her Majesty's ecclesiastical supremacy and attacking The Church of England. Henry Barrowe refused to recant what he had published and charged the government of The Church of England to be unlawful and anti-Christian. [1]

John confessed to the co-authorship of *"A Brief Description of the False Church"* and was interrogated by the court. While denying any attempt to incite people to rebel against the authority of the government and denying all further charges laid against them, John Greenwood and Henry Barrowe were sentenced to hang. The next morning, March 24, preparations were made for their execution. But there came a reprieve, as attempts were made once again to dissuade the pair.

John understood that the doctors and deans being sent to confer with them were simply ploys to convince them of their guilt and to prompt them to repent of their ways and renege on their beliefs. He saw no purpose in meeting with them unless it be in a public forum, which was denied. In pondering his impending execution, John reinforced his resolve.

"My heart is right with God, by His mercy alone. I have no false estimate of the whole or right of my character. I am a sinner, paying close attention to my conduct and actions as well as my motives. I can only now prevail on those who will perceive that I maintain supreme regard for a better world. I prepared my life for duty in God's service, to love Him in all His mercies, to submit to every trial, even walking in darkness. And now, I will not abandon the truth of what He has brought to my mind and heart through the scriptures. Indeed, I cannot." [2]

On March 31, 1593, preparations were again made for their execution. John and Henry were conveyed to the place of hanging in Tyburn and tied by the neck to a tree. There they were permitted to speak and began to address the accusations against them. They declared their innocence of all malice and exhorted the people to obey and love the Queen and magistrates, but to follow government and church authority only as far as Scripture would permit. However, they were once again reprieved in hope that they would ultimately recant. There was some fear that an execution could incite people toward rebellion. The ropes were removed from their necks and they were returned to prison. Attempts were made in Parliament to gain clemency, but to no avail.

Six days later, on April 6, 1593, in the pre-dawn hours of the morning, the two men were secretly taken to Tyburn and unceremoniously hanged. There was no commemoration. There were no crowds. John Greenwood, at thirty-seven years of age, would never go home to Heptonstall again.

6

Abel

Abel Greenwood [1] was more charismatic and light-spirited than his famous or infamous father, John Greenwood, depending on who you talked to. The years following his father's execution were difficult, yet life in the familiar village was one of comfortable routine. Isabella came from a family of weavers, as so many in Heptonstall did. Sheep grazing the hills provided the needed wool. Each spring the shearing would begin. Abel was a quick study and soon, through apprenticeship, could prepare, operate and maintain a loom. He and his mother rented a small room above a store on a busy street, and there they lived in relative obscurity. However, the gossip of the local busybodies never completely subsided after the shocking news of the hanging in Tyburn. The whispers lingered for years as gossipers recounted and embellished the demise of Isabella's beloved husband.

The village of Tyburn, itself being synonymous with hanging, held an eerie reputation as stories were told and retold. Two decades earlier, in 1571, the famous *"Triple Tree"* was set up to accommodate more executions on the gallows at one time. Now John Greenwood was a sorrowful part of the town's dark history. Later, in 1649, twenty-three men and one woman were hanged together as the public gawked.

Isabella [2], being only thirty-five years old when her husband was martyred for his faith, was determined to raise her son in the manner of which she knew John would desire, and within the deep conviction of faith which she herself held so dear. She refused to be tempted to converse on the details of John's death, but rather focused her heart and mind on the substance of his life. Attending St. Thomas was not an option for her. Most who knew her respected her decision, understanding her dedication to her convictions. Living so far from London made it easier to avoid legal ramifications.

By the time Abel came of age, he was well-versed in the scriptures through the steadfast teachings of his mother. Isabella created a loving and joyful home for Abel, with God at the center of their lives. Together they spent hours reading, walking, talking, praying and working side-by-side. Isabella worked hard to support herself and her son and was well respected for her abilities as an accomplished weaver. The loom became her companion and she enjoyed the hours preparing, spinning and interweaving the threads into sought after fabrics, which were then sold across England.

Abel Goes to Halifax

Waking early as was his custom, Abel slipped quietly out of bed. In the smoky light of dawn, not wishing to wake his mother, he crept across the floor trying to avoid the creaking boards that he knew by heart. He stirred the grey ashes of the fireplace, looking for the faint glow of orange embers from the night before. Grabbing a handful of kindling, he carefully set them in place and began to gently blow on the flickering ash. Soon small wisps of white smoke curled upward, finally bursting into flame, sending gold shades of shifting color across the walls and ceiling. He squatted by the fire for a time, enjoying its warmth, mesmerized by the dancing flame.

Isabella was now awake.

"I dread the deadly quiet just before dawn. It is so sweet to have you awake and the fire burning bright."

Abel turned to see his mother's face, like gold in the firelight.

"My hope was to not wake you. I see that I have failed." "Abel, you cannot steal off to Halifax without a solid meal and prayer. I will get the kettle going and send you off properly."

He heard a hint of worry in his mother's words.

"Let me get more wood for the fire," he said as he opened the door and stepped out into the darkness.

Halifax was a center for woolen manufacturing ten miles east of Heptonstall. Isabella did not like Halifax. It was notorious for its *"gibbet"*, a form of guillotine used to execute criminals by decapitation. A town that invented ways to execute people sent shivers down her spine.

"Halifax is a harsh town Abel, filled with sinful men. Be aware and keep God close."

Abel was to take a load of loom-woven fabric into Halifax for trade. Even at the youthful age of eighteen, he was known as an amiable and gifted negotiator and he relished the opportunity to haggle the best price. But he also had another reason to venture into Halifax and it had a name - Elizabeth Mitchell.

As he rode into town, the streets bustled with activity. Halifax was so much more than Heptonstall. The town was crowded and his oxen were agitated by the unfamiliar sounds and commotion of the street. Eventually setting up his wares, he began negotiating and selling. It had rained heavily through the night and dense clouds continued to roll across the sky. The air was fresh with the smell of damp woolen fabric, open air cooking pots and wood smoke. Abel felt a rush of excitement. The day went well and as he sold his last piece to a bright-eyed elderly gentleman, his eyes began to dart quickly around, taking in as many faces as he could, looking for one in particular.

Not spotting Elizabeth in the crowd, Abel's disappointment showed on his face. Gritting his teeth, he muttered to himself,

"What did you expect? Truly, what did you expect? You are indeed a fool!"

A chubby-faced girl, about his age, with bright red hair and a freckle-covered nose, stopped in her tracks as she walked by. Squinting her unnaturally huge eyes and tipping her head she questioned,

"Are you speaking to me in such an indignant tone?"
"That I am not. I only speak to myself out of frustration.
I apologize had I offended you in any way."

Just then, her father stepped up.

"Sir, am I to assume that you have suffered my daughter
an indignation and try now to worm your way free from
this indignation? Such a deep indignation is not so easily
dismissed."

Abel was both stunned and confused at the misunderstanding. Never
before had he heard anyone use the word *"indignation"* so many times.
Abel dare not chuckle to himself, should he inadvertently escalate the
situation even further, as strange as it all seemed. An awkward silence stood
between the three of them as the daughter feigned weeping.

"There need be recompense to appease the deep offense that
my daughter has suffered at your careless and cruel words,"
the father demanded.

Abel mustered his courage, as he now understood that this was some sort
of conniving shakedown. Yet he did not want to cause a scene and attract
any more curious attention than was already building. After all, his mother
had warned him to be careful, this is Halifax.

"Sir, I have offered no offense at all toward your lovely
daughter. This be only a misunderstanding of the simplest
nature."

Just as the father began to forcibly object to Abel's self-defense, a strong
voice from the growing crowd interjected:

"William Buckland, ye are treading on delicate ground, my
friend. This lad be under my care and I fear that ye slander
both his good intentions and his honorable name."

Abel was startled and then pleased to recognize the familiar face. John Mitchell [3] was an imposing man, with broad shoulders and an unmistakable air of authority.

> *"John Mitchell, this be not your affair,"* the father replied, giving no eye contact.

John Mitchell moved arrestingly forward and stated,

> *"Tis my affair because I make it my affair. I have seen the work of your trickery on other days. This day be not one. Now, William Buckland, you best move along to your home."*

The sheepish father and his surprisingly unfazed, now tearless daughter marched off, striving for a sense of dignity, but finding none.

Abel shrugged his shoulders and laughed, his big smile displaying teeth whiter than they should be for a boy his age. His mother always insisted that he scrub his teeth with a cloth before going to bed each night, a practice that he found annoying and unnecessary. He was taller than most of his friends, lean like his father, but with the eyes of his mother, almond shaped and dark. Girls found him quite handsome, but it was hard to differentiate between his natural charisma and his God-given good looks. In either case, he remained unaffected by this and held a deep and humble sense of his own culpable nature before a holy and loving God.

Abel had traded goods with John Mitchel over the previous years and had come to admire him as an honest merchant and good man. He had also come to be acquainted with John's lovely daughter, Elizabeth. John insisted that Abel go home with him and share in a meal with his family, saying, with a lilt in his voice,

> *"After your little ordeal Abel Greenwood, I should think that a good meal and healthy conversation are in order. Especially after ye were almost married off to William Buckland's first-born daughter!"*

Abel smiled, with raised eyebrows, knowing there may have been more truth in the statement than jest! Abel was quite pleased to join the Mitchell family for the evening meal. John Mitchell had been a follower of his father [4] and was now a fierce defender of the Puritan cause and those martyred for it. John Mitchell's face would grow pale and drawn as he spoke of the injustices surrounding the hanging of John Greenwood. It stirred Abel's heart to hear someone speak of the father he had known ever so briefly.

The political tides were changing with the coronation of James I scheduled to occur in a few days.

> *"The year 1603 may see a change in the winds, but alas, no one is to be sure in which direction,"* John casually commented, while tossing a log onto the fire.

Queen Elizabeth I had died in March. James I, the son of Mary, Queen of Scots, who reigned as King of Scotland for almost forty years, after succeeding to the throne at a mere one year of age, was now to succeed the childless Queen Elizabeth I. He would rule over the two distinct kingdoms, each with their own parliaments, judiciary and laws. John continued,

> *"Time and God's sovereign hand will tell the tale soon enough. The fortunes of our land rises and falls. The war in Ireland is finally settled, now only to see the plague raise its sickly head in London during the King's coronation."* [5]

John Mitchell wanted to converse on the political concerns of the land. Taxation, the Spanish War, The Established Church and the King's coronation were all that people talked about these days. But Abel was clearly distracted. Elizabeth Mitchell sat poised in a rocking chair near the fireplace. The fading light from the fire danced along the right side of her shining face creating a rhythmic golden glimmer. He could see a slight smile. He was sure that she was smiling at him. It was all he could do to respectfully focus his thoughts on the events and news of the day as recounted by her animated father.

Yet when John Mitchell began to speak of Abel's father, Abel's concentration was apparent. He hung on every word that others had to say about the man so many admired. John Mitchell, although not a Separatist, was a devout Puritan, but in a less radical sense of the fluid definition. He continued,

"John Greenwood, your father, was a godly and passionate man for the truth, while I continue to believe that the Church can conform and that we need not separate, indeed, I grow more and more restless and dare I say, critical. The offenses are expanding and The Church has ceased to break fully from Rome. It rides a fence between two worlds and fails to fall on the side of true reformation. In matters of ceremonies, church government, worship and discipline it has been unsuccessful in change and has overstepped the truthful boundary of Scripture."

Abel was torn. His father had died for Separatist views. He sat silently as John Mitchell verbalized what so many believed; The Church could be purified. There were great hopes for James I to achieve what had not yet been accomplished.

The hour was late and eyes were growing heavy. John insisted,

"Abel, it be prudent for you to stay the night, rather than risk peril on the dark road to Heptonstall."

Abel happily obliged. As he lay on the straw bed, restless and unable to sleep, his mind was spinning. Thoughts intertwined between his father, the reformation, the coronation and, of course, most notably, Elizabeth.

7

Abel and Elizabeth

Elizabeth Mitchell [1] held Abel's heart in the palm of her hand. She had been raised, much as Abel, in a middle-class environment. John Mitchell was a well-respected merchant in Halifax, and she enjoyed the benefits of her father's good reputation. [2] Elizabeth was strikingly beautiful. While Abel remembered her, from years before, as a gangly child, she had quickly grown as tall as her father yet lithe and willowy. Her dark braided hair tightly tied at the back of her head and neatly tucked under a blue bonnet accentuated her heart-shaped face, full lips and milky skin. Abel felt intimidated and even shy when he found himself in her company. She was full of charm and possessed an iron will.

Abel managed to see Elizabeth on several occasions over a period of two more years, after the "*William Buckland Matter*" as it came to be referred. He continued to have business dealings with her father, and often stole the opportunity to engage her in polite conversation. He enjoyed these encounters and would respectfully sneak quick glances in her direction. Her deep green eyes would coyly attempt to avert his, ultimately connecting, yet for only a proper moment, bringing a bright pink blush across her soft cheeks as she smiled at him. She was aware of his interest and, in turn, she found him handsome and a curious fascination. He seemed so innocently unaware of his own charisma and she liked that.

These sporadic and chance encounters with Elizabeth were proving a frustration for Abel. It was taking too much time and he wished to move

29

on with his life. He wanted Elizabeth to one day be his wife, and bravely he made the decision to approach her father and ask permission to officially court her. Beginning nervously,

> *"Sir, I have built a prosperous weaving business with my widowed mother in Heptonstall. I am of ardent faith and in good moral standing within my community. The prospects for my future are great and my desire is to now establish a family of my own. Your daughter, Elizabeth, is a fine woman and I find much to admire in her. I stand before you now, humbly asking your permission to court Elizabeth, wishing, with God's blessing and your approval, to make her my wife within the year."*

John Mitchell began in a stern voice, sending foreboding down Abel's spine, weakening his knees,

> *"Young Abel Greenwood, I have long wondered what has been your delay in asking. I grant you my permission to court my daughter."*

Life, Death and Political Unrest

Abel Greenwood and Elizabeth Mitchell [3] were married in Halifax, on a beautiful summer morning in 1605. They settled into life in Heptonstall, moving into a cottage on the outskirts of town, with a weaving shop in the front, where a large glass window of good quality allowed in plenty of light. Abel's widowed mother, Isabella, lived with them for the first three years, until her death at the age of fifty-three, [4] dying peacefully in her bed after a brief illness. Abel saw her death as one more blessing from an eternal, loving God. She did not suffer as his father, John Greenwood, had. Abel was deeply heartbroken, although grateful for the devoted and faithful mother that God had given him. And now he was at peace and filled with joy, knowing that she was in the presence of her Savior.

Life in Heptonstall fell into a comfortable rhythm for Abel and Elizabeth. Political and church policies seemed far away as day-to-day life functioned without serious interruption. Still, a kettle of unrest continuously brewed underneath the seeming calm throughout the country. The religious and the political were steadily heating toward a boiling point. Queen Elizabeth I had always pursued a balancing act between these two dominant influences in 17ᵗʰ century England. She felt that if she allowed the Puritans to have their way, the Roman Catholics, who considered her illegitimate (referring to her as "the bastard Queen"), would become even more alienated and all could be lost in relations with France and Spain. Yet if she were more favorable to Catholicism, the vast majority of her people would rebel. In reality, she had been a true daughter of her father, King Henry VIII, and her sympathies remained largely on the Catholic side. However, during her reign she purposely strove to appease both sectors.

Since the Queen's death [5] in 1603, James I had ruled as King of England. *"What wonderful hopes we now hold for this man to put everything right" was* the common sentiment among the Protestants. Yet James I, who was brought up under the influence of John Knox, [6] the leader of the Reformation movement in Scotland, would prove to be even worse for the Puritan cause than Elizabeth. For although King James I held great interest in theology, commissioning a new translation of the Bible, he set a decrepit moral tone in his court, earning it the name "Sodom" and remained strongly committed to enforcing conformity to the church, which induced continued persecution toward Puritans. He refused Puritan demands, while also sanctioning harsh measurements to control nonconforming Catholics.

With tensions mounting and confusion abounding, Abel and Elizabeth sought to isolate themselves from the conflict in order to thwart undue attention from the authorities, conforming only as far as was absolutely necessary to survive. Abel was tangibly aware that with the reputation of his Separatist father and his subsequent execution, there may be some who would be watching him and his family especially closely. They followed the obligatory, lawful expectations of the church, having their two children, Anne and Thomas baptized at St Thomas a Becket, when each was born. [7]

8

Thomas I

Thomas gleefully waved a pocket-sized black snake high over his head, while chasing his sister, Ann, around in circles across the yard.

"I will drop him down your back! Run! You better run!" he teased.

Just then his mother stepped firmly through the front door and with hands on her hips she scolded,

"Thomas Greenwood, put that snake down this second and tend to ye chores. That wood will not chop itself."

Ann spun around, smiled victoriously, stuck her tongue out at her little brother and marched away.

Elizabeth went back inside the house, smiling to herself at the impishness of Thomas. As she continued kneading the bread for their evening meal, she mused at her son's rambunctious ways. He was forever torturing his sister with his antics. Ann at the age of fourteen was quiet and reserved, and Thomas, one year younger, took full advantage of her meek nature. She never retaliated, and secretly Elizabeth wondered if Ann did not truthfully relish the attention her brother gave her, even if colorfully negative. Ann did not have any real friends and her shyness isolated her much of the time, while Thomas, with considerable self-confidence, was full of spunk and spit.

With the bread almost finished and vegetables in the cooking pot, Elizabeth sat down to meditate on a Bible verse that had struck her firmly that morning during her devotions. Thomas and Ann would be outside for a while longer, and Abel was still away on his trip to Reading, Berkshire.

> *"May God guide and protect him on his journey home,"* she silently prayed.

She didn't like it when he traveled so far to trade and sell but she understood that Reading was an important trading center, and these trips were necessary in order to prosper their loom-weaving business.

She read aloud the words from Romans that had touched her heart so profoundly that morning.

> *"For ye have not received a spirit of bondage to fear anymore, but ye have received the Spirit of adoption whereby we cry 'Abba Father.'"*

Elizabeth marveled at the words:

> *"The eternal God, who created the universe, is my loving Father! I am not bound by fear. I am His daughter, His child. I am held in His arms. Such amazing love!"*

Closing her eyes, she soaked in the tangible peace.

Hearing a wagon coming up the road, she gathered herself up, hopeful that Abel was returning early. Squinting against the brightness of the hot August sun, she saw that it was Timothy Miles, a neighbor and friend. Timothy's face was taut and drawn and Elizabeth instantly knew that something was wrong. Stepping onto the stone stoop he looked soberly into Elizabeth's eyes.

> *"Elizabeth, I bring sorrowful news."*

Attempting to control his emotions, Timothy choked out,

"It appears that Abel's horses spooked, and his cart overturned along the road just outside Reading. It rolled over onto him. I am so sorry Elizabeth, but Abel is dead." [1]

The somber bluntness of Timothy's words rang cold and bleak. Even as he tried to temper them, the news struck Elizabeth like an anvil. It all seemed so impossible. Abel was an extremely capable horseman.

"How can this be?"

she questioned, while still in a state of shock, knowing that there would be no satisfactory answer.

She trembled. Her hands began to shake and a defenseless panic threatened to overtake her. Fear.

Time seemed to freeze. Elizabeth's mind was spinning with a whirl of memories, all of them eluding a firm grasp. Suddenly a warm soft breeze shook her to attention and seemed to almost whisper her name, blowing the loose strands of dark hair, now tinged with grey, about her face. She remembered that she was not alone,

"Abel is held in the same arms that held me this very morning. Glory be to my God who cares for His children with perfect wisdom. I will not be afraid."

Tears streamed down her ashen face.

The long days of summer turned into weeks and months, becoming a blur of confusion over the return of Abel's body to Heptonstall. The distance was compounded with rains that seemed to never subside. Low heavy clouds hung motionless, dropping a dark and gloomy greyness over the land that seemed to mimic their hearts. Not until the dry coolness of autumn had arrived did Abel's body finally return to Heptonstall for burial, on the 14th of October 1623. He was thirty-eight years old. St. Thomas a Becket would hold another Greenwood in its cemetery and Elizabeth wondered what the future held.

The Legacy of John Greenwood

The Separatist church in London, which young Thomas's grandfather, John Greenwood, loved and for which he sacrificed his life, had continued to experience dire persecution. In 1593, the same year that John Greenwood hanged, a definitive and fierce drive to force Puritans into conformity for the sake of Church and Queen began. It was called the *"Act Against Puritans"*. Puritan beliefs were considered to be in direct contradiction to the teachings of the Church of England and in opposition to the authority of the Monarch, with banishment as the ultimate penalty. When King James came to the throne, he declared that he would put an end to church reform movements and deal harshly with radical non-conformists.

With godly, passionate young leaders like William Bradford, [1] many from the London separatist church and faithful congregations elsewhere sought to make the costly escape to Holland, where religious freedom was practiced. By 1620, these English Puritans, now banished to a foreign land yet still deeply proud of their English identity, began to recognize that their English children were becoming Dutch. Plans were soon underway to establish a colony of their own in the New World, America, where they could maintain their English heritage and continue to practice their faith freely.

Another contributing factor for the Puritans in their desire to make the dangerous journey to a new land concerned the European conflict, involving Spain and its complicated and volatile political relations, which included the Dutch, French, Austrians and Germans. War was underway. While King James I of England was ardent to remain free of involvement in the clash, the effects of European disputes and engagements were always far reaching. No one was safe. Puritan families were not only displaced, but now they were also surrounded by rumors and threats of war.

Thomas marveled at the reports of these brave, religious, unbreakable Puritan men and women who sacrificed everything for the sake of the gospel, and he felt a sense of pride and admiration for the legacy he knew he had inherited from both his grandfather and father. At breakfast one morning he thoughtfully shared with his mother,

"My faith is not merely for my own personal contentment. I have been blessed with the faith of my forefathers and have an obligation to carry it forward. With God's help, I shall do so. I do not go to scripture to strengthen my own resolve, but I go there first to begin with God, and then to honor him with my actions."

He continued,

"Doctrine without the fruits thereof in good works is merely a prideful and pointless practice."

Elizabeth was amazed at the insight that her once unruly son now shared with such passion. She praised God for the growth she witnessed in his young life. Abel's unexpected death had a profound and maturing effect on young Thomas.

At thirteen years old, when his father was tragically killed, Thomas Greenwood had suddenly found himself tossed into a new and unfamiliar role. He was now the man of the house. He took his duties seriously and Elizabeth saw forthright and tangible change in his behavior and attitudes. It seemed that overnight he transformed from an immature young boy to a contemplative, dependable young man. He threw himself into his apprenticeship as a weaver and concentrated his energies in caring for his widowed mother and devoted sister.

9

King Charles I and The English Civil War

1625-1651

The news came not as a surprise. King James I was dead. Rumors had been buzzing about for months of his ailing health. And now, on March 27, 1625, he was gone. Charles I immediately began his reign as the King of England and that same year he took Henrietta Maria of France as his Catholic wife, making her very unpopular in England. If life had been difficult under James I, it was only compounded with the reign of Charles I who implemented sweeping persecution. Charles I was a tyrannical, absolute monarch. He levied taxes without the consent of Parliament, and both Parliamentarians and Puritans strongly disapproved of his overreaching authority. Ultimately, Charles dissolved parliament, believing in his own divine right as King. His prerogative was to rule from his own conscience.

His religious policies, which were sympathetic to Catholics as well as High-Church Anglican ecclesiastics, generated deep mistrust among English Puritans. Ultimately, by mid-1642, overall tensions between the Parliamentarians (Roundheads) and Royalists (Cavaliers) grew into a multitude of skirmishes across England. The English Civil War was underway. As Yorkshire became embroiled in the fighting, Thomas was concerned that conflict could soon reach their peaceful village. The men of Heptonstall gathered at the grammar school, which had been recently completed, to discuss their options should a battle ensue.

Although most northern cities of England supported the Royalist Cavaliers (the King), Heptonstall and the rural farming villages and communities were solidly in support of the Roundheads (Parliament) and as the spring of 1643 celebrated the end of winter's bitter cold, Thomas Greenwood, at the age of thirty-three, was prepared to fight.

While holding his newborn son, Thomas II, in his arms, he watched as the morning sun burned thick fog off the distant hills, filling him with awe and thanksgiving, as well as an agonizing dread. Sarah, his young wife, slept peacefully in a rocking chair near the large fireplace with her black hair loosely tied in a braid and falling off her shoulder. His mind wandered back to the day they married. She was only eighteen and incredibly striking. He had waited to marry, though his mother, Elizabeth, and sister Ann had often coaxed him, giving him their eager, bold suggestions of eligible young Heptonstall maidens. But he had no time for courting, that is until he saw Sarah and finally surrendered his hesitations, making the time to court her. [2]

Now, as his heart welled up inside his chest and he thanked God for the gift of his family, Thomas pondered their safety. The Earl of Newcastle and his Royalist troops of 10,000 men were marching on the town of Bradford, only eighteen miles from Heptonstall. News came that a battle had raged at Adwalton Moor, with the Royalists success consolidating control of Yorkshire. War was closing in.

The Royalist army was not fed or paid well, and indiscriminately plundered the area. As autumn colors began to dot the hilltop forests, the pillaging and looting developed into a direct threat to Heptonstall itself. By November of 1643, tensions had risen to a fever-pitch, and strategic pickets were placed along the road leading up the hills in hopes of holding off any onslaught. Thomas volunteered for this position [3] and his shift was about to begin.

He gently woke Sarah, quietly watching as she rubbed her eyes, compelling them to open to the dimness of early morning. The dark circles beneath her beautiful brown eyes betrayed the fact that she hadn't had much sleep the past few weeks. She smiled weakly and stood to gather those belongings she would take with her, along with five-month-old, Thomas II. With tears she shared,

"I cannot help but feel fear this morning. My prayers are constant, and still my heart is bathed in dread."

"My love if I could whisk ye and our little one away to some other world this very moment, I would indeed do so." Thomas replied.

Sarah heard the stress in his voice. Opening the front door, Thomas was reminded to clean the rusted hinges as they squealed loudly. It seemed such an unimportant detail at this moment, yet how he welcomed the idea of the mundane routine of an unthreatened existence. They entered the street to begin the short uphill trek with many women and children to gather at the grammar school; it was the newest and strongest building in Heptonstall, and its location was centralized. [4]

Thomas soon found his position along the rough road behind a low stone wall, relieving the tired old man who had stood guard throughout the night. It was now Thomas's turn. With his matchlock musket, he settled in to watch for movement along the valley floor and the River Hebden far below. A long orange glow stretched along the edge of the eastern sky, until the sun found its path, breaking forth in long streaks of blinding light. A cold wind swept across his face. He shivered, his eyes glassy and red with fatigue. Thomas could see sheep peacefully grazing on the hillsides and carefully watched them for any disturbance.

The night before, Parliamentarians from neighboring towns and farms rallied at Heptonstall. The manpower increased by 750 men and Thomas felt confident that they could turn back any attack. At mid-morning a flock of birds fluttered out from a clump of trees on the far side of the river. Thomas scowled and squinted, focusing his attention there. Scattered flickers of red dotted the open plain in the distance. Then, the unmistakable venetian red coats of foot soldiers clearly appeared. The sheer numbers sent chills down his spine. Sounding the alert, every man ran for position.

"God was with us," Thomas would later recount.

Disaster struck the brightly colored Royalist army as they tried to cross the swollen Hebden River. The Parliamentarians took the advantage and Thomas helped roll boulders down the steep buttress. [(5)] Numerous Royalists were captured, killed or drowned in the initial onslaught. By late afternoon, the defenders clattered wearily back up the hill to Heptonstall, which remained peacefully untouched. The wounded were many, but gratefully only three Parliamentarian men were killed. [(6)] Thomas was exhausted and when Sarah saw the deep cut across his shoulder her heart jumped and she nearly fainted before he quickly reassured,

> *"Fear not my dear, this be only a minor injury. I cannot complain, others saw worse. The poor fellow standing next took a musket ball to his arm."*

This battle had ended, but the war was far from over.

The high views of Heptonstall were an advantage against attack, but by January [(7)] the Royalists gained reinforcements and launched yet another assault. This time they easily broke through the pickets and, upon reaching Heptonstall, torched fourteen buildings and pillaged the town. Thomas and Sarah were spared, but their home was destroyed. Thomas moved his wife and their son to a safer location with his mother, Elizabeth, [(8)] who had remarried a wealthy, widowed farmer on the outskirts of town. His sister, Ann, moved in as well with her four young children. Her husband, Timothy, was already fighting with The Parliamentarians in the south.

The decision to leave for the war with most of the able-bodied men from Heptonstall, on a dismal spring morning, was an agonizing choice for Thomas. [(9)] But the facts were clear, the cause was just, and Thomas felt God's call to fight. As he rode away, Sarah stood in the doorway of the picturesque farm cottage, holding baby Thomas in her arms with tears welling up in her eyes. Weakly waving, she watched to see if he would turn around in the saddle of his muddied mare, before vanishing over the hill. Just at the top, he stopped, spun his horse around, and simply stared at the scene below, impressing it into his memory. Then, he was gone.

If the Parliamentarians were going to succeed in this war, the internal discipline and religious zeal of its soldiers would require consolidation. The New Model Army was formed, consisting of 22,000 soldiers. Eleven regiments of cavalry, each of 600 men, twelve regiments of infantry, each of 1200 men, and one regiment of 1000 dragoons. With Oliver Cromwell leading them, they were now a force to be reckoned with. There was no shortage of cavalry volunteers, and Thomas, owning a strong and well-disciplined mount, was prepared to do his duty for God and country. Many who had fled to America now returned to fight.

Cromwell, a committed Puritan, accepted only soldiers and officers who were dedicated to Protestant ideals. He wrote to Sir William Spring in the autumn of 1643, *"I would rather have a plain russet-coated Captain, that knows what he fights for and loves what he knows, than what you call a Gentleman and is nothing else."* And indeed, that is what he got. The New Model Army was nicknamed *"Ironsides"* for its ability to cut through enemy defenses. But the most elite of its fighting force were the horse troops. Their discipline was markedly superior to that of their Royalist counterparts and Cromwell used them with precision.

Cromwell's power stemmed from his military ability and his unique relationship with his troops. He always led his army from the front and it took its toll, as he often sustained combat injuries. But his soldiers respected him, and Thomas was confident in his leader's capabilities to end the Royalist stronghold. With Oliver Cromwell as Lieutenant General of Horse in Manchester's Army, confidence was indeed high. Time and again Thomas recognized divine intervention and attributed successes on the battlefield to God's almighty hand.

In July 1644, a battle was brewing in the Moors. It had been a year and a half since the Royalists had sacked and plundered Heptonstall and the wound was still fresh in Thomas's mind. Skirmishes had continued all over the valley. Finally, the Parliamentary Dragoons scouted the Royalist army camped near Marston Moor and the cavalry was on the move to rout them from their position. Thomas rode his mare confidently, front and back breastplate secured over his buff leather coat, the edges flapping in the breeze as they were at a trot. The sun was coming up and it was already warm. The light armor he wore added discomfort, yet it provided some protection. His high leather riding boots were old and worn but had never yet been called upon to guard his legs from the slashing and sharp edges of swords in battle.

Thomas spoke calming words gently into the ear of his jittery horse. Two lines of enemy cavalry now faced each other. His heart was racing at the image before him - seasoned Royalist soldiers ready for battle.

"Lord, if I am to meet you today, may my life be worthy of your presence, through my Savior Jesus Christ."

Thomas, jolted from his prayers, heard something that perplexed him. It was the sound of distinct laughter. Tilting his head to the side, with eyebrows furrowed and confusion in his shaky voice, Thomas whispered to the fellow next to him,

"Do you hear laughing?"

With a snort and a half smile, the experienced Roundhead quietly answered.

"You are not becoming daft of mind. It is Oliver Cromwell. He has a propensity for laughter both before and after a battle"

As unusual as it was, this somehow brought a strange bit of comfort to Thomas.

The charge was sounded, and Thomas squeezed his mount into a full gallop. A frightful din followed. The noise was deafening with shouts of crazed men and panicked musket fire. Glittering swords flashed bolts of reflected light from the blinding afternoon sun. For a moment Thomas was mesmerized by the beauty of the clash, but only for a moment. A Royalist trooper rode fearlessly directly at him and took aim. Thomas ducked off the side of his horse, as the musket ball soared over his head. Combat was close now and swords were drawn.

Cromwell demanded that they hold the battlefield, and not a man turned to run. A spear found its mark, striking a rider on his left flank, spilling him off his horse as he crashed to the ground. Thomas's heart beat heavily, pounding in his ears. His burning eyes darted across the battlefield. The clamor of battle reached a roaring pitch while men smashed into each other. Thomas drew a ragged breath and pressed forward. Just as the heat of conflict cooled, a far-flung spear buried deeply into his side. Thomas fell from his wild-eyed horse. The world seemed to spin with dust and muted streaks of sunlight, while time lapsed into nothingness.

Soon the Parliamentarians broke the ranks of the Royalist Cavaliers, and then regrouped, as the dust from Royalist horses scattered their retreat into the distance. If General Cromwell ordered them to pursue, they were ready, and they would do so relentlessly. There would be no abandoning their duty to loot discarded enemy baggage, as the Royalists were prone to do. This was a disciplined army.

Cromwell was slightly injured in the neck. However Thomas lay on the battlefield, looking up at the hazy sun almost blotted out from smoke and the dust stirred by frantic horses' hooves, gravely wounded.[10] The enemy spear had found its way between his breastplates and penetrated just under his ribcage.. The air was heavy and stagnant. He felt no pain but knew that he was dying. Not attempting to move, he lay perfectly still, listening to rider-less horses running and whinnying in confusion, some wounded and frenzied. A song of muffled praise came to his dry lips and he quietly and haltingly sang,

> *"Thy death...life to me. Thy life my heart the only joy ...from Hell redeemest me...*
>
> *My fate my love my grace o Lord...to find you art my heart my only...."* [11]

He had no idea how long he lay alone in the solitude that approaching death brings. It did not really matter. A silhouette approached. A young man knelt beside him and took hold of his hand.

> *"Sir, your wounds appear beyond remedy."*

He spoke quietly, as in respect of the dead. Thomas turned his head to see the man's face. He recognized him as the farrier who had tended to the hooves of his mare earlier in the week, Henry Brooks [12].

> *"I fear it is true,"* Thomas responded, coughing hard, wincing in pain. *"I will not see a new day, but this I know, my Savior lives."*

He closed his eyes, and with a pleasant smile on his face took his last earthly breath.

The Battle of Marston Moor, with Oliver Cromwell fighting at the head of his troops, secured the north of England for the Parliamentarians, but failed to end the Royalist resolve for another two years until the formal surrender of the Royalist army at Oxford in 1646. By 1648 Cromwell's New Model Army consolidated its control over England. In 1649, King Charles I was tried, convicted and beheaded with one swift and violent stroke. His final words were these:

> *"I must tell you that their (the people) liberty and freedom consists in having government... It is not their having a share in the government; that is nothing appertaining unto them. A subject and a sovereign are clean different things. I shall go from a corruptible to an incorruptible crown, where no disturbance can be."*

10

Thomas II Immigrates

1665

As the salty west wind washed across his face, Thomas Greenwood II [1] threw his head back and laughed, his knuckles white as he clutched the side rails, while keeping rhythm with the tossing ship. Massive waves cresting with angry froth, pulling mist off the tops, seemed to pulsate with life. It was almost sundown and still the seas refused to give way to peace.

Thomas had remained below deck for most of the menacing day. Grey, worried faces, strained with tinges of seasick green, packed together in their low-ceiling cabins, holding back sickness as the ship lurched and pitched back and forth. The smell of sweat mingled with whiffs of vomit permeated the gun deck and Thomas needed air. Scampering up the ladder and through the hatch, he immediately lost his balance and slid on his back along the slippery upper deck.

Gathering himself, he struggled to regain his footing against the ship's constant rocking. Finally he staggered upright, grasping the wet cold railing, standing mesmerized by the grey pounding waves as they unleashed their fury. An unanticipated joy overwhelmed him. The ship creaked as the cargo shifted against the constant rolling motion and Thomas felt reckless and carefree. His dark hair soaked with water and his grey eyes stinging with salty spray, he felt alive.

A crew member checking the main mast saw Thomas and hollered above the roaring wind,

"Young man, ye best get below before ye find a watery grave!"

Thomas smiled and teased in loud response,

"A watery grave is not my intent, but only to dance with these tempestuous waves a bit."

"Well laddie, you are either crazy of mind, or simply full of pep and vinegar."

Thomas laughed again and turned back to his buoyant dancing partner.

At twenty-two years of age he was leaving everything he had ever known. There was no second guessing and there were no regrets. Everything that mattered to him was now gone. He wasn't running away, although there were plenty of reasons for that. No, he was beginning anew, in the Massachusetts Bay Colony. His mind wandered to memories of his mother, Sarah, and how weak and dependent she was on the strength of his grandmother, Elizabeth. He was not like his mother, who had been almost paralyzed with fear after his father, Thomas I, was killed in battle. Courageous and gutsy, he was undaunted and eagerly followed the call to the colonies.

The Civil War had finally subsided in 1651 and Oliver Cromwell reigned victorious as England was declared a "Commonwealth". There was no more monarchy and everyday life settled into a routine of relative safety. Throughout Thomas's growing up years, political news was filled with reports of Ireland's and of Scotland's continuing threats to England's ruling authority. War was a constant, as invasions and campaigns were devotedly launched. Oliver Cromwell died in 1659 and was posthumously beheaded two years later.

In 1660 the monarchy was restored. Charles II (son of executed Charles I) returned from his nine years of exile in France to rule as King of England, Scotland and Ireland. Penal civil laws were once again placed in effect to uphold the establishment of the Church of England against Protestant nonconformists and Catholics. The most drastic of these laws was the Clarendon Code which called for nonconformists to be excluded from holding public office, and the Book of Common Prayer being made compulsory, resulting in over two thousand clergy being forced to resign. Unauthorized gatherings for worship, defined as any meeting of more than five people who were not related, were forbidden. Nonconformist ministers were prohibited from coming within five miles of an incorporated village or town of their former congregations, and nonconformists were denied degrees from the universities of Cambridge and Oxford.

For five years Thomas endured the oppressions of what Charles II brought back to England. He longed to emigrate to the colonies. His mother, Sarah, now remarried and raising a hoard of children, was finally well settled after grieving the death of Thomas's father for several painful years. He only remained for the sake of his loving grandmother, Elizabeth, who had quickly after her second marriage become widowed once again. Having helped raise him into adulthood, she had been his rock. When she suddenly succumbed to heart failure the previous winter, and slept her final sleep, he knew that he was now free to go. (2)

The colonies' textile industry was dependent on English manufacturers for clothes, blankets, sails and dozens of other items vital for a growing society. Heptonstall had provided Thomas with a skill as a weaver. He knew that he could make a life for himself in the colonies. Prepared with a deeply instilled and determined faith, as well as a small inheritance left to him from his grandmother and the dream of a better world, he now sailed intrepidly alone across the Atlantic.

After two months at sea, the grey horizon gave way to the distant image of a crowded Boston Harbor. Stepping off the ship onto the sturdy wooden docks was a strange relief. His footing slowly adjusted to the feeling of solid ground once again. Glancing around, he was spellbound at the bedlam before him.

People, carts, livestock and baggage all mingled and jostled along. Having no particular destination, Thomas fell into the natural direction of the flowing mass. Walking for hours, all the while taking in the sights, sounds and smells, he soon found himself in Boston Common. He had read of how a law had been passed in 1646, declaring that this was to perpetually remain a public property. Thomas surmised that, if need be, he could sleep here while he sought to secure lodging. The hour was late, and he was exhausted. Finding a large tree, he sat down and leaned against it. His eyes heavy with sleep, he closed them and dreamed of a life free of oppression.

Waking early the next morning, he shivered with a chill running up his spine. Stretching his legs and surveying his surroundings, he saw that people were already scurrying about. The smell of hot baked bread made his mouth water and licking his lips Thomas searched for the source. Finding a small bake shop around the corner, he bought a loaf and sat outside to enjoy the warm bread fresh from the oven.

"Have ye just arrived in Boston?"

The Scottish voice came from a man, seemingly a little older than Thomas.

"Indeed, yesterday," Thomas replied.
"Are ye alone then? No family with ye?"
"I am. I am alone. And in need of some assistance to find myself lodging and I am seeking work,"
"What be your name, lad?"

Thomas thought it odd that he should refer to him as "lad", as the man could not have been more than a few years older.

"Thomas Greenwood, sir."
"It is my pleasure to make your acquaintance. I be James Maxwell." [3]

James went on to tell Thomas that he was a member of the Scots Charitable Society and that he, with his wife and five children, had only themselves lived in Boston for a few years. They had come from Dumfries, Scotland, on the left side of the Nith River, nine miles from Edinburgh. Thomas listened patiently to this stout, green-eyed Scot and could not help but realize that the problems he had faced in England were the same kinds of problems that James and his family experienced in Scotland. Wars and rumors of wars. Oppression and dreams of a new life. The world suddenly seemed small.

Thomas asked about the church meeting house and James told him about the First Church of Boston, founded as a part of John Winthrop's original Puritan settlement. It was just a few blocks away and Thomas was eager to find it. Thanking James, Thomas walked quickly in the direction of the meeting house, his muscular legs taking long strides in anticipation. His heart felt bold and blessed. God had given him a safe journey across treacherous seas, he had a good night's sleep under an old oak tree in Boston Common, he had warm bread in his belly and he met a Scot who gave him sound advice. Now, he stood on the threshold of the First Church of Boston. Remembering the martyrdom of his great-grandfather and the brave Puritans who had left England to worship in freedom, he shuddered with a sense of wonder and reverently opened the door.

11

Thomas II and Hannah "Anna" Ward

The First Church of Boston was not what Thomas expected. The aged Rev. John Wilson [1] was harsh in both his tone and manner and thus was quite unapproachable. His strict discipline, severe teaching and gruff style had been a source of conflict within the church for many years prior to Thomas's arrival. Wilson remained on sound theological ground, preaching that grace alone saved and stressing that works could not offer salvation to a lost soul. However, his perceived overemphasis on "*evidencing justification by sanctification*" was viewed by many in his congregation as reverting to a covenant of works, thus disregarding the free gift of God's grace.

It was this issue which led to what became known as the *"Antinomian Controversy"*. Beginning in 1635. Anne Hutchinson, a strong-minded woman and member of First Church, objected to the emphasis on morality and through meetings in her home she along with her brother-in-law, the Rev. John Wheelwright, gathered a following, believing that Rev. Wilson lacked "*the seal of the Spirit.*" Ministers and magistrates of Boston gathered in 1636 to discuss the theological errors and accusations brought against him and determined to come to a consensus opinion, which they failed to do.

The theological debate escalated, with members of the congregation launching an attack to submit charges against Wilson. Opinions and emotions were ramping up. Wilson met the onslaught with a quiet dignity and responded soberly to each of the accusations brought against him. Yet the crowd refused to accept his explanations and demanded a formal censure. Under advisement, he chose to temper his exhortations.

However, with Rev. Wilson now attempting to preach a more conciliatory message, Anne Hutchinson's followers only became more emboldened, continuing to accuse Wilson and the majority of the colonies' magistrates and ministers of preaching a "covenant of works". When Wilson rose to preach or pray, they walked out. By 1637, the fervor grew, and the General Court brought charges of sedition against Hutchinson's brother-in-law, Rev. John Wheelwright. He was banished, and Ann Hutchinson stood trial in November of that same year, accused of heresy. She was also banished and later excommunicated from the church. The absence of a wall separating church and state, carried over to the colonies from England itself, would continue to drive a devastating stake in the heart of the people.

Rev. Wilson continued to reunite his battered congregation who gradually regained an appreciation and respect for a man with a heart for God and a passion for godliness in the lives of God's people. Yet controversies would continue in the ensuing years. Thomas quickly learned the hard lessons of the political and religious workings of the community. Rev. Wilson was undoubtedly a man with a love and zeal for God, and Thomas noted that this complicated man possessed a sincere modesty. Yet Rev. Wilson was not a Separatist, and Thomas still longed for a place where the extended arm of the Anglican Church (Church of England) was less embraced. In his view, church and state were indeed an unhappy union.

But times were slowly changing. The intense Puritan devotion of a decade earlier was gradually waning in New England. The first generation of leaders were aging and dying, and those who replaced them were not of the same stature, lacking the fervor that once motivated extreme action. Prosperity brought a certain degree of worldliness and Puritan leadership concluded that the church in general was in a certain state of moral decline.

Thomas believed in a moral code, observing a modest lifestyle, while at the same time understanding the gospel message as found in Ephesians 2:8,9, *"For by grace are ye saved through faith: and that not of yourselves: it is a gift of God: not of works, lest any man should boast."* Using sound Biblical reasoning and a love for God he agreed with the call for greater personal modesty, as in a woman's dress and men's hair, as well as the condemnation of the more blatant sins of drunkenness and adultery. However, he could not hold with judicial decisions banishing individuals who held religious views that did not accord with Puritan beliefs. Any decision to execute Quakers who returned to the colony after banishment was far too severe for Thomas to accept. State enforcement of religious uniformity was repugnant to him, especially as he recalled the execution of his own great-grandfather, Rev. John Greenwood.

By the time Rev. Wilson died in 1667, [2] Thomas was ready to move on. Working in Boston as a weaver, he had established himself well enough financially to consider relocating. Choosing to settle on the south side of the Charles River, some eight miles from Boston, he made the necessary arrangements. Cambridge Village, [3] which consisted of mostly family farms and one room cabins, was a community more to Thomas's liking. He missed the rural feel that Heptonstall had provided him through his growing up years.

The Ward Family

Hannah "Anna" Ward [4] was an eighteen-year-old carefree young lady. Her ash brown hair pulled up into a messy bun, with loose strands falling out here and there was of no concern to her. She had a tendency for over exuberance and frankness that was easily overlooked by others, as her intelligence masked many flaws in her social graces. She cared little for impression and was not interested in casting any seductive demeanor to impress a gentleman suitor. The eldest child in a family of eleven children, Anna had little time for frivolity, yet her fun-loving nature bore out affectionate teasing, even as she worked to help her mother. The house was filled with noise and laughter.

Raised in Sudbury, MA, Anna's father, John Ward, [5] was a wealthy landowner and her mother, also named Hannah, came from a prominent Cambridge Village family. John Ward, a turner [6] by trade, was no one to be trifled with. Born in London in 1626, John was the eldest son of William Ward [7] who emigrated to the colonies in the spring of 1638. John, as a twelve-year-old boy, relished the outdoors and the adventure of the thick wooded hills, mountains and valleys of his new home in the colonies. With Indians living in wigwams within the boundaries of Sudbury, he quickly learned the instincts necessary for survival. Even as peace ruled the day, a general unrest prevailed in the endless stretches of wilderness among the native inhabitants.

Anna's mother, Hannah Ward (born Jackson), [8] was born in Stepney, England to Edward and Frances Jackson (born Taft), in 1634. She immigrated with her family as an eight-year-old in 1642. Her little brother was born at sea during the voyage and was named Seabas or Seabys. No one was ever quite sure how to spell such a unique name. Hannah Jackson was sixteen years old when she married John Ward in Cambridge Village. Her father, Edward, [9] was one of the first settlers and became a very wealthy and influential man. He conveyed to Hannah and John Ward forty-five acres of land in the east part of Smelt Brook upon their marriage.

John Ward ultimately accumulated more than five hundred acres and prospered, building a south-facing saltbox house for his growing family. There were two kitchens, with a fireplace on each end, with two bedrooms upstairs and one-bedroom downstairs. Anna shared an upstairs bedroom with her thirteen-year-old sister, Rebecca, her nine-year-old sister, Elizabeth and her seven-year-old sister, Deborah. The boys shared the other upstairs room.

Cambridge Village, often referred to as *"the south side of the Charles River,"* was the only home that Anna Ward had ever known and, as a young girl, she was fascinated to hear her parents tell of England, that magical unknown land. Somehow Anna had romanticized England, as images of knights and fair maidens whirled around in her young mind. *"Tell me about the castles and the Lords and Ladies again!"* she would plead with her mother. Her mother would smile with both amusement and exhaustion recounting stories that she had been told as a girl, for the fact was she didn't really remember much of her own short childhood in England. But she was always careful to include the darker facts of the England that they had fled.

> *"We were under persecution, Anna. England was a place where we were not free. We were told how to pray and how to worship God. There can be only one head of the church,*

Anna, and that head is not the King of England, but Christ alone. There can be no law for the government of the church, other than what scripture contains."

Hannah soaked all of this in and determined to read the scriptures every day, so that she could know for herself how to worship God privately as well as publicly.

Settling and cultivating this land in the middle colonies was difficult. Forced to struggle with a rigorous climate and the hard and rocky soil, there were few who had the crushing tenacity required to risk everything, while building communities and villages along the way. Hannah's family was fortunate. Her grandfather, Edward Jackson, saw to it that they had the land needed to farm, raise cattle, sheep, pigs and chickens. The deep shadows of a seemingly haunted forest was not a deterrent for houses to be built and for fruitful crops of corn and wheat to be planted.

What to do About the Indian

Anna rose early and silently tiptoed down the stairs. The house was still dark, but she instinctively was able to make her way to the large fireplace. Kneeling, she began to gently puff over the grey ashes, revealing the tiny orange embers underneath. White smoke curled toward the chimney as she laid pine needles in, waiting for them to burst into bright flames. The fire would chase the chill from the dark room. Shadows soon swayed randomly across the wood plank ceiling. Hannah wanted to give her mother a little extra time to sleep if possible. The new baby, Mercy, had been up crying most of the night. She was a fussy baby and was wearing on everyone's nerves.

Padding across the floor in her bare feet, Anna lit the lantern, grabbed her wool shawl and the milk bucket and headed across the yard for the barn. Suddenly realizing that she had forgotten her shoes, she spun back around toward the door, when from the corner of her eye she caught a fleeting movement. It came from the side of the house. Anna froze in her steps, her eyes adjusting to the quickly changing light of dawn.

The figure stood brazenly still; their eyes locked. He was painted in frightening splashes of color, like the brightly colored parrot she had once seen at a sideshow in Boston. A large chalky-white circle spilled down the middle of his forehead and three royal blue lines streaked across each cheek. His head, painted red, was shaved except for a patch of mohawk hair across the top and two feathers attached from the right side of his head. Hannah wanted to scream, but nothing came. And then, as quickly as a startled deer, he was gone.

Dropping the bucket, Anna scrambled into the house and quickly slid the wooden latch behind her. Leaning with her back against the door, she tried to catch her breath and slow her racing heart. She closed her eyes and prayed,

> *"Lord, I do not know if what I just saw was a dream or if indeed, he was there, but I pray for your loving hand of mercy for us this day."*

Waiting, she heard nothing but the soft crackling of the fire, until Mercy once again began to fuss.

Anna's father did not question her account.

> *"Anna, ye be not one prone to imagine or invent a tale. If say ye the Indian, I believe ye."*

John gathered his musket from above the fireplace and went to investigate. Natives in the area had been mostly peaceful, but as of late, they were becoming more and more agitated, causing John to take greater precautions. As he walked around the outside of the house, he found shallow moccasin tracks. This Indian appeared to be alone. John followed the tracks a little further across the field and into the deeper woods, until he lost them.

Reviewing the plans with his family once again, John stressed the importance of immediate barricade should an attack be imminent. Their house was a garrison house, a defensive structure heavily fortified. The well was near the house sheltered by a large elm tree, making water more easily accessible should a siege be prolonged. Friends and family would retreat to the Ward house in the case of any Indian attack. Anna felt secure with her family.

It was the Sabbath. After the morning service, John assembled the men of Cambridge Village and the surrounding area to discuss what Anna had seen. Each man was aware of the possibility of an Indian uprising, although everyone thought it to be unlikely.

> *"I be somewhat anxious that this shameless native dare to venture within two miles of the village, let alone creep about a garrison house. He be either a scout or crazed. I say he be crazed, and we need not be of any great concern,"* shouted Isaac Williams.

There were many supporting this view, shouting, *"Aye! Aye!"*, until a challenging opinion was raised.

> *"So indeed, should we be more feared of a scout gathering particulars than an unstable Indian capable of behaving well outside the boundaries of competent behavior? I see danger in either case, and it causes me pause altogether."*

Thomas Greenwood was new to Cambridge Village. Twenty-five years old, educated and already respected for his opinion, although there were some who thought him impertinent to the elder status of Isaac Williams. Tempers flared and shouting ensued as the men of Cambridge Village debated the course of action, should any need be taken. In the end, patience ruled the day and all journeyed home to their families simply reminded to be diligent in their watch.

Finding Peace of Mind

John Ward liked Thomas Greenwood and chuckled quietly to himself when Thomas's words caused such a ruckus. After the meeting, John approached Thomas and invited him home for the evening meal with his family, which Thomas gladly accepted. He lived alone, renting a small room in the village. He was a terrible cook, and a home-cooked meal with a prominent family was a welcome prospect.

Hannah welcomed Thomas warmly, while bouncing the wildly squawking Mercy in her arms, apologizing for the din. Anna had taken charge of the meal preparations. Savory venison stew was simmering over the fire with the aroma of fresh meat, onions, carrots and potatoes filling the room. Thomas's mouth watered with anticipation. The meal tasted as good as it smelled, and using his bread to soak up the last streaks of sauce from his bowl, Thomas commented with a tone of fondness,

> *"To serve a meal as delectable as this, ye be a fine wife for any man someday, Anna Ward."*

Anna cringed at Thomas's unfounded familiarity with her, assuming that he saw her as an immature schoolgirl who would swoon at such a compliment. For once in her life, Anna was speechless. At seventeen years of age, she recoiled at any implication that she was not a grown woman. Finally finding her words, she glaringly replied,

> *"Mr. Greenwood, ye should judge me wholly on a meat stew?"*

Thomas's grey eyes flashed with amusement and he thought to himself,

> *"This girl is formidable."*

John Ward, fearing his daughter's propensity to continue with speaking her mind, dutifully interrupted with an offer to show Thomas the livestock.

John Ward and Thomas strolled around the property, a full moon assisting the lit lantern John carried, observing cows, pigs and oxen. But Thomas's mind was still lingering on Anna. Her image would not leave his mind: the firelight dancing across her face, biting her bottom lip to hold down a smile, and then her unfettered and infectious laugh that would spring up unexpectedly, filling the room with joy. He knew that he would meet this girl again, and hopefully make a better impression.

Anna could not sleep. She argued silently with herself most of the night,

> *"Who does he think he is? That arrogant attitude. And he is not really all that handsome. He is too tall and skinny. Maybe he does not eat well. Maybe that is why he is so skinny. He speaks crudely with that Northern English accent. Actually, he really is quite good-looking, although his nose is too sharp. His eyes are too.... too.... something!...beautiful? No!"*

Fitfully, she finally fell into an exhausted sleep. It was almost light when Anna finally woke the next morning. Her mother had already stoked the fire and baby Mercy slept peacefully in the cradle next to her mother's chair.

"Anna, is there something you'd like to talk about?"

Hannah asked her daughter, with a sly look on her face. Anna apologized for her tardiness and spilled out her confusion and the feelings that she had never had before. Her mother quietly listened as she rocked the baby's cradle. Anna clearly needed time to work through these unfamiliar emotions. But there was no time now, with the younger children stumbling down the stairs and wanting to eat. Anna took charge and her mother warmly smiled down at Mercy.

As the weeks eased into months, Anna continued with her usual duties of daily chores. Now, almost six months since she had first met Thomas Greenwood, her heart held a hollow ache of perplexity. It was early autumn and the day was brisk. Fresh air held the smell of wood smoke from the chimney low to the ground, as morning gave way to afternoon. Anna hauled water, made lye soap, baked bread and plucked a chicken. There remained spinning to do on the loom and tallow candles to make, yet Anna's eyes were on the grove of silver birch that stood just over the rise to the north. A silent wind caught the leaves off the old elm tree and tossed them joyously into the air. Iron grey clouds swirled in tumult to the west. Anna ignored the threat and hopefully asked,

> *"Mother, I have done as ye asked this morning. Would ye allow me some time alone this day to walk and pray?"*
> Hannah sighed, *"Much work is still to be done."*

Anna held her breath as her mother continued, with a tone of hesitation,

> *"Be back before darkness falls."*

Anna kissed her mother's soft cheeks and grabbing her dark green woolen shawl, bolted from the house.

The expanse of towering trees, boulder strewn gullies and wide valleys were beckoning to her. Humming softly as she walked, she found herself engulfed with a deep sense of God's presence, while a misty rain drizzled from the dark pine trees looming overhead. Her mind found comfort and her heart was settled in peace as she shuffled along the wet pine-strewn path, tears rolling down her cheeks for reasons she knew not. She trusted her future into God's hands and prayed that it be so with Thomas Greenwood. When the Charles River began to shimmer through the tangled deadfall, she realized that she had wandered too far.

The rain had sputtered itself out and clouds had given way to the milky sky. It was beginning to get dark and John was readying his horse to search for Anna when she came running from over the hill, her dress and shawl fluttering in the wind like some wild moss-colored bird.

> *"Where have ye been, my girl?!"*
> *"I walked too far, to the river. Time slipped away from me, Father. I am greatly sorry to have troubled ye,"* Anna exclaimed, panting to catch her breath.
> *"Ye have not been yourself of late, Anna. I am worried!"*

Anna smiled broadly, her eyes beaming with delight.

> *"My heart is settled, and my mind is at rest. The Lord has my future in His loving hands. No more will I fret over a husband. Nor will I fret over one particular man who is ever so slow to act,"*

she declared, with her arms folded and a smile matching the joy of her heart. Throwing her head back, she laughed and spun around, skipping toward the house singing. John shook his head:

> *"I will never understand the nature of womanly thought."*

As the moon began to crest, shedding its timid light, dark narrow eyes watched, blending unseen through thick underbrush.

A Match is Made

Thomas had waited for what he believed was a respectable amount of time before approaching John Ward for permission to court Anna. While Anna had agonized in her belief that Thomas gave her no thought, the reality was that Thomas thought about her almost constantly. Seeing her each Sunday at the meeting house and exchanging polite greetings only caused him more anguish as he longed to make her his wife. Finally, Thomas mustered the courage to awkwardly and fearfully ask her father,

"Sir, I have admired your daughter, Anna, for these many months and have fond feelings toward her. I have established myself in business and have seen my trade grow. Soon I will be able to purchase my own land and I now wish to ask your blessing that I might court Anna."

John Ward was hesitant. He would not be swayed into giving his blessing based on untrustworthy fickle emotions. Romantic love did not figure into his mind. John's desire for his daughter had always been that she marry into a family of great respectability and prosperous influence. Thomas Greenwood had no family. He was a fine godly man, yet he had not truly proven himself with time and accomplishment. John pondered carefully. He understood his daughter's feelings, but he was unsure of Thomas's future prospects.

"I will consent to wait one year before making any contrary arrangements for Anna's future. This will allow Anna to remain in my care, where she will continue to aid her mother with the care of the younger children and household duties, while providing you, Thomas Greenwood, ample time to prove yourself to me and the community."

One year later, Thomas gained John Ward's blessing and the following spring, on June 8, 1670, nineteen-year-old Hannah "Anna" Ward, of Cambridge Village, Massachusetts Bay Colony, married twenty-seven-year-old Thomas Greenwood, of Heptonstall, England.

12

Cambridge Village and King Philip's War

1673-1675

Thomas and Anna settled in Cambridge Village. The skills that Thomas had gained from his apprenticeship back in Heptonstall so many years before had provided him with opportunity and respect within the community. His determination to steadily "modernize" spinning and weaving in his village, using recent inventions and methods being incorporated in England, proved to be profitable. Focusing on one kind of woolen cloth, he could produce large quantities for both sale and trade.

Anna was soon with child and thrilled at having a baby of her own. However, her joy soon melted into grief when, in the seventh month of her pregnancy, she went into labor and their first son, Thomas, was stillborn. Anna, with a broken heart, sought solace and understanding from the Lord.

> "O God of all comfort, you know the depth of my sorrow. My tears have been my food both day and night. Help me, I pray, to place myself under thy guiding, loving care, trusting You with all things. Thou hast done for me all things well and have indulged me with your many blessings. Yet all my desires have not been gratified. If fulfillment of my wishes be my ruin, I pray, spare me, but if not, wipe away my tears and bless me with motherhood."

While Anna was still grieving the loss of her firstborn, her mother, Hannah, gave birth to two more sons, Edward, born in 1671 and Eleazer, born in 1672, creating a strange mixture of emotions within Anna's already wounded heart.

Ultimately, on July 15, 1673, Anna's tears were wiped away as God doubly answered her prayers with the birth of twin boys, Thomas III ("Tom") and John. [1] That same year Thomas purchased seven acres adjoining John Ward's property, and with the added acreage he expanded his sheep shearing shed and increased his livestock. At thirty years of age, Thomas Greenwood was gaining both respect and wealth.

The Frontier Under Siege

Thomas woke to a sharp rapping at the door. Growling with sleepiness, he stumbled down the stairs to find his father-in-law, John Ward, impatiently pacing back and forth across the porch.

> *"I received a dispatch. Swansea [2] is under siege. Metacom and the Wampanoag are enraged and on the warpath. We are to be on full alert."*

John was speaking loud and fast, with a twinge of fear in his voice and Thomas knew not to underestimate the seriousness of the situation.

In January 1675, John Sassamon, a Massachusetts Indian, had warned the governor of Plymouth Colony, Josiah Winslow, about impending Indian attacks being planned by Metacomet, the Wampanoag sachem (elected chief) otherwise known as King Philip by colonists. In his early teens, Sassamon was introduced to Christianity by John Eliot, the first minister of Cambridge Village. Becoming proficient in speaking English, Sassamon became a skilled interpreter and eventually studied at Harvard College for one year.

Sadly, John Sassamon's body was found in an icy pond the same month he provided warning of potential native attacks. Accidental drowning was first suspected, until closer examination revealed that his neck had been broken. In June, three Wampanoag Indians were charged for the murder. Further evidence came from the testimony of an eyewitness named

Patuckson, a Christian convert who testified to having seen the murder. A jury of twelve colonists and six Indian elders found the men guilty and sentenced them to be executed.

Thomas and the men of Cambridge Village were well aware that King Philip was outraged at the executions and were growing more and more concerned at Wampanoag aggression and rumored military strategies.

"This war is a long time coming,"

Thomas mused as he sat with Anna at the kitchen table, the fire's orange glow warming the air and pushing the morning chill from the room. Anna remembered the terrifying image of the painted Indian with whom she came face to face eight years before.

"Aye, a long time,"

she quietly replied. Chasing the memory from her thoughts, she bounced three-year-old John on her knee, with his twin brother Tom playing on the floor beside her chair.

Thomas understood, as many others did not, that land ownership was an unthought of concept to the native inhabitants of the colonies. Anna's uncle, John Howe, who married Elizabeth Ward (John Ward's sister), was a fur trader. Thomas spent many hours with John Howe discussing the native mindset. In 1656, John Howe [3] built his house at the intersection of two Indian trails known as the Nashua and the Connecticut. He spoke the language of the Algonquian, gaining confidence and goodwill among them. John Howe would often rant,

> *"Indian's build villages and use the land for some years and then relocate to new fertile land, leaving the used land to rest, while we whites view land as permanent acquisition."*

Neither understood the other. He continued,

> *"Owning land is as foreign an idea to Indians as not owning land is to whites".*

The encroaching white population, with farms, villages and towns quickly multiplying, was causing a growing mistrust and a yearning to strike the whites and drive them out.

This festering sore, being poked year after year, became increasingly inflamed until all-out war broke out in 1675. Metacomet (a.k.a. King Philip) had sought to live in harmony with the colonists. However as colonial expansion grew, hostilities grew as well. In an effort to block the intrusion of white settlers, Metacomet led the native uprising against the colonial English, with the goal of repulsing Puritan expansion, hoping to ultimately push them out of New England. It would prove to be barbaric on both sides, as raw furor swept the colonies.

Marlborough and Massacre

Smoke rolled high over the tops of standing pines in the distance, like a dark boiling thundercloud. Thomas and his party of eight men, including his father-in-law, John Ward, cut across a steep slope, moving slowly, watchful of detection. Stumbling once, Thomas grabbed a dead cedar bough to balance himself; it cracked loudly, and everyone froze, with eyes darting along the bottom and top of the deep ravine. There was no movement and only the sound of a squirrel leaping from branch to branch overhead. They clutched their muskets more tightly and continued to move up and over the hill.

Finally reaching the outskirts of Marlborough, they were sickened by what they saw. The destruction was complete, as the smoldering remains of what once was an active village lay in ruins. No living thing was spared that was not protected inside of the fortified houses.

Many had fled Marlborough after the first attack had occurred in March, but William Ward, John's father, at seventy-three, had refused to leave. And now, one month later, when the Algonquians returned to attack again, they destroyed almost every remaining structure. Thomas found William with mostly women and children inside the garrison that was William's home.

"We be safe. The ruthless painted raiders would not give up. They loitered here many a day, with cunning and evil

intent to kill us all, but we remained firm, and have most of us survived,"

William exclaimed, with unchecked emotion. It was obvious that he suffered from extreme exhaustion, yet the adrenaline was still pumping heavily through his aged veins.

"Most of the men have gone on to Sudbury town to provide reinforcements there. If ye travel forthwith, and being cautious, ye might join them there before Sudbury meets the fate that we have seen these days." [4]

Thomas, along with John Ward and the other men from Cambridge Village quickly agreed to join the reinforcement party. Following the heavily wooded road from Marlborough to Sudbury was not safe. Skirting the road, they made their way cautiously, pausing often to listen in motionless silence through the dense, mossy forest. Wading in a narrow stream, with the icy water numbing their legs, they found themselves traversing through what seemed to be a dark green tunnel of heavy overgrowth. Pressing forward, they suddenly caught the sound of faint yells, high pitched screeching and gun fire perhaps a half mile in front of them. Wading from the water, they squatted together and spoke in whispers.

"We should hurry to the commotion. There be indeed a fight directly over those hills,"

John Ward commented, his voice shaky with emotion. There was consensus, but with an awareness of being small in number, they knew they were extremely vulnerable.

A stiff wind had picked up, muffling any noise they made, for which Thomas silently thanked God. More panicked voices. Louder. Closer. When they finally reached the top of the hill overlooking the road below, all was eerily quiet. Thomas could see what appeared to be bright red coats lying motionless and scattered in clusters across the ground. There were no Algonquins in sight, apparently having moved on. Cautiously maneuvering down the hill, Thomas and the others quickly realized the extent of the massacre. The scene was horrific beyond description, the likes of which Thomas had never witnessed before.

Smoke from the battle whirled in the wind close to the ground, adding a foggy mystical impression to an already brutal sight. His eyes burning, Thomas collapsed to his knees and wept when he found the body of Eleazer, John Ward's seventeen-year-old half-brother and William Ward's youngest son. He was shot in the temple and lay on the edge of a ditch not far from the road, his young life brutally extinguished.

John Ward found his brother-in-law, John Howe, not far from Eleazar's body. It was apparent that he had died trying to protect Eleazer, but to no avail. Thirty more men lay across the road and in the woods. Tracks indicated that the remainder of the surviving militia, some twenty men, had scattered in all directions, running for their lives. As Thomas and the eight others with him began the gruesome job of gathering the dead, a half dozen of those men who had fought so fiercely and only withstood by running, returned from their flight and recounted the ambush, which had taken them completely by surprise.

Cambridge Village Becomes New Town

The horror of that April day would remain as Thomas battled nightmares, waking night after night in a cold sweat. His only peace was found in the scriptures as he pored over them, finding therein *"the only rule of truth"*. Anna grieved the loss of her family members, while finding a degree of comfort in the joy of her two young sons. Tom and John were growing straight and strong.

> *"I praise thee, O God, for thy steadfast love and mercy, both given and promised."*

Thomas threw himself into his work as well as matters pertaining to Cambridge Village, which had been crippled through the three long, terrifying years of King Philip's War. In person and property, residents were now burdened under the great expense of rebuilding what had been destroyed. Cambridge Village was laden with the task of enlarging their meeting house, as well as building a new house for the minister, Rev.

Nehemiah Hobart. [7] Under lawful requirement, based on increased population, they were also charged to build a school. These responsibilities, combined with paying taxes and tithes to the town of Cambridge on the north side of the river, was more than they could bear.

On May 8, 1678, Thomas Greenwood, along with fifty-one residents of Cambridge Village petitioned to be separated from Cambridge and to become an entity unto itself. Edward Jackson, Anna's grandfather, a distinguished citizen, author of the petition and representative to the court for many years, was the first signer. Her father, John Ward, who was involved in drawing up the petition, also signed. Cambridge vigorously protested and the matter was delayed in the courts for nine years. Finally, in 1687, the village was granted the right to secede. [8] Edward Jackson never saw the fulfillment of the numerous years he spent aggressively petitioning for an independent town. He died June 7, 1681, at seventy-nine years of age. Anna grieved the passing of her grandfather and marveled at the accomplishments God brought about through his life. The new town was, very appropriately, named New Town (later to be "Newton").

13

Death and War

1686-1690

"Thomas, the Lord has seen fit to bless us. A baby will come this year. Let us hope He does not bless us with twice more, for I doubt my energies can sustain the bedlam that twins would bring again to our home!"

Anna made her cheerful announcement to her husband with an enormous smile on her round face. Thomas had suspected that she might be with child; her morning sickness and lack of appetite had hinted at it for several weeks. But he could not hide his concern, for she had almost died delivering the twins. At thirty years old she was still well within the age of childbearing, but a nagging doubt weighed heavy on Thomas.

Young Tom and John worked side-by-side with their father, learning the woolen/weaving trade. John was especially adept at sheep shearing and tending to the livestock, while Tom could often be found with his nose deep in a book, especially the Bible. John, being born twenty minutes after Tom, teased his "*big*" brother,

"Sheep have no need in understanding the sovereignty of God, Tom! So ye best help them find shelter lest they freeze!"

With colder weather approaching, both boys labored diligently in order to get the young ewes and lambs sheltered before the winter snows arrived.

The weather was turning quickly, and they knew that the young sheep would not survive when exposed to extreme elements. The shearing had been completed the day before using stud combs, leaving more wool on the animals for greater protection. But with menacing storm clouds gathering in the west, they needed to quickly get the sheep inside the protection of the roofed shelter.

Their father had been in town all day and was not expected back before dark. As justice of the peace and constable of New Town, his community responsibilities took more and more of his time. The boys wondered if the weather would hold out long enough for him to return that night. Heavy snow began to fall just as they herded the sheep securely inside the shed. It was dusk and they were exhausted and famished. They shared laughter and conversation as they walked back to the house, their hands and feet numb with cold and their bellies rumbling with hunger. As typical thirteen-year-olds, it seemed that they were forever hungry. They often heard their mother cheerfully complain,

"Ye both be eating us out of house and home!"

The house was eerily dark, quiet and cold as they burst through the door. The fire had gone to embers and no candles lit the mantle. No mouthwatering smells permeated the room as they had expected. With a twinge of confusion and concern, they tossed their gloves and coats on a chair and called, *"Mother?"* A soft, pain-filled moan came from behind the table. Anna lay on the floor, her face etched in agony. *"Mother!!"*

John ran to the barn and saddled the horse, a brown gelding named Diligent. He prayed that today she would live up to her name. Riding hard toward town, snow was a flurry of freezing white bullets chasing past his head, as he prodded Diligent at full gallop. Struggling through the wind and blowing snow they forged on. Filled with alarm for his mother while at the same time fighting fatigue, John struggled to stay alert, being somewhat mesmerized by the horse's raspy rhythmic breathing and the steady beat of its hooves. *"Stay awake John! Ye must reach father and the midwife or mother may die!"* he continually repeated to himself.

Tom gently cradled his mother's head in his lap, while stroking her hair and praying for God to keep her alive until help came. But it was not to be. Anna took her last breath, leaving young Tom in a state of disbelief. As the storm raged outside, he held her lifeless body through the cold night, waiting for his father and brother to return. She had remained conscious for several hours, aware that she was dying. Her excruciating sorrow at losing her unborn baby along with her deep love for Tom overwhelmed her mother's heart. She assured Tom, in weak whispers, over and over: *"I go to be with Jesus, Tom. No worries. No fear. Befriend faithfulness."* [1] Tom wept over his mother in the silence of the dark house, never to forget her words. He was very familiar with the Psalm that she quoted to him in her dying breath; it had been her prayer for her sons every day.

John and his father fought their way home in the blinding whiteness of the snowstorm that continued to bluster its fury. Wading through deep drifts and against blizzard conditions, John had intercepted his father on the road the night before. Thomas made the difficult and painful decision to find shelter for himself and John, rather than risk becoming lost and freezing to death. By mid-morning they finally reached the house. Thomas, in a state of exhaustion and with a sense of panic, leapt from his horse and ran into the house, only to discover his beautiful Anna lying lifelessly, yet serenely in the arms of his oldest son.

King William's War and Captain Wiswall

Captain Noah Wiswall [2] was an imposing man. At fifty-two years, his six-foot stature showed no signs of shrinking. An incomparable marksman and a man of dangerous fighting capability, his infantry militia would trust him beyond question. He had led many an expedition over the expanse of the colonies throughout King Philip's War, and now King William's War which was also known as "The War of the Grand Alliance", had begun in 1689.

His guttural voice, sounding as if raked over gravel, had evolved from years of barking out orders to undisciplined men. New France [3] and their Indian allies, the Wabanaki Confederation, [4] had attacked and seized Fort Loyal [5] in Acadia and were freely attacking settlers along the New Hampshire frontier without reprisal. Captain Wiswall had seen firsthand the horror of gruesome and brutal violence used against men, women and children. Feeling a sense of urgency, he prodded his men at a quick pace to bring retaliation and relief to a terrified frontier.

New England was again engulfed in the cruel flames of a bloody clash. Captain Wiswall felt grateful for the allied warriors joining his force as reinforcements. The Iroquois Confederation consisted of Mohawk, Onondagas, Oneidas, Seneca and Tuscarora. It was not for love of New England or the English that the confederation sided against New France, but primarily for the purpose of trade. The Confederation had dominated Great Lakes fur trade and continued in conflict with the French over those rights since 1680. They now willingly fought the French, with bitter hatred engulfing both sides of a seemingly endless conflict.

Although the Iroquois Confederation fought with the English against the French, they vehemently resisted the concept of conducting themselves as subjects of the crown, refusing to behave in a subservient manner, and often playing both sides against each other depending on the advantages. Appeasing their less than subservient allies, the English encouraged and rewarded the Iroquois in attacking New France. The Massachusetts Colony had expanded their settlements northward into Acadia and the resulting disputes over land required the assistance of this powerful Confederation of skilled and merciless warriors in securing increased occupation over the French.

The warm breeze of late spring caught Captain Wiswall's attention as his horse plodded alongside his men. *"Spring doth revive my soul,"* he absentmindedly observed to himself while stroking the stock of his flintlock. He had shed his jacket and his black tricorn hat for comfort. The gold-colored buttons on his white vest glistened in the sun. He sat up a little straighter and taller in the saddle, should his men sense he was not vigilant in his duties. Suddenly there was noisy commotion among the ranks as a dispatcher rode in furiously, kicking up dirt and dust as he passed. The message was short and to the point, *"Bloody Point* [6] *ravaged by attack. Reinforcements required posthaste."*

Several houses still smoldered in ruins as the Wiswall's militia arrived the next day. Too late. Wiswall stopped a man, clearly dazed, his face blackened with smoke and soot. His wife stood by, trance-like, her grey dress dirty and torn at the shoulder. Recounting in staggered phrases the wretchedness of the attack, his watery eyes never left the ground, seeming to conceal some regrettable shame.

"People are dead and gone. I could not help them."

Several were killed and even more carried into captivity. Bodies lined across the front of what was once the meeting house, covered in blankets and ready for burial. Wiswall shuddered at seeing the tiny blankets, knowing that innocent children lay beneath.

Death at Wheelwright Pond

Finding the enemy was a difficult challenge. They had seemingly melted into the wilderness. Phantoms of an inscrutable forest of ancient giants. Scouts fanned out, relaying outdated and inaccurate information back to Captain Wiswall who was becoming increasingly impatient with every passing hour. Always one step behind. Time was slipping away, and the enemy continued to attack up and down the frontier. Just one month prior, the infantry militia had helped to dig graves at Bloody Point, and now frustration and boredom replaced nervous energy. They had vigilantly pursued their adversaries, only to be too late after a surprise attack on Exeter [7].

Spring had now given way to summer heat. The sun was high and horse flies were biting.

Ensign Walker [8] whispered to Lt. Flagg [8], while prodding his horse across a fallen log,

"I think we could be in for rain."

The thought brought a mixture of emotions, glad for cooler temperatures while also dreading the anticipation of wet, musty clothes. Albeit, the weather was a mere distraction, as Walker shifted in his saddle, having the strange sense that he was being watched.

Wheelwright Pond glistened in the sunlight through a mask of thick green forest. Captain Wiswall could feel the tension; his untamed, grey hair was matted with sweat under his black tricorn hat. Suddenly, a colorfully painted figure leaped in front of the column. His chest shimmering with bear grease; his hands covered with blood-red paint; his wolfish face streaked with a blue diagonal line crossing his arched nose; a band of three feathers rising prominently from his head; red zig-zag "lightning bolts" running from his shoulders down across his belly. His sudden and shocking appearance brought an immediate sense of panic among the soldiers. Wiswall's horse pulled back and reared, almost tossing the captain from his saddle. *"Ayeeeeeeee,"* the painted warrior shouted in a long piercing howl, his mouth twisted in a cruel sneer.

A storm of warriors surged from the cover of the surrounding trees, swarming the militia like a frenzy of buzzing, screeching bees, wielding hatchets, tomahawks and knives. Shrill screams came from the woods and the pop of gunfire quickly filled the air. Lt. Flagg, calling for his men to make a defense, died instantly as a ball of lead tore through his heart. Ensign Walker cocked his gun and fired, with the orange stab of flame and puff of smoke blinding him, as a warrior caught the side of his head with a tomahawk.

Captain Wiswall dismounted his horse and ran for nearby bushes, seeking cover while wildly barking orders. Crouching low, he fired. One Indian crumbled in mid-stride. He quickly reloaded, but never fired again. A young warrior, his dark cat-like eyes clouded with fury, smashed the butt of his rifle across Captain Wiswall's [9] temple.

The tattooed Iroquois in deerskin breechcloths and leggings, alongside the infantry militia in their bright red jackets, battled valiantly in unnerved confusion. A feverish madness swept across the battlefield. Deer-tailed headpieces on painted skulls, feathers and torn strips of brightly colored trade cloth, entangled with the screams of wounded and dying men. A nightmarish scene, as men struggled against violent death.

Singling out officers first was a common strategy, causing the infantrymen to flounder without direction. Before the battle was over, fifteen men as well as the three officers would die at Wheelwright Pond. [10] The battle was a defeat, but the war would ultimately be won as the English eventually pushed back the territory of New France, giving them more land and greater domination.

14

Rev. Thomas "Tom" Greenwood III and Elizabeth Wiswall

1670's-1720's

Tom had waited a long time to marry Elizabeth Wiswall. As children and second cousins (once removed) Tom and his twin brother, John, would "torture" Elizabeth and her younger sisters with their practical jokes; making a general nuisance of themselves. Their fathers, Thomas Greenwood and Captain Noah Wiswall, had been friends, while Tom's great-grandfather, Edward Jackson, was a brother to Elizabeth's grandfather, John Jackson.

Elizabeth, being four years older, viewed Tom as simply a child for most of her life. *"Foolishness shall not get ye very far in this life, Tom Greenwood,"* she would scold, trying her best to sound sternly authoritative. She devoured books and spent every possible minute reading, which generally meant straining her eyes by the dim candlelight of dark evenings.

When Tom matured from childish foolery into young adulthood, he too found himself mesmerized with books, and the two became odd friends of sorts, conversing about every imaginable topic, which at times led to arguing over matters of faith, the church, Shakespeare or anything else that struck their fanciful imaginations. Neither thought of each other beyond occasional companions caught up in thought-provoking and sometimes adversarial conversation. Both were bright and both could hold their own in debate.

When Elizabeth's father, Noah, was killed at Wheelwright Pond, Tom found himself in a different role that summer as a comforter for Elizabeth.

With Elizabeth's head on his shoulder, he stroked her auburn hair and relished the way she felt in his arms. Her tears soaked his white shirt and when she looked up to thank him for his kindness, her narrow, deep set eyes strangely reminded him of his mahogany desk at Harvard [1], dark and rich. He almost chuckled aloud at how, even now after having graduated, he still had difficulty redirecting his thoughts away from school. Silently scolding himself, he quickly focused his attention back on Elizabeth, and together they recounted the finality of death and the legacy of her father's life.

> *"Answers will not bring comfort, Ye must look to the Lord, for He is present in times of trial. As the Good Book says in Isaiah, "Fear thou not; for I am with thee, be not dismayed; for I am thy God."* Then he added his mother's familiar words, *"Befriend faithfulness".*

The satisfaction that he had felt with his achievement at Harvard was quickly offset by the tragedy that was Noah Wiswall's death. Tom was well acquainted with death. The heartbreaking circumstances of his mother dying in his arms several years prior had left an indelible imprint on him. His great-grandfather William Ward's death three years later in 1689 left him with a deep and abiding grief. Indian threat and the horror stories of capture, torture and death permeated his mind with their images throughout his youth. Life had been difficult to be sure, yet Tom saw God's sovereign goodness at work through it all. God had been faithful to him, and now Tom sought to be faithful to the Lord and possessed a strong desire to serve God full time in the ministry of the gospel.

Noah Wiswall had not sought any marriage arrangements for his daughter before his death. Elizabeth's mother, Theodocia, [2] now found herself a widow with seven children remaining at home. Marriage for Elizabeth was not top priority in her mind. At twenty-two, Elizabeth was the oldest daughter and supporting her mother and siblings was now paramount. Her daily duties occupied most of her time and energy. There were floors to sweep and clean, cows to milk, meals to cook, candles and soap to make, along with a never-ending list of the needs of her brothers and sisters.

Her mind would ponder the possibilities of her future, but never could she imagine a life beyond New Town and the requirements of her family in the exhausting mundane, if not chaotic, demands of each day.

> *"My course is set by you, dear Lord. I refuse to worry or be disturbed in my spirit for what lies ahead or what could have been. My life is in your hands, Father God. Why should I connive or attempt to manipulate toward what I believe would be for my good, when you have my good in your loving control, whatever it may be. Yet my prayer would be that thy hand would reach firmly down and guide Tom Greenwood to love me, the way I most affectionately love him."*

Elizabeth Wiswall found it easy to be honest with God.

Tom was well aware that a wife would enhance the effectiveness of his ministry. With his attention completely consumed with securing his ordination and a position with a congregation, he had given marriage no serious thought at all. His brother John [3] was aiming to wed Hannah Trowbridge [4] and was preparing to present himself to her father soon. John worked alongside his father, Thomas, in the family weaving business and was realizing his strengths as a man and as a leader. His path ahead was clear. Whereas Tom was less decisive and prone to great reflection. John would often chide his twin brother,

> *"Ye mind be as a bucket without a bottom and ye heart without affection and full of leaks."* [5]

It was true, Tom was an academic and "frivolous emotion" figured little into his life. It was not that his emotions were shallow or easily disregarded; they were simply unexplored. In his fervor to hold fast to the gospel, he pushed aside the secret sorrows and longings of his own heart. The tragedies that had befallen him were guarded behind a wall of intellect and knowledge. But God had other plans.

Soon, that crushing enemy, death, swept down upon his life yet again, as greedy as a starved wolf. Tom's father, Thomas Greenwood II, while repairing the shingled roof of the sheep shed, fell, striking his head. [6]

He died two days later, on Sept. 1, 1693, just one month before Tom was ordained to become the minister of the First Congregational Church [7] in Rehoboth, Massachusetts Bay Colony. Tom later recorded in the church registry, *"My hon'rd father has dyed, (Friday), Sept. 1st, in the evening of the day."*

Elizabeth Wiswall was there, her ivory face framing her mournful dark eyes, as she sat rigidly straight, her calloused hands folded in her lap, while the funeral service proceeded. Sitting in the back pew, never taking her eyes off Tom, watching the tilt and bowing of his head, her heart longed to comfort him. Thomas Greenwood's young widow, Abigail, whom Thomas had married the year after Tom's mother, Anna, went to glory, had her hands full with one-year-old, William and three-year-old James, who insisted on jumping up and down on the pew. Following the service, the beloved and respected man, Thomas Greenwood II, of Heptonstall, England was buried. He was fifty-years-old.

For Elizabeth, the vivid autumn colors seemed to mock the grey-colored grief that hung over her heart. She slowly walked home, trying to absorb the mixture of emotions stirring within her - grief, confusion, a sense of failure, and some feelings of shame. Tom had not acknowledged her presence at the funeral, which she understood, but which also caused her to feel sadly ignored. She prayed, kicking a stone along the road,

"Let me not despair of the smallness of my selfish heart. Grant me thy grace to go forward for the utmost honor of my Lord."

"Elizabeth! Elizabeth!", an urgent voice called from behind her. It was Tom.

Rehoboth and Witch Trials

It was a bleak and blustery Monday, the twenty-eighth day of December 1693. [9] Family and friends filled the meeting house. The justice of the peace solemnly pronounced them to be husband and wife, *"'til death doth thou part"*. John Greenwood slapped his brother on the back,

"Ye did well Tom! Ye did very well!"

Packed and ready for travel the next morning, [9] Tom and his blushing wife, Elizabeth, pulled out of New Town, never to call it home again. Rehoboth, some forty-five miles away, where Tom was to be the new minister, would be their future. The previous minister, Samuel Newton, [10] had recently resigned after being widowed and the congregation looked forward to Rev. Thomas Greenwoods arrival. Elizabeth marveled at the quickness of God's hand in her life, in what initially seemed a never-ending sentence as a maid and caregiver. Her mother had tearfully given her blessing to the union, and quickly Elizabeth had become the respected wife of a minister and on her way to an unfamiliar community.

Rehoboth, in Plymouth Colony, had been on the front lines of King Philip's War seventeen years earlier. The memories of that bloody conflict which raged throughout New England remained fresh in this close-knit community. Anawan Rock, in Rehoboth, was one of the final episodes of the war which played out in August of 1676. The story, told and retold, held intrigue and mystery as well as the frightening aspect of what some believe to have been supernatural phenomenon.

The colonists' conflict with the Wampanoags over the issue of encroachment had been escalating, when Metacomet was killed on August 12th and Anawan, his chief advisor, led the remaining warriors. Pursued by colonial militia, they sought to evade capture by changing camps every night. Making camp at the base of a huge dome of rock, 25 feet tall and 75 feet wide, in Squannakonk Swamp just outside Rehoboth was a strategic move. With their backs to the rock, Anawan and his sixty warriors felt safe. Dragonflies acrobatically hunted the air over the thick underbrush while spiders trapped insects in dew-heavy webs across the soggy marshland. The silence was interrupted only by the heavy droning of bees and the occasional croaking of frogs. Feet sink deep into the dark and blackish mud. The possibility of an attack seemed unimaginable.

Yet Capt. Benjamin Church, with six of his men in an outrageous and daring maneuver, climbed down from above, and in a surprise attack captured the Indians without bloodshed. Years later, stories would circulate claiming that *"ghost fires"* hovered over the rock at night and voices could be heard, chanting *"lootash, lootash!"*, meaning *"Stand and fight!"*. The haunting of Anawan Rock would be legendary.

Rehoboth was, in a very real sense, a typical colonial village, experiencing the effects of ongoing strife all around them. As they were recovering from the Indian and French conflicts, political and religious pressures were increasing across New England. The British government was pushing for a new political and economic system. Massachusetts in particular had maintained a great deal of autonomy, with its own courts, coinage and religious requirements for citizenship. London was never happy with this arrangement and began to focus on bringing them back in line. Royal authority became far more ambitious and local self-government severely curtailed.

Arbitrary taxation, threats to the established system of land tenure, and heavy-handed attempts to bolster the influence of the Church of England threatened Puritan way of life and the values they held. Britain was emerging as a world empire and the New World (New England) would have no choice but to be a part. Anxiety and profound anger ran deep in the hearts of colonists. The bells of injustice began ringing louder.

The strains of war, decimating tragedies, British oppression, weakened moral conviction, hardships of daily life, mystical forests and a quagmire of political and religious perplexities over the previous thirty years would finally explode in the town of Salem in 1692. Leading up to this, the courts had become very familiar with charges of witchcraft. In 1675, Northampton resident Mary Bliss Parsons was accused of witchcraft, but was soon exonerated. Eight years later in 1683 in Hadley, Massachusetts, Mary Webster [11] was found guilty of being a witch and was sentenced to death by hanging. Adding to the intrigue is the fact that she survived the hanging. Then in 1688, Ann Goody Glover had the same charge and sentence brought against her in Boston. Accusations were common although convictions were rare, until the Salem witch trials.

The atmosphere was ripe for the madness that would follow. Rev. Tom Greenwood was skeptical of the medieval tests used for identifying witches, as were many of his colleagues. He never doubted the power of the devil, yet the public frenzy that resulted in the testimony of hysterical teenage girls was not convincing enough for him to believe that they were ever reliable witnesses.

> *"It is possible that it were not witches who afflicted these girls,*
> *but that they be deluded into accusing innocent people,"*

Thomas openly commented to Judge Samuel Sewall. [12]

Judge Sewall liked Tom and Elizabeth Greenwood and often enjoyed time at their home when he made his official rounds in the area of Rehoboth. As a judge in the Salem witch trials, Sewall was faced with determining God's will in matters of life and death.

The stage had been set in Salem and Judge Sewell was caught up in manic misjudgment and paranoia, beginning with the rantings of three young girls in this small village. In the end, over two hundred people were accused and twenty executed. By 1693, the Salem witch trials hysteria began to lose its steam and finally came to an end. In the ensuing years, explanations and attempts at justifying the hangings abounded. Judge Samuel Sewall was the only judge to publicly issue an apology. He handed a sheet of paper to his minister, the highly respected Samuel Willard of Old South Church, [13] Boston, to be read in the meeting. He humbly asked for the *"pardon of men and God"* for his role in the trials. After the confession he experienced relief, but never fully recovered from the guilt and damaged public persona that would haunt him.

In the beginning, when the accusations began to insidiously spread and public fervor was spiraling to a frenzied peak, Sewall was no doubter. He, along with fellow judges, condemned twenty people to their death. But later, sitting alongside the fireplace hearth, a warm cup of tea in his ink-stained hands, this portly man confessed to his friend Tom Greenwood,

> *"My conscience is dismally wounded. To have such pride in knowledge of God and in understanding the laws of man is of no value at all. I am no object of valuable price. I am a shell full of dust."*

Tom understood his friend's admission, and in reply carefully chose his words.

> *"Only God can heal a guilty conscience, support a tottering frame and uphold a departing spirit. May God expel from ye mind all sinful fear and shame, so that in firmness and courage ye may confess before men, zealous with the knowledge of God and filled with His wisdom."* [14]

Sickness and a Search for Renewed Faith

The first faint light of dawn cast its dim glow across the table. Elizabeth's head was bowed in weariness, sitting slumped in the wooden rocker that her father had made long ago. She had been up throughout the night with four-year-old Noah. His fever had spiked again, and he cried out with excruciating back pain as chills racked his small body. The bumpy rash covered his chest, arms and back. The vomiting had stopped, but the nausea remained. She rubbed his aching muscles and applied cool cloths to his matted blonde hair. There was nothing more she could do but pray.

Nine-year-old Hannah and six-year-old John were staying with Elizabeth's sister, Hannah, and her husband Caleb Stedman in Roxbury, forty miles away, until the danger passed and Noah [(15)] was well again. Smallpox was extremely contagious. The widespread epidemic of the previous year had seemed to spare them - until now, March 1703. Her mother, Theodocia, who had remarried the former minister of the Rehoboth church, Samuel Newton, was a source of loving comfort as well as help in caring for Noah. Noah held an especially treasured place in Theodocia's heart, being the namesake of her beloved first husband and Elizabeth's father, Noah Wiswall.

Tom, Elizabeth and Theodocia sang quietly as Noah labored for his last bit of breath. Finally, his small body went limp and was released from the pain and agony he had suffered for so many weeks. Tears flowed down Elizabeth's hollow face. Her baby was in the arms of Jesus and no longer in hers. Tom, with red-rimmed eyes and assured voice, prayed aloud as Elizabeth had never heard him pray before.

"Streams of grief overflow my path. Yet I give Thee thanks for our high calling in Christ. Taken from darkness to light, death to life, sin to victory, Ye bring comfort in the truth of Thy word. I ask of Thee nothing, but to take our son, Noah, in your loving arms and ease him with Thy love. Tho' my mind says "nay", my heart entrusts him to Thee, for Thou hast redeemed him from this life to the next. I bless and adore Thee, the eternal God, for the comfort of these thoughts, the joy of these hopes."

Tom's words were sweet and tender. Yet Elizabeth knew that Tom's words did not reveal all that was going on in his wounded and weary heart. He had struggled severely with the thought of God's goodness in the light of life's tragedies, and his faith had weakened. While still clinging to it, he felt it slipping away.

At thirty-two years of age, death had become too close a companion and required some wrestling. Their baby girl, Esther, had lived only three weeks the previous spring, and now Noah was gone. The church was of little comfort for Rev. Thomas Greenwood. Shepherding the flock and bringing messages from God's Word had become as dry bones, lifeless, lukewarm, rather than the effective and joyful call of God upon his life that he had once experienced. His soul was miserable and weak, as he went through the familiar motions and recited the correct words.

To be sure, Tom still believed; faith itself had not been torn from him. And he continued to perform his duties as a beloved minister to the church at Rehoboth. Yet he could not deny the inner turmoil and emptiness that stirred within. He cried out to God for the peace that he so longed for, and for the love that seemed to be growing as cold as the winter winds. But the silence from heaven remained deafening, as the weeks turned into months of seeking relief for his anguish. He longed for a revival of his own ever-shrinking heart.

Coming home from the meeting house on a crisp September Sunday morning, Tom felt physically weak. Before reaching the doorway to his house, he collapsed. Elizabeth and the older children carried him inside. Beads of sweat puddled in droplets across his broad forehead as he lay on his bed, dreaming in delirium. A fever surged through his body. Elizabeth kept the older children quiet, as she nursed two-month-old, Esther, who had been given the same name as her older, deceased sister. John, their only surviving son, was twelve now and dutifully assumed greater responsibilities, while his father languished for days. Tom was growing dangerously frail as a rattle developed in his lungs and breathing was labored. The doctor was at a loss and death seemed imminent.

Judge Sewall was making his rounds and as was his custom he stopped to visit the Greenwoods. He did not remain long and after a heartfelt prayer for health and recovery he went on his way, heavy in his spirit. As he lifted his bulky figure onto the carriage seat, Elizabeth stepped to the porch, and with tears she requested,

"Please, would ye continue to hold Tom in prayer, and if ye would, please acquaint Caleb Stedman at Roxbury of the situation? He will then inform John, Tom's brother, in Newton." (16)

However, death was not to have the victory over Tom Greenwood so soon. God brought his healing hand and Tom recovered to everyone's wonderment. The time required for regaining his strength gave him opportunity to reflect and examine himself.

"My doctrine be secure and reformed to the essence of the gospel, yet my soul has not been so quickened, warmed and refreshed as it once had been."

Repentant of his own sinful contentious pride, conditional love for others and a lukewarm love of Christ, Tom found a renewed spirit, springing from genuine humility, motivating his life and ministry. But even more, he now looked at others differently, engaging his heart and soul as well as his mind, and now seeing them through the eyes of Jesus. God had placed a love into Rev. Thomas Greenwood's heart that had not been there before.

The difference in Tom's life did not go unnoticed by his young son, John. Loving ways now overruled what had been the cold, intellectual side of his father. He had suddenly become approachable, possessing a gentler heart. Even as his father never backed down from preaching the hard lessons of scripture, never diluting the truth concerning those who die in their sins, he now did so with compassion in his voice and tears in his eyes.

"Brothers and sisters, we are all liable to God's righteous judgement, and it is only by His grace and mercy that we can know Him as our loving heavenly Father. Therefore, let us walk in His good paths."

Regardless, there were those who reprimanded his preaching, saying,

"Why do you preach terror and judgement to those who are already under great terror, instead of comforting them?"(17)

Rev. Thomas Greenwood's response rang in young John's ears for a lifetime:

> *"If I go about to terrify persons with that which is not true, I am to be condemned. But if I terrify them only by holding forth the light of truth and their spirits are awakened by the Spirit of God, enabling them to see their case, then I should terrify them all the more."* [18]

15

Rev. John Greenwood
and Lydia Holmes

1720-1743 - 1st Great Awakening

"Mr. Greenwood has finished the race; much lamented."

Judge Samuel Sewall wrote in his journal, as a chilly autumn breeze rustled the linen curtain in front of the open window. [1] His words appeared cold on the written page as he solemnly remembered his good friend. Their time spent together in deep reflection, debating the vital things of life, death and everything in-between, made him smile. Tom could always make his point with great clarity, causing anyone debating with him to thoughtfully ponder his words and carefully choose their response. Sewall greatly respected Rev. Thomas Greenwood III and would miss him. He put pen to paper again:

"Though great our loss, in Greenwood's bless'd transition. Yet well-fill'd pulpits bless the little nation…." [2]

Elizabeth buried her dear husband. In the minister's graveyard, the blue slate tombstone read, *"Rev. Thomas Greenwood, Late Pastor of the Church of Christ in Rehoboth, died Sept. 8, 1720"*. He was forty-seven years old. Elizabeth slowly ran her hand across the carved words. *"Tom's legacy on this earth,"* she thought to herself. Twenty-six-year-old Hannah, married now, holding her one-year-old son in her arms, quietly wept alongside her mother with her husband, Capt. Adam Cushing. Tom and Elizabeth's youngest girls, Esther and Elizabeth, stood near their mother with sad and somber faces, their tears drained dry through the previous days. The fever that had so threatened their father's life eleven years before had returned with a vengeance, quickly robbing him of his life. All were in shock at his sudden death. [3]

Young John Greenwood, now twenty-three years old, with his coffee brown eyes cast down toward the leaf-covered ground, remained distant from the funeral crowd. The sadness of his spirit put him in no mood to receive condolences. Catching his eye, his mother nodded her head motioning for him to join them near the gravesite. He shuffled his worn black boots obediently to her side and wrapped his right arm tightly around her small shoulders. John knew that his mother's loneliness in the coming days and weeks would be profound.

John Finds His Ministry and Love

After graduating from Harvard three years earlier, [4] John Greenwood sought a ministry position and began to do some temporary preaching at Seekonk, thirteen miles from Rehoboth. The experience was uplifting for him and he soon realized that preaching the gospel was his passion. In the meantime, Rehoboth needed a schoolteacher. The selectman inquired as to whether John would consider the position, and upon offering him a generous rate of pay, John agreed.

Playing a rough game of bandy-wicket [5] with the boys under his tutelage, John, with his athletic build, was a competitive force. With bandy stick in hand and his long black hair flopping as he ran across the field, he extended no mercy to the energetic schoolboys who relished the fierce nature of the game. Exercise was an important aspect of a healthy life and taking a break in the middle of the day was always welcome. Dutifully returning to their studies, with the smell of their sweaty bodies filling the classroom, was always a disappointment to all, including the teacher himself. But this day required an early dismissal, for John was to meet with the elder council to discuss filling the empty pulpit that his father's death had left.

February 13, 1721 would remain a constant reminder of God's sovereign hand upon young John's life. On that day votes were cast and concurring with the church's choice, Rev. John Greenwood became the new minister in the west part of Rehoboth, his father's former parish. The vote was 119 in favor and 5 against. [6] It was recorded, *"Whereas the church of Christ at Rehoboth, having made a choice of Rev. John Greenwood to preach the gospel amongst us for the present, the question being put whether the town would concur with the church's choice, voted by the town to raise 70 pounds per annum till we have a minister settled in amongst us."*

Rehoboth was founded and established on the east bank of the Ten Mile River. As the town expanded many settlers moved east of the Palmer River, some distance from the First Congregational Church on the west part of town. Wanting to worship regularly, they petitioned the General Court in Boston to have the town divided into two precincts for the support of a second church. When Rev. David Turner was ordained on November 29, 1721 in the Palmer River Church, John gained a friend and an ally. Roughly the same age, these young men began serving side-by-side. Both being unmarried, David had his eye on lovely Sarah Bowen while John was already engaged to wed.

Marriage consumed John's mind. On his sister's wedding day two years earlier and before his father's death, he had met the most enchanting girl he had ever seen. When she walked into the meeting house that afternoon, John stood spellbound. Her honey blond hair pulled back into a tightly twisted bun, was perfectly smoothed under a loose, cream-colored bonnet. Small and lissome, the corners of her thin mouth turned up in a slight smile as she found her seat with the women.

John was undone, his eyes darting discreetly in her direction, until finally, his sister and her groom, Adam Cushing, came around, arm in arm.

"John, I would like to introduce ye to my cousin, Lydia Holmes," [7] Adam gleefully shouted.

He was obviously in a giddy mood, anticipating the night ahead with his lovely new wife. But John was completely unaware of Adam's demeanor, as his eyes now locked on Lydia. She respectfully smiled and John bowed slightly.

Polite conversation followed this introduction, all the while John memorizing her smooth, oval face and sky blue, wide-set eyes, which she boldly kept focused on him. She was not a flighty, silly girl, for which he was thankful. A great disappointment would have resulted had she been. Rather, he found her charming and insightful. His mother, Elizabeth, noticed and quietly commented to her husband,

"I do believe that our son be smitten with that girl."

Tom replied with a twinkle in his eye,

"I think we be seeking who her family be."

It always pleased John that his father had enthusiastically approved of Lydia, and he smiled to himself at the memory of that day and of his father.

For two long years John had worked to prove himself to be a worthy provider and a respected man within the community. With his appointment as minister, he was now confident that he could marry Lydia. Her father, Nathaniel Holmes, [8] a large landowner and tradesman, had died when she was fifteen. Her mother, Sarah Holmes Cushing (b. Thaxter), a strong entrepreneurial woman, who in widowhood had petitioned and been granted by the selectmen of South Boston a license to sell strong drink from her home, passed away the year Lydia and John had met. Lydia's stepfather, the Honorable Judge John Cushing, took great care to ensure that her future was one of stability; cautiously screening possible suitors. He finally approved the match with John, and on May 25, 1721, Rev. John Greenwood and Lydia Holmes were married, three months before he became the new minister in Rehoboth, Plymouth Colony.

John and Lydia

A pleasant smile now lit upon Elizabeth's face. She watched her son take his vows, her ashen complexion framed in gray-streaked hair, neatly secured under a light green cap. Memories swept her back some twenty-eight years earlier when she and Tom stood before the justice of the peace and pledged their lives to each other. Time had proven a test of trouble, yet God was faithful. Her heart swelled with joy. God had his good hand of love and mercy on them and she silently praised Him with a hollow vacancy in her heart. It seemed impossible that Tom had passed away just eight months earlier.

"*Your father would be greatly pleased this day,*" Elizabeth whispered in John's ear, her eyes blurred with tears.

John and Lydia settled into the one-and-a-half story wood-shingled house, set behind a low stone wall along a quiet road outside of town. With its large brick center chimney and an entry at the right side facing south, Lydia immediately felt at home. A large barn with a stone foundation provided shelter for the small amount of livestock required to sustain their needs. On the west side, a separate shed provided housing for the two horses. The vegetable garden in the back was already beginning to sprout carrots, cabbage and herbs. Lydia began her work, while John began his.

The Great Awakening

Rev. John Greenwood served his congregation year after year with as much dedication as he could muster, although the years began to take their toll on his patience. Bitter backbiting and untamed gossip seemed to flourish in the hearts of the people. His duties to care for and teach his unruly flock often seemed a fruitless effort. Self-serving consideration and prideful gain dominated most motives while a tepid desire for God commanded little attention.

Ministering to the sick was one service that he found more satisfying than most. It seemed that illness often brought out the reflective, if not a downright malleable nature in people. John would often comment,

> "*Fear may limit and narrow vision, but it can also open a hardened heart.*"

Yet he never expected Richard Jenkins to be softened by a healthy dose of fear. Richard Jenkins was an honest, straight talking man. There was no pretense or wavering. John liked him.

> "*I rejoice to find that the people continue to be pleased with you and your preaching, but you must remember that, though it is, "Hosanna, hosanna" today, it will be "Crucify him, crucify him tomorrow,"* [9]

Jenkins competently remarked. He had called for the minister to come to his home for prayer, as he had been suffering with serious infirmities. Rev. Greenwood courteously replied,

> *"Ye are of a good heart, Mr. Jenkins. Yea, I shall be watchful to the wolves dressed in sheep's clothing."*

Sauntering home at a slow and methodical gait, his aged horse seemed to relish the warmth of the afternoon sun. John reached down and patted Brown Beauty's smooth neck, thoughtfully evaluating Mr. Jenkins' biblically descriptive comment. *"Hosanna today, Crucify him tomorrow."* Although he had not confided in Mr. Jenkins, the truth was the undeniable hypocrisy and faithlessness lurking within the hearts of men and women troubled him greatly. Loudly he vented, alone on the road,

> *"For twenty years I have preached, served, prayed for and buried the people of my church, and still, where is the longing after God?"*

His horse snorted, as if adding, *"Amen"*. John laughed, but then acknowledged,

> *"Brown Beauty, of all hypocrites, I pray that I may not be counted as one!"*.

Truth be told, like his father before him, he was experiencing the dry bones of faith.

Revivals were sweeping across the colonies and John was skeptical. Yet as he read George Whitefield's [10] writings he admittedly was convicted of his own rebellious nature. He was prone to wander toward the love of the world. He silently prayed,

> *"Lord, the more I do, the less I am, the more I know, the less I understand, the more holiness I gain, the more sinfulness I realize. Give me a broken heart that yet carries home the waters of grace."* [11]

The smell of rabbit stew and roasted cornmeal bread coming from the house made John's mouth water as he brushed Brown Beauty and stabled her, rewarding her an extra portion of straw for being his listening ear. He could hear the boisterous voices of his seven children, each it seemed venturing to overpower the other. Laughter intermingled with screams of indignation. The girls competed over most everything.

Hanging his hat and coat on the hook inside the door, he glanced at Lydia who was busy stirring the pot of stew over the fire. She brushed a loose strand of hair off her dewy cheek, stood straight and gave him a jaunty smile, shrugging her shoulders. Time had not diminished her beauty. Other women her age sagged with wrinkled, sour faces, dull and drooping. Somehow at forty-five, he mused to himself, she remained undeniably elegant.

Sarah and Molly came running around the table, spinning their mother in a circle. Lydia's russet-brown linen skirt, secured with a white apron tied tightly around her narrow waist, was swinging wildly like an autumn leaf in a violent wind as the girls chased each other around and around their smiling mother. Laughing, Lydia caught Molly by the arm and wrapped her up tight, giving Sarah the opportunity she needed. She tickled her little sister mercilessly.

That evening, as Lydia sat with knitting in her lap, humming a pleasant tune to herself, John began to talk about the day and the spiritual struggles he was processing.

> *"The ordinances of the church are doing little to quicken hearts. A dead and barren time has been upon us and 'tis a sad state of religion. For many years, even as my father witnessed, the influence of God's Spirit seems suspended, the consequence being the gospel has had little effect on the hearts of men and of women."*

Lydia set down her knitting and questioned John,

> *"How be ye so confident in God withholding His showers of mercy among us? Have we not seen His good hand and His works in the lives of faithful ministers and serious Christians?"*

While he understood her questioning, Thomas responded firmly:

> *"His good hand is always present, although true conversions be few and dubious, Lydia. I believe that God has grown tired of our weak faith and is doing a great work. A work no man can claim credit, but glory be to God alone."*

The issue was not black and white, but a dreary grey, which slowly was becoming brighter with God's hand of grace at work through faithful men like George Whitefield and Jonathon Edwards.

John went on to explain,

> *"When I heard Jonathan Edwards speak, in the year past, he referred to the "outpouring of the spirit."* [12] *If indeed, this is a great awakening brought by God, I must be careful not to condemn it. I have witnessed the spiritual drought of our time. I have known it in my own heart."*

Lydia responded with concern in her voice.

> *"I welcome God's outpouring. And yet this revival has divided people and churches. There are those who totally oppose it. They be orthodox, godly men who may hold the same theology as Rev. Edwards, but rightly, they dislike and yea, even fear the emotional element and the novelty. They view this revival as extravagant and impermanent."*

> *"Lydia, that be true, and there be men at the other extreme as well, wild men, guilty of folly. Two sides. Two extremes. There be condemnation both for fear of uncontrolled emotion as well as zealous enthusiasm leading to radical foolishness."*

John waited. Lydia boldly lifted her eyes to her husband's.

> *"Who be ye, John Greenwood? What side be ye?"*

Weighing his words carefully, John concluded,

*"Neither. I cannot condemn an evident work of the Spirit and
I cannot condone mindless emotion. I stand in the balance.
In that balance, my fear be that I be lukewarm for the gospel
of Christ."*

Gradually, John began to see changes in the hearts of the people. From
thoughtless indifference toward their faith, they turned and confessed their
wayward ways and embraced a personal merciful God, rejoicing together
over the reality of having and knowing Jesus as their loving Savior. John
could not walk through town in the evening without hearing psalms sung
in the homes of different families on every street. [13]

*"Sanctifying grace directly from heaven did the business for
us, and nothing else,"*

John would often state for years to come.

Elizabeth, John's mother, widowed for over fifteen years, embraced
this great awakening that whirled all around her. Her faith had been
revived and strengthened as John had never witnessed in her before. At
sixty-seven years, she lay on her deathbed with a smile seemingly frozen
on her face and shining eyes transfixed toward an otherwise unseen vision.

"Jesus, my wonderful Jesus,"

is all she uttered as she took her last breath on January 24, 1736. The
experience left John and Lydia with a sense that they had been standing on
holy ground. Members of the family, as well as the community, watched
with sorrow as Elizabeth Greenwood (b. Wiswall), the beloved wife of Rev.
Thomas Greenwood III and greatly loved mother of Rev. John Greenwood,
departed this world for the next at the age of sixty-eight.

The prior year, 1735, had proven epic. God's mighty hand moved
in powerful ways that transcended denominational, racial and political
boundaries, creating a common evangelical identity in communities across
the colonies. Walls of division that had stood for decades were broken
down, to the glory of God.

United, But Different

Rev. Turner was of a different bent. He and John would often engage in lengthy discussions over God's sovereignty, the role of the Holy Ghost and works righteousness vs. grace in order to be saved. John would state,

> *"Conversion is not merely intellectual assent to Christian doctrine, but rather, deep personal conviction of one's need of a savior and then responding to that conviction to receive the free gift of salvation offered by the loving hand of Christ alone."*

To which Rev. Turner would respond,

> *"Be that as it may, works cannot be cast aside. Moral expressions must abound, turning the sinner to holiness."*

In frustration, John would hotly reply,

> *"Abound they must, but in response to salvation, never to gain it. My works are as filthy rags. I am dead in my sins. My works alone can do nothing for me. The grace, love and mercy of Jesus Christ is my only hope. As the Holy Book in Romans says, "And if by grace then it is no more of works; otherwise grace is no more grace."*

Yet even in disagreement, the two men respected each other as friends and colleagues and bonded together whenever circumstances required it, especially when approaching the town elders with requests for greatly needed increased salaries. Together they petitioned Rehoboth in 1728, 1736 and 1739 and successfully received the town vote required for deserved increased compensation. A report in town records states, *"Rev. Greenwood and Rev. Turner received raise to 200 pounds annually for the support of ministry."*

Sickness Threatens Lydia's Life

July was oppressive. Swarms of horse flies buzzed the stable. Brown Beauty continually shook her mane and swung her tail to relieve herself of the bites. Trees stood languidly docile under a clear cobalt sky. With doors and windows open, eighteen-year-old, Sarah had hoped to find some relief from the sweltering heat. There was none. Sweat poured down the back of her green cotton shirtwaist. Her tanned face soaked with perspiration, as she knelt alongside her mother's bed, gently wiping her fevered forehead with a cloth.

Lydia had not been feeling well throughout the morning and by mid-afternoon, headache and fever had brought on delirium. She moaned and thrashed, while Sarah fought to bring any measure of comfort that she could to her mother. Liddy, [14] Sarah's older sister, had risen early and taken a carriage with her friend, Mary Healey, to visit Mary's grandparents in Bristol thirteen miles away. Sarah knew the true reason Liddy was so amiable to ride along in Mary's carriage, in this dismal weather. His name was Cpt. Joseph Reynolds.

Molly, fourteen, was watching the younger children, while attempting to prepare the dinner meal. Their father paced outside the bedroom door. He had sent for the doctor. Sarah felt helpless and alone. She waited nervously for the doctor to arrive, for she hated the thought of "bleeding". Dr Curtis was very fond of the practice and Sarah knew that with her mother's condition, he would most likely administer this technique.

When Dr. Curtis arrived, as expected and to Sarah's utter disgust, he ceremoniously announced, *"We shall need to adjust the blood level."* When he finished, tightly wrapping both of Lydia's arms with white linen cloth to stop the bleeding, he smugly pronounced in his nasally, prideful voice, *"Please send for me, should she take a turn for the worse."* Sarah disliked him very much.

The night was fitful and Lydia was in and out of consciousness. In the morning, Sarah attempted to feed her mother warm clear broth. It dribbled down her chin and onto her nightgown. Her lips were dry and chapped and as Sarah looked closer, she noticed a mottled yellow cast to her mother's normally flawless skin. Horror struck her heart. *"Yellow Fever,"* [15] she whispered to herself. Lydia's breathing became more labored, and crying out in her feverish madness, she fought to get out of bed. Sarah and her father held her firmly down, each whispering reassurance in her ear,

"Ye be fine, ye be fine. Rest now. It be time to rest."

After two agonizing weeks Lydia began to recover, having narrowly escaped death. Her husband rejoiced at the miraculous recovery. He would be granted by God to have more years with his beloved Lydia, and her children would continue to have the mother they adored. Eighteen-year-old Sarah wept with joy and gave praise to God.

16

Sarah Greenwood and
(Rev.) Benjamin Sheldon

1740-1757

Benajah [1] was an adventurer. Benjamin, his twin brother, often recalled how when they were younger, Benajah would climb to the steepest peak of the stable roof and with wooden sword in hand, stake a claim.

"For God and Country!" he would yell at the top of his lungs.

Then one fateful day, he fell from his perch and broke his foot, and only then resolved to settle on conquering the lower mounds of hay bales. Benajah could always make Benjamin laugh.

Benajah and Benjamin Sheldon were different sides of the same coin. If it were not for their appearance, one would never guess that they were brothers, let alone twins. Both had shaggy, sandy-blonde hair, bleached from the sun, which they smoothed to the back of their necks into a braided queue. Deep-set, storm-gray eyes, with sweeping eyelashes were the envy of their little sister. At twenty-one years old, they had worked the docks for most of their lives. Tall, muscular and sunburned, their thick arms often taunted burly sailors to a challenge of arm wrestling. Benajah cheerfully welcomed these provocations to demonstrate manly vigor, while Benjamin merely shrugged it off.

It was spring and the fishing boats were packed with sailors and adventurers. Whaling was an exciting and lucrative job for a young man. Ship captains barked commands, while warm southerly breezes freely wafted over salty decks. The smell of wood smoke and fish mixed with the humid sea air, while livestock bellowed their complaints and men cursed the crowds. Hundreds of masts pointed to the sky, as galleon, schooner and clipper ships lined the harbor. While grateful for this coastal heritage that had been a part of life in Providence for over one hundred years, [2] Benajah was anxious to break free, venture out and make his own mark.

Benajah chose to forego the outer banks this season, where yellowfin and blackfin tuna filled nets to overflowing, and amberjack, king mackerel and grouper were just waiting to be hauled in. Nor would he sign on with a whaling ship to search off the coast for right-whale. Benajah had different plans. He would join a trade ship out of Newport. The sloop, *Mediator,* [3] was ready to sail for the West Indies with a load of lumber and fish. The ship was also carrying twenty enslaved men and women, traded from Africa, now bound for Suriname. Benajah was against the cruelty of the slave trade but rationalized that this commerce had nothing to do with him. He surmised that he would simply attend to his own business and perform his duties as a crewman.

This maritime trading web connected the lives of millions of people from Europe, Africa, the West Indies and the colonies. Vessels from Rhode Island bound for Africa with rum and other cargo would trade for slaves, gold dust and pepper. From there they sailed to the Caribbean and South America where they would trade for slave-produced sugar and molasses. The market for sugar and its related product, rum, was lucrative. The demand for unpaid labor in the over five hundred plantations of Suriname alone, made slave trading an extremely profitable business.

Benjamin and Benajah had given the slave trade very little thought, until a year earlier when the cargo ship *Brookes* [4] docked at Newport, en-route for the West Indies, one hot summer afternoon. The vessel was overloaded with more than five hundred African slaves, crammed and chained to maximize space. Benjamin was appalled and sickened by the conditions these men and women endured.

"Benajah, these people are not treated as human! They live like animals, naked and shackled together. They are underfed

JENNIFER BROOKS

and suffering from scurvy, dysentery and dehydration. The inhumanities are inconceivable.", he exclaimed, feeling sick to his stomach.

"Yes brother, 'tis sadly true. Plantations are demanding more laborers, and slave traders are more than willing to comply."

Benajah's thoughts desperately moving away from the dreadful sight, sound and smell of the burdened *Brookes.*

As the two moved on from the appalling slave ship, they walked toward home discussing what they had seen. Benjamin reflected,

"This trade is depraved and unchristian. The greed of the owners and traders cannot be justified on the backs of human suffering. This sin is astounding!"

It is despicable to be sure, yet, the slave trade is vital to commerce, is it not?" [5] Benajah rhetorically questioned.

"Commerce must be of secondary and separate consideration.",

came Benjamin's firm reply. Benjamin understood that his brother was attempting to ease his own conscience yet could not allow Benajah to swiftly sweep the issue under the proverbial rug, adding.

"If these poor creatures are to be recognized with the dignity of being made in God's image, then God forbid that we should ignore their suffering."

Benajah shuffled his feet as they silently walked, and Benjamin let the debate drop. He would never understand how his brother could justify looking to a future that included the transporting of slaves. Benajah did not want to consider *"black mankinde."* He could not allow himself to see it for what it was, pushing any moral aspects from his mind. He was going to sail the Atlantic on a merchant ship, slave trade or not, and his future was set.

As his brother gave a last wave from the deck of the *"Mediator",*

Benjamin [6] felt a deep emptiness. His mind wandered back to the times of their childhood. As boys, the reckless abandonment of Benajah had played out into numerous mishaps and mischievous adventures. A mixture of amusement and worry followed Benjamin's thoughts.

> *"Benajah, may God go with you,"* he silently prayed as the ship left the port and disappeared from sight.

A Fateful Trip to Providence

Sarah was bored. She had been cooped up in the house for weeks caring for her mother and she wanted fresh air.

> *"Mother, our daytime dresses are all but in tatters. I hear that traders in Providence have imported Indian cottons and chintzes. With your permission, may I travel to purchase fabric? How exciting would it be to have fresh dresses in the new softer pastel colors! Possibly I may even find lace and ribbon!"*

Travel to Providence, RI was only eleven miles from Rehoboth, MA, yet Lydia was cautious in allowing her eighteen-year-old daughter to travel that distance alone. Smiling at Sarah's unabated enthusiasm, Lydia replied,

> *"You have worked so hard throughout my illness. A little adventure would be good. You may go, but only under the supervision of your father. If he agrees to attend you for the day, then be happily on your way."*

Rev. John Greenwood was also glad for an excursion to Providence with his daughter.

> *"I have no urgent business that requires my attention in Providence, however I am sure that I can occupy myself with old acquaintances and thus come upon the most recent news. Yes,"* he said with a smile, *"A trip to Providence does indeed seem a pleasant thought."*

He laughed as both Lydia and Sarah smiled; all three knew that Sarah had a way of getting her way with her father.

"I know - wrapped around her little finger," he mumbled as he walked out thedoor to hitch the horses to the cart.

An added truth was the fact that Lydia's illness had taken a lot out of him, and a day of diversion was welcome.

Providence was bustling. Sarah was amazed at this growing maritime city. It had been a year since she had last traveled there. With a population of several thousand, it was a far cry from the quieter rural feel of Rehoboth.

"No worries. I will stay with you,"

Sarah's doting father assured her, discerning a look of being a bit overwhelmed on his daughter's face.

"I am not afraid, Father, only befuddled at so many people crowded together. It seems they all clatter about, jousting for position, and for what purpose I cannot imagine! Busy as a cow's tail in fly time."

Sarah had a colorful way with words.

Taking his hand as she stepped off the cart, John could not help but feel a sense of pride in his daughter. Her plain dress, worn and patched, could not disguise the charm and beauty that was hers. So much like her mother. Sarah's large hazel eyes glanced up at him quizzically.

"What is it father?"
"Nothing dear, nothing, only thinking of where to find the finest fabric."

The day was warm. After locating a shop and successfully purchasing chintzes, lace and ribbon, they strolled toward the docks to catch the cooler sea breeze and watch the bustling activity of traders, laborers and slaves. Sarah was enthralled with life in Providence. Fishermen, whalers, tradesmen, soldiers and all of the brawny and distinctive jargon and odors that surrounded them. The energy was palpable. So different from Rehoboth, where farming was the energy of life and a simple pessimism seemed constantly connected to the weather. Sarah commented,

> *"I wonder that it might rain soon, Father,"*
> *"The good Lord knows we've had too little rain,"*

John replied. Sarah smiled to herself, momentarily appreciating life in Rehoboth.

> *"Excuse me, but are you not Rev. John Greenwood?",*

came an unfamiliar voice behind them. John spun around to see a tall, tanned, square-jawed young man with his hand outstretched.

> *"Yes I am."*

> *"Pardon my intrusion, but I recognized you from the funeral of Nathaniel Carpenter some years ago. My name is Benjamin Sheldon."*

Love, Marriage and Responsibility

The Sheldons, Greenwoods and Carpenters [7] of Providence and Rehoboth had a long and intertwined history. Sarah's sister, Esther Greenwood, married Elisha Carpenter and her Aunt Elizabeth Greenwood had married Ezra Carpenter. Benjamin Sheldon's great-grandmother was Fridgewith Vincent (b. Carpenter), the sister of William Carpenter, [8] co-founder of Rhode Island and instrumental in its development as a colony. Family connections stretched for generations.

Sarah had not met Benjamin before that fateful day in Providence and was immediately smitten with his handsome, rugged looks and his good character, as well as his respected family name. Benjamin had seen many a girl struck by his persona. But it was not until he'd met and courted Sarah Greenwood that he found the love he had patiently waited for. May 4, 1743 was the joyful day of their wedding, and both twenty-year-old

Sarah and twenty-three-year-old Benjamin Sheldon counted themselves blessed by God.

Rev. David Turner presided over their marriage and was now a barrel-chested, heavy-set man. Sarah watched sweat roll down and drip off his bulbous nose, and she held in a deep yearning to laugh aloud. Verbose, he droned on and on, as she became increasingly impatient and much less amused. Finally, he pronounced,

> *"Benjamin Sheldon and Sarah Greenwood are now wed before God and this company; let no man tear asunder."*

Sarah's four sisters and two younger brothers surged forward with hugs and congratulations. Her father waited for the commotion to clear before thanking his old friend, Rev. Turner and extending a hand to Benjamin, officially welcoming him into the family. Her mother, Lydia, shed some tears of joy.

The day was especially bittersweet for Benjamin. It would forever remain a year remembered as a mixture of joy and sorrow. He happily wed the beautiful Sarah Greenwood and at the same time sadly wished that his twin brother, Benajah, could have been there to rejoice with him. Earlier that year, the Maroons [8] of Suriname in the West Indies had staged a violent attack, and Benajah had been caught in the middle and killed. The specifics were never really known, but the report included a gruesome particular that Benjamin would never repeat.

After finishing his schooling, [9] Benjamin took a position as minister in Tiverton, RI, twenty miles south of Rehoboth. With Sarah's older sister, Liddy, soon to be married to Captain Reynolds and living in Bristol, she felt it her duty to remain in Rehoboth. This allowed her to help her parents as they were aging and in need of care. Each week Benjamin travelled the twenty miles between towns, spending three or four days away from Sarah. His congregation was small and could afford to pay only a minimal stipend, so in order to help supplement their livelihood, he farmed a small plot of land near the meeting house in Tiverton. The following year, Pawtuxet Baptist Church was also in need of a minister. Benjamin became an itinerant minister to these two communities. [10]

It was Benjamin's love of the sea that drew him to these congregations.

It was in his blood - the smell of salty ocean air, the slippery docks loaded with wet nets and flopping fish, seagulls floating overhead and ship's bells clanging - all of it called to him. Tiverton was bounded on the west by Mt. Hope Bay and on the Sakonnet River, across from Bristol and Portsmouth, where farming, blacksmithing, tavern keeping, shipbuilding, whaling, trading and ferrying were a way of life for the vast majority of the population. Gently rolling farmland slopes from the river eastward, divided into fields with rubble stone walls topped with flat stone slabs. The sea provided alternative or supplementary occupations for Tiverton men, who fished and engaged in coastal trade, in addition to farming and operating ferries between Bristol and Portsmouth.

Larger farms operating with a greater demand for manual labor used black and Indian slaves to get their produce to market in Newport. Benjamin understood slavery was not only accepted but valued among many of his own congregants. The Congregational Church experienced active growth due to the rapid population increase in the southern part of the town itself. Adjusting to this fledgling church took some time, but Rev. Sheldon was soon acclimated to the community and quickly realized that to keep things at an even keel he would need to simply preach the gospel and stay away from political debate, including topics of slavery and loyalty to the English crown. He often felt cowardly in this approach, but with his growing family, he did not wish to risk losing his position.

The Joy and Grief of Childbirth

Lightning struck a tree nearby. The intense flash and thunderous crack caused thirteen-year-old Betty to jump. Throwing her hands across her face she wanted to cry but knew that it would do no good. The midwife was late. Her sister, Sarah, had begun labor early that morning and progressed rapidly. Betty did everything she could to help but was of little assistance. The day before, Benjamin had remained overnight in Tiverton after Sunday evening services, and the storm now caused his delay in returning to Rehoboth. The sky had opened up and torrential spring rain washed the countryside in a murky muddy green, the roads flooded with water.

Sarah screamed with each close contraction and prayed in-between. Finally, Mrs. Crawford pushed through the front door, soaking wet and breathing heavily. Her muddy feet tracked a wet path across the carpeted hardwood to find Sarah in the bedroom.

"No need to worry my dear girl! I am here now. All will be fine," she assured Sarah, while wiping her own soggy, dripping, grey hair with a towel.

"Bless you Mrs. Crawford! You've arrived just in time!"

"It certainly won't be long now, Sarah!"

Less than an hour later, with a final hard push, Sarah collapsed back on the bed.

"It's a boy! You have a strong boy," Mrs. Crawford gleefully pronounced.

Sarah, her body shaking with exhaustion, smiled weakly and stretched out her tired arms to hold her firstborn son.

"We will name him Benajah, for Benjamin's brother,"

Adjusting this unfamiliar little bundle as best she could, preparing to nurse him, her heart was filled with wonder. Young Betty stood in the corner of the room, biting her lip and crying freely now, with a great sense of relief.

The following year baby Sarah was born but survived for only two months before the croup took hold of her delicate lungs and ended her sweet life. One year later baby Lydia, named for Sarah's mother, was stillborn. Sarah and Benjamin grieved the loss of their two girls and prayed earnestly that God would protect this fourth pregnancy with His almighty and sovereign hand. The frigid winds of February howled and whipped across the snow-covered ground, building white mountain drifts. Sarah was busy knitting a woolen scarf for Benjamin, laughing and smiling as she watched her belly roll from side to side.

"You are an active one!"

Four-year-old Benajah played with wooden blocks at her feet.

Contractions began. Sarah was used to it now. She knew what to expect, although she feared the unknown, realizing full well the potential dangers. Mrs. Crawford gingerly trudged her way through ankle deep snow and up the slippery walkway. Her rosy plump cheeks flushed with cold and her thick red cape fluttered in the breeze behind her, like a cardinal hurriedly escaping a predator. Stomping the snow from her shoes, she knew the way to Sarah.

"No worries my dear! I am here now! All will be fine!",

Sarah had heard those words before. Sometimes they were true, sometimes not.

Benjamin paced the floor, waiting for the cry. He could hear Sarah's determined pushing. Worry spread across his face as he could not help but remember their last baby, Lydia, the cord wrapped around her neck choking her life away. He prayed harder than he had ever prayed before, his hands clenched in white-knuckled fear. Suddenly, startled by the intensity, a baby howled from the bedroom. Mrs. Crawford cried out,

"It's a boy and a good set of lungs he has at that!"

Jonathan Sheldon was born February 16, 1749. He was strong and healthy with a full head of black hair which his father, Benjamin, coveted. With his hair growing thinner on top, Benjamin had taken to wearing a powdered grey wig, tied in a queue, according to the fashion. The wig also made him look older than his twenty-nine years, which garnered more respect from his older congregants.

*"Blessed be the day, my little son, that your hair be your hair
and none to judge you for it!"*

Benjamin laughed as he held his newborn son, Jonathon, peacefully on his chest, gently rocking in front of a warm fire.

A Mothers Death, a Husband's Sorrow

Late on the afternoon of September 8, 1757, Lydia Greenwood took her last breath and, after living sixty-one years, passed from this life to the next. Thirty-two-year-old Sarah fell across her mother's bed and wept uncontrollably as she cried out,

> *"Jesus, conqueror of death, hell and all opposing might, accept my blessed mother into your presence with joy! Thy death is her life, thy resurrection her peace, thy ascension her hope, thy prayers our comfort now and forever. Amen."*

For Rev. John Greenwood, Lydia had been a love that he could never replace. He thanked God for the thirty-six years they spent together. His children and his grandchildren would fill his days with joy and his ministry would continue to fulfill his calling to honor God with his life, yet he would never be the same after Lydia's death.

It wasn't long before Sarah was noticing her father's failings. He was short of breath and often confused the simplest of things. John had been a pillar in Rehoboth for almost sixty years, his entire life, but now his infirmities were stripping him of his abilities to perform the necessary duties of his calling. She knew that a conversation was required, an exceedingly difficult conversation. Praying and asking the Lord for wisdom and grace to give her the right words, she began:

> *"Father, you know that you are greatly loved. You are loved by your family and by this community and by this church, which you have faithfully served."*

John sat up in his chair a little straighter, suspecting what she was about to say. [11]

Reluctantly, he presented his letter of resignation to the congregation at Rehoboth after thirty-six years of faithful service, stepping down from his position due to *"bodily infirmities"*. He was grateful for God's blessing, never forgetting the words of caution from old Mr. Jenkins, long since gone to glory:

"I rejoice to find that the people continue to be pleased with you and your preaching, but you must remember that, though it is, 'Hosanna, hosanna' today, it will be 'Crucify him, crucify him' tomorrow."

The minister who succeeded John Greenwood would experience the full truth of Mr. Jenkins warning. Rev. John Carnes was ordained into the Rehoboth church in 1759. But after only five years the congregation sought for his dismissal before the General Court. The long series of difficulties would greatly hinder his usefulness and arouse much ill-will and bitter controversy among men professedly godly in heart and mind. After an investigation, it was determined by the court that

"Mr. Carnes is blameless, having proved himself a good minister of Jesus Christ, but there appeared an unhappy alienation of affection in his people and an incurable riff which was the true case of our advising to his separation."

The situation was distressing for both the church and the pastor and unquestionably barren of positive spiritual results.

Too Young to Die

The winter of 1763 had been especially bitter, and Sarah Sheldon had suffered through continuous bouts of deep chest congestion. A sharp cough persisted well into spring. In April, she awoke in the middle of the night with severe difficulty breathing, almost completely unable to speak or swallow. She was seven months along with her fourteenth child. The doctor was called and, not being a believer in bloodletting, she refused to allow the doctor to perform it. Frustrated with his uncooperative patient, he left the house in a prideful huff. But her deepest concern was for that of her unborn child.

Having given birth to nine more children after Jonathan was born in 1749, five having not survived birth, she desperately pleaded with God for the life of this baby. The older children kept up with the daily chores, as day after day Sarah was unable to leave her bed, racked with fever and chills. The youngest, two-year-old Daniel was energetic and full of mischief. Sarah worried that he would grow up without discipline or focus. She couldn't help but worry even as she silently recited memorized verses.

> *"Peace I leave with you, my peace I give unto you; not as the world giveth I give unto you. Let not your heart be troubled, neither let it be afraid."*

She lay in her bed and rehearsed her thirty-eight years of life. She understood that she was dying and that in all likelihood, her unborn child would not survive. The anguished grief of losing so many of her children in infancy, the grievous loss of her mother, Lydia, the never-ending war with the French, the challenges of being a ministry wife, the wrangling's and backbiting of the Rehoboth church congregants, who she loved so profoundly in spite of the bickering - all combined with an apprehensive fear of the future. Her heart was troubled, not at the thought of personal death, for she knew her Lord and Savior, but for the future of her children, the lack of spiritual health of the church, and the overall peace of the colonies. It seemed that war was an almost constant in all realms of life and she sensed that it would eventually touch them all in devastating ways.

Holding Benjamin's rough hand while her father, Rev. John Greenwood, sat sullen and frail in a chair on the other side of her bed, Sarah smiled weakly, her eyes gazing upward as she peacefully breathed her last. [12] She had encouraged Benjamin to remarry, knowing that he would need the help and support of a wife to continue on as a father and in ministry. With tears streaming over his bearded cheeks he had dolefully agreed, but in his heart, he knew that he never would. Benjamin wrapped her small limp body in his arms one last time and wept without shame. Sarah Greenwood Sheldon had been a devoted wife and mother. She died, taking with her their fourteenth unnamed child on May 24, 1763.

His heart stricken with inconsolable grief; John Greenwood wondered why the Lord tarried in taking him to his final home. With his beloved Lydia gone to glory and now, his precious daughter, Sarah, gone as well. He was ready. Ailing with gnarled arthritic hands and painful stomach infirmities, his sixty-nine-year-old body had seen enough. Soon he was bedridden and called for the minister. He required no doctor.

"We don't always know what God is doing, but we know who He is. I am ready to meet my Savior face to face."

When Rev. Ephraim Hyde was ordained at Rehoboth in May of 1766, following the disastrous ministry of Rev. Carnes, John Greenwood had been wary. Rev. Hyde was young and inexperienced, yet in time he proved to be capable of handling the position. John liked him and was grateful to have him at his bedside that December, as his life slowly ebbed away. As Rev. Hyde [13] prayed, John Greenwood, with a smile spreading across his wrinkled face and his eyes shining with delight, died to this life and passed into the next. On December 1, 1766, his earthly journey came to an end, [14] nine years after his beloved Lydia and three years after his precious daughter Sarah.

Benjamin Sheldon, at forty-three years of age, would not remarry. Rather, he dedicated himself to the raising of his living children and to the gospel, although his attentions were admittedly torn. His devotion to serving the Lord was sure and unwavering, yet he remained deeply connected to the sea. Possibly it rose from memories of growing up with his brother, Benajah. Possibly it came from simply the tranquil vastness of the ocean itself. Regardless, Pawtuxet, thirteen miles from Rehoboth, offered the familiar environment that would sooth the rough and painful edges of his grieving soul.

He was a humble man, but not a weak one. Rev. Benjamin Sheldon understood his strengths and admitted his shortcomings. As much as he admired his father-in-law, he understood that he could never accomplish the social status that had belonged to Rev. John Greenwood, for although he exercised a most wholesome influence, always on the side of good order and strict morality, Rehoboth was the legacy of Rev. Greenwood and he would never begrudge that fact.

Life continued for Benjamin. Turning the dirt in the heat of summer, watching his crops grow in the small garden next to the house and harvesting the fruits of his labor in the fresh autumn air provided him with a great sense of satisfaction. But often he would also find himself walking the shipyards, taking in the smells and the sounds of his youth. He would daydream of the salty ocean wildly splashing his face and soaking his clothes as the whaling ship sliced through deep blue-green water. And in his mind's eye, he could almost hear his brother, Benajah, yelling, *"This be a good life Benjamin!"* In those moments he would smile to himself and softly reply, *"Indeed. Indeed, it is!"*

Grassy meadows and rolling hills line the Pawtuxet River and dam, leading to the deep-water cove. Pawtuxet itself was filled with memories for Benjamin and he relished walking the streets and reliving in his mind adventures with his brother so many years before. Nostalgia consumed many of his thoughts. Yet he remained vigorous in mind and body, continuing to minister to the church in Tiverton, and assisting with the Pawtuxet Baptist Church, which had begun in 1764 when Abraham Sheldon had donated the land for *"religious purposes."*

He was a forty-six-year-old widower [15] with seven surviving children ranging in age from seven to twenty-three. Benajah, the oldest, was married and raising children of his own. Jonathan, so much like his mother, was a teenager testing his wings. Daniel, [16] the youngest son, was in need of significant motherly guidance and with his beloved wife, Sarah, having fallen into the sleep that knows no waking, Benjamin prayed that God would give him strength. He was especially grateful for his two middle daughters, seventeen-year-old, Rebecca and thirteen-year-old, Molly, whose diligent attempts to provide young Daniel with the moral and educational guidance that was required never faltered. That being said, Daniel was strong-willed and independently minded.

17

Jonathan Sheldon and Mary Durfey

1754-1769

Widespread unrest prevailed in the western wilderness of 1754. [1] French presence in the Ohio valley had not only blocked British colonial westward expansion but threatened the very existence of the colonies as a whole. British and colonial militia march in a combined force against the thinly populated region called *"New France"*, with native warriors bolstering their forces. Beginning in Canada, New France was enormous in size, extending from the Great Lakes south to the Mississippi Valley. Under General Edward Braddock, the British intended to take possession of this land, expanding their sphere of influence. Braddock began building a road across the Appalachian Mountains in order to reach and do battle with the French and their Indian allies.

Many, including the eccentric Benjamin Franklin, believed that the sixty-year-old British General Braddock was ignorant and ill-equipped for fighting in the wilderness. Franklin issued a dire word of caution to Braddock concerning travelling through the thickly wooded forests in a single file column, believing it could easily lead to a devastating attack. Braddock ignored the warnings. His tactics were conventional and impractical. Yet the general population sees Braddock as victor, even before there is actually a victory. The fear of French and Indians sweeping freely through the settlements of the western arena; killing, pillaging and looting farms and towns have people fervently on their knees in prayer for a swift British triumph. The threat is real. Braddock is perceived as their savior.

Discarding repeated advice, General Braddock replied to Franklin's warning,

> *"Those savages may indeed be formidable to your raw American militia, but upon the king's regular and disciplined troops, sir, it is impossible they should make any impression."* [2]

The truth was that the "savages" were the most experienced and adept fighting force on the battlefield. Energetic, nimble young warriors were eager to test their skills against the invasive colonists and the power of the British army.

After six weeks and 290 backbreaking miles, General Braddock and his fighting force have finally moved into New France, advancing on Fort Duquesne. [3] The French and their Indian allies are ready, blocking the advance. British regulars are flustered at the sight of the enemy, hardened men on the French line, wearing brown moccasins and leggings of their native allies. These young men from England, Ireland and Scotland are terrified, yet obey orders to engage the enemy.

The French have established themselves onto the perfect killing ground. The British draw first blood and the French quickly dive for cover. Initially frightened, as the constant pounding of British canister and grape rip through limbs and torsos, the French combatants cower behind ancient oak and walnut trees. French commander General Beaujeu is shot and killed and the French troops and Indian warriors are undone, fleeing the battlefield in confusion.

British troops are elated and rush forward in what they believe to be a swift victory. However, it is a fatal mistake. Not all of the warriors had fled, and their knowledge of this landscape and the tactics required is beyond British comprehension. Their troops fear the French, but never as much as they fear the Iroquois and the Delaware. The horror of being captured and tortured haunts them and unexpectedly their worst nightmare is about to come true.

Rather than stand in one place and fight as the British expect in the manner considered honorable, these phantoms of the woods run like deer, bounding over boulders and hiding behind trees to reload. High-pitched war cries pierce the air, and a brutal carnage ensues. Mind-fogging fear grips the British troops. Desperate, terrified red-coat soldiers turn and run, pursued by brightly painted warriors, their quivers covered in outlandish designs, feathers and torn strips of gaudy trade cloth fluttering from their weapons. Muskets, tomahawks and war clubs beat down stragglers.

George Washington [4] had long feared this type of loss and had advised General Braddock to give up the bright red British uniforms and adopt the "Indian dress" for camouflage and for ease of movement. He also advised against the traditional straight lines in fighting. But the air of disdain that had long defined the British attitude toward colonists prevailed. Braddock ignored Washington. The British were routed, and General Braddock was mortally wounded, leaving the colonies, once again, defenseless against French and Indian attack. [5]

Shortly after this defining British failure of 1755, known as *"Braddock's Defeat"*, more than four hundred settlers in Pennsylvania are slaughtered and scalped. The French and Indian War, as it eventually came to be known, raged on for eight more years until Great Britain and France ultimately came to terms, with the conclusion of the *"Seven Years War"* which had engulfed Europe. France ceded to Great Britain its territory east of the Mississippi.

When the French and Indian War began in 1754, Benjamin and Sarah Sheldon's second oldest son, Jonathan, [6] was but a child of five years. When it was concluded in 1763, the same year his mother died, he was an impressionable fourteen-year-old. Seasoned men came home with horrific stories of valor and bravery, embellished with each retelling. Many had been at Fort William Henry when it fell to the French in 1757 and had survived the bloody massacre by Indians as they marched away, under the terms of surrender, to Fort Edward. Over two thousand British, colonial militia and their camp followers, including women and children, had been ambushed when a war whoop sounded, and warriors seized upon the column. The atrocities included killing and scalping the wounded and sick. Over two hundred were reported killed or captured.

Rhode Island maintained a small militia. They had supplied troops to assist in this conflict against the French. Over the winter of 1755/56 Rhode Island retained only 185 men in military service, one hundred at home and the rest at Fort William Henry. By late 1756 a draft, which included every man between sixteen and sixty years of age, was instituted. British regular forces took a leading role in regulating colonial provincial and militia troops to non-combat roles, using them primarily as pioneers and transportation troops, leaving the bulk of the fighting to the British Army. Even so, the wretchedness of war was equally cast upon American militia and British troops alike.

Jonathan Sheldon felt a sense of disappointment. He was eager to stand and fight for a cause. But he was born too late for this war. His father, Rev. Benjamin Sheldon, was a man of the cloth. While he longed to serve as a chaplain, he chose to remain at home to care for his family. Sarah, his wife, suffered with poor health, having given birth to thirteen children within a span of seventeen years, and the idea of leaving to serve in the military was unthinkable. [7] Little did either father or son suspect that a greater war was just around the corner and it would change their lives forever.

Marriage: A Suitable Match

Frigid winds whipped across Narragansett Bay in October of 1771, as twenty-two year- old Jonathan Sheldon anticipates his marriage to Mary Durfey. It was dark when he awoke. The house was quiet as he swung his long legs over the side of the bed to stand, ducking to avoid hitting his head on the low ceiling beam. Standing in the gloom of pre-dawn, he mumbled,

"Today is a good day, Jonathan Sheldon"

He quickly pulled on his breeches and buttoned them up, shivering in the cold morning air as he threw a loose white shirt over his head. As quietly as he could, he stepped down the ladder to the second-floor landing when a voice teased from the darkness,

"You are a brave one. You would sooner sleep in the airless, musty attic, with bats, than crowd in with two little brothers in a cozy second floor bedroom."

"You understand me so well, Molly!", he laughed with obvious sarcasm.

His seventeen-year-old sister had risen early. Together they made their way to the lower level and sat down at the kitchen table in the quiet of the house.

> *"I am feeling most nostalgic this morning. God's sovereign plans sometimes leave me bewildered of their purpose,"* Jonathan mused.

Absentmindedly, he sipped his tea and pushed the ham around his bowl with a piece of bread. Molly frowned. His usual carefree manner seemed replaced with contemplation and Molly was confused. He glanced up to see her reaction and asked,

> *"You think that I have not more than simplistic thoughts, sister?"*

> *"Indeed not! Do you not remember admitting this very morning that I understand you so well!?"* Molly smiled.

Then, recognizing his reflective mood, she added,

> *"Jonathan, who can fathom God's immeasurable ways? But this we know, He exceeds our rational senses. We live here in a finite glimpse, but there we shall see all things clearly. And until then, we can trust Him."* Pausing to catch her breath and reign in her emotions, *"But I miss her too, brother."*

He was always amazed at how Molly seemed to read his mind.

The house was filled with memories of his mother, Sarah. Even after eight years he still expected to see her bending over the fire, stirring a pot of stew or sitting in the rocking chair with a baby in her arms and smiling up at him. He had grown up here, in Tiverton, in this house. Situated near the Sakonnet River, on Dartmouth Road, [8] the two-and-a-half story house, with a large brick center chimney and a veranda across the front, framed with two large maple trees. The large garden in the back had provided vegetables and herbs, supplementing the income that Rev. Benjamin Sheldon received from the town. [9] Jonathan had spent most of his childhood working side-by-side with his family in that garden.

Shaking off his morning melancholy, Jonathan prepared for the afternoon. He had known Mary Durfey his entire life. In school, as children, he had tormented her with boyish pranks, and she had found him annoying and immature. Her proper attitude and prim behavior never seemed terribly convincing, and Jonathan was usually annoyed at her dismissive ways. By the time Jonathan was sixteen he had grown into a tall and rugged-looking young man with a strong-jutting chin and brown wide-set eyes that gave the appearance of perpetual distraction. He found girls to be mostly uninteresting. Mary found Jonathon intriguing, but in her opinion, in need of maturity and, as she was fond of saying, *"social graces."*

Romantic love was not a respectable motive for marriage. Both Mary's family and Jonathan's were notably established in the community and their families agreed that economic and social benefits were suitable for the young people. Mary agreed, assuming a superior, albeit, conciliatory approach to the idea of a union. Jonathan hesitated, but in the end agreed, hoping that Mary's opinionated ways would mellow and make for a happy home. It was a suitable match.

> *"In short, I am of the opinion that a married state if entered into with proper motives of esteem and affection will be the happiest for ourselves"*,

Jonathan confided to his best friend, James Durfey, [10] as they sauntered, kicking autumn leaves along the road, toward the meeting house that morning. James reflected,

> *"My little sister will make you most respectable in the eyes of the world, and as a couple you will be the most useful members of society. Whether you grow in affection is another matter, yet it is my fond hope that you both grow sensible to each other's merits and find the happiest of lives together."*

With all her admirable qualities of prudence, tenacity and faithful integrity, James understood that Mary was a difficult personality, and that Jonathan would have his hands full.

Continuing with his thoughts, Jonathan confided,

"As good an economic and social consolation as this marriage be, dare I admit to you, as being her brother, that although I will honor my commitment to this union, I am not at this time attracted to Mary. Her demeanor is more sullen than I would prefer."

James threw his head back and laughed,

"You are truly an honest man Jonathan Sheldon! But I must caution that you not share such sentiments beyond our conversation. As we walk toward your eminent wedding vows, remember, your wife-to-be, my sister, is a strong woman and a good cook. You should not want for her to discover arsenic as a seasoning."

Two hours later Jonathan and Mary married in Tiverton and began their new life together. Settling on a small plot of land provided by Mary's parents, they built a modest house. Economic times were hard, and Jonathan soon found a position on a whaling boat. Life with Mary was quite satisfactory from his perspective, for she never burdened him with the ideals of romantic notions. She was practical and orderly. And as for her propensity toward a sullen disposition, Jonathan found her serious-minded and straightforward nature a source of clarity in their relationship. Love was not of great concern for either and they functioned in a kind of easy harmony.

Mary, as Jonathan's wife, was not his highest priority and she understood it. There was a side of his character that could not be penetrated, an aloof reserve. Mary would proudly state,

"I do not require more than a husband faithful to our marriage bed and committed to the cause of independence for our future."

She was forever a patriot. There was talk of open rebellion against the crown and both she and Jonathan were ready to do their part when the time was right. It was, indeed, a suitable match.

Faithfully consummating his marriage, babies began to arrive, while the rapidly changing outlook of political affairs perpetually preoccupied both Jonathan's mind and time. The state of the colonies eroded into further discontent and the winds of underlying dissent were swirling in strength. Talk of throwing off the shackles of English rule became more common and openly discussed in public debate. No majority consensus was established, yet unrest could be found in every corner.

Whaling

"Thar she blows!", sang out the familiar call from the barrelman stationed in the "barrel" of the foremast some fifty feet above from where Jonathan stood. Adrenalin surged through his body as men thundered across the deck to launch the whaleboats. *"She be a sperm whale, two miles south by southwest!"*, came rough directions. The long hours of boredom were over, and the frenzied excitement of the hunt began. Two whaleboats dropped into the sea and men scurried onboard, settled in and began frantic paddling, while dipping their oars as quietly as possible, so as not to spook the giant mammal. Each boat hustling to arrive first.

Jonathan remained onboard the large schooner. As the ship's cooper, his responsibilities did not permit that he join the whaleboat crew. But this day had developed into a unique opportunity of another type. This day he found himself master of the ship. His apprenticeship was not yet complete, but when old Caleb Bowen went down to sickness three days earlier and languished in the hull of the ship. Jonathan was suddenly and unexpectedly assigned master.

His responsibilities dictated that he navigate the ship, guiding her toward the whale and the whalers in the smaller boats. A large, menacing tail fin sprung from the cobalt blue ocean, gracefully waved and then submerged below the surface. The whaleboats moved closer as the boatheader shouted orders, admonishing the men to row harder. Straining every muscle, they surged forward, rising and falling on the languid ocean swells, drawing near their enormous, unpredictable prey.

Jonathan squinted his eyes against the bright sun to watch in the distance as the harpooner on the first boat picked up his weapon. His muscular arm throwing the six-foot long barbed whale iron deep into the blubber, like a hook, the animal was now securely fastened to the whaleboat. As the fifty-ton whale thrashed in pain and fury, causing huge waves to roll across the otherwise tranquil surface, the small boat rocked wildly. Uneven swells build in intensity. Immense power is unleashed. The whaler boat backed off to a safer distance. The whale plummeted down, taking the harpoon with it, as the crew let the line out keeping the boat from going down as well. The line smoked with friction, men shouted, and the boat careened back and forth violently. A seaman was thrown overboard. Frantic hands grabbed at his desperate arms flailing in the open water. He was pulled safely back aboard.

Coming up for breath, the whale began to swim along the surface in an anguished attempt to escape, pulling the boat behind, waves slapping and splashing over the sides. Jonathan barked orders,

"Don't lose sight of them, men! We give chase!",

knowing that a whale that size could drag a whale boat quickly out of sight. Marveling at the speed and power of this amazing creature, he ordered all eyes on the whaleboat as it bounced along the shimmering expanse of ocean blue. The salty wind whipped his ruddy cheeks and snapped his shoulder-length dark hair around his face.

Finally, after what seemed an eternity, the whale slowed from exhaustion. The crew began to pull the line, drawing the boat closer to their prey. Jonathan was tense as he watched through his telescope. He had seen this go very badly in the past and he prayed silently as the harpooner and the boatheader changed places. With the lance poised high over his head the boatheader plunged it into the whale's lung, and with each desperate breath its life was gradually ebbing away. The whaleboat backed off again, with the crew waiting, watching, as the enormous beast swam violently in tight circles. A flurry of panic. The end came with its tail slamming down against the water. With an uncontrolled shudder and a slow roll to its side, death had arrived.

The captain and crew, weary and drained from the extended exertion, now towed the whale back to the sloop. They were grateful that Jonathan had kept so close, making their work easier.

"Youth be persistent and resourceful, young Jonathan! You proved yourself as a capable master! An extra mug of rum for you! Well deserved!", the captain exclaimed.

Jonathan was pleased, praying to himself,

"Father God, your hand of grace was on me today. I thank you!"

18

Captain Jonathon Sheldon

1770-1775

Tensions were accelerating in the colony of Rhode Island, just as they were across the whole of the colonies. Jonathan sat with friends and neighbors long into the night to debate and rant over British oppression. Jonathan sat on the edge of his chair as he expressed his frustration and anger.

> *"The war with the French is over, does British rule now have no limit to it's greed and abuse?"*

> *"Aye! Aye!"*, came the response to the rhetorical question.

Lot Shearman [1] spoke up and added,

> *"Without respecting the most essential rights and liberties of the colonies and the grievances held by reason of several illegal acts of Parliament; British authority has imposed its sovereignty beyond legal and moral bounds."*

He continued to speak as men grew in their fury:

> *"I stand with the lawyer from Virginia, Patrick Henry.* [2] *'If this be treason, make the most of it.'"*

In British attempt to alleviate massive debts after the war with the French, Parliament had passed several *"Acts"*. Tremendous anger was building over these oppressive taxes and proclamations imposed on colonists. On March 5, 1770, a street fight broke out in Boston. Unwelcome British troops opened fire on a Patriot mob, who threw snowballs, sticks and stones at their adversaries. Several colonists were killed. It would later be known as *"The Boston Massacre"*. King George viewed the colonists as mere children and required that they unquestionably obey the proclamations of Parliament and the Crown, including:

- *The Royal Proclamation of 1763* - no colonists permitted west of the Appalachian Mountains
- *The Sugar Act of 1764* - tax per gallon on imported molasses
- *The Quartering Act of 1765* - the quartering of His majesty's officers and troops in private residences if barracks are overcrowded.
- *The Stamp Act Of 1765* - tax on all printed materials
- *The Declaration Act of 1766* - for better securing the dependency of His majesty's dominions
- *The Townshend Act of 1767* - taxes on glass, paint, oil, lead, paper and tea

The HMS Gaspee Affair

The first faint light of dawn crept over the eastern horizon. Pawtuxet was waking. Jonathan rubbed his eyes and blinked hard, focusing on the low ceiling above him. Stretching his sore muscles, he finally rolled to his side and carefully eased himself from the bed. He could hear his father stirring about downstairs and he cringed at the thought of the coming conversation. Benjamin Sheldon was sympathetic to the Patriot cause, but fearful that the Sons of Liberty were too radical to achieve the compliances that were being demanded from Britain. He believed that diplomacy and patience would result in a peaceful compromise, whereas Jonathan believed that they were clearly beyond that point.

Benjamin was fifty-two years old and having had removed permanently back to Pawtuxet from Tiverton, with only Esther, fifteen years of age and

Daniel, eleven, remaining still at home. Pawtuxet was the nostalgic seaport hamlet of his youth. He was well acquainted with growing anti-British sentiment, although he was now less consumed with future political events and more contemplative of sweet personal memories of days gone by, as well as the spiritual health of his congregants.

Jonathan entered the room. Holding his side he walked haltingly and sat down at the table across from his father. Sipping his morning tea, Benjamin glanced up and with tenderness in his voice, asked,

"Are you injured badly?"

"No, only bruised ribs and maybe some pride,"

"You have a wife, with a baby soon to enter this world, Jonathan. Your considerations must provide for their well-being. To risk your life in a daring scheme and a foolish venture is irresponsible."

Jonathan understood and respected his father's concerns.

"Father, I can do nothing else but stand with the just cause that I believe God has sovereignly set before me. I pray for divine protection daily. God governs the affairs of men and he has given me abilities to assist against inequity."

"Jonathan, bearing arms against the sovereignty of Great Britain? How can this be right?"

"Father, diplomacy has been tried. It has failed. We have no representation in Parliament. We are at their mercy and have received nothing but exploitative policies of forced taxation, all to pay off British debt."

Jonathan grimaced in pain as he spoke.

The night before had indeed been foolhardy but demonstrated the severity of the crisis that was upon them all. Lt. William Duddington, of Her Majesty's ship *HMS Gaspee*, a British customs ship, was responsible for patrolling the waters of Narragansett Bay. Duddington was an arrogant and opportunistic man who abused his power for personal profit. His reputation was that of an overzealous and heavy-handed enforcer, boarding and detaining ships and confiscating cargo, often without warrant, leaving merchants without recourse for repossessing their impounded goods. Harassments continued and losses mounted, as did deepening discontentment and anger.

Earlier that spring Lt. Duddington had seized a ship called *"Fortune"*, owned by the powerful Greene family of Providence. He and his crew had severely beaten Rufus Greene, who commanded her. Duddington then condemned the ship and her cargo, which included rum, a prize of customs enforcement. Duddington's aggression continued into late spring.

When the packet sloop *"Hannah"* had cleared customs in Newport, on June 9th, loaded with a cargo of rum, Capt. Lindsay anticipated an encounter with the *Gaspee*. With the wind blowing forcefully against his face, as sails billowed proudly, he had deliberately decided that he would not yield to Duddington's demands this day. As the *Gaspee* came into sight, she signaled for the *Hannah* to lower her flags. She declined. *Gaspee*, armed with eight cannon and twenty-six crew, fired a warning shot across the bow of the *Hannah*, yet still she refused to comply. Choosing defiance, Capt. Lindsay decided to try to outrun the much larger and heavier *Gaspee*. Duddington gave chase, but his zeal overshadowed his skill and wisdom.

The *Hannah* intentionally moved into shallow waters near Namquid Point where the *Gaspee* ran aground. Capt. Lindsay and crew sailed for Providence. Arriving in port, news spread quickly. The despised Duddington and his hated ship were stuck on a shallow sandbar and vulnerable to attack, only six miles south near Warwick, south of Pawtuxet.

The city's leading merchants and citizens convened at Sabin's Tavern to plan revenge on the now-immobilized *Gaspee*. John Brown of Nicholas Brown and Co. bolstered the flames of anger.

> *"Men! Now is the time to make our claim! The rights afforded us have been trampled! Tyranny has offered its day of reckoning! Let us not disappoint!"*

They quickly dispatched a man to march up and down the streets of Providence, pounding a drum, announcing the misfortune of the *Gaspee*, and volunteers began arriving at the tavern eager to seek vengeance.

Sixty-four men zealously arrived at Sheldon's Wharf and set out before midnight in eight longboats, headed for the warship which floundered as helpless as a beached whale. Christopher Sheldon, who owned the wharf, forty years old and an experienced mariner, served as captain on one boat while his first cousin, Pardon Sheldon, captained another. Both men, distant cousins to Jonathan, were well respected in Providence and Pawtuxet. As they proceeded down the Providence River, they passed Pawtuxet and two more long boats joined their force. As Jonathan took his seat on the main thwart in Christopher's boat, near the left-hand side, facing forward, he gripped his gun tightly in his right hand. Sweat was rolling off his face, even in the cool evening air. Two rowers, each on either side of him, silently focused on the task at hand, their oars muffled as they dipped into the smooth black water.

By 1 a.m., Jonathan could see the enormous shadow of the *Gaspee* against the starry sky. A shiver went through him. Looking around, the camouflaged, blackened faces of men he had known his whole life, were now unrecognizable. As they approached, the *Gaspee* spotted them and sounded the alarm. Lt. Duddington appeared on the deck, with a pistol in his hand.

"Identify yourselves forthwith!", he demanded.

Jonathan cringed as the sheriff, Abraham Whipple, adding a string of cursing to his angry tirade, hollered,

"I am the sheriff of county Kent!! I have a warrant to apprehend you on legal charges!"

Whipple had been trying to serve Duddington with papers after the Greene's had filed a lawsuit against him, over the *Fortune* and the beating of Rufus Greene.

The sheriff demanded a surrender. Duddington refused. A shot rang out and Duddington was hit. Another shot and he was hit again.

Jonathan and the Providence men quickly boarded the *Gaspee*. As he climbed over the side railing, a short, muscular sailor drew back his fist and caught Jonathan in the ribs. Doubled over, Jonathan anticipated a second blow, but it never came. A fellow patriot smashed the butt of his rifle across the back of the sailor's head, sending him crashing to the deck floor. The fight lasted but a few minutes. The crew of the *Gaspee* was promptly overtaken.

Lt. Duddington had been hit in the arm and groin, neither fatal. A medical student and a participant in the raid, John Mawney, dressed the lieutenant's wounds. Duddington and his crew were herded onto small boats and taken to shore. Humiliated, they could only watch as the Providence raiders torched their warship. The flames licked high into the sky, with the popping of dry timber and on-board ammunition being heard up and down the river. By morning, the *Gaspee was* a smoldering skeletal hulk of charred wood. [3]

As Jonathan conveyed the details of the raid to his father, Benjamin shuddered with somber concern.

> *"The crown will not rest until it secures and punishes those involved in this affair."*

Jonathan spoke with a tone of somberness:

> *"Father, I believe this insurrection is only a glimpse of what is to come. I, as you also, have long-feared that this escalating conflict between the powers of Great Britain and the colonies would end in rivers of blood."* [4]

Jonathan continued with emotion in his voice:

> *"Just as we first realized that religious power resided in our own hands rather than in the hands of the Church of England or any other authority, besides God's own written word, we have now come to realize that political power need not reside in the hands of the English monarch, but in our own will to self-govern."*

Benjamin knew that those were the words of sedition. The truth was, in his youth, he would have joined the raiders of the *Gaspee*, but age had softened him. The look in his dimmed brown eyes said it all, expressing without words his grave concern. He thoughtfully picked up his cup, and said,

"Indeed, Jonathan, I know. But for now, let us simply see to your bruised ribs and drink some tea."

A Cause to Fight For

Their small farm plot suffered, with Jonathan's growing attention being given to the state of the colonies, along with the whaling season now taking him away for months at a time. It was evident that full-on war would soon be upon them. Mary did not have slaves to help her, as some of her wealthier neighbors did. She fervently yoked oxen and harvested autumn crops with her own hands, often with a baby secured in a sling at her breast and toddlers following behind. Parry Sheldon was born in 1772, the year of the *Gaspee Affair*, as it came to be known, with Prudence and Joseph following quickly behind; every two years like clockwork it seemed a baby arrived.

Mary worked resolutely without complaint, assuming chores that were customarily reserved for men. The necessary outdoor duties did not engender masculine habits in her or cause her to become less agreeable in her proper sphere, as social norms dictated. She clung dearly to the decorum she held in such high regard, while willingly sacrificing them for a greater purpose. In this, her husband grew in deep appreciation for her. Forfeiting the eminent prescribed graces of refinement, Mary, with steely determination, accepted the duties of what she understood would inevitably be a military life in a violent struggle with the mother country, England.

The Tea Act in the spring of 1773 had sparked widespread riots and demonstrations. The financially troubled British East India Tea Company, in an effort to reduce the massive amount of tea held in its London warehouses, influenced the British government to pass the Act which granted the company the right to duty-free export, while a greater tax was imposed on the colonies and collected by force. In Boston, the resistance culminated on a cold December night in what would be referred to as the Boston Tea Party. Colonists, disguised as Native Americans, boarded tea ships anchored in the harbor and dumped forty-six tons of cargo overboard.

Tensions continued to escalate between Great Britain and her unruly colonies in the Americas. The First Continental Congress met in Philadelphia in September of 1774, representing thirteen colonies, [5] and issued a declaration and resolves to organize colonial resistance in response to Parliament's Coercive Acts. [6] Colonists, for the most part, were inspired to throw off the shackles of British oppression and embrace their independence. What that looked like would vary in the eyes of the people. Men like Patrick Henry made bold and radical statements:

"Give me liberty or give me death."

Others took a more cautious, loyalist approach, believing in Great Britain as sovereign over them. To rebel against the Crown came with serious consequences. High treason was punishable by torture and a violent execution.

King George III is livid with America. He is a strict man and continues to view the colonials as children needing severe discipline. On one occasion he states to his friend, John Montagu:

"I am of the opinion that once these rebels have felt a smart blow, they will submit."

While the king believes that the colonies are required to obey and provide support to the motherland, colonists hold that Parliament has no authority to levy taxes on them without representation. The seeds of sedition run deep, much deeper than King George III understands.

April 18, 1775, Paul Revere and other riders were hastily sent to sound the alarm that British soldiers had mobilized from Boston. Farmers, merchants and townsmen respond in force, gathering their muskets and ammunition, making ready for a confrontation.[7] On April 19th, British troops, marching to confiscate a secret stash of weapons, encounter hordes of untrained, enraged colonial militia in Concord and Lexington and along the roadside as they marched. Defeating seven hundred highly skilled professional soldiers in a surprise victory bolstered colonial confidence for what lay ahead. The first shots of the revolution have been fired, the so-called *"shot heard 'round the world."*

The Continental Congress commissioned George Washington as Commander in Chief of the Continental Army on June 19, 1775. America was inching closer and closer to full out rebellion against King George III and Great Britain. The thousands of militia who responded at Lexington/Concord remained in the area and their number grew daily, placing the British forces in Boston under constant siege, blocking all land access to the peninsula and trapping them. Yet Boston Harbor remained under British control. Due to naval supremacy, the colonials could do nothing to stop the British from being resupplied and from carrying out raids against patriot communities along the coast.

Tryall, George Washington and Boston

Twenty-seven-year-old Jonathan Sheldon could not determine where the gray sea ended, and the gray sky began. Weak rays of sunlight struggled to crack through heavy clouds. A vast expanse of emptiness surrounded the sloop, *Tryall*, as her sails fluttered weakly in the light breeze. Clad in a warm woolen jacket and a green knitted scarf, Jonathan scanned the horizon for signs of British merchant ships. Growing impatient, he ordered,

> *"Turn about. We need head for the Connecticut coast, off New London."*

Men scrambled to the fore and aft rigging. The mainsail swung wide and the sloop gradually changed course. Adjusting to a northwest bearing, they soon spotted Block Island off their starboard side. Skirting around it toward Connecticut, they kept their eyes trained on the horizon before them. The wind was picking up.

Col. John Cooke had been engaged in maritime warfare under a commission of war issued by the General Assembly. His sloop, *Tryall*, [8] a 43-foot, single mast, 25 ton boat with a six man crew, was small but useful, especially in providing valuable communications, running small amounts of cargo and accompanying larger vessels on cruises as a tender. [18] Mr. Cooke had earlier approached Jonathan:

> *"Your reputation as a qualified seaman has preceded you. Jonathan, your eagerness to make your mark in this rebellion against the motherland is well noted. I entrust you as the master on Tryall, to carry on all forms of hostility permissible at sea by usages of war, including attacking foreign vessels and taking them as prizes. Sail off the coast and God be with you."*

Jonathan smiled to himself as he stood at the port bow on the slippery deck, remembering Mr. Cooke's words. He thought to himself, *"A lofty speech that was!"*, as the *Tryall* pitched hard, cutting across six-foot swells.

> *"A sloop-of-war she will never be, but she be quick and hard to catch; a good ship for the master of a privateer,"* [9] he uttered aloud.

> *"Sir, she have but one cannon, and that be a small one."*

Jonathan spun around to see his deckhand, Richard Cooke, [10] calmly standing behind him.

> *"You make a good point!"*

Jonathan laughed, his dark brown eyes shifting over the gray churning sea that stretched before him. Squinting through a telescope, Jonathan spewed,

> *"For almost a year the British have continued to resupply Boston by sea. Now, with this frigid weather, their supplies must be running shorter by the day and colonial resolve is running hot. Give me more cannon and ammunition*

and I will bombard them with all the strength God has given me!"

He watched as the sails of an armed merchant brig disappeared over the horizon, presumably toward the frozen Boston Harbor. Young Cooke assured,

"Aye, no worries. A larger and better armed privateer will make short work of her, sir. The Katy [11] *be in those waters and Capt. Whipple has a deep hunger for prize!"*

Jonathan felt a tinge of covetousness. The truth was Jonathan's orders were to avoid confrontations of any kind with warships or armed merchants. *Tryall* was not equipped for battle. Her quickness was her advantage. Reporting British movements and confiscating prize from smaller cargo ships, while easily being mistaken for a merchant or a whaling vessel [12] was what made her so profitable to the cause.

February winds were wrought with brutal cold and Jonathan longed for the hearth of his fireplace and the warmth of family. Privateering along the Rhode Island and Connecticut coastline, he had seen success. Jonathan's men were seasoned sailors and not afraid to take risks. Seizing several smaller cargo ships enroute from the West Indies with rum, sugar, salt rock and molasses, they overcame even a few larger ships by sheer intimidation and brawn. Young Richard Cooke was learning life lessons of the cruder, more colorful kind, and as much as Jonathan appreciated his crew, he also reprimanded them on many occasions for their salty language and inappropriate conversation regarding the fairer sex.

Finally, in March of 1776, the welcome news came. *"The British have evacuated Boston."*[13] British soldiers, officers, and loyalists alike were boarding ships bound for Halifax in a retreat from the besieged city. Collapsed, looted and burned buildings lined the once pristine streets of Boston. Garbage piled high brought with it disease and vermin. Plagued with malnutrition, smallpox, scurvy, dysentery, respiratory infections and typhoid, the evacuation was a mix of relief and demoralization for the citizens of Boston.

Gen. George Washington had outmaneuvered the distracted British General William Howe, gaining the favorable ground of Dorchester Heights and positioning the American Army in bombarding Boston day and night with cannon shot. British contempt for the colonials was complete and with it came a continued underestimation of their capabilities.

To the shock and embarrassment of England, Gen. Washington had won his first great engagement and he had yet to go into battle. He sat victoriously on his prized gray horse, "Blueskin", watching across the bay as the English evacuated. Sitting in the waters several miles offshore, Jonathan let out a guttural shout of celebration as he and his men watched the unfurled white headsails of the British fleet sail out of Boston Harbor.

A Vote for Independence!

Nicholas Cooke, re-elected to governorship of Rhode Island, in May,1776, boldly declared independence from Great Britain, by *"Rescinding oaths which pronounce allegiance to the king."* Correspondingly, in Philadelphia in June, the Continental Congress debated a vote for independence. The war, to this point, had been waged in hopes to force King George III into rescinding his disciplinary acts against the colonists. Americans are still British subjects and even a year ago the idea of independence was radical at best, treasonous at worst. A vote for independence changes everything.

Jonathan went home to Tiverton. The harsh winter was over, and his focus returned to his farm and family. He enjoyed the solace as he walked behind Buck, plowing up the black earth to be ready for planting, and soaking in the warm sun and the humid breeze. *"You've lost some of your vigor, Buck,"* Jonathan commented, as the old ox strained against the yoke, pulling the blade through the hardened ground. *"After ten years of faithful service, I think maybe a greener pasture will be in store for you soon, old boy."* The thought caused Jonathan to feel surprisingly sad.

Sitting at the table, eating his usual breakfast of ham, fresh bread and coffee, a furious knock came at the door. Mary, startled at the interruption, fumed.

> *"Why indeed, need a person nearly break the door down to make his presence known?! A gentle rap would suffice."*

Jonathan silently observed Mary's propensity for re-establishing decorum and proper posture in all areas of life. Her proud and somewhat pompous ways often put him in a black mood, although he continued to value her devoted love for him and for their children, as well as her willingness to drop the pretenses when the greater duty called. She opened the door, but before she could even muster a sour greeting, a dark figure brushed abruptly past her.

Mary's brother, James Durfey, wild-eyed, rushed to where Jonathan sat. *"America has severed her ties with England!"* Catching his breath, he continued.

> *"The Continental Congress has voted to declare independence! Thomas Jefferson has drafted a document resolving that the united colonies ought to be free and independent states and totally absolved of any allegiance to the British Crown."* [14]

Jonathan sat silently stunned. James added with a sense of glee,

> *"The taverns are brimming with celebration!"*

In the distance, church bells began to ring.

Ready to Fight

The sultry heat of July brought sweat across Jonathan's tanned brow. Memories of perilous encounters along the coastline with the sloop *Tryall* both haunted and exhilarated his mind, as he toiled in the cabbage garden, harvesting the inner cabbage head and leaving the outer leaves to root, for a second harvest in the fall. War was upon them and he would be forced to make difficult decisions regarding his role as a godly man, a patriot, a husband and a father. Mary, always a stout patriot, boldly proclaimed,

> *"I fear only the failure of efforts to bring a better life to ourselves and our children. All other fears are groundless, and I have none."*

Sitting in rockers outdoors in the cooler evening air, a light breeze brushed across Jonathan's face and he marveled at his wife's resolve, while carefully weighing his options. Jonathan mused,

> *"With war comes suffering and sacrifice. I believe that suffering is necessary in this life. It strips away the pretense that life needs be reasonable and safe. Life is not, we know this full well, Mary. It is not logical and good. Evil surrounds us, if not outwardly, in our own hearts and minds."*

Mary wondered where the conversation was going but knew not to interrupt. He continued:

> *"God is the only good. The satisfaction of our souls comes only from God himself, through his beloved Son, Jesus. It is wrong to look in other places."*

Mary nodded her head in agreement and waited. Jonathan raised his clenched fist high in the air and exclaimed,

> *"With that truth in my heart, I have no choice but to defy injustice and the evil bonds that strap us into servitude to anyone other than the Almighty. The English Crown is not my sovereign and I will fight the idolatry of a ruling government that forces upon us loyalty and allegiance to a King of inequity. I will fight. I can suffer no less."*

Mary understood what that meant and hastily gave her full support. Col. Cooke had offered Jonathan the chance to privateer, once again, on *Tryall*, and he would go. This time, it was an absolute war.

19

Revolution and New Beginnings

1776-1790

Sanctioned and encouraged by the General Assembly for privateering, *Tryall* set sail, with Jonathan Sheldon as Master of the Sloop and a new crew. Fifty commissions had been issued in this year of 1776, and there was an enthusiastic zeal for putting a foot on the back of the British Navy which had been ravaging the patriot coastline and American merchant ships.

It was hard to imagine the horrors of war while peacefully patrolling between Montauk Point and Block Island. The ship gently creaked. Waves seemed to almost sleep as the *Tryall* made placid wake across glistening cobalt water. Off his starboard side, Jonathan mused at the majesty of the privateer schooner, *Witch,* [1] her regal white sails framed against the opulent blue sky. Behind her tracked the two-hundred ton *Two Brothers,* [2] a sloop out of Providence. Looking up at the billowed sails of *Tryall*, Jonathan felt a surge of pride as a tender with these two powerful ships and prayed that God bring them prize before the weather turned again. It was not to be.

Capt. Samuel Spencer, [3] on *Witch*, was experienced and hungry for an encounter. The skies became dark and heavy with a roaring rain, blinding them for two days straight. Lightning flashed across the sky in dazzling and deadly display. Finally, the ocean flattened, and the clouds thinned. Scanning the horizon, the crow's nest called out,

"Sails off the port!"

The crew of *Witch* scurried into action, climbing ropes and rigging, manning stations, readying their guns. *Witch* slowly began to turn, and *Two Brothers* followed course. Jonathan called out,

"Man your positions and turn about!"

Adrenaline pulsed through the veins of every man. Jonathan recognized the massive HMS frigate, *Guadalupe*. She carried eighteen guns and escorted the severely damaged and dismasted British merchant ship, *Betsey*. Outnumbered, Jonathan wondered if *Guadalupe* would fight or run. The flash of fire and the boom of cannon soon answered his question. Smoke rolled over the wooden side of *Guadalupe* as cannon shot off, one by one, in a barrage of aggression. *Witch*, in position off *Guadalupe's* starboard side, let loose her armament. Hot balls of iron wrecked across the decks of the enemy ship. Men screamed and officers shouted orders above the din.

    Two Brothers, maneuvering around the stern of *Guadalupe*, was ready to unleash when the enemy ship shifted her course. The thundering clamor of guns silenced as *Guadalupe* suddenly turned and sailed north, leaving *Betsey* as a privateering prize. Cheers could be heard floating across the calm water as crews relished their quick victory. Jonathan and his exhilarated crew were the first to board *Betsey*, her crew, beaten down and exhausted from the ordeal that they had experienced.

    The captain of the brig, *Betsey*, explained the series of her unfortunate events.

> *"Carrying lumber and rice, we had been enroute to the West Indies when the fierceness of the storm damaged us beyond repair. Dismasted, we were limping back to the Charleston port when two privateer schooners seized us. Guadalupe appeared and swiftly recaptured us just one day hence."*

Jonathan chuckled to himself and responded,

> *"You indeed have a checkered and unlucky past! For now, you have been captured thrice."*

Black smoke rolled high into the bright blue sky as *Betsey* burned. Having removed the cargo and crew, *Witch*, *Two Brothers* and *Tryall* sailed as hastily as the wind would take them from the fiery wreckage, eager to return to Newport with their prized cargo and to disembark the crew of the *Betsey*, which uncomfortably outnumbered the crew of *Witch*. There had been many instances where prisoners succeeded in overpowering their captors, taking possession of a ship. This thought had crossed Jonathan's mind, as it did Capt. Spencer's, but the fact remained, the crew of *Betsey* had no fight left in them. Their demeanor proved that they were resolved in their capture and assumed that, as was often the case, when arriving at Newport, they would be paroled.

Setting a course for Newport, eyes searched the horizon diligently. Cruisers from the English Navy had a special hatred of privateers and sought every means to destroy them. They were often successful by virtue of their heavier armament, although the superior speed of privateers often enabled escape, while daring and cleverness also provided success. One such instance became a story retold again and again in taverns and church meetings alike.

Capt. Oliver Reed, a prominent Rhode Islander, commander and privateer, received a report that the British had captured a privateer sloop named *The Spy*. [4] Reed devised a risky plan. He patiently waited with his crew on his sizable sloop at the entrance of New York harbor. *The Spy* came sailing in under the British flag and anchored, waiting for a pilot to guide her into port. Reed rowed out to her with a few reliable men and offered his services, posing as a trusted harbor pilot. After a short and friendly parley, Reed was given control of *The Spy*. He held his direction but a short time, when suddenly taking advantage of a stiff breeze, he shifted direction and laid a course out of New York Harbor heading for Newport. The British commander, confused, remarked, *"We are going to New York, are we not sir?"* To which Reed replied, with a profoundly deep bow,

"No sir, we are not. We are going to Newport."

The British flag was lowered without a shot. The pure audacity of the scheme along with the determined, threatening looks of the hardened men around him, convinced the English officer to surrender without a fight and *The Spy* was brought safely to Newport. [5]

The British Occupy Newport

December of 1776 brought with it frigid weather. Blowing warmth into his freezing hands and stomping his feet to fend off the cold, Jonathan stands along the shoreline and watches, his brown eyes large with horror. White sails crowd the horizon as far as he can see. The wind is bitter cold and snow flurries whirl in the air. *"A more majestic sight can never be seen,"* commented an exuberant local observer standing next to him.

Newport is filled with a good number of Loyalists, who now see the buttress of their loyalty sailing toward them in grandiose power. A welcome sight for the many loyal Tories now cheering the arriving British occupation.

A crusty, eccentric old man, who generally opposed what others approved, hobbled along the walkway, with his cane for support, and commented loudly,

> *"Nothing to celebrate today. Ignorant Tories don't know their front from their backsides."*

Jeers and glares shot in his oblivious direction as he continued along, mumbling epitaphs against the Crown.

Jonathan wisely remains a quiet onlooker. Tensions are elevated and suspicious eyes dart back and forth. The British fleet arrives unopposed as Newport gives up authority. The celebrating Loyalist population is exhilarated at the approaching occupation. Gen. William West of the American militia had overseen the Loyalists in Newport, exiling several of its more vocal and influential citizens to northern Rhode Island in the previous months. The tide has now turned in total favor of loyalist citizens, who had been secretly supplying the British.

Remaining in Newport is certainly now an extremely dangerous proposition for staunch Patriots, while others, more flippant with their allegiance, remained. Ardent Loyalists, who had previously fled Newport, gleefully returned in support of the King. No one knew who to trust, as suspicions and hearsay abounded.

As the powerful British fleet sailed closer, [6] Jonathan watches the faces of known Patriots standing around him lose color, not from the cold, but from the realization that now they must choose to either remain or abandon their homes, while Tories, loyal to the crown, celebrate in the streets. Jonathan's thoughts went to a pamphlet he had read by Thomas Paine:

> *"Tyranny, like Hell, is not easily conquered; yet, we have this consolation with us, that the harder the conflict, the more glorious the triumph."* [7]

Newport was a strategic location. It had been eight months since Boston had fallen to the Americans and five months since the Declaration of Independence had been signed. With their eye on New York, Newport was ideal as a British stronghold and a natural base of operations.

Just that morning Jonathan had crossed on the ferry from Tiverton to attend a public forum at the Colony Meeting House.[7] As the debate centered on the defense of Newport, should British and Hessian [8] forces attack, church bells began to ring. Pandemonium broke out as people scrambled from their homes, their businesses and local taverns hastening for Long Wharf to watch. The force was unimaginable in its grandeur. Seven warships, four frigates, and seventy transports. Onboard were 6,500 British military personnel and about 1,500 civilians.

Two very harsh winters would follow this bitter winter of 1776-77, and tensions and miseries would rise to a fevered pitch. Increased military population on Aquidneck Island brought with it dramatic impact both physically and environmentally. Battling the hard frost and deep snow, almost every tree was ordered cut down. The town and surrounding area was laid waste. Vacant buildings and fences were leveled and used as firewood. With the frigid, subzero temperatures, sentries froze to death at their posts, their muskets at their side.

Even though most Patriot families fled their homes, [9] housing was limited and countless soldiers and officers quartered with the Loyalist families [10] who remained. Spies were everywhere. No one knew who to trust. Rumors and accusations abounded. Movements were constrained. Written permission was required to hunt or fish. Patriot sympathizers were rooted out and punished. Women could move about more freely than men, but public visibility increased their chances of abuse from soldiers. God-fearing women remained less conspicuous, while women of ill repute, flaunted themselves boldly.

Resilience, Fortitude and Strength

The oppressive early morning air only served to remind Jonathan of what the afternoon would bring. [11] The glaring orange sun was just beginning its tyrannical journey across the cloudless blue sky. Heat. Men wandered the streets in exhaustion, slow and lethargic, both from the scorching heat as well as their hunger. Mary had been working day and night, baking bread in her stone oven, to help feed the thousands of Continental troops and militia that had been streaming into Tiverton from neighboring states. Jonathan was worried. She had recently given birth to their fourth child, Oliver. The baby appeared sickly and Mary had not yet regained her strength from the difficult delivery. She insisted, when Jonathan suggested that she rest,

> *"I will do my part! I will not settle back to simply nurse a newborn and not lift a finger to feed these honorable and brave men who have come to help liberate us,"*

Mary's father, Samuel Durfey, quartered several Continental officers, including Gen. John Sullivan. [12] It was August 28, 1778 and the hurricane damage of just two weeks earlier had come at a tremendous cost. The French had officially joined the war in March and after taking three months to cross the Atlantic they were ready, with twelve massive ships and over 4,000 troops to help America gain victory against British dictatorial rule. Just as they prepared to do battle in the open ocean, the fierce wind and looming waves of the gigantic storm built to enormous proportions, separating the two enemies. The badly mauled French ships retreated to Boston for repairs on August 20th. Almost as quickly as they had arrived, the French had retreated, having never fired a single cannon shot.

Gen. Sullivan of the Continentals was enraged. Samuel overheard Sullivan's rant, after receiving an urgent correspondence.

> *"D'Estaing is a coward. This is treachery in its highest order. Our troops are ready for an assault on Newport but we now have no support from the sea. The Frenchh ave gone back to Boston to lick their wounds."*

A subordinate asked,

"Shall we retreat from Tiverton and rejoin Gen. Washington, sir?" "No. We shall attack."

His voice was firm, yet a hint of doubt was easily detected.

Battle of Rhode Island
August 29,1778

Sweat poured down over Jonathan's forehead, stinging his eyes. He was serving with John Cook's 2nd Regiment, from Tiverton. They had crossed over to Aquidneck Island at Howland's Ferry. Eleven thousand men, from all walks of life, soggy and smelly from heat and humidity. Looking back across the Sakonnet River, Jonathan could see the bluffs of Tiverton rising high above the low granite ridge of shoreline. Fort Barton stood silhouetted against the brightness of the sky, ready to lay a barrage of cannon blast. This was his home. Glancing around him, he recognized men he had known his entire life - Benjamin and Abner Chace, Andrew Cory, Pardon Gray, Thomas Osborn, Joseph Durfey. The British were fighting for a faraway King and Country, while these men were fighting for their homes and families.

Jonathan's mind wandered back to May 25th. [13] *"How can it be just three months past? It truly feels like a lifetime,"* He would never forget that daybreak. The terror of hearing musket shots and men screaming orders. A party of 150 British regulars made a preemptive strike directly on Tiverton after receiving reconnaissance that Tiverton militia were preparing an attack against them. Under God's sovereign goodness, a spy in Newport had provided previous warning to the residents of Tiverton. The militia turned out with formidable vigilance and secured effective defensive positions.

Jonathan directed Mary and the children to barricade themselves in the cellar with instructions not to emerge until, God willing, he returned. Their eyes huge with fear, each child hugged their father's neck tightly. Jonathan teased,

"You best let me go, lest I meet my demise from choking right here!"

As he waved goodbye, he gave Mary a look she understood and scrambled up the steep ladder.

Fortified behind a stone wall near the bridge, vigorous musket fire was exchanged for nearly an hour and a half. The attack had not been the surprise that the British had hoped. They only managed to wound several militiamen and burn a house along the shore along with the lower mill before retreating.

"Come back and fight like men, you cowardly cockalorum!", [14]

came the emotional whoop from a stocky, balding militiaman and local blacksmith. Others joined in with stronger sentiments, disappointed not to satisfy their revenge against the hated redcoats.

Shaking the memory from his foggy mind, Jonathan wiped the sweat from his forehead and focused on the mission ahead: Newport. With the French refusing to offer support from the sea, a victory was doubtful. In July, the British had reinforced themselves with 2,000 additional troops.

As he marched with his fellow patriots, one pessimistic militiaman offered,

> *"I am not hopeful that a land attack alone can penetrate the British line. I am more inclined to believe that we would have as much success if we merely asked them nicely to leave Newport to us."*

Jonathan responded with a laugh and inquired,

> *"Should we ask with common British refinement or with American vigor?"*

"American vigor is all I know, sir," came the man's jovial reply, as he scratched his stubbled cheek.

The humidity gave way to a dreary gray drizzle, affording momentary relief from the harsh and taxing heat. Marching south, they sought to establish a defensive line that cut across the island, denying the British the high ground in the north. Gen. Sullivan directed operations from Fort Barton in Tiverton. Cannon roared and columns of white smoke filled the air. The unmistakable sound of an approaching army sent shivers down Jonathan's spine. Whinnying horses, creaking caisson wheels and the fierce discord of aggravated officers shouting commands all melded into a drumming bedlam. The clouds cleared and the sun beat down. Men collapsed in the unrelenting heat, some dying.

The terrible squeaking sound of deadly canister shot buzzed through the windless air. With each volley men dropped, the clusters of iron spheres ripping through limbs and torsos. The American forces were no match for the British onslaught. They fought, but to no avail. Withdrawing to the northern part of the island, the British pursued, with a sluggish cannade. Gen. Greene, on the west advance position, turned his militia to engage the British in hand-to-hand combat, driving them back. It was a bloody clash.

By three o'clock, the Americans withdrew to Bristol and Tiverton. In the end 200 American men and 260 British troops were lost. The land attack could not penetrate the British line without support from the sea, and Newport was left in British hands. The next day, the militia returned to their homes and the Continental troops rejoined Gen. George Washington in New York. A small force was left at Fort Barton. They maintained cannon shot on any British vessel who dared venture that far north along the Sakonnet River.

American military resilience confounded the English. Outnumbered, out-trained, out-disciplined and out-maneuvered, over and over, and still Washington seemed to find a way to bolster his underfed, underdressed and often demoralized troops. His stoic countenance and optimistic nature rose above one humiliating defeat after another. King George III was losing his mind, both figuratively and literally. The English Parliament was divided on the correct approach to take with the disobedient and childish Americans.

Gen. Howe, commander of the British troops, commented that the behavior of Americans amounted to *villainy and madness of a deviled people.* King George lamented,

> *"I still hope that the deluded and unhappy multitude will return to their allegiance."*

Neither man has any respect for Americans, while the war continues on much longer and with much greater a cost than the English ever imagined. The arrogance and egotism that once defined British sentiment toward waging war with America is slipping away.

After the Battle of Rhode Island, Jonathan returned home. Fall quickly turned to winter and it arrived with a vicious fury. The weather turned brutally cold with blinding and drifting snow covering the ground. The bitter temperatures reminded Jonathan of the merciless winter of the previous year. The oft-told stories of Valley Forge [15] horrified and discouraged the colonists. Washington had camped his troops at Valley Forge and men were dying of starvation, typhus, smallpox, dysentery and influenza. They did not have appropriate clothing to defeat the cold; many did not have shoes but wrapped their feet in rags. Standing in front of a small fire and turning in continuous circles in order to face the warmth of the flames was the only way to keep from freezing to death on many nights. A deep despair waged its effective talons on hearts and minds. Desertion became commonplace. It seemed an impending doom settled across the land.

People were losing hope and beginning to believe that the war was lost. Jonathan shared his deepest fears.

> *"Mary, I do not see how we can stand against the military power of our opponent. The weather itself seems to be against us."*

> *"I know our fight to be honorable and true, Jonathan, and I must believe that God's will prevail through us."* Mary gently patted her growing belly: another baby was on its way.

In the darkness of the quiet evening, Jonathan mulled over her words. He silently wondered,

> *"How do we continue on against such military might, when all appears so hopeless?"*

Poring over his Bible by the light of a single candle on his desk, he read from God's Word: *"Finally, be strong in the Lord, and in the power of his might. Put on the whole armor of God, that ye may be able to stand against the wiles of the devil…. Stand therefore, having your loins girt with truth and having on the breastplate of righteousness."* [16] Jonathan's thoughts went to something his father, Benjamin, had told him,

"Only the courageous speak truth to power, for they risk losing their friends, their freedoms or their very life." Jonathan once again resolved, *"Stand firm. This I shall do."*

The following year, 1779, brought reports of what felt like a stalemate for the American cause. It had been over a year since the French had joined the war, and their impact had been minimal if not disappointing. An American victory at the Battle of Newtown, in Elmira, New York was only countered by an American defeat at the Siege of Savannah. In August, a plan was approved by Congress stipulating independence and British evacuation. In September John Adams was appointed to travel to France to negotiate terms of peace with England. By the time he arrived in Paris, conditions were unfavorable for peace negotiations, as the war was going badly for the Continental Army. The British were in no mood to compromise.

British Evacuate Newport

The sun split through the dark gray clouds, igniting the copper and red leaves of maple trees into a fiery brightness across the distant hillsides. The air was crisp and fresh. Jonathan and his oldest son, seven-year-old Parry, cheerfully picked apples from the small orchard in the back of their house. Hearing the fast-paced gallop of a horse, Jonathan stepped down from the ladder, putting his hand over his eyes to block the glare from the sun and squinting until he recognized his friend and distant relative, Alexander Balcom.

> *"The British are evacuating Newport!"* [17] he declared, his face brimming with a toothy smile.

Cheers could be heard coming from up and down the streets of Tiverton. At the British occupation, many Patriot families had fled Newport and sought refuge in this tiny nearby village. Alexander added,

> *"They are abandoning Newport to concentrate troops in New York!"*

Jonathan's knees almost buckled under him in joy. He scooped up Parry and spun him through the air, in a jubilant circle. After three wretched years, the English were finally leaving Aquidneck Island.

Finally, the French Arrive

Less than a year later, July 1780, the French fleet arrived in Narragansett Bay [18] with an army of 450 officers and 5,300 infantrymen, sent by King Louis XVI and commanded by Marshall Jean-Baptiste Donatien de Vimeur, comte de Rochambeau. Newport became the base of operations for the French. Given earlier events and the perceived failure of the French to perform as expected, there was no certainty that their collaboration would meet the standard or that they would ever be of real assistance to America. Doubts abounded, yet the fact remained: French military aid was vital to American independence. An insidious apathy was permeating the hearts and minds of many colonists concerning the war. Doubt that England could be defeated, even with the assistance of the French, was growing. Nonetheless, the people of Rhode Island, and especially Newport, worked hard with their new allies to overcome the cultural barriers that separated them. For most of the 12,000 French soldiers and sailors who eventually quartered in Rhode Island, it was their first exposure to America and Americans. The staunch and unwavering support of the French was the only mark of eroding optimism that remained.

It would be one more year before Rochambeau mustered his troops out of Newport to ultimately engage the enemy. Along with Gen. Washington, the plan was to march a formidable joint force to Yorktown, Virginia, trapping Gen. Charles Edward Cornwallis V and his British troops against the sea, as the French fleet of twenty-nine warships, carrying three-thousand additional marines, was expected to arrive from the West Indies at any time. Already late, there was great anticipation for the French fleet's arrival. Without it, there could be no victory. In July 1781, Rochambeau removed his troops from Newport to Providence in preparation for what was hoped to be a decisive march against Gen. Cornwallis and the British. But by the middle of September, the French fleet still had not arrived. [18]

American Victory Over the British

Twenty-nine-year-old Mary Sheldon had proven to be a devoted and industrious wife. After the infant death of her fourth child, Oliver, Mary gave birth to her fifth child in May, a girl they named Ruth. Mary focused her attention on her customary daily chores as summer quickly approached. Desiring to be of aid during the war effort, her evenings were spent knitting woolen caps for the troops, anticipating their torturous winter encampments. With the uncertainty and chaos that had surrounded their community for so long, their lives were wrought with despair. They had endured so much. Looking down, fearfully, at Ruth peacefully sleeping in her arms, she wondered to herself,

"*Will war never end?*" [19]

After the British permanently vacated Newport, Patriot families slowly returned, finding their city devastated and essentially in ruins from the long occupation. Facing a bleak future, Newport would need to reinvent itself. Tiverton returned to a more peaceful measure, while suspicions and accusations of treason or espionage filled the air with secret whispers. Loyalists were growing in number as a Patriot victory looked less and less reasonable at that time.

Life had indeed been replete with suffering. It seemed the ashen pale of death lay all around, and yet glimmers of hope continued to shine its light of encouragement from time to time. Jonathan and Mary were resilient and strong in both character and fortitude. Although the war continued on perpetually, battles now settled well south of them. The British were evacuated from their lives and the French had finally withdrawn from Newport as well. The summer of 1781 was time to rebuild the pieces of what was left. Farming their small acreage of land, Jonathan appreciated the fruits of his hard work more than he ever had before.

When autumn came around again, there came an additional and welcome revelry to the already boisterous color pageantry of the wooded hillsides.

> "*Cornwallis surrendered at Yorktown! Over eight-thousand British troops are now prisoners!*"

It was indeed welcome news and cause for celebration. French ships had finally arrived and successfully blocked British retreat by sea, and Cornwallis had no choice but to abdicate. Bells rang out in celebration. The war was not officially over, yet the American victory was sure to seal the fate of English domination. America with its ill-equipped, untrained army of farmers, merchants and laborers had defeated the most powerful and disciplined army on earth. Jonathan and Mary danced with their children across the wooden floor of their sitting room. There was optimism that soon there would be an official and lasting peace. [20]

Gen. Cornwallis, in command of the British army, had made an arrogant tactical error. Encamping his nine thousand British, Loyalist and Hessian troops on a bluff overlooking the York River, American and French ground forces formed a perimeter at their front and the river at their back. On September 28, 1781, when the French fleet finally arrived, there was no escape. It was now Washington's turn to drape the noose around the necks of the British forces.

In a stunning defeat, Cornwallis was forced to surrender at Yorktown on October 19, 1781. The war virtually came to an end that day, with the Siege of Yorktown proving to be the last major battle, though it would not officially end for another two years on September 3, 1783, with the Treaty of Paris.

Celebration Turned to Sorrow

Christmas Day of 1781 was especially joyous. Jonathan hitched the sleigh to his old brown mare, Belle, and with the children bundled in warm clothes and wrapped in blankets, the family huddled close together, as they bumped along the snow packed road to church. Inside, the atmosphere was jubilant. Happy greetings were all about with firm handshakes, heartwarming smiles, slaps on the back and spirited hugs. They worshipped with a new sense of freedom. The message that day was one of acknowledging God's abundant blessings through the birth of Jesus and great hope for their new nation.

Jonathan and Mary looked forward to the afternoon and evening, a time of celebration with friends and family. The pleasant aroma of a feast permeated the room. Ham, turkey, jams, breads, pies and desserts spread across the long wooden table. The noise of conversation mixed with laughter, the smell of evergreens, holly and laurel decorating the window ledges. [21] Gathered together with the people they loved, they ate, drank, danced and sang. *"Joy to the World"* was especially rousing, and Benjamin Sheldon held back glad tears as the chorus finished. Jonathan watched as his father, Benjamin, sang, in his deep baritone, with gusto in his voice and tears welling up in his aged eyes. The memory of that evening for Jonathan in the years to come would be of considerable comfort, as his father, Rev. Benjamin Sheldon [22], would die just six days later, at sixty-one years of age, while sitting in his chair sleeping in front of the fireplace.

Jonathan's voice cracked.

"I find it difficult to imagine my life without him,"

Mary, whose plump body rested next to him under heavy wool blankets, wasn't quite awake and rolled toward him with her eyes still closed.

"He was a good man, Jonathan, an exceptionally good and godly man. You were Blessed to have him as a father. And it was indeed a blessing from God that such a patriot and man of God as Benjamin Sheldon lived to see the defeat of the English, even if just by two months. God is gracious."

Ruth cried out, and Mary quickly tossed the bulky bedding aside and reached for the hungry infant.

The Routine of Life and Death Returns

With peace finally settling across the new nation, life developed into a satisfying routine. While Jonathan worked hard to provide for his growing family, Mary continued to give birth every two years. Jonathan Jr. was born in 1783, only to die from a tree branch falling on him at five years old. Mercy was born in 1785. An unnamed *"little angel"* was stillborn in 1787, and a baby girl was born in 1789, yet to be named until it was assured that she would survive. Mary deeply grieved the deaths of her children, nevertheless the rigorous demands of life did not allow for wallowing in sorrow for any extended time.

Death was an accepted, painful part of life. But even more than being accepted, it was quietly expected, an ever-present shadow grown accustomed to. It was no friend, but a consistent unwelcome visitor. There was no choice but to accommodate death, it was always the ultimate victor, while at the same time it never defined life itself. Hard work shaped who they were. But it was family giving the hard work purpose and a new free country that gave the hard work a means to advance, flourish and thrive. Faith in a sovereign God wrapped it all up, giving light, hope and peace in the face of that enemy...friendless death. By no stretch was life easy, but then again no one expected it to be.

Mary was thirty-eight years old when she died unexpectedly in 1790. [23] It was an unforeseen accident. Tripping and plunging down the steep cellar stairs, hitting her head, she lost consciousness, never to wake. She had shared nineteen years of marriage and nine children with Jonathan Sheldon, seven of whom survived. Now she was with her Lord. Parry was eighteen and working as an apprentice in the shipyard. Sixteen-year-old Joseph remained unsure of his future. The middle children dutifully saw to their chores and responsibilities at home. The youngest, referred to simply as "*little angel*", [24] was not two years old, with no legal name yet decided.

Jonathan grieved the loss of his beloved wife and regretted the early years when he bemoaned their marriage. He prayed, asking God to forgive him for his immature and foolish heart, and then thanked God for this faithful woman who had loved so well and sacrificed so much. "*We will name the child "Mary" after her dear mother,*" Jonathan stated. He buried his wife, Mary, in Tiverton and many grieved her passing.

20

Jonathan Sheldon and
Priscilla Manchester

1792-1815

The wagon bumped along beneath huge oaks lining the dusty road. Two new oxen, still adjusting to working as a team, labored under the heavy load. Jonathan, Parry and Joseph prodded them from the buckboard seat or walked in front, guiding them forward. It was slow going. The older girls mostly walked, while Jonathan's new wife, Priscilla [1] and the youngest, four-year-old, Mary, rode in the back.

The weather had cooperated, and roads were dry and free of mud, although cavernous potholes created from previous rains were hazardous, once bouncing Priscilla off the back of the wagon. Landing hard on her right hip, she rolled over several times before stopping, her skirts flying as if caught in a windstorm. Tucking her ash brown hair back inside her crooked bonnet, she laughed and complained,

> *"This road is straight from the pits of Hades itself and beyond repair!"*

Ruth and Mercy laughed, while little Mary's eyes were huge with concern. Parry rolled his eyes and shook his head in bewilderment at how his father's recent wife could be so graceless. Jonathan helped Priscilla up and dusted her off. With a twinkle in his eye, he said,

"If you wanted to get out of the wagon, all you need do is ask, Mrs. Sheldon,"

She returned the banter.

"I find 'tis quicker to be jostled off by an inept driver, like common baggage, Mr. Sheldon."

Parry felt a twinge of resentment. His mother, Mary, had been gone for only two years.

Priscilla Manchester believed she would never marry. Having passed the thirty-year mark, both she and her sister, Lois, had given up the thought of a husband. Time and events robbed them of their prime. Priscilla was sixteen years old when the war began and Newport fell to the English, just across the Narragansett Bay from Little Compton. Life became a struggle for survival. Manufacturing and trade came to a stop and the unbelievably harsh winters brought hardship, hunger and isolation. Her older brother, John, went off to fight and she, with Lois her sister, was left to help her parents and five younger siblings. [2] There was no time or even consideration for courting. No young men came around.

The Manchester family was well known in both Little Compton, Tiverton and Portsmouth. Tiverton being located 10 miles to the north. William Manchester, Priscilla's father, was born in Rhode Island along with his father before him and his father before him. Priscilla's mother, Mary, [3] was born an Irish. Her great-great-grandfather, John Irish, arrived in Plymouth Colony from England when he was eighteen on the ship Talbot, in 1630, as an indentured servant. He agreed to *"serve, remain and abide"* with Timothy Hatherly, a well-to-do felt maker, for five years. In late 1659, he relocated his family from Duxbury, Massachusetts Bay Colony to resettle in Saconnet Neck (now Little Compton). Three generations later, Mary Irish, Priscilla's mother, was born in Little Compton in 1734. Priscilla knew only Little Compton and Tiverton her entire life.

When the war concluded, John Manchester, [4] Priscilla's older brother, had moved west to Granville, MA, and his description of bounteous, unspoiled land was enticing - crystal clear mountain streams cascading over moss-covered boulders and rocky falls; steep rolling hills brandishing pine, oak, ash, chestnut, maple and evergreen. The mountainous region was not so well-suited for farming, but apple orchards flourished, and English hay could be grown in poor soil. Livestock, especially sheep, roamed the hillsides. John painted an enticing picture of Granville, MA.

Tiverton was overcrowded and the land overworked. People were migrating west. The promise of cheap and abundant land was compelling, compared to the worn out, overpriced fields of Rhode Island farmland, which could be divided among family members only so many times. There was a bright and promising future in the west. A spirit of idealistic ambition drove them to pack up their families and leave everything they had ever known.

John Manchester, having had no real opportunity in Little Compton or Tiverton, at the age of eighteen [12] had packed his meager belongings and travelled the one-hundred and forty miles just one month before those fateful shots rang out at Concord/Lexington in April, 1775, signaling the beginning of the Revolutionary War, and John was eager to join in the conflict, serving for three years. [13] After the war he returned to Granville to meet and fall in love with young Phoebe Stedman, marrying her in the autumn of 1781. They went on to have many children.

The push west reached beyond the Appalachian Mountains. After the victory in the war with England, the American government was deeply in debt to France, Spain and the Netherlands, owing over $75,000,000. Selling 160,000,000 acres of land at one dollar an acre was very conducive for addressing that financial burden, as well as encouraging colonists to venture west. Americans flooded over the mountains, despite the inherent dangers. For although the British had been severely weakened in the Ohio Valley and the sanctioned fighting had been over for nine years, the frontier remained a war zone, with native peoples rising up in violent protest to whites flowing over the Appalachians.

When Jonathan and Priscilla made the decision to move west in 1792, [5] Indian attacks had been increasing across the Ohio Valley. Unrelenting pressure was forcing the Indian Nations to move out of the way, but they would not go easily. By 1793, the flow of settlers was grinding to a halt, with over 2,500 settlers killed in guerilla warfare attacks across the Ohio frontier. For the Sheldons, choosing to relocate as far as Granville, MA seemed the more cautious and wiser thing to do, avoiding the dangers of pioneering too far west into the wilderness of the Ohio Valley. Joining Priscilla's brother, John Manchester and his family, seemed a safe and forward-looking venture. For now, they would make Massachusetts their home.

Behind the team of sluggish oxen, they continued down the rutted, uneven road. Jonathan and Priscilla sat tightly together on the wagon bench and talked. Jonathan asked,

"Do you worry about your father's wellbeing?"

"I more grieve for my sister, Lois. [6] Since our mother's death three years ago, she has labored without rest. Guilt finds its way into my heart at leaving her behind. My father [7] is in need of attention and assistance, it's true, but his life is nearing its end. Lois, with her selfless nature, has never had the opportunity to truly live hers."

Priscilla adjusted sleeping Mary in her arms. Jonathan pondered her words for a moment.

"Guilt is not what the Lord would have you to know, Priscilla. Sorrow is natural and pity be true, but regret or shame is not yours to carry. Lois is in God's hands. You must hold her up to His care."

Priscilla appreciated his genuine consideration, although a cloud of regret continued to follow her.

A lithe woman, with intense blue eyes, thin lips and small in stature, Priscilla was not a natural beauty. Her hair pulled straight back in harsh firmness, with a tight bun secured on top, gave a stern and serious impression, belying her certain good-natured character. Kind and gentle, there was rarely an occasion when her feathers ruffled, or her temper flared. For the older children, she would never replace their mother, Mary, but for Little Mary and eventually, seven-year-old Mercy, she was every bit their mother. Loving the children deeply, Priscilla prayed for wisdom in this new and foreign role.

Forty-two-year-old Jonathan found Priscilla's company to be engaging and most pleasant. When it was initially proposed that a marriage between the two would be beneficial to both, he was cautious. He knew her only as the unmarried daughter of William Manchester. He did not wish to marry an *"old-maid"* simply to help him raise his children. An agreement to court her, within the confines of a mutually agreed upon understanding, was set upon. If either chose to forgo the ultimate intention of marriage, the courting would end with no further commitments required. And so, with his hat in his calloused hands, Jonathon called on her. Sitting in her father's parlor, he felt as if he were a young man again, seeking a wife, and the entire situation felt quite uncomfortable.

Musing over those introductory, awkward, early months of marriage always brought a smile to Jonathan's face. Priscilla had more than met the expectations that he held. At thirty-two years old when they married, her youthful prime was gone, and yet over the years, he grew in deep attraction. Their marriage bed was at first graceless and even bumbling, but over time there came *"plain sailing"* as Jonathan would jokingly tease. Her wit was quick, and her mind was sharp. Priscilla was everything a frontier woman needed to be.

Arriving in Granville after eight slow days on the move over one-hundred miles of rough and rutty roads, the family began the arduous task of creating a homestead west of Granville. As they built the house on the seventy acres of land he had acquired, Priscilla worked side by side with her new husband, even as she anxiously awaited the birth of their first child. Her courage and confidence, combined with a rarely swayed contentment in the midst of difficult circumstances, made for a joyful home, and the older children began to warm to this amiable woman who had so suddenly, it seemed, come into their lives.

The land was exactly as Priscilla's brother, John, had described; rugged, mountainous and beautiful, yet the soil was poor and rocky. Settled by colonists in 1736, Granville was officially incorporated in 1754. In those days, settlers could get a hundred acres for free, providing they built a house and put in four acres of English hay. Situated eighteen miles west of Springfield and nine miles southwest of Westfield, with the border of Connecticut sitting on the south, Granville was highland country with steep rolling hills, deep cuts and whitewater rivers flowing as tributaries into the Connecticut River.

Settling six miles southwest of the center of Granville, in an area ultimately incorporated in 1810 as Tolland, near the Connecticut border, the Sheldon family began to work the stony land. Small tracts of clay and sandy loam made for difficult growing conditions, however the grandeur and beauty surrounding them sparked a contentedness that had been lacking in their lives for so long. The Revolutionary War of ten years earlier had taken an enormous toll on them in every way. The freshness of this new home began to wash their spirits clean. Several fast-flowing mountain streams cut through deep green valleys, and sheep grazed peacefully along the steep hillsides. Life was simple and pure.

Isolated from the larger Granville population by several miles, community involvement was mostly limited to the weekly trek to attend church services. Priscilla had been raised Methodist Episcopal and she held deeply to the tenets. Since there was no Methodist Episcopal Church in Granville at that time, they settled in with the Congregationalists. The Congregational Church [8] gave Priscilla a sense of belonging, yet she missed her Methodist roots. The teachings from God's Word were comparable, and although there were specific doctrinal beliefs that differed, she found herself content for the time being.

Before Jonathan reluctantly adhered to Methodism, he and Priscilla spent many long evenings discussing the merits of their apparent conflicting doctrines in light of the Biblical text. She explained,

> *"We are not so far apart, Jonathan. Our common belief in the authority and inerrancy of God's word remains truly secure. Our understanding of God's plan of redemption rests solidly in truth; we are dead in our sins and consequently, separated from God. We are justified by faith alone and our faith produces inward and outward holiness...not perfection, but a mind toward honoring Christ in all that we are and do. God's grace is acquired through Christ alone, not on our own merit."*

Jonathan responded,

"I cannot argue with you Priscilla. We indeed agree at every point you have set forth. And yet you are suffered to be of one opinion and I of another concerning the doctrine of universal redemption. Nay, I believe many have been misled. God's truths are clearly revealed in His Word. In defense, I must use great plainness of speech, leaving the consequences to God. John Wesley, as pointed out by George Whitfield, proceeded with illogic in his published sermon against the doctrine of election and predestination." With her voice rising in pitch, Priscilla replied, *"But if there be election, then is not all preaching in vain? Preaching to save souls is void if they are elected with or without it. And it would seem useless to those that are not of the elect, for they cannot possibly be saved."*

Jonathan waited patiently, knowing that she had more to add. Feeling flustered, she continued:

"And furthermore, Wesley wrote, 'the doctrine of election wholly takes away those motives to follow after it.' Election directly tends to destroy holiness in the life of a follower of Christ."

Jonathan smiled broadly, the deep creases in his tanned forehead seeming to dance a bit as he stood to get another log for the fire. He loved to see her riled with that fiery emotion when she spoke of faith and the Methodist Episcopal Church. After a few minutes, he finally responded.

"First and foremost, the gospel itself speaks to the truth of predestination and election, although we may not like it or understand it. To your first objection, we do not know who are elect and who reprobate. The gospel must be preached to all. The preaching and hearing of God's Word to those God hath ordained to eternal life quickens and enables those to believe. God effectually calls his elect, for we are dead in our sins, and a dead man can do nothing on his own. To your second objection, that the doctrine of election tends to destroy

holiness, it would be quite to the contrary. A true disciple of the Lord Jesus Christ strives to be holy for the sake of being holy, living for Christ out of love and gratitude, without regard to the rewards of heaven or the fear of hell. Priscilla, I am a reformed Congregationalist, and you follow the tenets of John Wesley. We both hold to the need for conversion and new birth for sinful man. Ultimately, God will do what man cannot, namely, make us both of one mind, but if not, at least unified in the saving grace of Christ."

She frowned, but with the slight hint of a smile.

"You can wrap this up in that package if you so choose, Mr. Sheldon, but I believe that you simply enjoy being contrary."

Chuckling to himself, he walked out the front door.

"The sheep need tending," he quietly mumbled.

She laughed, knowing that he was amused, but praying that he would see her point of view.

A Flurry of Children and Grandchildren

With the spinning wheel and a loom, Priscilla knitted and sewed clothes. In her small vegetable garden next to the house, she grew corn, squash and beans, drying and canning as much as she could for the bleak winters. With a natural flowing spring nearby, water was readily available, and so there was no need to depend on beer or corn whiskey, although she was sure to make cider each autumn.

The traditional role of women's work concentrating primarily inside the home, safe from the more physical and "manly" outdoor endeavors, remained a luxury that no one could afford. Priscilla did what she needed to do without complaint. She had never been one to fuss with vanity over the sun burning and weathering her fair skin. Life was hard work, but it was good. Pretentious airs never entered her mind. She would often reflect that her lot in life could have been cast in easier circumstances, but not necessarily in happier ways.

Labor pains began in the middle of the night.

"I am afraid. Should I die, my family will be in an awfully hard way,"

Priscilla shared with Phoebe as she squeezed her hand tightly, trying to catch her breath. Jonathan had sent for his sister-in-law, John Manchester's wife, to attend to Priscilla when the contractions came close. Phoebe was a no-nonsense personality, yet, she also had a caring soul. She chided Priscilla,

"You shall be fine. God will see to you. Now let us concentrate on meeting this little angel. When I say 'Push', you do it!" "Push!"

Bearing down, Priscilla's oval face turned bright red as she curled herself up, grabbing her knees and giving one final effort. Falling back on the bed, she heard the cries.

"You have a son, Priscilla. A son!"

Jonathan was more than pleased.

"A son! We will call him Daniel, after my departed brother." [9]

Priscilla liked the name. She understood why Jonathan chose it, having heard the story of how young Daniel, only twenty-eight, had drowned at sea on a privateer ship loaded for Suriname. The sea had claimed many loved ones over the years. Priscilla's younger brother Shadrack had also been a sailor. She shuddered to think that Jonathan too could have so easily met a watery grave. Daniel nursed hungrily and Jonathan solemnly reflected,

"Davy Jones locker."

Life soon became a flurry of change. Jonathan's older children, born with his deceased wife Mary, embraced their unfamiliar surroundings in a new land and quickly began independent lives of their own.

- *Parry* found an apprenticeship, thirty-five miles south, as a cooper in Hartford, CT. He married twenty-two-year-old Rhoda Sutlief in 1794.

- Nineteen-year-old *Prudence*, always prone to impulsiveness, immediately fell head over heels in love with twenty-four-year-old local boy, Timothy Ives Hall, and married a mere year after arriving in Granville in 1793. They would go on to have eleven children.

- *Joseph* moved to Hartford, met and married Catherine Olcott. Joseph had a heart for God and entered the ministry. He moved with his family to Tiffin, OH, where he would die in 1821, at the age of forty-five.

- *Ruth*, more shy and plain, worried that she may never marry. But the Lord answered her prayers after she moved to Hartford to help Parry's wife, Rhoda, with their new baby. There, in 1806, at the age of twenty-six, she met Elihu Moses Beach and they married in 1807. They would have six children, the middle boy dying as an infant.

- *Mercy* married Archibald Black in Granville in 1810. He was born and raised in the area and Mercy had known him as far back as she could remember. It was not love at first sight for the eight-year-old children, but over time a spark blossomed into like, and like then matured into love. They went on to have two daughters.

- Little *Mary* was only four years old when they arrived in Granville in 1792, held devotedly in Priscilla's motherly arms. She met Osmond Williams while visiting her Aunt Phoebe and Uncle John Manchester and her cousins in Colebrook, CT, in 1810. They married in 1812. She was twenty-three and the following year gave birth to their first child, a girl who did not survive. Heartache followed Mary's life, as almost half of her thirteen children would not survive to adulthood.

As her stepchildren were beginning lives of their own, so too Priscilla and Jonathan were adding to their family quiver. Giving birth to eight children over the course of eleven years provided all the joys and sorrows that accompany the challenges of frontier life and childhood survival. After Daniel was born, Priscilla found that she was quickly pregnant again. The work was never ending, and although tired from sleepless nights and a colicky baby, she gently tilled the ground of her garden. Grateful that baby Daniel slept peacefully in a basket alongside her during the day, she wished that he would sleep during the night hours instead.

Standing to stretch her back, she tilted her head back and allowed the hot sun to bathe its heat across her face. Her dry, cracked hands were dirty and as she wiped the sweat from her forehead, she giggled to realize that she now had mud smeared from ear to ear. Rubbing her large rounded belly, her demeanor fell. A deep foreboding came from somewhere inside. Looking down, she said,

"Sweet baby, I fear that you will not survive in this world."

Two months later, baby Chloe was born. She lived only a few days and Priscilla was heartbroken to bury her little daughter. Yet there was no time to sink into the abyss of vast sorrow, let alone grieve for what would feel like an appropriate amount of time. It was fall and harvest time. All hands were needed if they were to reap the hay and tobacco before the weather turned. With that also came preparations for winter. Food had to be safely stored and sheep had to be shorn for carding the wool that would then be spun into warp. Daily chores were never ending, even after death took its toll. Death: always living nearby and knocking at the door.

Prudence and her husband Timothy lived a few miles up the road, and the joint work efforts brought ease to the load as well as rewards in the physical labor required to work the land. They often travelled between houses to share in meals or to simply relax on a cool evening. Baby Timothy had been born to Prudence and Timothy just four months before baby Daniel. Each with babies, Priscilla found a new bond with her stepdaughter, Prudence. Watching the two baby boys interact together; crawling across the floor, pulling themselves along, almost ready to walk, brought delight to the adults.

In 1795, Prudence and Priscilla were on track to have babies in the same year once again, while Parry and his wife, Rhoda, having moved to Hartford, CT, were also expecting. When baby Lois was born to Priscilla and Jonathan, their hearts were filled with gratefulness. The umbilical cord had been wrapped around her neck, and the quick-thinking midwife, Hannah Slocum, responded without hesitation to free the blue Lois Sheldon and breathe life back into her little body. It was a difficult way to enter the world, but Lois rebounded well and began to flourish quickly. Prudence delivered baby Huldah Hall with no complications and Rhoda had no difficulties at the birth of Curtiss Parry Sheldon. Jonathan would shake his head in amusement when his little daughter and his grandchildren gathered. Being the same age, Lois, was an aunt to the cousins Huldah and Curtiss. It felt complicated on one hand yet perfectly natural on the other.

Family Life in Granville

Priscilla woke to an empty room. A thin linen curtain held back grey morning light against the small glass paned window. Contractions had begun in the night and in between the sharp stabbing pain, she was able to sleep albeit restlessly. She called out,

"Mrs. Slocum, are you there?"

and was relieved to hear the seasoned midwife's reassuring answer.

"Yes, dear, just making some tea while we wait."

It had been two years since Lois was born, and now once again she was ready to give birth.

"This baby be a big one. Either that or you have been blessed with two," Mrs. Slocum casually commented, sipping her

tea as she sat down on a straight backed chair next to the bed.

Ignoring that overwhelming possibility, Priscilla asked about the children and was reassured at Mrs. Slocums response.

"Oh, they are well taken care of and happy as larks. Prudence came and took the lot of them to her place."

Priscilla was especially concerned for eight-year-old Mary, who had been feeling neglected with the attention that Daniel and Lois required.

By midday, June 6,1797, Jonathan Jr. was born. A healthy boy, who they would call *"Jon"*. Priscilla breathed a sigh of relief as she watched Mrs. Slocum clean off her new son. But something did not feel right. Contractions continued,

"Mrs. Slocum, I believe you were right! There is a second on the way."

Baby Jonathan cried with a healthy set of lungs as Phoebe, who had arrived to help, quickly wrapped him up tightly in a blanket and whisked him off to another room. Priscilla lay back, exhausted, and prepared herself to deliver again. After several more hours, the second baby refused to come. Mrs. Slocum was concerned and called for the doctor, but before he arrived, baby Joan was born. She was beautiful but had been deprived of oxygen for far too long and only survived long enough for Priscilla to hold her but a minute, before her tiny body gave way to death's sting.

And so, Jonathan and Priscilla buried yet another child. Baby Jonathan "Jon", never having had the opportunity to know his twin sister, grew happily in mind and body. Four more children came after, with Benjamin being the last, born in 1805. [10]

As they grew, the children attended school, but most for only a short while. Mary and Mercy stopped travelling the long steep road to the schoolhouse in the third grade, believing that girls, after learning to read and write, should concentrate on the more practical duties of cooking and raising children. The boys, Daniel, Jon and later Benjamin, studied longer, although they found little enjoyment in schooling. Sitting on wooden benches, with only a single fireplace off to one side, the schoolhouse was chilly, if not downright cold, and perpetually uncomfortable. Children's literature was rare and school supplies inefficient. The New England Primer was used and included *Aesop's Fables, Robinson Crusoe* and always the Bible, but otherwise, learning tools were inept.

Daniel, the oldest, was especially rambunctious and had difficulty with concentration and proper behavior. He saw no sense in schooling and simply preferred to be in the field working or tending the sheep. The teacher was, *"Spinster Sally Sherman is so homely, we are squirmin"*, as the children sang behind her back until she up and married Josiah Remington in 1807. [11] Mr. Remington was a fearsome man of momentous height, with powerful arms and a massive beard. He was known to strangle a wolf with his bare hands and fell a bear with a pocketknife, or so the story goes. Regardless, the wide-eyed children believe every sordid word, and Miss *"Spinster Sally Sherman"* gained a whole new respect as *"Mrs. Remington"*, and the silly rhymes stopped.

Most teachers punished ill-behaved boys with whips, dunce-caps and cards hung around their necks reading, *"Idle Boy"*, but Mrs. Remington only had to glance a wary eye in a boy's direction, and he snapped to attention. Although some boys went on to college as young as twelve, others joined the workforce as soon as they could read, write and "cypher". Daniel was the latter, while his younger brother, Jon, discovered a love of books. Albeit, together with their many Manchester cousins, the Sheldon children were a force to be reckoned with.

A Crisis of Faith

William Manchester, who was Uncle John's and Aunt Phoebe's oldest son, was extremely industrious and forward thinking. A serious young man, and three years older than Daniel, he rarely played the raucous games of blind man's bluff or kickball with the other boys. In 1803 at the age of thirteen, he took an apprenticeship twenty-two miles across the Connecticut border in Colebrook. He would eventually own the sawmill and turning shop that he worked in, but his true passion was to establish a Methodist Episcopal Church [14] in town. Prior to this,

Colebrooke had seen fourteen years of dissension over Congregational Church issues.

Dr. Jonathan Edwards Jr., son of the prominent Jonathan Edwards associated with the *Great Awakening,* was installed as minister of the Congregational Church in Colebrook in December 1795, at the age of fifty-five. It was believed that he could bring order and peace, so long ago forgotten. Edwards had previously been dismissed from his church in White Haven, which he had served for twenty-seven years. Colebrook was looking for a man of strong character and ability who could mandate a much-needed respect, in order to restore unity throughout the congregation and community at large. On the day of his installation, Mr. R. Robbins enthusiastically proclaimed,

"Well gentlemen, the sea is before us, now, dive, dive!"

Edwards was clear in thought and style, acute and logical. As a theologian he had no equal, although he lacked the powerful imagination and creative thought of his famous father. The town of Colbrooke benefited from his ministry, but only until in 1799 when he took a bad fall from his horse and it was feared that he suffered a concussion of the brain. At that point, he relocated to become president of Union College, dying two years later in 1801 of overwork and exhaustion.

While Dr. Edwards was still in the throes of beginning his new ministry in Colbrooke, Jonathan decided to pay the esteemed minister a visit.

"Why must you speak with him? There is no sense in it," Priscilla fumed.

But Jonathan was undeterred. His hat in his hands, he calmly brushed an annoying fly from his slightly balding head.

"This man, Dr. Edwards, holds a legacy. His father touched the heart of my grandfather, Rev. John Greenwood, years ago. The providence of this has greatly affected me. I purpose to pay respect to him and honor God in this way."

He pushed his hat firmly down on his head, swung his leg up and over his aged brown horse, kicked the animal's sides and trotted off down the dusty road.

As he rode, he considered what indeed he was doing. He was not seeking advice or interested in theological debate, for which he was sure that he could not win. He was not as educated a man as Dr. Edwards who graduated from Princeton. Doubting himself and thinking aloud, he decided,

> *"No. I only desire to shake his hand and thank him for his faithful service to the Lord and to acknowledge the impact that his great father had on our family."*

Arriving in Colebrooke, Jonathan was impressed with the progress of the town. Above the bridge there was a clock shop, and on the north side of town, a grist mill and a sawmill. He had heard that Elihu and Timothy Parsons operated a tannery on the bank of the Colebrooke River, but he had not known of the carding mill on the west side of the river, north of Jane Carpenter's. [(15)]

Dr. Edwards greeted Jonathan warmly and was most gracious and pleased with his brief and encouraging conversation. They exchanged short stories, and before Jonathan rode the fourteen miles back to Tolland, they prayed together, each asking God to bless the other. Jonathan appreciated being held in respect by a theologian of Dr. Edwards caliber. For as a simple man of comparably little education, Jonathan understood that it would have been extremely manageable for Dr. Edwards to step into pious judgement from a place of intellectual superiority. As he slowly sauntered home on the back of his tired horse, it was with a renewed sense of appreciation for the wide spectrum of God's saving grace. And in his heart, he believed God was calling him to preach the Word, the good news, the Gospel of Christ, as his father and grandfather had done.

Jonathan, becoming more and more convicted of the need for strong Biblical teaching in the lives of people, commented to Priscilla one rainy spring morning:

"Once a man sees his sin, then he must see his Savior. My heart is constantly drawn to this good news of the gospel. My prayer is that God can use me for His glory to save the lost and rescue the downhearted."

Priscilla, just stepping in the door, dripping wet, swinging a milk pail in her hand, giggled out loud, as Jonathan looked up from his Bible.

"I understand your zeal, my dear, but may this conversation be delayed until I have wiped my rain-soaked face and shed this milk sodden apron to the hook?"

Jonathan joined in her laughter.

"I am sorry. My timing for in-depth conversation is not always the most thoughtful."

Growing up under his father's ministry he had learned much simply by observing, although it was his father's wise counsel that remained fresh in his mind. Memory would steal him away and he could still see Rev. Benjamin Sheldon, his long hair white as snow, and hear him say as he so often did,

"The Gospel should not be too exclusively concerned to be "helpful" to man- to bring peace, comfort, happiness, satisfaction - and too little concerned to glorify God. It's first concern need always to give God glory." [16] His father never tired of proclaiming the gospel.

Jonathan now found himself impressed with new observations. William Manchester, his young nephew, with devoted resolve to bring the Methodist Episcopal denomination to the area, provided a profound impact on Jonathan to conform his strict Congregational roots and to at least partially embrace the tenets of Methodism, while the words of George Whitfield would forever ring comfort in his ears,

"Why fear that the Lord Jesus Christ will not accept of you? Your sins will be of no hindrance, your unworthiness no

hindrance, if your own corrupt hearts do not keep you back,
nothing will hinder Christ from receiving you."

Bringing unity of heart and mind to his family was Jonathan's priority, as long as faith itself was solely based on the truth of scripture. Whitfield's words became a confirmation that Christ is sovereign overall, including a call to faith. Jonathan could live with that, even if he had to stretch Whitfield's meaning to conform to his own understanding of the gospel message. And so, continuing to hold staunchly with the rational and philosophical views of atonement consistent with Congregationalists and Methodists alike, which were generally adopted throughout New England, Jonathan commanded the highest respect as a man of faith and vision, holding a firm hand, tempered with patience and diplomacy. With these personal virtues as his foundation, he began to preach, believing that every doctrine that comes with the truth of God, leads men to God and if it does not produce a desire for holiness, it is not of God.

While Jonathan labored tirelessly to provide a life for his family and a future for his children, a new prospect kept arising, like wildflowers in a spring garden, appearing routinely and in unexpected places. The winds of opportunity were in the air once again and the signs were sure.

21

The Connecticut
Western Reserve

1783-1815

Following the Revolutionary War in the year 1783, [1] the newly formed United States government granted a particular portion of land to the Colony of Connecticut in the Northwest Territory. It was located over the formidable Appalachian Mountains in what was known as The Ohio Valley. In 1786, Connecticut released its claim to a large segment of western lands and relinquished them back to the United States. Despite ceding sovereignty to the United States, it retained ownership of the northeastern portion, south of Lake Erie, known as the *"The Connecticut Western Reserve"*. In 1795, Connecticut sold *"The Reserve"* to a group of investors operated by the Connecticut Land Company, who in turn sold it to speculators and settlers.

The Connecticut Western Reserve was immediately wrought with problems. In 1795, after the Connecticut Land Company bought these three million acres of endless wooded wilderness, they encountered continuous conflicting claims by various eastern seaboard states. As a land speculation company, venturing into a prized part of the lucrative northwestern territory, there were immediate disputes as to who had the right to govern the land and the legitimacy of land titles. Connecticut refused to guarantee land titles, causing many would-be settlers to reject offers to invest their futures in these uncertainties. Due to mismanagement and weak land sales, they were forced to lower their prices and give away free land in order to encourage settlement. Continuing conflicts with Indians in the region also slowed sales and development.

During the Revolutionary War, between the years 1776-1783, there was not a single permanent white settlement to be found in the Northwest Territory, often spoken of as "the vast interior" or "the howling wilderness". The following ten years saw wild land speculation fever sweeping the colonies, as pioneers streamed over the mountains and into the frontier lands. By the mid-1790's, thousands of pioneers were building new lives in the unspoiled wilderness and Indian hostilities exploded. Wyandot, Delaware, Chippewa and Ottawa finally repulsed the flood tide of migration, while Colonists who had already made the dangerous and problematic journey into the wilderness were no longer safe.

A great expanse of dark forest lay across endless miles of uninhabited woodlands, untraversed except for the indigenous people and the occasional trader. Hundreds of busy axes sent an alarm ringing through the inhospitable wilderness. Approaching destruction was near. As the white man's fields replaced their beloved hunting ground, anger and revolt surged through the native peoples like a forest fire. Steadily being driven back from set boundaries provided by uncertain and often unenforced treaties, apprehension and tension continued to build. The inevitable finally happened, with war suddenly erupting like a volcano on the frontier. A reign of blood and carnage for white settlers had begun, with over twenty-five hundred Americans killed by disgruntled and enraged native warriors in savage butchery.

After peaceful attempts failed with treaties broken on both sides, the United States believed it necessary to compel obedience by use of arms. Vigorous means for the relief and protection of white settlers was called upon. Initially, unrelenting warriors prevailed and were bolstered with optimism and support from the embittered British, believing that they could once again reclaim lands. But that all changed on August 20, 1794.

Gen. Anthony Wayne with the new army, The Legion of the United States, [2] marched north from Fort Washington in Cincinnati, building a line of forts along the way. Wayne commanded approximately thirty-five hundred men as well as Choctaw and Chickasaw warriors used as scouts. Encountering the enemy along the Maumee River, a final battle was fought where a stand of fallen trees had been blown down by a recent storm.

Wayne's soldiers closed in and pressed the brutal attack with a bayonet charge. It ended very quickly. Nearly every chief of the Native American Tribes of the Western Confederacy was killed.

The Battle of Fallen Timbers [3] secured the northwest territory for white settlement once again, as the Treaty of Greenville yielded native claims to lands east of the Cuyahoga River. This put to rest asserted ownership of the lands and ultimately opened the door for The Connecticut Land Company.

With the Indian wars subsided and the area experiencing relative peace, an expedition of surveyors commenced their journey for the Western Reserve in 1796, ascending the Mohawk River in four flat bottom boats. At Fort Oswego, [4] a trading post in the Great Lakes region, the fifty-two-person crew, composed of five surveyors, one physician and forty-six chainmen and axe men, encountered difficulty getting past the British who were garrisoned there. Although dispatches had arrived earlier announcing the ratification of *"Jay's Treaty"* of 1795 between the United States and England, stating that navigation of the lakes should henceforth be free to all American vessels, permission to pass was denied.

Time was precious and anxiety to arrive at the reserve was great. After deliberation, it was agreed by the expedition leaders that they should attempt to pass by deceit. A decoy boat was sent ahead, throwing off the garrison, while in the dead of night the other three boats passed by the fort unobserved, joining their decoy companions on the waters of Lake Ontario days later.

First touching the soil of the Connecticut Western Reserve on July 4, 1796, on the day commemorating the 20th anniversary of America's independence, Moses Cleveland, the land company's agent, and Josiah Stow, commissary, along with surveyors, Augustus Porter, Moses Warren, Seth Pease and the other members of the party were animated with emotion as they celebrated together, infused with patriotic devotion and a good share of celebratory whiskey, of which the flow both smoothed and helped exacerbate any undercurrent of misunderstanding with the Native American "friends" they quickly encountered.

Ultimately, after four more long years, surveying was completed and the discrepancies and squabbling over land rights was settled. In April 1800, President John Adams signed into effect *The Quieting Act,* establishing Connecticut's right to govern the land and guarantee the legality of land titles. The *Act* was meant to encourage and speed up the settlement and development of the area, resolving the political uncertainty. In pursuit of profits, The Connecticut Land Company was at last able to sell surveyed lands to eager investors. Land was usually sold several times before it finally was purchased by someone who would actually settle and develop it.

By 1804, forty-two thousand pioneers would take advantage of the newfound stability and pour over the mountains. A map, using colorful and enticing descriptions of the Western Reserve in order to stimulate interest and excitement among prospective investors, circulated through the mail in the east. The romantic, unrestrained life and great expanse it suggested became vividly impressed upon the imagination of Jonathan Sheldon. The dream of a new life, with the promise of a brighter future for his children and their children, tugged on his heart.

In a broader scope, President Thomas Jefferson, elected in 1801, understood that the powerful Empires that surrounded the relatively new United States remained a threat. Great Britain continued to hold designs on northwestern America, the French occupied the south, while the Spanish held the southwest. Jefferson believed that there was only one way to protect this new and vulnerable country: expand. Many did not share Jefferson's vision for the importance of expansion, arguing that it was unconstitutional to acquire more territory. Jefferson agreed that their new Constitution did not contain explicit provisions for acquiring territory but that his constitutional power to negotiate treaties was sufficient.

The President secretly took a risk and negotiated with Napoleon to buy the French port of New Orleans. Napoleon, in need of financial support for funding his military, with the prospect of renewed war with Great Britain, sells all of the Louisiana Territory. Thus, The Louisiana Purchase of 1803 gives America control from the Mississippi River to the Rockies and from the Gulf of Mexico to Canada, doubling America's size overnight.

As Jonathan read the news of America's profound expansion, he could not help but to begin pondering the possibilities for his family. It was a difficult decision and one that would initially place enormous hardship on everyone. Yet Jonathan continued to consider the prospects and weigh the options. Although there appeared to be relative peace throughout the region, Jonathan was apprehensive to move his family until there was absolute assurance that conflict and war between the British and their Indian allies was over.

Jonathan understood the devastating hardships and overwhelming hazards of war. He had experienced it and had seen what it did to his family, especially his first wife. He did not want that for Priscilla or for himself. He had been involved in horrific battles. Rhode Island had seen extensive warfare throughout the Revolution and Jonathan was often haunted by memories of brave young militiamen and hardened privateers risking their lives in hand-to-hand conflict and on the ocean currents for the American cause. He could almost smell the gunpowder from cannons, the sweat of men months at sea without bathing, the salty air and the hot fires for the cooper's metal hoops. It was a dangerous time. Foreboding fog, monstrous waves rolling across the surface and always the danger from enemy vessels. Fire. Destruction. Death. An age of great uncertainty, yet an age filled with hope. The struggle had seen victory and Jonathan now relished a peaceful life.

War seemed like a lifetime ago; it was indeed a lifetime ago, as he mused,

> *"How my life has changed from those days. Now, here I am, a farmer of sixty years of age, dreaming of pioneering a wilderness land!"*

Shaking his head, he quickly reminded himself,

> *"I cannot allow my perpetually restless spirit to put my family in harm's way. We shall wait until the territory is secured and deemed free from conflict."*

Jonathan's decision to wait before venturing further west was a wise one. By 1812, President James Madison signed the declaration of war against Great Britain. The reason and justification for the war was not as obvious as it was for the Revolutionary War, and as a result it suffered serious unpopularity among the American people, especially those in New England. Jonathan was against the war. The town of Tolland (formerly unincorporated as part of Granville, MA) sent no soldiers or volunteers to participate.

Meanwhile, settlers on the frontier were once again subjected to violent Indian raids, especially by the Indian chief, Tecumseh and the Shawnee nation. Westward expansion came to a standstill. The war with the British revolved around land acquisition, trade and ultimately the security of America as a sovereign nation. In 1814, a British raid burned the capital, although Americans subsequently repulsed British attempts to invade New England and capture Baltimore.

The War of 1812, ending in February of 1815, resulted in both sides being repulsed in their invasion attempts, as well as the defeat of Tecumseh and his Shawnee nation, bringing peace to the country once again. With the war ending, the time and circumstances finally felt right for Jonathan to move his family to the western wilderness, finding new opportunities for future generations. Along with thousands of others seeking new beginnings, the pull to the idealistic and romanticized virgin land was powerful.

Granville's population had expanded quickly after the Revolutionary War, and by 1810 Tolland, MA incorporated as its own town, six miles from Granville, and its population peaked at over 2,000 settlers. The Farmington River washed the western border, providing a power source for a small tannery, and at first glance the progress and future of Tolland potentially looked bright. However there remained great uncertainty in providing for a large and growing family, and with a strong desire for one's children and grandchildren to have a better life, people were ready to continue the push over the mountains to the west, where the promise of abundant land waited.

Titus Fowler [5] had boasted for years concerning the availability of land in the west, purchased by his cousin Samuel Fowler, of Westfield, MA. More than 16,000 acres of dense unbroken forest in the eastern portion of The Connecticut Western Reserve was there simply waiting to be settled. Jonathan spent many hours discussing the land and the prospects of moving to the frontier wilderness. Solicitors were aggressively at work encouraging families to move and settle the unspoiled land. Advertising circulars were distributed, captivating and sparking imaginations. *"The enchanting beauty and inexhaustible fertility of New Connecticut"* was an enticing prospect. Jonathan had long dreamed of the rich fertile land promised in the west.

The poor quality of the highly elevated land in Tolland was a constant battle. The soil was as bad as his brother-in-law, John, had warned years earlier. Almost wholly mountainous, there were fertile valleys, but overall, the rocky clay was only advantageous for trees and grazing livestock. Eighty acres provided ample grazing land for Jonathan's stock, but there was never enough grain. Every year he found himself purchasing feed from Westfield, nine miles away. Butter, cheese, maple sugar and molasses were plentiful, along with apples and peaches, but the overall limitation of the land was ominous, and the prospects for his children's future was limited.

By 1815, Jonathan's and Priscilla's children were quickly growing to adulthood. The oldest, Daniel, with a restless and rebellious spirit, one day disappeared over the foreboding mountains in search of adventure and fortune. No word had come from him in over a year, and the family did not know where he had settled or even if he was alive. Priscilla's mother-heart clung to the hope of his safe return home, every night praying for the day when she could once again hold him in her arms.

Twenty-year-old Lois, petite, with yellow hair and eyes as bright as a blue sky, had a flirtatious and bold personality. Zaphna Stone, after meeting her, was immediately smitten with her beauty, and proposing after only one month of courting, they soon married. Lois, moody and prone to fits of depression, remained an emotional entanglement to those who knew her best. Yet Zaphna, aware of her erratic tendencies, chose to love her for better or worse. They very quickly welcomed their first baby, a boy, Philemon. Since the birth of the baby, Lois suffered several unexplained episodes of bizarre behavior, hallucinating and hearing voices, giving evidence of some very disturbing and concerning mental and emotional issues.

Jonathan and Priscilla held great concern for Lois's well-being. Jonathan thoughtfully contemplated,

> *"Could it be that her difficult birth has affected her irrational mental state?"*

Priscilla replied, with worry in her voice,

"I do not know. Perhaps. I pray for her and her family. She seems to be a lost soul."

The future would prove her worries well-founded in the most tragic of ways.

Jonathan Jr., "Jon", at eighteen years of age, was eager to spread his wings and soar toward the heights of his own personal exploits. Growing into a man of uncommon strength and great force of character, he possessed an empathy for the downtrodden and a wisdom beyond his years. His deep-set grey eyes, with eyebrows angling sharply down-word, gave him a stern appearance when his face was in a resting position. Well over six-feet tall, a strong square chin, thin lips and thick dark brown hair; Jon was modestly unaware of his attractiveness and naively oblivious to the flirtations of the opposite sex.

Jonathan and Priscilla were watchful for a good match for their son, while realizing at the same time, that customs and expectations had changed. With some frustration Jonathan spouted,

"Romantic love is blind to possible defects. When taking in all other considerations, a well-made match by well-meaning parents is so much more effective than the emotion of two young people in heat for each other,"

Priscilla continued washing a pot and scoffed,

"You are too cynical when it comes to love, my dear."

"Perhaps, although I understand that this rise of individualism is potentially healthy, indeed we would not have a nation without it, yet there must be something said for a parent being more interested in a child's future security and social position than merely in future happiness. If happiness should be a by-product, that is truly the best of all circumstances, but it should not be the basis for a future." Jonathan's voice was lifting with some emotion.

Priscilla sought to smooth the churning waters of Jonathan's mind.

"Our son has a sensible and level head about him. You need not worry about his choice when it comes to marriage. Besides, he is nowhere near ready. His mind is on his work. Let it be Jonathan. Trust him to the Lord."

Changing the subject, Jonathan stood and stretched his long body.

"I spoke with Samuel Fowler today. He was in Tolland visiting Titus."

Priscilla's tone revealed her suspicion,

"Really? I am sure that he has once again promoted "Westfield" in the Western Reserve." [6]

"Indeed, he did. As a matter of fact, he offered me a proposition. A trade. My eighty acres for seven-hundred and ten acres of land in the western territory," Jonathan said, with a gleam in his eye. Priscilla spun around; her eyes opened wide in bewilderment.

"Jonathan Sheldon, I know you too well. Tell me what you are up to immediately!"

"I accepted!" Jonathan announced in boyish excitement along with a little husbandly trepidation. [7]

His intention to build a future in an unknown wilderness made perfect sense to him and he hoped that his wife would eventually see his point of view.

For a man in his sixties Jonathan was of solid stature and sharp mind, a strong, resolute and determined man, whose courage was fully tested thirty years earlier in the Revolution and whose body bore the scars of battle. His mind was now centered on plans for pioneering across the mountains, while Priscilla's strongest impulse was focused on her family. Her youngest and last-born child, Benjamin, was ten years old. Her anxious thoughts concerned how to provide a proper start in life for all her children. Accustomed to sharing the toils of life with Jonathan, at fifty-five she inseparably linked the whole of her destiny to his, although her hopes for her children and their future are of paramount importance. Weighing the circumstances, she willingly began preparations to leave the home she has worked so hard to establish for over twenty years.

Pioneering Over the Appalachians

Priscilla stepped back as sparks from the hot fire singed her skirts. Wiping her brow, she leaned back to stretch her back, pausing to watch the sun slowly set behind a distant hill. Refocusing on dinner preparations, she called to fifteen-year-old Sarah,

> *"Fetch the bucket and bring up water from the stream,"*
> nodding her head in the direction of the nearby ravine.

Sarah quickly did as she was told. Ten-year-old Benjamin hurried behind her, calling out,

> *"Mother, I can help her! May I drink coffee tonight?"*

Priscilla smiled; Benjamin was in a hurry to grow up.

Dinner was meager yet satisfying enough. It had taken several hundred miles before Priscilla had perfected baking bread in ashes. Considerable failed attempts resulted in blackened crust with a doughy middle.

> *"You'd think that I could remember how to cook over an open*
> *fire, but it's been so long. Tiverton to Tolland seems ages ago!*
> *No worries, it will come back to me. In the meantime, we'll*
> *just have to scrape off the burnt."*

The smoked pork usually managed to fill their empty bellies at the end of an exhausting day, and no one dared complain. It had also taken a while to adapt to drinking coffee with no sugar or milk as they were accustomed. Travel had definitely simplified their way of life. [8]

The Conestoga had proven a reliable wagon. Five metal bows arched over the bed and a thick white canvas was stretched across, giving it a distinctive silhouette. Jonathan had purchased six heavy draft horses from the money made by selling off unneeded household items. The horse's tall stature and muscular build made them well suited for pulling the bulky, cumbersome wagon. With no suspensions, it was a rough ride even over smooth ground. The women walked apace with the wagon, unless weather, injury or fatigue required them to ride inside. Several heads of cattle were herded along by Jon, Sarah and twelve-year-old Rhonda.

Leaving Tolland early in April, snow dotted the shady side of wooded hills. The farm disposed of and old furniture sold except for as much as would be absolutely needful in their new home, they began the long journey. Priscilla shivered under her woolen shawl.

"Tis a cold morning,"

she said to her stepdaughter, Mary, as they walked alongside the lumbering wagon. Her mingled feelings of doubt, regret and anticipation were temporarily hidden beneath benign chatter. Jonathan rode ahead of the wagon on old Dora, buoyant with hope and impatient for the day he would lay eyes on the new land.

Mary held her infant baby, Mercy (named for her sister) in her arms as they walked. Osmond Williams, her husband of three years, guided his team of horses and their wagon behind Jonathon's. Mary, trying to lighten the mood, asked Priscilla,

"Do you remember when we traveled from Tiverton on that bumpy road and you were tossed from the wagon?"

"I do indeed," Priscilla softly replied with a chuckle, reflecting on that time, *"but I doubt that you do. You were but four years old."*

"True, but I have heard it told so many times, I feel as if I do remember!"

"That was an adventure. I suppose that this is also an adventure, although uncertainty and fear haunt my heart. I suppose that my age has made me more cautious and adverse.

I am trusting God and the wisdom of your father to carry me through my doubts."

"You have been a true mother to me. I would not want to make this journey without you."

Priscilla smiled and brushed away tears,

"Thank you Mary. Now, where has that Benjamin gotten off to? That boy! If I did not keep my eye on him every minute, he would be swinging from the treetops!"

Traveling the thirty-five miles to Hartford, they reached Parry Sheldon's family loaded and ready for travel. Mercy and her husband, Archibald Black, with their five-year-old daughter, Larena, anxiously pulled ahead, rather than wait for the final preparations that Parry's family was making. Archibald had several head of sheep and keeping them in line was proving difficult when at a standstill.

The promise of new beginnings had bitten all as they eagerly anticipated the future. Up the road a few miles from Parry's house, Ruth and Elihu Beach scurried around to gather their five children. Ruth carried one-year-old Amanda in her arms, while sixteen-year-old Phoebe carried little Thomas, age two. Miles, seven, and Benoni, four, had climbed a tree and were whining loudly, not wanting to leave and refusing to obey their mother. Ruth stood at the foot of the tree, giving them a stern talking to, but not until their father commanded that they return to the ground did they reluctantly lower themselves, one branch at a time.

It was mid-morning, and if they hurried, they could get several miles behind them. The entire caravan consisted of five Conestoga wagons each pulled by teams of six to eight draft horses, and several head of cattle as well as sheep being herded by the older children. Smaller children walked alongside their mothers or ran around in circles inventing new games to play, often tattling on each other. With so many cousins it was endless revelry, if not flat-out pandemonium.

The women chatted freely with each other, enjoying the company, happily distracted from the potential dangers and pitfalls that may lay ahead. The men concentrated on the team, the road and any possible problems before them. Travel was tedious and slow moving. Priscilla would soothe her impatient and tired children and grandchildren with songs and then playfully quip,

> *"A journey of five-hundred miles begins with one step! Now children, step in line and look sharp. There are lots of one-steps today!"*

Having resupplied in Cumberland, Maryland, Priscilla was careful to ration their necessities and reserve delicacies, like sugar, for special occasions or milestones. Covering eight to fifteen miles a day depending on the weather and terrain, by early May the Appalachians and the Cumberland Road [9] finally loomed before them. Three years before in 1811, reconstruction on the road had begun, resulting in it becoming a jumping off point for the thousands of pioneers crossing into the western wilderness. But these improvements only extended a few miles into the mountains. [9] The primitive and rutted dirt pathway offered challenges of mudslides, fallen trees, and steep rocky inclines that strained the abilities of horses and men alike.

As the white canvas-covered wagons rocked and bumped slowly along Wills Creek, Jonathan could see the central ridge of the Cumberland Narrows, [10] lying between Wills Mountain and Haystack Mountain. The rugged landscape and majestic sloping heights, with the prominent rocky outcropping on the south end of Wills Mountain known as Lover's Leap, loomed ahead of them with seeming intimidation.

With dinner finished and the livestock and horses secured with ropes and make-do brush fencing, fatigue caused even the hard ground to offer some relief. Sleep came easily. This subsequent leg of their journey would offer the greatest test. The uneven, dangerous and winding tracks through deep passes and over steep ridges would require deliberate heedfulness and serious scrutiny. With the sunrise, the family joined together to offer prayer and thanksgiving to God for his many blessings. Jonathan prayed,

> *"May we be thankful for your mercies, O Lord, forever humble under your loving correction, so that we may serve*

you with joy, be content in our circumstances and more useful to others. Your hand has been upon us over these many miles and we are most grateful. Guide us this day under your strong protection as we proceed by faith into the unknown. Amen."

A gray steady rain spewed endlessly. Fog gathered in the valleys, as mountain tops seemed to spring from white clouds. Water poured off the canvas. As the little ones huddled inside the wagons, a steady drip made for a fun game of who could catch it. There was no place to be dry, so they made the best of it, making up silly songs about "drippy, dropsy raindrops", "squishy mud between my toes", and whatever else they could think up, helping the time pass inside the uncomfortable, crowded, soggy wagons.

Ascending a slightly elevated slope as rain continued to drizzle down, Parry's right rear wagon wheel slipped deep into a sinkhole. Rhoda and the children were thrown with a jolt, bumping heads and squealing with bewilderment. No one was seriously hurt. Osmond, Elihu, Archibald and Jon quickly helped Parry secure the team, calming the jittery horses. Jon held the reins tightly, all the while speaking calming words to the agitated, wild-eyed team. The men, now joined by Jonathan who had been a short distance ahead on the road with Priscilla and the younger children, pushed the wagon from behind, their feet slipping in the sodden terrain, as the horses strained to pull the wagon free. Suddenly the axle broke with a loud crack, dropping the wagon violently and precariously close to the edge of a steep ridge.

Deep, soft mud made the repair extremely difficult, but by unloading most of the wagon's contents of clothing, heirlooms and farming tools, they lifted the slippery wagon corner, and the axle with the wheel were ultimately replaced. The team, although unnerved, soon pulled the wagon to more stable ground. Wet, cold, dirty and exhausted, they made camp early that day, everyone feeling exhausted and discouraged.

With the wood wet, it was difficult getting the fires started for cooking. It seemed everything was becoming more difficult with every passing mile. The weather was taking a toll. Several of the children developed coughs and chills, and the women struggled with how to dry clothes that had remained wet for almost a week. Priscilla prayed that they would see a break in the weather, and she knew that she wasn't alone in her pleas.

"Lord, give me a deeper trust, for I am bound by worry. When all things come to life in spring, it is indeed rain that makes it so, and for that I am thankful. But Lord, we have seen enough rain. You alone have power over all your creation. I ask you now, dear Lord, please give us some relief. Please stop the rain, and bring the warmth of sunshine, to dry us and to give renewed health to our children."

The next morning, Priscilla blinked quickly, squinting against the brightness. A narrow piercing beam of light sliced through a small hole in the damp canvas above her head, directly into her eyes. Laughing, she exclaimed jubilantly,

"Thank you, Lord! I praise you, for you are indeed blindingly good!"

"Arise, arise!", came the familiar morning call by Jon, who early in the journey had become the self-appointed rooster. The entire caravan was immediately transported from somber grayness to the joyful brightness of a fresh sunny morning. Birds chirped incessantly in the shimmering green trees and squirrels clucked their annoyance, jumping clumsily from branch to branch, releasing water showering down from the leaf-covered branches. A swollen stream nearby offered the opportunity to wash sticky mud from worn trousers and skirt hems. Wet clothes hung on every available surface, happily drying in the warm morning sun.

Cows were milked as breakfast sizzled over the fire. After Jonathan concluded reading aloud from a chapter in the Bible, the children ran about laughing and playing blind-man's bluff. The women worked to finish baking bread and packing up the supplies, while the men repaired harnesses and greased wagon wheels. Refreshed, dry and rejuvenated by the warm sun, the bullwhip cracked through the air, and the four wagons began their lumbering pursuit over the mountains.

22

Fowler

By the time they traversed Braddock's Road and reached the Ohio River at Pittsburgh, they were joined by other immigrant families. The women were especially pleased to share conversation with fellow pioneer wives and mothers, trading stories of the adventures and mishaps of their travels. When first meeting Margaret Dwight, Priscilla was impressed. A niece of Yale University President Timothy Dwight, Margaret initially presented a very sophisticated air, until her caustic and judgmental conversation revealed her true colors.

> *"I should not have thought it possible to pass a Sabbath in our country among such a desolate, vicious set of wretches as we are now among. At least fifty Dutchmen have been here today to smoke, drink, swear, laugh, speaking Dutch, and continually staring at us. It is dreadful to see so many people that you cannot understand or converse with."* [1]

> *"She's cold as ice,"* came Jonathan's response when Priscilla told him of Margaret Dwight's rant.

Pittsburgh was a welcome relief, offering a much-needed touch of civilization. With a population of well over a thousand people, it offered general stores, bakeries, and hat and shoe shops. Neat houses sat along tree-lined streets. Manufacturing capability was growing, and Pittsburgh was producing steel, brass and glass.

The boatyard was of special interest to Jonathan. He wandered about the docks, giddy as a schoolboy, striking up conversation with workers, discussing ships and his vast experiences at sea. Most of these men had never even seen the sea, even as they were busy building a sizable ocean bound sloop which was almost complete and ready to be launched into the Ohio River.

Jonathan returned from the yards, exhilarated, with entertaining tales to share. As the family sat around the supper fire, he raised a quizzical eyebrow, and with his eyes twinkling with excitement, he began:

> *"I have a story to tell. A Captain Brevoort, of the ship Western Trader, presented papers for his vessel and its cargo of flour and pork, in Livorno, Italy. Just imagine - Italy! Well, the captain was trying to convince the customs office that Pittsburgh was a port city, and the official looked at the documents and angrily accused the captain of lying and giving him forged papers, asserting that no such port as Pittsburgh existed. Furthermore, he would be more inclined to believe that the Western Trader had traveled to the moon than to the interior of the United States. So, here is what he did: Brevoort asked for a map of the United States and proceeded to chart a course from the Gulf of Mexico, up the Mississippi and to the Ohio River with his finger. When the captain's finger reached the headwaters of the Ohio River, he stopped and exclaimed to the official, "Pittsburgh, the port I sailed from!"* [2]

Everyone laughed at Jonathan's animated tale, but it was Jonathan who laughed the loudest, warming Priscilla's heart immensely to hear it.

It was mid-June now, and with roughly seventy miles to Youngstown, Jonathan could almost smell the new land. Their white covered wagons, now faded from sun and dingy with dust, moved beneath tall majestic trees through a belt of solitary wilderness toward the village of Youngstown, in the Mahoning Valley. Youngstown had been a part of the Western Connecticut Reserve, originally intended for Revolutionary War refugees from Connecticut. It was included as part of the Northwestern Territory which Connecticut refused to cede over to the United States, and which it then sold to the Connecticut Land Company. In 1800, the territorial Governor, Arthur St Clair, established Trumbull County (named in honor of Connecticut governor, Jonathan Trumbull). In 1803 Ohio became a state. In 1813, Trumbull County was divided, with Youngstown comprising much of Mahoning County.

Youngstown was a mustering ground for families immigrating to their land in the Western Reserve. Having purchased a month's supply of provisions in Pittsburgh, the Sheldon caravan was well equipped as they approached Youngstown. Arriving as the sun was setting behind the dark forest, the four wagons and their tired occupants made camp along the Mahoning River. The men sauntered off to talk to neighboring sojourners camped nearby, gathering information and discussing plans. The women prepared the supper meal and settled the children down to sleep. The air was heavy with humidity, although there was no threat of rain. Mosquitoes and deer flies buzzed incessantly, and Priscilla hesitantly concocted a "recipe" of rendered bear fat mixed with mint and other herbs to provide some relief for herself and her children. The foul smell was at least more bearable than the persistent bites.

It was decided that the women and children would remain in Youngstown, while the men traveled on to Warren and from there would venture out to the lands they had each procured. As the men left Youngstown, they traveled along the winding trail past the salt springs some twelve miles southeast of Warren. They were in a jovial mood and engaged in light conversation and a few practical jokes as the horses strained against the weight of the supply wagons. Eager to reach the lands they had so long dreamed of, while at the same time entering an abyss of uncertainty, an unknown world lay ahead of them.

Warren had been organized as the Trumbull County seat by Ephraim Quinby in 1801, fourteen years earlier. As their wagons meandered into town, Jonathan was surprised by the development that had already occurred in this small community of less than two hundred people. Four acres had been set aside for a village square, a city hall had been established, and several wood frame houses sat along well-maintained streets. Locating the clerk's office, Jonathan, along with eighteen year old Jon, sat across from George Parsons, [3] the Clerk of Courts, with a large county map laying on the desk between them, confirming the survey and the purchase of seven-hundred acres of land in Fowler Township.

Mr. Parsons was very enthusiastic and helpful.

> *"Mr. Sheldon, you and your fine son here will find your investment heavily forested with swales and small creeks, dividing the land into a number of varying ridges and undulating elevations of moderate height. Once cleared, you will discover the soil to be rich and fertile. Fresh water springs are abundant, providing pure, cold water for you and your family."*

Jonathan genuinely thanked Mr. Parsons, who had also verbosely continued to share tales of colorful local legends.

> *"In the early days you'd find old James Hillman* [4] *wandering these parts. A brave and useful character he was. He possessed rife knowledge of Indian disposition, an attribute that saved his scalp more than once and settled plenty a disagreement peaceably."*

> *"What became of him?"* Jon asked.

His father gave him a light kick under the table and a quick disgusted glance, wanting them to be on their way. Jonathan was eager to make some distance toward Fowler while there was still some light, rather than continuing to lollygag over myths and folklore. Taking a deep breath, Mr. Parson's began...

> *"Well, my boy....",* but that is as far as he got, with Jonathan interrupting,

> *"Sir, we thank you again for your assistance, but we must now be on our way. Time's shadows are chasing us down."*

> *"Certainly, Certainly! And may God be with you!"*

Jonathan and Jon were already through the door walking a fast pace down the street toward the wagons.

Parry, Elihu, Archibald and Osmond had already secured and confirmed their deeds and surveys for Vernon Township, nine miles to the northeast of Fowler. As the sun was midway across the sky, they cracked their whips, prodding their teams and livestock toward Fowler. Stopping to make camp about five miles outside of Warren, they lit a small fire and chewed on hardtack, excitedly talking about the future.

Bedding down, Jonathan stretched his sore muscles against the hard ground, his thin blanket faded and worn from use. He studied the heavens glistening in the night sky, with his mind wandering back to Mary and their years in Tiverton and Little Compton, Rhode Island. He thought to himself,

> *"Mary would not like it here. She would be horrified at her daughters digging in the dirt and working the land; the sun burning their delicate skin. Although, her four girls find this pioneer life a pleasant contrast to the inactive life of the older settlement. But I do believe that Mary would be pleased with the strong and capable husbands her daughters have married."*

His tired eyes glanced over at his oldest son, Parry, leaning against a tree with a knife and a small piece of wood in his hand, whittling in the firelight.

> *"Lord, if you are of a mind, please tell Mary that her children are well."*

New Land on the Western Connecticut Reserve

Jonathan stopped to remove his hat and wipe the sweat from his brow. He had preserved, to an unusual degree for his age, a youthful elasticity of both mind and body. A man in his sixties slightly touched by gray, an erect carriage and quick in movement, he was well equipped for the ominous task before him. Subduing a wilderness was no place for the faint of heart or the weak of body. Restless to finally begin clearing his own land, he worked with the vigor of a man half his age. It had taken two weeks to clear a road that would reach his lot lines before he and Jon could begin clearing land to build a cabin. He was especially eager to have a cabin built so that he could retrieve Priscilla, the younger girls and Benjamin. Leaving them in Youngstown had been a difficult decision and yet one that he did not regret.

Once they had reached Jonathan's purchased tract, Jonathan reluctantly said goodbye to his faithful son, Parry, and his three sons-in-law, sending them on their way as they continued to Vernon Township. He and Jon were left alone to begin clearing their acreage in this truly unspoiled and wild land. Absolute quiet seemed to envelope them, only interrupted by the buzzing of ravenous mosquitoes. Jon swatted the back of his neck as he and his father stood side by side, each with an axe in hand. Jonathan finally broke the silence.

"Well son, find a tree and make good use of that axe. Time is the only coin we have today. If we use it wisely, soon we will reap great benefits."

Understanding the nature of the land proved compulsory for survival. Wild and predatory animals roamed freely. Wolves were plentiful. The bleating of sheep and clamor of cowbells signaled an enticing invitation for dinner. With the livestock penned close by, Jonathan and Jon bedded down each night to the unfamiliar, dismal howling and the cheerless whistle of the wind. In one part of the forest a wolf would raise a cry, those near him would repeat at intervals, others further away would answer, and soon the forest would resound with a thunderous howling, the pandemonium shaking the most stalwart of nerves.

Jonathan feared wolf attack, but as the days passed, he soon realized that the abundance of wild game in this wilderness secured relatively good behavior among the would-be predators. Wild turkeys, partridges, rabbits and other smaller animals were easily caught and consumed by the larger carnivores, who also came to quickly know and understand the effects of the white man's rifle, which was always close at hand.

The township of Fowler, formerly known as Westfield, was first settled by Abner Fowler, (brother to Samuel Fowler who originally purchased the 10,000 acres). Abner received one-hundred acres as compensation for services rendered in surveying the land. In 1799, Abner built the first cabin. His wife had previously died in Massachusetts and he lived alone in the area until other settlers arrived. It was Abner who had first introduced Jonathan Sheldon [5] to the possibility of locating in Fowler so many years before. He was a most convincing solicitor.

Jonathan had been sad to hear of Abner's passing. His was the first death recorded in the township in 1806. Levi Foote, with his wife Milly and their large family, moved from Westfield, Massachusetts, sometime before 1805, earning them the distinction of being the first family to settle in Fowler, with their daughter Lydia being the first white child born, on July 5, 1805.

From 1806-1812, immigrants arrived slowly, settling primarily in the southeast corner of Fowler Township in an area called Tyrrell Hill, where Elijah Tyrrell and his wife Clarissa built a cabin. Justice Meeker, Lemuel Barnes, Hillman Fisher, Drake Fisher, John Vaughn and Mathias Gates [6] were just some of those early pioneers who braved the unknown wilderness with their families to begin a new life. Wandering bands of Indians still camped and hunted, but rarely caused any undo disturbances, unless whiskey was involved.

Remnants of broken Indian tribes, generally harmless, no longer possessed that proud loftiness of character commanding admiration and respect. Discouraged and beaten down, they became objectless wanderers, ready to absorb the vices of the white man's civilization. The life they had so proudly lived had been stripped, leaving them to flounder without the clearly defined identity they had once enjoyed. Whiskey and strong drink obtained a mastery over many of them and was generally the root cause of prevailing crime, from which the whites could not claim ultimate pardon.

An unfortunate incident occurred on a hot July day around the year 1810. [7] Joseph McMahon and his family had cleared about four acres of land for corn and built a cabin. Three hundred yards along a steep ravine was an Indian encampment, where a large number of tribe members gathered and were frequently joined by whites to enjoy a drunken frolic.

One fateful afternoon they ran out of whiskey. Mr. McMahon, as a part of the festivities, secretly rode to Warren for a resupply. Upon his return, the Indians discovered his deception and expected that he would share, but instead McMahon claimed that he had no whiskey. Two or three Indians soon arrived at McMahon's cabin and began to insult Mrs. McMahon with brutal proposals. Threatening to kill her and her children if she did not give them whiskey, they hit one of the children over the head with the back end of a tomahawk, causing injury. The family fled to Warren for safety.

In Warren, Capt. Ephraim Quinby was called upon to help resolve the situation. With a reputation as mild-mannered and judicious, it was hoped that violence could be avoided. Capt. Quinby advised a conference with the Indians but thought it wise to go in with sufficient numbers for self-defense, should negotiations go poorly.

The next morning most of the young and middle-aged men of Warren mustered out to address the situation, thirteen in all. Each man had a gun, though no one expected to use it. Once reaching the encampment Capt. Quinby called a halt, and it was agreed that the men remain outside the camp, while he went in alone and learned accurately what the true state of affairs was.

The Indians were lulling around the camp aimlessly and obviously unconcerned that any possible conflict was approaching. Capt. Quinby located Capt. George (a Tuscarora) and John Winslow, called "Spotted John", because he was half white. Spotted John spoke fluent English and explained the difficulty between the Indians and the Joseph McMahon family.

> "Old Joe, a fool! The Indians don't want to hurt him or his family. The whites drank up all the Indians whiskey and then wouldn't let the Indians have any of theirs. They were a little mad, but don't care anymore about it. The McMahons may come back and live as long as they like. The Indians won't hurt them."

Capt. Quinby felt satisfied that no further attention was required over such a trivial matter. He started back, expecting to see his comrades where he had left them. But they had moved along the ravine, closer to the encampment. When Capt. Quinby finally discovered their location, he quickly shared the results of the conference. Mr. McMahon was furious and seeking revenge continued boldly toward the camp. Capt. Quinby called for him to stop, but he refused.

McMahon and two boys who were with him, boldly entered the camp. Capt. George, a large, muscular man was sitting at the base of a large oak, leaning against the trunk, when McMahon approached him, yelling,

"Are you now for peace? Yesterday you had your men, today I have mine!"

George sprang to his feet and grabbed his tomahawk, which was lodged in the tree above his head, swinging it wildly at McMahon, who quickly jumped back out of reach, while bringing his rifle to bear. He fired, the ball piercing George's chest.

McMahon turned instantly and shouted to the men who had now arrived on the scene,

"Shoot! Shoot!"

By now, the other Indians had seized their rifles and, taking cover behind trees, were taking aim and ready to fire. Several flints snapped on both sides, but the morning was damp, and the guns misfired. Richard Storer took aim at Spotted John, whose rifle was pointed in his direction. He fired. John's squaw was directly behind him, endeavoring to screen herself and her children from the attack. Unbelievably, the ball passed through John's throat, continued its path breaking his son's arm, then through the neck of his daughter, and ultimately grazing the hip of his squaw.

The scene was wild with chaos and confusion. The two boys who had been with McMahon fled. Screams and commands resounded, and bedlam ensued as men, women and children ran for cover. Hearts beat as loud as drums. But it was soon over. When Spotted John fell, the whole Warren party of men retreated quickly. The Indians were grief stricken, remaining long enough to bury their dead, then fleeing west to Sandusky along the old trail. Spotted John's widow carried her wounded children nine miles to the cabin of James Hillman where, in desperation, she arrived, incredibly, in just an hour and a half.

McMahon was later arrested and taken under guard to Pittsburgh, the nearest place a prisoner could be secured. No one who accompanied him on that fateful, brutal day was arrested. It was determined that they were men of integrity; upstanding citizens not anticipating any difficulty. No blame of criminal intent was attached to them. It was only McMahon who had entertained violence and faced imprisonment for his actions.

American natives across the entire western wilderness had lost all hope of recovering and protecting the life and land that they had always known. Their way of life had been pushed to a breaking point. Yet a faint glimmer of hope rose up among the Shawnee tribe. A uniting of all tribes was being aggressively pursued. The Shawnee chief, Tecumseh and his brother, Tenskwatawa, known as "The Prophet", were attempting to form a united front of all Indian nations west of the Appalachian Mountains, believing that if the various tribes worked together they would be able to stop white encroachment of western lands. By 1811, large numbers of Indians from various tribes had moved to an area called "Prophetstown", near the Tippecanoe River in Indiana Territory.

With the Indian population steadily growing, white settlers in Indiana and Ohio were becoming increasingly concerned for their safety, demanding the government do something to protect them. In the fall of 1811, William Henry Harrison [8] led an army against Prophetstown in the Battle of Tippecanoe, driving off the Indian settlement and the American army burning Prophetstown to the ground. Disillusioned with the promises and false hopes that Tecumseh and his brother offered, the dream of united Indian nations was abandoned, never to recover. The Prophet lost his influence and became an outcast. Tecumseh, in desperate attempts to regain his reputation and power, allied himself with the British the following year, coinciding with the beginning of the War of 1812.

During the War of 1812, Ohio was on the front lines of this conflict between the United States and Great Britain. Violent fighting raged in the northeastern section. Ohio volunteer units served under the command of Brigadier General William Hull, governor of the Michigan Territory. With a few scattered families in Fowler Township, the militia of Fowler and Johnston Townships was put under the command of Capt. Elijah Tyrrell. Capt. Tyrrell was ordered to draft one half of his men, totaling nine. The service of these men, including Capt. Tyrrell, Alfred Bronson,

Hoyt Tyrrell, Roswell Tyrrell, Isaac Farrow, Cable Meeker and three of the Gates, was approximately three months, although some stayed for six months. John Gates was killed in the first engagement he was in. Much consternation was wrapped in a blanket of despair, as half of the able-bodied men from Fowler Twp. were mustered out, leaving women and children alone to face the uncertain future.

Good Neighbors, Lending a Hand

"Jonathan, I do declare, that was a rough patch for sure!"

reminisced Alfred Bronson, [9] a Methodist preacher. He continued with a chuckle,

> *"When I came back from that war, Newman Tucker and his family had moved into my house! That family had a hard time of it though - dirt poor, the children coming down with whooping cough, and Newman himself real sick - and it was my God-given honor to see that they were assisted."*

Jonathan liked Preacher Bronson. He was jovial and a good-hearted man who loved God and loved people. He had ridden his spirited horse out to meet Jonathan and Jon early that morning. Jon laughed as he watched the preacher approaching on his high-stepping horse, with the skinny Preacher Bronson's arms flailing about and the reins flapping in the breeze.

"That is a resolute man right there!", commented Jon.

Jonathan looked up and leaned against his rake, replying,

"And the horse has equal resolve!"

They laughed together and continued to watch with amusement as the rider and horse drew closer.

Preacher Bronson was especially pleased to discover that Jonathan too preached the gospel. It was rare to find a kindred spirit. Although the good preacher was half Jonathan's age, he was fascinated to know Jonathan, and in turn Jonathan was intrigued with this unique little man and his tenacity. It was hard for Jonathan to imagine Preacher Bronson, two years earlier, engaged in battle, prepared to shoot a human soul. It seemed so contrary to his nature. But duty was important to Preacher Bronson and he would never shirk his duty. That Jonathan understood very quickly, and soon very personally.

In early July, Jonathan and Jon woke to a distant thundering rumble. Unsure of its source, they were greatly on edge until several teams of oxen pulling wagons and loads of men carrying saws and axes came into view.

"Ahoy, you old sailor!", came a friendly shout.

Alfred Bronson was waving wildly with a huge grin spread across his thin face.

"Your neighbors from miles around are here for a clearing party, and have come to sweep your first acre, so that your cabin can be built and your precious family will join you!"

Jonathan was humbled and extremely thankful for their great kindness. Jon breathed a huge sigh of relief. He had been very uncertain that he and his father alone could accomplish the ominous task of clearing such dense forest.

Preacher Bronson made some quick introductions,

"This be Wakeman Silliman, he is "captain" today and will be supervising the project."

"It's my great pleasure to meet you, sir." Jonathan said, vigorously shaking Wakeman's hand.

"The pleasure is mine, sir. Now let's see what we can do to get an acre free and clear."

Wakeman was a no-nonsense man of action, with a strong character and a commanding presence. With introductions made, he quickly began unloading the wagon of needed supplies and shouting out directions to the men. As the day progressed, Jonathan learned the names of many more neighbors: John Kingsley, the first Justice of the Peace, Abijah Tyrrell, the blacksmith, and Harvey Hungerford, who built a flouring mill on the north side of Yankee Creek, and too many Meekers and Footes for Jonathan to sort out.

Jonathan was astonished at the speed and expertise these men displayed. Wasting no time and with jovial exchanges, they came together, swapping jokes and news as they worked side by side. *"Heave, ho, Heave, ho!"* came masculine shouts and calls from across the tract. Men divided into two parties with each party taking a side. Competition pushed each team to excel in a test of strength and endurance. Axes rattled and the teeth of saws squealed back and forth through thick trees, which Jonathan and Jon had already girdled. [10]

Hearty laughter and a spirit of camaraderie energized the men as they cut out underbrush and rolled logs for a future cabin, finding great pleasure in the severe struggle they all shared. Well-filled jugs of New England rum and corn whiskey only added to the merriment. Wives and daughters had also accompanied the men. Setting up cooking fires with Dutch ovens while sharing stories, they prepared a noon meal for the ravenous men of steaming wild meats, cheese and corn cakes.

Shy young girls whispered to each other with giggles and batting eyes, making Jon feel most uncomfortable. Turning his back to their obvious attentions, he scarfed down his meal as quickly as he could and made himself look busy tending to the yokes of an oxen team. Grateful for the captain's call to return to work, he all but sprinted back to his axe and the vigor's of physical labor. Social graces had never been his strong suit, and he regretted his awkwardness when it came to the fairer sex.

Hoisting Wakeman Silliman triumphantly on their shoulders, the clearing party concluded the day with victorious cheers. Having cleared an acre of tillable land, large straight grained oak logs were now ready to be split into clapboards to be used on the roof and for flooring. Smaller trees had been cut for the cabin walls and flat stones placed at each corner of the foundation. Two heavy logs had been adjusted, across from each other, notched every four feet, with straight poles laid across serving as joists. Skilled axe men stood at each corner, and as each log was set in place, it was then notched, ensuring the next crossing would rest securely. One log at a time, the four walls were raised until reaching approximately eight feet. Chinked and daubed with mud, the structure was a modest yet livable eighteen by twenty-four feet in size, with a rudely constructed door and windows consisting of mere holes in the sides of the cabin walls, which would eventually be pasted with oiled white paper, keeping out some of the cold while letting in the sunlight. [11]

Jonathan mused to Jon late that evening, as darkness fell, and the party had travelled back to their respective homes.

> *"This is a good life, Jon. A life that God will bless and provide for a favorable future. Tomorrow, we go to Youngstown and bring your mother, sisters and brother to this place."*

Laying in silence for a while, watching the stars twinkle across the silent sky, Jon finally reflectively responded.

> *"This is a good life, Father. Thank you."*

He had relished the time they had spent together, and although he looked forward to the family being reunited again, he would miss having his father all to himself as he had these past two months. A few mosquitoes buzzed about his face, and swatting them away, he rolled over to fall into a deep sleep, resulting from both exhaustion and a sense of deep satisfaction.

Re-United for Frontier Farm Life

It was August. Priscilla had had enough of waiting. Tempted to simply load the wagon, hitch the team and follow the marked trees the eighteen miles from Youngstown to Warren herself, she paced back and forth, wondering when Jonathan would return for her and the children. Two months had been a long time. Summer had been especially hot. Her energy was spent on providing the basic needs for their children and worrying for their safety. Streams and rivers were swift and dangerous; rattlesnakes were prevalent; wild animals of the forest were legendary. The children flourished in this new land, their imaginations running free with romanticized images of American Indians, French trappers and British soldiers.

When Jonathan arrived, Priscilla thought she would faint with joy. Running to him, she threw herself into his arms and simply broke down into a puddle of muffled tears. He stoically held her until she was ready to free him, a bit surprised at her emotional display, yet understanding its cause. Her normal steady, unflappable disposition was apparently off the tracks, so to speak. After gathering her wits about her, she choked out,

"We did not expect for you to be this long gone from us! And where is Jon?"

"He stayed back. Wolves are always a consideration with the livestock. He remained at the cabin to guard and care for them until we return."

"Well, we should not delay! We are ready to see our land and Jon!"

Priscilla was on edge and there was an anxiousness in her voice.

The next morning at dawn, they set out. The wagon bounced gracelessly along the rutted track and Priscilla eagerly chatted news and stories of their two months in Youngstown, with Jonathan quietly listening and taking it all in.

"Lois and Zaphna came through in mid-July. It warmed my heart to see her, although she looked tired and I continue to worry for her health. Baby Philemon is fussy and Lois seems to be unsure of how to comfort him. Zaphna has purchased acreage in Gustavus Township. It is good that they will be so close. My understanding is that it may only lay eleven miles from us."

"We will do everything we can to help them."

Jonathan was already thinking of what might be done to help Lois.

The crude little cabin stood heartlessly against a wall of trees, but

Priscilla smiled pleasantly, knowing that this would be their new home. She knew that it would take time to make it feel like "home," to give it a life, a heartbeat of its own. Her eyes immediately darted about, seeking Jon. Waving from behind an old draft horse and a wooden harrow, Jon spotted them, and dropping the harness, began running, tripping and tumbling to the ground only to dirty his face even further. They were finally together again.

Priscilla was shocked at the changes in Jon. In only two months he was almost unrecognizable. His thin six-foot frame was now filled out and muscular. Tanned, his strong white teeth seemed to shine in contrast. His hair had grown long and hung in wet dark strands to his shoulders under his sweat-brimmed hat. Brawny hands were dirty and calloused. His shirt hung down almost to his knees, tattered and soiled. She thought to herself, *"Jon is a true pioneer. The necessities of life include a whole new set of definitions."*

The cabin, roughed out, had the floors laid and the roof weighed down. The heavy work was finished. Now, Jonathan and Priscilla, along with the children, began to complete the structure. Pressing down rough edges, they filled gaps with stick and mortar made of mud, mixed with leaves and grass. Cutting an opening on the gable end, Jonathan laid flat stones as a foundation for the enormous outside chimney, five feet deep at the base. Soon, the chimney was complete, and Priscilla was busily preparing meals and enjoying the warmth of a fire just as autumn began.

Life was so vastly different from the home they left behind in Tolland. The wood framed house with a porch and glass windows they once enjoyed was replaced by a roof of clapboards and walls of split oak logs. Glass was a luxury that few could afford. Even the door was rudely constructed, hung by two large wooden hinges secured with wooden pins. The bedsteads were made in the back corners of the cabin, with posts forming bed rails and hickory cords stretched from side to side, supporting a matting of husks or leaves. Linen curtains hung around the bed for privacy. Furnishings were sparse. Two chairs, which Priscilla had insisted be transported with them from Massachusetts, sat on either side of the fireplace. Priscilla had also required that the dining table make the trip west and it was now lined with roughhewn benches.

Jonathan and Jon continued to girdle trees in preparation for spring clearing. Burning off underbrush, they had tilled enough of the acre they had cleared for the cabin to plant a small garden. Carrots, cabbage and beets were sprouting, and Priscilla was anxious to add them to their daily fare of venison, bear or squirrel meat. Game was bountiful. After this first season, Priscilla knew that she would have much more to work with, potatoes, beans, onions, lettuce, cabbage. In the meantime, neighbors were helpful and generous, bringing corn, cheese and wild honey, as well as welcoming words and encouragement. Groceries were difficult to obtain, requiring a trip to Youngstown.

Priscilla was especially fond of Milly Foote, whose daughter Lydia, ten years old, was the same age as Benjamin. Milly had an unusually happy disposition, making friends easily and seldom losing them. Hearing Milly recall the stories of her early arrival in Fowler over twelve years prior, Priscilla and the children would sit, fully enchanted, their eyes wide with wonder as Milly spun a tale.

> *"My mother-in-law, Miss Bathsheba Burr, was a relative of Aaron Burr,* [12] *a distinction which has caused no little conflict in our family. But that is neither here nor there in this story. Miss Burr has long been called Auntie Thompson, and I am to assume that you, too, shall call her by that name if you should have the opportunity to meet her. She married two times after her first husband, Asa Foote, died. Her last husband was Mr. Thompson, so that explains That. She experienced many a hardship of this pioneer life, but none quite so harrowing as the wolf incident."*

Milly paused for dramatics sake. The Sheldon children sat motionless, eagerly waiting to hear the story.

> *"Well, while Mr. Thompson was out hunting, a bold and voracious wolf came circling the pig pen, right in the middle of the day! The hungry beast crouched low and singled out the little porker he desired for dinner. Seizing the helpless piglet by the throat, the wolf attempted his escape, just as a gun blast knocked him flat! Auntie Thompson had shot that wolf senseless. Picking it up, she carried its limp body to her*

doorstep and clubbed him in the head, just for good measure. This brought the wolf to consciousness and it sprang to its feet growling and snarling at Auntie. Her gun still in her hands, she quickly got off another shot and dispatched that wolf in a permanent way." [13]

Milly sat back with her arms folded and a satisfied look spread across her face. The children were duly impressed.

Children

Children worked hard because daily life required it. Most boys and girls learned how to plow, mend fences, skin animals, dress meat, fish, shoot, hunt, ride a horse. Although in the midst of all this work, children were still children and found time to play or sit spellbound by a good story. Boys played ball, and girls played with dolls made of rags and cornhusks. Sled in winter, swim in summer. Read books and practice arithmetic. Often, work itself became entertainment. Breaking a feisty horse could be a competition. Racing to the barn or teasing one another over who could work better or faster at one thing or another infused a sense of fun throughout their daily lives.

Life itself was tied to the seasons. Winter was bleak and gray, and Priscilla was relieved to finally see the beginnings of spring. Snow had kept them housebound for what seemed like weeks on end and she was ready to get out and socialize once again. She was also ready to attend church. Walking that distance in winter was a very cold and sometimes dangerous prospect, but with the dawn of spring, new energy abounded. Preacher Bronson was holding services in the cabin of Milo Duga, who also owned the land on the north side of Yankee Creek. The Sheldons were intent and disciplined in their church attendance. Jonathan preached on occasion, but circuit riding to reach those in more remote areas with the gospel gave him the most joy, fulfilling a higher purpose and satisfying his desire to honor God with his life.

Spring brought news of new life. Mercy and Archibald, living in Vernon, had their second girl and named her Amelia. Mary and Osmond had a boy, Jonathan, named for her father. The baby died shortly after birth. The family support in Vernon was strong, with Parry and his wife, Rhoda, as well as Ruth and Elihu all living in Vernon Township with their numerous children. This pleased Jonathan very much and he knew that their deceased mother, Mary, would be very pleased as well.

Vernon, located nine miles from Fowler, allowed many opportunities for family gatherings on special occasions. Lois and Zaphna, in Gustavus, were also close enough to participate in family activities, although Lois was becoming more and more removed emotionally. Expecting her second child cast her into a season of dark depression. Battling the destructive demons of her mind, resulting in a confusion over faith, a demanding perfectionism and doubts regarding salvation, silently haunted her. Lois was spiraling downward into a much deeper and darker place than anyone imagined.

While his older siblings busily cleared their own lands in Vernon and raised their ever-growing families, Jon, along with young Benjamin, worked side-by-side with his father in Fowler. Building a secure enclosure with high walls, which guarded the sheep at night protecting them from wolf attack, gave Jon a sense of accomplishment. Cows, with their heavy bells, were turned out to pasture in the fenceless woods until a suitable barn could be built. He never tired of the work and found great satisfaction in developing the land, caring for the livestock and raising structures.

Sixteen-year-old Sarah was devoted to her mother and spent hours each day carding, spinning, weaving, cooking, and in the evenings perfecting her needlepoint. Shy and unassuming, she was quite content in womanly duties. Whereas Rhoda, at thirteen, was quite the opposite. Jon was constantly chasing her away from the fields, where the heavier work of cutting and clearing trees continued.

> *"Go help mother, Rhoda! The garden needs weeding and the pot is boiling for soap making. You are of no use out here with the men!"*

He would often chastise Rhoda who was restless and easily bored. Rhoda's lack of attention to her expected duties concerned Priscilla, as she commented to Jonathan,

"She cannot sit still long enough to see one thing to completion,"

Jonathan was less disturbed, passing Rhoda's immaturity off with a shrug.

"She has a curious nature, to be sure. She'll grow out of it."

Wolf Eyes and The Changing Land

Benjamin, the youngest, sat cross-legged on the floor playing with twelve glass marbles he had received as a gift many years before. Having scratched a circle onto the floor, he mindlessly played against himself, knocking his "opponent" outside the circle in rotating fashion. The evening had immersed itself in the darkness of a storm. Thunder rumbled overhead and a crack of lighting startled him. His eyes shot up, focusing on a small crack in the mortar between the wooden logs on the wall. Staring into the seam for several seconds, two glassy eyes peered back, flickering with the firelight.

"Father! Jon! Come quick!",

Jonathan had just finished his evening meal and Jon was cleaning his gun.

"What is it Benjamin? And do not yell inside. You startled everyone," Jon scolded. Benjamin sniveled,

"A wolf is watching me!"

"Ah yes, eleven-year-old boys make wonderful meals," Jon teased, not believing his brother.

The next morning proved Benjamin's claim correct as wolf tracks were found all around the cabin.

The following year, clearing fires seemed to break the spell which had so long reigned over the forest. Wolf sightings became fewer and fewer, as they moved further from civilization and deeper into the western wilderness. The land was changing, and everything was affected. Roads were improving. Once only passable with teams of draft oxen struggling to pull a wagon over rutted, narrow strips of clearing lined with brush, now became wider and easily traversed by horse-drawn teams.

While many settlers arrived only to discover that life in the deep wilderness was not for them, soon returning to civilization, others stouter in heart readily endured the hardships of pioneer life. Hezekiah Reeder cleared and fenced four acres, planted his garden and raised his house, only to leave and never return. In the meantime, Hillman and Daniel Meeker developed a successful sawmill, Harvey Hungerford built a flouring mill, Elijah Tyrell increased the size of his blacksmith shop, and a Mr. Parker, of Kinsmen started a water-powered scythe factory. By 1820, Fowler had a growing number of permanent settlers as well as its first doctor.

Deep Concerns

Zaphna was hesitant to walk the three miles to church without Lois and the boys, for the previous evening had been especially alarming. Cyrus, ten months old, had fallen and hit his head on the corner of a jagged stone as he sat outside watching his brothers play. His crying had unnerved Lois to the point of utter despair, rendering her useless in tending to the bleeding cut oozing from the baby's temple. Five-year-old Philemon ran inside for a rag and tried his best to help his brother, while three-year-old William enthusiastically patted the baby's back and chattered,

"You be okay, baby Cy. You be okay. Don't cry. You be okay!"

All the while, Lois sat vigorously rocking in her chair, mumbling something about heaven and unforgivable sin.

When morning came, Lois appeared to be a changed woman. She rose early, milked the cow, gathered some eggs and made a hearty breakfast. Humming quietly, she gently rocked Cyrus as he nursed. Zaphna sat at the table watching her closely and as her eyes caught his, she smiled warmly and stroked Cyrus's blond head.

*"You should go on to church this morning, Zaphna. Truly we
will be fine. Philemon and William can play, and I will keep
a close watch on Cyrus to be sure that he takes no other spills."*

Zaphna was encouraged by her demeanor; calm and rational. It seemed
that she had returned to him, tranquil and beautiful.

Lois stood at the front door waving as Zaphna walked down the
muddy road, around the corner and out of sight. Wearing his leather shoes
which he saved to wear only on Sundays, she thought to herself,

*"He is a good man. Never thinking of himself, but always
others and seeking to serve God."*

The sun felt warm on her face and she threw her head back to soak in the
rays, all the while bouncing Cyrus on her hip. He laughed, looking up at his
mother. Philemon and William began chasing each other around the yard.

Spring was a welcomed relief from the cold seclusion of winter. While
heavy May showers seemed to hold a steady bleakness over Lois, clouding
her mind like the sky itself, today was different. The sun broke through.
She found herself grateful for the brightness of the day and the renewed
clarity of mind that she was feeling. Believing herself finally free from the
clutter of confusion that had wrapped itself so doggedly around her like a
prickly blanket, she called to the boys,

"Let's go down to the stream and catch some frogs!"

Philemon glanced at William in confusion. Their mother had never invited
them to play before.

The church service ended with Rev. Joseph Badger offering a rousing
benediction. David Shipman [14] with his young wife, Lydia, turned to
greet Zaphna.

*"I pray Lois soon recovers from her illness and is able to join
us again,"* David offered.

And as they stood, Zaphna expressed his deep concerns for his wife's
mental state.

"She did not fare well through the winter. My prayer is that now, with spring, she will find peace again. Her mind holds dark memories of discovered sinfulness, without a view of God's great forgiveness through our Lord Jesus. Turmoil is lodged deep within."

Meanwhile Lydia Shipman bounced two-year-old Charles on her hip as he fussed and squirmed. David's thirteen-year-old younger sister Patty noticed Lydia's endeavor to empathize with Zaphna while keeping baby Charles happy. Patty reached out to him, and Charles threw himself into his young aunt's waiting arms. Zaphna went on to explain in more detail.

"She continues to expound on unforgivable sin and holy perfection. I have gone over the grace of Christ with her again and again, but she is as stuck as a wagon wheel in the mud. She won't be budged."

"Perhaps Rev. Robbins can help."

"Yes, I will speak with him, but I must be getting back. Thank you for your time and your prayers."

And with a nervous nod Zaphna walked quickly away, anxious to return home.

Unfathomable Tragedy

Three-year-old William spotted a butterfly and began running across the clearing. Stumbling over a tree root, he tumbled to the ground skinning his knee. Lois ran to him and kneeling she inspected his injury. And with a cheer, she exclaimed,

"No serious hurt here my love! Com'on, I'll race you to the stream!",

Clinging tightly to baby Cyrus, her striped skirt waving in the wind and whipping around her ankles, she raced along, careful to allow the laughing boys the "win". Philemon's five-year-old legs outran his little brother. He shouted,

"I won!"

William began to cry.

"I want to win."
"It's alright boys. You both are winners today because today is a special day and even baby Cyrus will win."

Reaching the house, Zaphna's heart began to pound. He called out,

"Lois?!"

Though the sun was at its highest, the house was dim and gloomy. Silence. Stepping through the door and squinting to scan the yard a second time, there was only a disturbing quiet in the air. Then he heard it. Singing, a faint voice being carried along through windless air. Following the sound, he could make out the tune of a familiar hymn:

"Father, I stretch My hands to Thee
No other help I know.
If Thou withdraw Thyself from me,
Ah! whither shall I go?
What did Thine only Son endure,
Before I drew my breath!
What pain, what labor, to secure
My soul from endless death!
Surely Thou canst not let me die;
O speak, and I shall live.
And here I will unwearied lie,
Till Thou Thy Spirit give.
Author of faith! to Thee I lift
My weary, longing eyes:

O let me now receive that gift!
My soul without it dies." [16]

Side by side lay three small, lifeless bodies, looking as though they were simply asleep while dripping wet. Lois sat next to them, legs folded, clothes soaked, and her hair combed smoothly back and tied in a twist knot. Zaphna, breathless and in a state of utter shock, raced down the embankment and fell upon Philemon's cold body.

"No! No! Lois! What have you done!"

Reaching out for William and then Cyrus, he wrapped all three boys in his long arms and wept uncontrollably. Lois softly said,

"They are in heaven now. They are safe from sin and death."

After finally composing himself, Zaphna ran to the house to get some quilts for wrapping their bodies. He laid them in the back of the wagon, and with Lois sitting by his side, he slowly prodded the oxen team down the road toward the Shipman cabin. Saying nothing, Zaphna's mind was a blur of confusion and grief, while Lois hummed softly, as if on a family outing.

David Shipman heard the wagon coming and stood in the yard waving a friendly greeting. Lydia stepped outside as well and began to wave, but then dropped her hand down to her side when she saw Zaphna's face, sensing that something was terribly wrong. Young Patty had ridden home from the meeting place that morning with her brother and sister-in-law to help with Charles, as Lydia was pregnant. She started to walk outside, but Lydia grabbed her arm and firmly stated,

"No child. Remain here for a moment,"

Patty watched from the doorway as David and Lydia walked to the back of the wagon. Lydia's knees buckled and David caught her before she collapsed to the dirt. Unsure of what was happening, Patty's eyes were huge with wonder as she watched David and Mr. Stone (Zaphna) talking quietly, while Mrs. Stone remained on the wagon, her face seemingly dark and hollow. Zaphna got back in the wagon and pressed his team around and back down the road, while David rushed to the makeshift stable and fitted his horse, leaving Lydia to walk back to the cabin alone.

> *"May God have mercy,"* Lydia cried, as she fell into Patty's young arms.

> *"What has happened?"* Patty asked, her voice trembling.

> *"Mrs. Stone has murdered her children. She drowned them in the creek this morning."*

The words seemed surreal and were impossible for young Patty to digest. How could a mother drown her own children?

> *"Why?"*

> *"Her mind was troubled beyond reason. Insanity can drive a person to commit great evils,"*

Lydia picked up baby Charles and hugged him tightly to her chest, as if protecting him from the shock and horror whirling through their minds and hearts.

David rode hard, racing the eleven miles to Fowler. Zaphna had given him rough directions on finding Jonathan and Priscilla Sheldon's cabin, but he knew that he would never find it in the dark. The sun was dropping behind the dense forest and evening shadows fell long, uneven ridges across the potholed road, when he finally spotted gray smoke curling above the silhouetted tree line. He breathed a sigh of relief, while at the same time dread gripped his heart.

> *"Mr. and Mrs. Sheldon, my name is David Shipman. I am a friend of Zaphna Stone. He and Lois are neighbors and friends."* He took a deep breath and blurted out,

> *"I am afraid that I bring tragic news. Your three grandsons have died.*

In shock and utter disbelief, Priscilla screamed,

> *"What?! No! No! How can this be? What happened?!"*

> *"I don't know how to tell you this, but I am afraid that Lois drowned them. I am so sorry to have put this so bluntly. I am so, so sorry. Zaphna has asked that you come as soon as possible."*

It was decided that to attempt to travel the road in darkness was foolish. David would stay with them the night and the three of them would leave first thing in the morning and arrive well before noon. Jonathan gathered as many details as David could provide, while Priscilla sat, numb with grief, with intermittent episodes of silent tears rolling down her cheeks.

> *"I blame myself. I knew that her instability was serious."*

Jonathan quickly responded:

> *"There is no possible way that you could have known she would be capable of such an act. It is true, we saw that in the deepest straits of her soul, she could not seem to grasp reality... the fullness of God's grace and forgiveness, but no one could have understood the depth of her inner darkness. There is no one to blame, not even Lois."*

The wagon lurched along. Drawing closer to the Stone cabin, they could hear the ring of a hammer. Priscilla shuddered at the sound. Zaphna had worked through the night to finish the first small coffin for baby Cyrus. He was working on the second, for William. Simple pine boxes. Jonathan and Priscilla sadly greeted Zaphna with hugs and tears. Lois was inside the cabin.

> *"Lois?"* Priscilla gently called.

Sitting in her rocking chair, Lois lifted her head to face her mother.

> *"Oh dear. I must have dozed off."*

Priscilla pulled a bench close to Lois, putting her hands on her daughter's knees. Lois looked directly into her mother's eyes and with love and tenderness in her voice, confessed,

"I set them free, Mother. They are no longer in bondage, but are free from the sins of this world once and for all. They are free, Mother. Free."

Priscilla knew that her daughter's crazed and irrational mind had warped and distorted the gospel, and that this was not the time to attempt a rational conversation. And would it ever be?

Priscilla chose to address the immediate situation.

"Lois, your babies lie together in the back of your wagon, wrapped in quilts, ready to be buried. Your husband is building coffins. Your brother, Jon, has gone to Fowler to bring the constable."

She then proceeded to deal with inevitable consequences.

"My beautiful daughter, you will be charged with murder. Can you comprehend any of this? Do you understand what I am telling you?"

Priscilla's hands covered her face as she sobbed for her three grandsons and her lost daughter.

Lois reached out to comfort her mother.

"Do not grieve, mother. Heaven awaits us all."

John Hart Adgate, the coroner, declared murder by drowning. The sheriff of Trumbull County, David Abbott, committed Lois to the log-built county jail, but soon she was released when the Justice of the Peace, John Kingsley, [17] dropped all charges on the basis of insanity. Zaphna stood by her side, advocating for her freedom. Preacher Bronson, along with her father, Jonathan and her half-brother, Rev. Joseph Sheldon, spent many hours with Lois over the following year, helping to bring her out of her delusion and to a place of relative sanity. Reading scripture to her and praying with her, she was ultimately restored and deeply grieved her actions from that dreadful day, a day that would linger with sadness for Zaphna and Lois for the rest of their lives.

Young Jon Focuses on Work

Jon Sheldon struggled to forgive his sister. In many ways the drowning of his three little nephews put a blight on the family, as rumors and gossip became exaggerated and distorted. The strapping twenty-three-year-old secluded himself from social events, choosing rather to concentrate on developing the land into fertile, productive fields of corn, wheat and beans. Hauling logs or a sled of grain to the mill and weekly attendance at church services were the only social occasions he allowed himself, immersing himself instead in the drudgery and toil of day-to -day farm labor. The land itself became a source of solace for Jon, a landscape of picturesque beauty with its stately trees of maple, chestnut and oak, its gurgling streams, along with the satisfaction of the planted fields and the harvesting of crops. It was a solace that he could not find in people.

Overall, the weather was of constant concern and generally a topic of daily conversation. Even as hurdles invariably emerged with occasional drought but more often over-saturation, and with the stiff, tenacious clay resisting the plow, an inner peace could be found in relentless work. His clothes were ragged from climbing over logs and through thickets, as clearing was a never-ending prospect. There was no cobbler to repair worn out shoes. Mostly he went barefoot, except in winter, saving the leather on the only pair of shoes that remained somewhat wearable, for church. Life was straight forward and clearly defined. God was center most and hard work never ended.

Money was a scarce commodity. Exchange by trading was most common. Although Jonathan disapproved and practiced temperance when it came to corn whiskey, Jon seized the opportunity, as most did, to reduce corn and rye into the drink and haul it to the shore of Lake Erie, near Ashtabula, or to Pittsburgh. At these two points, currency would be received and for a while this was all the money that would come in to help the family survive the early years. [18]

23

Jonathan "Jon" Sheldon and
Martha Patricia "Patty" Shipman

1830-1876

"Jon, I am as old as the hills." Jonathan boldly stated.

Jon knew there was some fatherly advice about to come his way, as his father continued.

"And you are no spring chicken; it's time you find a wife."
"Father, I am thirty-three, not one-hundred and three. I will find a wife soon enough."

Jonathan called over his shoulder, as he meandered toward the cabin, his body straight as a rod,

"If you flit around here like a dizzy moth much longer "soon" will be too late,"

Even at eighty-plus years, Jonathan Sheldon Sr. looked as fresh and fit as many a man half his age and remained boundless in energy. His mind was still quick as a wink. That being said, he had no delusions of immortality, and he wished to see his boys settled, as he would often say, *"before the good Lord's hand reaches down from heaven to snatch me up."* Young Benjamin was twenty-three and already had his eye on Ada Ames, the younger sister of his friend Ezra. She was only fifteen and her father had made it clear that his oldest daughter would not be married off at so tender of an age. In the meantime, Jon, ten years older than Benjamin, had no prospects in sight, even as a myriad of women batted their eyes and flashed demure smiles in his direction.

Priscilla as well prayed that her sons would soon marry, but also felt somewhat compelled to take matters into her own hands. One warm afternoon she casually commented,

"Jon, your friend William Shipman has a younger sister, doesn't he?"

William and Jon had become fast friends ten years earlier, when "the tragedy" had occurred, when Jon's sister, Lois, drowned her three young sons. The large Shipman family had settled in Gustavus some years before and had endeared themselves to the Sheldon family through their Christian love and benevolence. David Shipman Jr. formed a deep bond with Zaphna, Lois's husband, while William, David's younger brother and Jon, being of the same age, found much in common with each other. [2]

Jon responded with a patient tone.

"Mother, I know what you are thinking. And yes, William Shipman has a younger sister. Her name is Martha, but they call her "Patty". And yes, Mother, she is a fine woman, kind, thoughtful and industrious."

Priscilla prodded a bit further, while seeming to continue concentrating on her needlepoint.

"It seems to me that you think very highly of her. Does she currently have any suitors?"

The truth was Jon had been thinking a lot about Patty Shipman. Although rather plain in looks, there was something very appealing about her. Her manner was sincere, and her intelligence was obvious when engaged in conversation. She wore her light brown hair parted starkly down the middle and then swooping loosely over her ears before gathering into a bun on top of her head. Jon wondered about that.

"Is she hiding large ears?"

But he kept his question to himself. Patty was tall with close set brown eyes, a sharp thin nose and matching thin lips. Her face was not one that most would consider beautiful, but rather instead, wholesome. It was her demeanor that Jon found the most attractive. She laughed easily yet wasn't prone to silliness. Blunt honesty came effortlessly, while at the same time she had a sweetness about her, a gentleness. Patty Shipman came from hearty stock, so to speak, and she understood what it took to work the land, to become a part of it and allow it to become a part of her.

Two Covenants

"Jonathan "Jon" Sheldon Jr. and Martha "Patty" Shipman, I now pronounce you man and wife," the aging Rev. Bronson declared.

Cheers filled the air as Jon scooped Patty up and swung her around, her white veil catching in the wind, *"Like the spinnaker of a ship,"* Jonathan thought to himself. Jon turned to his father and mother, embracing them each with love and gratitude. He whispered in their ears, sweat pouring off his forehead in the summer heat, [3]

" It is a good life. Thank you!"

The squawking fiddle began, announcing the program for the night's celebration, for not only was it a wedding, it was also a celebration of America's independence from British tyranny fifty-four years ago to the day, the 4th of July. Many old men still survived that war, as Jonathan had, and for them there was offered special thanks. Family and guests moved about in great enthusiasm, round dancing and high stepping. Children chased each other with laughter. A bountiful spread of wild meats, corn cakes, cheese and breads were being enjoyed by all, while whiskey flowed freely, to the concern of those who belonged to an ever-growing temperance society. [4]

Looking across the rolling hills, with knee-high fields of corn as far as he could see, Jonathan marveled at what fifteen years of physical strength, ambition and courage had provided. He pulled Jon away from his new bride for a moment and said, with emotion in his voice,

> *"When we arrived in this wilderness, there were but four acres in all of Fowler Township cleared of dense timber. With God's blessing and your help, Jon, we have begun a productive and profitable homestead of tilled land. Today, as you marry, I give you two-hundred and eighty-five acres. In return, my only request is that you care for me and for your mother in our declining years."* [5]

Jon, quite overwhelmed, tenderly put his hand on his father's shoulder.

> *"Father, you know that I will be here for you and for mother. Thank you for your generosity and trust."*

Years Bring More Life and More Death

Jon and Patty moved into the old log house with his aging parents. Patty quickly found herself with child and on April 11, 1831, [6] Chauncy Sheldon was born, just nine months after their marriage. Two years later baby Edith arrived, and the cabin was quickly becoming expressly crowded. With another baby on the way in 1835, Patty was anxious and ready for Benjamin, Jon's younger brother, to marry and get on with his own life. Benjamin, now thirty, remained living with his parents, waiting patiently until he ultimately secured permission to marry the petite Ada Ames.

Mr. Ames was a stubborn and ornery man who delayed as long as he could in giving his eldest daughter the freedom to marry, exclaiming,

> *"Eight children! We need Ada to stay right where she is to help her poor mother with the chores and caring for so many mouths to feed."*

Mr. and Mrs. Ames' newest little bundle, Horace, had been born in March 1834. Ada was twenty years old and ready to establish her own life with Benjamin, who waited so faithfully for so long. Finally, Benjamin convinced her father that if he would allow Ada to marry him, he would promise to stay and work the land with him. This greatly pleased Ada's father, who suddenly realized that he wasn't losing a daughter, but gaining a "son" or a field-hand, whichever way you look at it. And so, Benjamin and Ada were set to be married March 20, 1835. Jon and Patty were happy for Benjamin, but they were even more happy for the increased space as well as privacy, which had been in short supply for quite some time.

The civil wedding ceremony took place with a small number of family and friends in attendance. As the liturgy concluded, Benjamin asked that his father pray a blessing. Jonathan was touched by his youngest son's request. He was now eighty-six, his body frail and his voice weak with age, but at that moment, the vigor that had been his for so many years returned, and with deep inner strength Jonathan Sheldon began,

> *"Lord, you are the giver and taker of life. It fades like a passing shadow, Yet, we come before you this day, to acknowledge your sovereign hand and to ask your special grace on these two young people."*

Jonathan choked back emotion as he glanced up to see Zaphna holding three-year-old baby George. Lois was gone; her troubled life and mind had been healed, only to be lost, quite ironically, in childbirth. She was just thirty-seven when she died. Pausing for a moment to regain his emotions, he continued.

> *"There will be hardship and heartbreaks, but you O Lord are faithful! I have sailed the seas, fought for truth, pioneered a new land, preached the gospel and have found you always to be true. Place your almighty and loving hand on Benjamin and Ada this day and always. Bless and keep them, dear Lord. It is in the loving name of Jesus that I pray. Amen."*

Life itself was so tenuous and death, as always, was so final. Tabitha Shipman [7], Patty's mother, succumbed to cholera in October of 1833, three years after Jon and Patty married. Two years later, on August 8, 1835 Jonathan Sheldon Sr, the patriarch of the Sheldon family, departed this life for glory at the age of 86, succumbing to injuries incurred in a tragic logging accident. [8] While harvesting the scattered great strands of white pine and hemlock for the sawmill to transport downstream from Youngstown, [9] Jonathan slipped from the wagon, striking his head. After languishing for a short time, he took his last breath, leaving this world for the next.

Priscilla wept over her husband of forty-four years.

> *"I tried to convince him that he had no business at his age harvesting logs, but he was as stubborn as the day is long,"*

Yet even in her grief and frustration she couldn't help but to admire his strong will and tenacious spirit. Many grieved the loss of this brave and adventurous man, while lauding the accomplishments of his life, character and faith. Eulogized with great respect, the Western Reserve Chronicle printed:

> *"Jonathan Sheldon manifested those splendid qualities of manhood, justice and impeccable integrity, which he carried through his long and useful life. Possessing a keen sense of responsibility, fine dignity and considerable physical stamina, he devoted his life toward the higher ideals of faith, family and citizenship. He bestowed generously of his time to the encouragement of those less fortunate, spreading the saving gospel of Christ to the lost. He was a pioneer to this land, blazing a trail for others to follow. His life saw the calamities and perils of the Revolutionary War, fighting for the freedom we now take for granted as a country. He was a warrior patriot, a man of the sea and a man of the earth, a cooper, a preacher, a pioneer, husband, father and grandfather. Jonathan Sheldon can be measured well by the accomplishments of his life, and yet, he would be the first to reprimand those who declared his accolades without first giving praise and glory to the God and Creator of all and to His Son, Jesus Christ."* [10]

As summer crept into autumn of that same year, further anguish came with it. David Shipman Sr, Patty's beloved father, fell victim to illness, going by the way of all flesh and passing from this life to the next on October 6, 1835. [11] He lived a long and useful life, faithful in the Lord to the end. Pausing to take in the brilliant golden colors of the distant hillsides while hanging laundry on the line, Patty pondered the delicate nature of life itself. Her growing belly, preparing to bring yet another life into the world, brought her joy while her father's recent death remained heavy on her heart. She deeply sighed,

"Life and death, such an endless cycle. No one can predict its ways but the Lord God alone."

Mariah Sheldon, Jon and Patty's third child, was born strong and healthy in December of 1835 and the endless contrast of grief and joy culminated another year. [12]

Patty's Loss and God's Blessing

Patty stitched clumsily as her arms stretched once again around her ever-growing belly. Yet another baby was on its way. The needlepoint served as a distraction from the oppressive August heat. Five-year-old Chauncey raced around the yard, chasing butterflies and all manner of flying creatures, while three-year-old Edith sat next to her mother's chair, laughing at her brother's antics. The house was stuffy and still. There was a light breeze outside, and Patty had decided to take a break from her everyday inside chores.

Pulling a chair into the yard under a shade tree, she continued to attempt her needlepoint. Frustrated, she said,

"Let's go down to the stream and dangle our feet."

She pushed herself up from her chair with difficulty, the buttons on her loose-fitting wrapper dress stretched across her wide waistline. Straightening herself, she took Edith's small hand and they slowly followed Chauncy who was already well on his way down the hill toward the creek.

Lifting her skirt to her knees she slipped her bare feet into the cool clear water and was soon wading ankle deep, while Chauncy and Edith splashed each other without mercy. Edith cried out,

"Make him stop!"
"If you are going to give it, you must be willing to take it."

Patty laughed and thought to herself, *"I sound like my mother. I suppose all mothers say that."*

Watching the water flow across her feet, Patty's mind wandered back to that day, almost twenty years earlier, when Lois Sheldon had drowned her children in a very similar stream. Watching her children laugh and play, she could not even begin to imagine such a desperate and evil act. She whispered to herself,

"I was only thirteen, but I can still see the expression on Zaphna's face when that wagon pulled up to my brother's cabin, with those three small, lifeless bodies."

She shivered at the thought. Shaking it off, she stumbled up the embankment.

"Let's go, children. We need to help grandmother with dinner and check to see if baby Mariah is awake."

Priscilla had already begun a pot of potatoes boiling in the dutch oven when Patty and the children returned. Smiling as they walked through the door, Priscilla exclaimed,

"You are all wet!"

Edith immediately piped up blaming Chauncey,

"He did it, Grandmother. He splasheded me!"

Priscilla laughed, *"No matter who "splasheded" who, Edith, let's get you dried off,"* and began tousling Edith's strawberry-blond hair with a towel.

Suddenly there was the crash of a bowl falling to the ground. Priscilla spun around just in time to see Patty drop to the floor in a crumpled heap, with glass shattered around her limp body. The children began to cry. Priscilla attempted to calm them while at the same time supporting Patty in her arms, stroking her flushed face trying to bring her to consciousness. Groggy and unsteady, Patty finally came to and tried to help prepare dinner. Priscilla stated very firmly,

"You must go to bed and we will send for the doctor,"

"I am fine. Just overheated," Patty argued, but Priscilla insisted.

Dr. Bostwick ordered strict bed rest until the baby was to come. Laying on her back hour after hour was not a simple task, but there was something different with this pregnancy, and so with reservation, she acquiesced to the doctor's orders. The children did not understand. Little Edith demanded,

"Get up Mommy!"

"Mommy needs to rest for the new baby to be safe. But let's read a book together," she replied, trying to sound as cheerful as possible.

As she read to Edith, she suddenly became aware that she had felt no fluttering all day; the baby had stopped moving.

Patty prayed for her unborn child, as she longed for her own mother's comfort. Having gone home to Heaven over two years earlier and she still missed her mother's level head and whimsical ways, always putting a positive spin on any difficult situation. Patty asked, with hope in her quiet voice,

"Please send for my sister Desdemona in Gustavus. Ask if there be a way for her to come and tend to me,"

Concerned that it be too difficult for Jon's mother, now seventy-five, to assume all the household duties and care for her and the children as well. Desdemona was her only hope.

Desdemona, unmarried at the age of thirty-one, was considered by many to be an "*old maid*". Truth be told, Desdemona was so devoted to her parents' care that she had little time to consider matrimonial aspects. First her mother languished for months, and then two short years later she found herself occupied caring for her father, David Shipman Sr., until his death. Those autumn leaves seemed to perpetually signal an end to life, and meanwhile time was robbing Desdemona of her youth. Nevertheless, her cheerful spirit and faith in God did not allow her to wallow in self-pity. Her joyful heart prevailed through the tragedies of life

It had been a full year since her father had passed, and Desdemona was unsure of her future prospects. She was free from caregiving for the first time in many years and now welcomed the opportunity to provide help and care for her sister, Patty, giving her life purpose once again. Patty was grateful and Priscilla was relieved. The help was a welcome support.

In a burlap sack, Desdemona packed up a few essentials and immediately focused her mind, prayers and energy on getting to her sister. She was grateful for the improved roads, remembering only a few years before how practically impassable they were. It took only three hours to travel the eleven miles to the Sheldon cabin in Fowler from Gustavus. Upon arriving, Desdemona took charge, doing everything she could to aid Patty through the pregnancy, but in the end, it was all for naught. Patty's worst fears were realized when she gave birth to a stillborn baby girl. Her heart ached as her arms gravely held her tiny daughter. The baby remained unnamed.

Mr. Smith, the cabinet maker and undertaker in Fowler, was contacted and a small coffin was built. Mr. Smith was the father of Orpha Smith, who was married to Jon's well-known and highly esteemed cousin, Henry Olcott Sheldon [13]. The following year, Patty would once again give birth, this time to a baby boy, whom they would name Henry, and three years later in 1840, a baby girl joined the family and was named in honor of Patty's sister, Desdemona. Patty and Jon went on to have nine more children, with Laura, the youngest, being born in 1850 when Patty was forty-three and Jon being fifty-three. The previous two decades had proven to be a continuous cycle of life and death.

Priscilla Sheldon died on August 19, 1847. She outlived her husband Jonathan by twelve years, and at the age of eighty-seven, she died peacefully after falling asleep one evening and never waking the next morning. (NOTE) She had survived the Revolutionary War, the rigors of childbirth and raising her children, and the many hardships of pioneer life. She had lived her life with patience, tenacity, humor, love and an abiding faith in God. Her children, stepchildren and grandchildren rose up and called her "blessed". She was the last of her generation.

Chauncey was sixteen years old when his grandmother, Priscilla, passed away. He remembered her as *small but mighty.* Reflecting on what his father and grandparents had endured in order to settle a wild and untamed wilderness, it was nearly impossible for him to imagine it all. Modernization and innovation were reaching forward in what seemed like a race against time. The old ones were being left behind as the country sat on the edge of a new future. Railroads were beginning to spread their iron tentacles across the land, the telegraph was revolutionizing long-distance communication, the discovery of gold in California was luring many to head west, the women's suffrage movement was taking shape, and abolitionists were fighting against the injustice of slavery. The social climate of the nation was rapidly changing right before their eyes.

A Matter of Morality and Conscience

Patty opened her eyes to the dark silence, listening carefully, certain that she had heard a low rumbling sound in the distance. Swinging her tired legs over the edge of the bed, her feet hit the cold floor. She shivered and grabbed a nearby shawl. Easing herself up, she tiptoed to the small window, peering up at the stars twinkle like diamonds across the cloudless sky.

"No clouds. No thunder. Strange," she whispered to herself.

Standing quietly for a few more minutes, she shrugged it off and slipped back into bed. Jon continued his rhythmic snoring as she closed her eyes and drifted back to sleep.

The next morning Roswell Abel [14], Jon's longtime friend and fellow Democrat, [15] rode at a gallop around the bend in the lane, pulling his horse to a stop in front of the Sheldon barn. Swinging his leg over the saddle and losing his balance, he fell to the ground. Jon, watching from inside the barn, let out an audible laugh and said,

> *"The forces of time have not improved your horsemanship, Roswell." "Laugh all you like Jon Sheldon, your fifty years of life have not served you much better!"*

Wiping his hands on his trousers and stepping outside, Jon's voice was now serious with concern,

> *"At this early hour, I assume you ride with news, Roswell."*
> *"Runaway slaves, Jon."*
> *"Can't say I have seen any around these parts. Is there trouble?"*

Straightening his hat and spitting on the ground, Roswell reported,

> *"Slave owners out of Kentucky came through last night in a foul mood. Seems the underground railroad has been moving slaves through here all the way to Canada. Figured they may have stopped here checking for runaways. But they must've passed on by your place."*

Jon smiled a nervous smile,

> *"No one came knocking. Patty heard them. Thought it was thunder a way off, but it must have been the horses. They were chasing something or someone because they'd have to be riding hard to make that kind of noise. Well, thanks for the warning. I'll keep my eyes open, but it's a fight I plan to avoid. None of my business."* Roswell clumsily swung himself back on his horse,

> *"You take care, Jon!"*

"Likewise, Roswell."

Jon returned to the barn, but his mind was not on his work. The slavery issue was becoming a serious thorn of contention. Just then, fourteen-year-old Chauncey walked in holding an axe.

> *"Ready to chop some wood to fill the wood box, Father. Is everything alright? I saw Mr. Abel. Is there bad news?"*

A worried look spread across Chauncey's innocent face. He had always been a curious boy, and Jon wasn't sure how much to share with his son, fearing his young mind may become consumed with apprehension.

> *"Nothing to be distressed over, son. There are matters of disagreement among men regarding the issue of slavery. It will resolve itself in time. You can go ahead and feed the livestock, Chauncey. The wood pile can wait. I need to run an errand."*

Jon saddled his old mare and started off down the road. He'd decided rather spontaneously that he needed to talk to Dr. Chauncey Fowler. [16]. It was well known that the doctor's sympathies lay deeply with the care and protection of runaway slaves. He was a vocal abolitionist who had suffered a great deal at the hands of pro-slavery radicals. Jon simply wanted to hear why he was willing to risk so much for a cause that could split a nation.

Mary Fowler, Dr. Fowler's wife, answered the door with caution. Recognizing Jon Sheldon, she breathed a sigh of relief and invited him in.

> *"You have come a long way for nothing, Mr. Sheldon. I am afraid that my husband is not taking patients today, for he is under the weather himself."*

> *"I have not come seeking medical care, but wish to speak to Dr. Fowler on the matter of slavery,"*

Dubious of his intentions, and aware that Jon Sheldon was known as a staunch Democrat, she cast a wary eye and asked him to be seated in the living room while she consulted with her husband in the other room.

Dr. Fowler limped as he came toward Jon with his hand outstretched and a toothy smile on his face. Jon immediately stood. Dr Fowler vigorously shook his hand and offered a genuine greeting,

"Good to see you, Jon!"

"Good to see you as well, Dr. Fowler. May I Inquire as to your injury?"

"Please, call me Chauncey. It seems I am getting a bit old to be chasing around on horseback in the middle of the night. Jacob Barnes and I were attending an antislavery meeting in Ellsworth two nights ago when some pro-slavery hooligans set our wagon on a pole and shaved our horse's tail. Returning home here to Canfield, an angry mob began the chase, with full intentions of tarring and feathering both Jacob and me. Riding a single horse, we knew that we could not outrun them, so Jacob jumped onto an overhanging tree and hid himself in the branches, as I continued on. Needless to say, I was riding for my life. Those pro-slavery men were out for blood. Well, I managed to get home safely, but then, after all of that, I tripped over the front step upon entering the house! Can you believe it? I hurt myself on my own front porch!"

Dr. Fowler laughed and then added,

"And Jacob is fine. No harm came to him. But it gave us both a fright I must say!"

Jon expressed his regrets that such a thing should happen. Taking a deep breath, he then went on to inquire,

"No one should be attacked the way you have yet you willingly put yourself into this position. Why? Why risk everything as an abolitionist?"

Dr. Fowler admired a man who was not afraid to ask questions and search for understanding. He paused and leaned in toward Jon.

"Last week, I peeled back a dirty rag to reveal a deep laceration and fractured lower leg. The young boy was bleeding to death, a fractured bone. His mother and older sister were desperate. They were runaway slaves from a cruel and heartless master in Kentucky. Their only hope was my medical care and safe passage to Canada. When I see their faces, I know that I have a moral obligation to do what I can to save them. They have no voice other than those of us who will defend them."

Jon briefly paused thoughtfully before responding.

"Please understand, I do not condone slavery. I actually oppose its expansion. But I believe that where it already exists is a matter of states' rights. The foundation of my political belief stands with the states retaining as much power as possible. The federal government need only step in when necessary for the nation to function."

Dr. Fowler rubbed his head and replied,

"Jon, let's be clear, slave owners also favor this message, fearing the federal government might try to end slavery."

Jon could feel his blood pressure rising and his frustration growing stronger. With tension in his voice he said,

"The economy of slave states depends on the implementation of slavery. That economy and the decisions made concerning it, should rest with the individual state. The individual rights of the people must be of first and foremost concern. The rights

of slave holding states to create and maintain their own laws and statues is the basis of our nation and the freedom we claim."

In a calm and consoling tone, Dr. Fowler concluded their conversation.

> "You must wrestle with these issues on your own and before God, Jon. To bury your head in the sand and refuse to face the truth does not gain you anything. I only challenge you that the life of a slave is as much a human life as yours or mine. Where are the slave's individual rights to freedom and happiness? Does a slave state have the moral right to deny them freedom? Or should, in this case, the federal government intervene to end the injustice of slavery?"

Jon thanked Dr Fowler for his time and offered a final thought,

> "The tide of change is forever moving forward, and we shall see where it takes us. I pray for a promising future but fear the whirlwind of conflicting ideals will bring with it a violent upheaval. Thank you for your time. You have given me much to ponder."

As he climbed on his horse and sauntered down the lane, his heart was very troubled.

24

Chauncey Sheldon and Harriet Trumbull

1854-1884

Chauncey gritted his teeth as he signed the mandatory draft registration. [1] He stood in line with other men from the area to record their names, knowing that it was now compulsory for them to serve if called up. Most were silent, but their tense expressions revealed the anger that many felt. Stepping back into the street in front of the Warren County courthouse, Chauncey took his handkerchief from his shirt pocket and wiped his brow. It was unseasonably hot for June. *"A rich man's war, but a poor man's fight!"* he heard someone call out. Chauncey had heard the slogan before. He sadly thought to himself.

> *"This war was thought to end in a matter of months and now we are two years in with no end in sight. How many poor young lads will lose life or limb before it's over?"*

His mind was spinning with conflicting ideals, as he fumed to himself.

> *"My duties are torn. My duty to God must be foremost, yet even my church is split over the issue of slavery and the rights of the individual states. My duty to family is paramount. How do I leave a wife and three young children to fight? I believe in the Union and I support the constitution of the*

*United States. Yet I do not support the overreaching power of
the federal government and President Lincoln."* [2]

Jon sat on the porch of his newly built house, [3] as Chauncey pulled the
curricle close to the hitching post, looping the reins securely. The old
rocking chair creaked as Jon slowly swayed back and forth, his pipe in
hand. Chauncey noticed how his father had aged over these past years.
At sixty-six, his hair still as thick as a young man's and as gray as his eyes,
which narrowed into deep creases at the corners. Most notably, his father's
eyebrows, heavy with age, swooped thickly down on the outer edges to give
the ever-present impression of irritation. Before Chauncey had a chance to
express his deep outrage, Jon said,

> *"Say what you must say, son,"*
> *"Father, this is an affront to personal liberty,"* [4]

Chauncey spewed in anger, taking two steps with his long legs to easily
reach the porch.

> *"If I am called up, I do not know what I will do. They are
> taking single men first. If this war concludes soon enough, I
> may be deferred from forced service. But if it continues, I may
> be called to fight. Father, you know that I am not afraid. I
> come from a long line of brave and daring men, as you well
> know! And I am not sympathetic to slavery!"*

Leaning forward in his chair Jon calmly responded.

> *"Chauncey, sit for a while."*

Chauncey sat on the top step of the porch leaning against the railing.
Feeling calmer, he continued his thoughts, while his father listened
attentively,

> *"I fear I am unfairly judged by friends and neighbors who
> assign false motives to my objection to this war,"* Chauncey
> said with a deep sigh. *"Even our Methodist convention,*

historically anti-slavery, has seen a series of changes and splits over the issue of slavery. But that is not the source of my resolve against this war. Being a Democrat, I hold to the belief that the federal government does not have the right and should not have the power to limit slavery's existence. As much as I personally abhor the practice of slave ownership, this war is a violation of states' rights. I fully and emphatically support the union of this country, and yet I dispute the federal government's right to impose a draft, forcing men to serve. But I am no coward."

Jon waited, holding the end of his unlit pipe firmly between his back teeth, allowing the silence to wash over them for a long moment. Finally, he spoke.

"Your grandfather, Jonathan Sheldon and your great-grandfather, Jonathan Shipman, fought to free this country from the strong arm of British tyranny in the Revolutionary War, some eighty-seven years ago. Time links us to our past, just as it presses into our future. Many allow the lessons of days gone by to fade into obscurity, as time dulls memory."

His eyes squinted tightly in thoughtful reflection and he continued, slowly rocking back and forth, the chair offering a rhythmic squeak.

"Several years back I had a similar conversation with Dr. Fowler, a staunch abolitionist and participant in the underground railroad. He challenged me thatburying my head in the sand doesn't make the truth any less real. Ignoring the truth of slavery does not make it less evil. In holding so tightly to convictions, Chauncey, you are refusing to take an honest look at the issue of slavery itself. This has nothing to do with your courage. It has everything to do with what you understand from history and the power of any government to strip freedom from individual lives. What you are missing is the fact that a whole race of

enslaved people has no power, no rights and no voice at all. While it is true, just as England once ruled with an iron hand of domination over us, our own federal government now, whether with good intent or not, reaches for power in overriding states' rights. But can the purpose, in this case a war to end slavery, be more important than the process? Granted, power Is dangerous in the hands of an overreaching government. But on the other hand power also has the potential for good. There lies your dilemma. The tension between the rights of individual citizenship vs. the responsibility of an individual fighting for a noble cause. Which one is greater? The right or the responsibility?"

Chauncey smiled,

"I cannot answer that yet, but you always seem to have the words I lack."

Jon stood to stretch his unstable legs.

"Words are only as good as the actions behind them. You are a good man, Chauncey. God will be your guide."

Chauncey arrived home just before the supper hour. Harriett knew to wait patiently until he was ready to talk. He had come home in a pensive mood. The compulsory draft had set his mind on edge. Five-year-old Eva and three-year-old Ellie played with rag dolls on the floor, occasionally arguing over which doll belonged to whom. Infant Charles, three months, nursed at Harriett's breast, while she waited for the bread to finish baking in the cast iron Franklin wood stove. Chauncey glanced around the small room at his growing family [5] and felt God's hand of peace, even in the midst of the turmoil that swirled in his heart.

Harriet held different views concerning the war. They had discussed the topic many times and she was careful now to hold them quietly until Chauncey was ready to have another conversation. [6] Ultimately breaking the silence, she began,

"Chauncey, I know that you wrestle with the political aspects of this war. I am sympathetic to your stand. I understand what it is that causes you to drive a stake in the ground. Although I may disagree, this I will tell you for sure, and for certain, you are a man of conviction and no one can fault you for that!"

Chauncey shrugged his shoulders.

"No matter what my convictions, I am between a rock and a hard place. I stand against slavery and yet I cannot support the over extension of the federal government. And thus, I am either perceived as a coward or I am forced to go against what I believe."

Harriet felt it was time to explain her position and clearing her throat she began.

"First and foremost, I would never doubt your courage. Secondly, may I be clear, my desire is definitely not to see you fight in this war."

Chauncey gave her a knowing nod and she continued.

"You are my husband and a father. The truth is that you are needed here to run this farm and to provide for our needs. I do not wish you to risk your life or possibly suffer such cruel injuries as we have seen in the men who have returned wounded so severely. Yet..."

Harriet paused. Chauncey raised his eyebrows knowing what was coming next. She continued with her thoughts.

"Slavery is a great evil. It is for the injustice and cruelty of slavery that I must advocate for a solution to their persecution, even if it be such a divisive and bitter war as this. And should that solution involve President Lincoln exceeding the norms

or laws of his proper authority, such as suspending the right of habeas corpus so be it. President Lincoln made his case in which he laid out the importance of suspending the rules in order to put down the rebellion in the South and free the slaves."

Chauncey smiled as he lit his pipe, surprised at the fire in Harriet's green eyes.

"And furthermore, the Dred Scott vs Sandford case in Missouri illustrates a broken-down, beastly state of affairs when it decreed that slaves are property, not citizens or even human beings. How can you, a godly man, not rise up to condemn this evil? The southern states seceded for fear that President Lincoln would free the slaves, thus splitting the union for the sovereign right to hold slavery in place. Chauncey, this is an honorable and proper war."

"Your earnestness is unmistakable, Harriet. I have known it since I first met you, and I married you anyway," he laughed. *"Together, God willing, we will raise our children, work the land* [7]*, grow old and continue to disagree on a myriad of subjects. And I shall love you through it all."*

Harriet smiled wryly and stood to carry sleeping Charles to his cradle. With her once slender figure now rounded through three babies in seven years, and her thick dark hair thinning slightly, Chauncey still found her the most attractive woman he had ever known.

He first met Harriet in 1851. He was twenty years old and ready to secure a wife and settle down with a family of his own. Harriet was the daughter of Orson Trumbull. She was born July 6, 1834 and had grown into a very curious minded sixteen-year-old. Fowler Township was now fully transformed from an industrial center to a farming community and Orson Trumbull, fairly new to the area, was already a successful farmer, owning several acres in various locations throughout the county.

Orson's wife, Lydia, was an outwardly passive woman; guardian of the moral purity of all who resided within her household, seeking to shelter Harriet from the harsh realities of the outside working world. Her desire was for Harriet's primary education to be focused on ways to maintain a home as a haven of comfort and quiet.

All of that is not to say that Harriet did not also experience the hard work of farm life. Each morning brought the usual duties required to run a successful farm and put food on the table. Harriet understood her role. There was little relief from the everyday necessities and unrelenting tasks of housekeeping. Still Harriet found time to read, expanding her knowledge of the world around her. She was not an absent-minded girl, but instead lent herself to contemplation and the required productivity that also provided her a sense of worth.

So, when Harriet went into town that bright spring morning, it was out of character for her. Shopping seemed a bit like a waste of time. But this was a special occasion and she was excited. She slipped on her muslin everyday dress with extra care, its brown striped sleeves beginning to fade. The high collar, stained with sweat from years of wear, made her feel a bit self-conscious. She tipped her head down to hide it with her chin, her blue bonnet, securely in place, revealing several strands of dark hair. She dutifully tucked them back up inside of her tight bun and realigned her bonnet.

Her father hitched the horse to the wagon and she and her mother started for town. Her mother had ordered a Sunday dress from a merchant in Pittsburgh and they were on their way to the Fowler post office to pick it up. It was the first dress she would own that wasn't made by her mother and she was beside herself with delight.

Receiving that package with it's brown paper wrapping tied with string was the closest she came to heaven, she thought to herself. Stepping from the post office in childlike joy, clutching tightly her package, she walked straight into Chauncey Sheldon, almost knocking him over. Harriet's initial impression of Chauncey was one of caution. His tall, thin stature, square chin and intense brown eyes made her feel slightly squeamish. She reverted to casting her eyes to the ground while mumbling *"Sorry"*, and quickly moved past him.

If Chauncey thought Harriet to be a demure, unassertive girl, he was later to be happily mistaken. But that day he simply noted who she was and as he watched her and her mother cross the road and climb onto their wagon, he thought,

"That is an attractive girl. I should inquire about her."

After a short courtship, Chauncey Sheldon (23 yrs. old) and Harriet Trumbull (20 yrs. old) married on October 19, 1854.

News, Death and Inheritance

Two years after the unpopular mandatory draft of 1863 was instituted, Gen. Robert E. Lee surrendered to Gen. Ulysses S. Grant on April 9, 1865. The war of the states was over. Chauncey was never called up to serve. [8] He and Harriet continued to farm their land in Fowler, Ohio, and life settled into the simple and straightforward manner that farm life requires, and three more children were born: Warren in 1868, Leslie in 1871 and Louise in 1873.

Chauncey's parents, Jon and Patty, lived comfortably in the house they had built together, enjoying the fruits of their many years of hard work and dedicated faith. The newspapers, which for four years of war had riveted the masses with the stories of battles fought and victories won, now took on a more local flavor, while at the same time keeping the people abreast of the happenings across the nation. *"CHICAGO IN RUINS!"*, blared the headlines of the great Chicago fire of 1871. *"CORRUPTION IN NEW YORK"*, announced the formal arrest of William M. "Boss" Tweed, an influential and corrupt politician who stole millions of dollars in taxpayer money.

The *Warren Reserve Chronicle* provided the most up-to-date information regarding the ongoing ramifications of the Union victory. The *Ku Klux Klan Act* passed in 1871, giving the seventeenth president, Ulysses S. Grant, the power to send in troops to enforce the 14th Amendment, addressing citizenship rights and equal protection under the law as related to former slaves. Yet, as developing political and social change slowly evolved, the day-to-day life of farmers like the Sheldon's took more personal and often heartrending turns.

Jonathan "Jon" Sheldon Jr passed away on June 1, 1871 at seventy-three years of age. His grieving widow, Patty, had shared forty-one years of marriage and twelve children, six girls and six boys, with Chauncey being the oldest. Young Charles, Chauncey's third born, was ten years old when his grandfather died and as he would remember in later years,

> *"I recall my grandfather being sought to participate in the conduct of many local offices and yet he never sought office. He was well respected for his fairness, foresight and experience. He is greatly missed."*

A life lived well into old age is celebrated and honored with stories and remembrances. Grief is real and experienced with deep loss, while at the same time is tempered with the truth of the inevitability and finality of death. Jon had lived a full and rich life. Although he was a man in his seventies, the vitality that was his had never diminished. One day he simply collapsed while out in the barn, and he was gone from this life and ushered into the next. The coroner said it was a massive heart attack, sudden and painless. [9]

Long before his death, Jon had relinquished the care and ownership of the land to his children, dispersing it as fairly as he thought appropriate. Of course there was dissension, as there often is in such matters, especially when so many children and their spouses are involved. Edith, Jon and Patty's first-born daughter, was particularly put out.

> *"I do not understand why my brothers are to receive twice the acreage that my husband and I do."*

Jon's reply was to the point,

> *"Your brothers have put in twice the back-breaking work that you have and your husband is flat out lazy. I would not trust him to plow, plant and harvest any more land than I have allotted to you."*

Edith huffed away to complain to other siblings and stir the pot of unrest. Eventually several factions emerged. In the end, it was all for naught. Jon Sheldon would do what he saw fit regardless of heedless squabbling. [10]

Patty sought unsuccessfully to make peace among her children, with her heart breaking over the petty wrangling.

Henry O, sixth born in the family, received the largest allotment of fifty-four acres. Of all the children, Henry truly understood the land, and his passion for it translated into financial gain. Chauncey, the oldest, with fifty acres, worked hard, but his health was slowly diminishing and there was growing concern. Patty was especially worried for her eldest son's weakened physical condition. He was losing energy and a ragged cough persisted.

Harriet, being Chauncey's concerned and often anxious wife, consistently experimented with herbal remedies, as the doctor seemed to be of little help and her uncooperative husband resisted the doctor's advice and prescriptions, commenting,

> *"Wife, if the provisions of nature cannot heal whatever it is that ails me, then let it be so. I will join my father in heaven whenever God sees fit."*

This logic frustrated Harriet, as she would fret over the many possible serious and deadly diseases that lurked in the back of everyone's mind.

Although a Dr. Edward Jenner, of England, had developed a method to protect against smallpox in 1797, the disease was not eradicated and there was yet to be a vaccine. Yellow Fever decimated Philadelphia in 1793, killing thousands. Polio was an ever-present fear, especially for children. Diphtheria as well as tetanus were also constant concerns, and newspapers were reporting an epidemic of cholera sweeping the Americas. [11]

Charles, as Chauncey's oldest son, had stepped up to provide his father with much-needed help on the farm, as Chauncey's health waned between a seemingly strong constitution and a total lack of vigor. Plowing, cultivating, and harvesting had all become second nature for Charles as he dutifully worked the land, picking up the slack that his father's illness left. As time went by, Chauncey gave his son more and more responsibility, and at sixteen Charles began to work full time on the farm, discarding his schooling in 1876. Although Fowler provided schooling for the higher grades since 1864, [12] Charles was eager to relinquish his formal education for the more practical aspects of farm life. [13]

25

Charles Robinson Sheldon and Ella Viola Boyd

1861-1885

James Boyd [1] and his wife Margaret arrived in America from Scotland by way of Liverpool, as poor as church mice, on May 18,1846. The potato crops of the Scottish Highlands had been devastated by a severe blight. Beginning in Ireland, the crop failure advanced throughout the 1840's causing widespread famine. Destitution and malnutrition, compounded with especially cold and snowy winters, raised the alarm for relief. Immigration began as a partial solution, mostly to Canada. [2]

"Tis a new land of opportunity, James, and it appears to be no secret,"

the older James slowly commented, with his deep Scottish accent, to his eighteen-year-old son, also named James, as they watched from the ship's deck. Black smoke streamed upward toward the low-hanging gray clouds overhead. Hundreds of distant chimneys stretched across the landscape that was New York.

The population density was astounding. Moving along the docks, the family inquired as to possible lodging and were directed to an area referred to as "Five Points" [3]. Walking the crowded streets. young James felt as if he were trapped in a smoky, dirty urban jungle. Unfamiliar sights, sounds and smells made him feel sick to his stomach and dizzy. Young children with coal smudged faces and ragged clothes played with sticks and cans in the street during the day, while women of the night made themselves obviously available on every corner. Gangs of young men roamed with the menacing strength and arrogance that numbers provide. Violent crime was rampant. Disease and child mortality rates soared within the ranks of the urban poor.

Older James secured temporary housing in the rundown, overly crowded tenement of "Old Brewery", [4] where it was rumored a murder took place every night of the previous ten years. Thin walls and tight quarters provided little privacy. Rats prowled the hallways freely. The Boyd family knew farming in Scotland, and plans were made as quickly as possible to escape New York City and relocate to the farmlands of Ohio, while cautiously protecting the small amount of money they had saved.

Once they secured arrangements to make the overland trip to Johnston, Ohio, where several Scottish relatives had previously settled, the younger James found himself, for the first time in a long time, excitedly anticipating a brighter future. Arriving in Johnston, the senior James purchased eighty-one acres of farmland covered with heavy timber. Eventually building a small yet comfortable cabin, the family settled in to make new lives for themselves.

However, misfortune soon followed. Both parents soon died of typhoid fever within weeks of each other, leaving young James unable to meet the payments on the farm. Alone and without options, the farm was repossessed, and James hired out to work for larger more established farms in the area and for the coal mines when they were hiring.

When young James Boyd eventually met Janet Hamilton, [5] there was an instant attraction. She was Scotch, smart, fun and easy to look at. After a whirlwind romance, they married, much to the chagrin of her parents who had hoped that Janet would marry someone with a more stable and fixed future. The marriage was not to last long, as Janet, at twenty-two years of age, died of tuberculosis in the epidemic of 1851. James Boyd, only twenty-three years old, overcame his sorrow by focusing all his attention and energies toward locating continued work to support himself. For ten years he scratched the ground for a future, shoveling stables, tending sheep, plowing fields and occasionally working the mines.

Jane Howe [6] was feisty and independent. Born in 1840, she was twelve years younger than James when they married on April 24, 1861. It was the same month and year that the war between the states began. James [6] was thirty-three years old and still struggling to survive. The string of "bad luck" had continued to follow him. Work was inconsistent and hard to find. He and Jane prayed for a better life. And yet as hard as he worked, nothing seemed to fall into place.

In 1861 when the war began, James, with a new young wife, was desperately grasping for a new beginning. He considered volunteering, but chose instead to hold out, hoping for a quick resolution and a Union victory. And with so many men off to fight, James hoped to secure more permanent work. Their first baby, Ella Viola Boyd, was born in April of 1862. When the 1863 draft was instituted, baby Ella was an active and crawling one-year-old. James completed the mandatory registration, fearful of being called up, yet feeling hopeful that he would not, due to having a wife and infant child to provide for, and he was correct. The war would end without him.

Life remained a constant challenge for survival itself. Harvest time was always the most lucrative, and the family was careful to save enough money to get through the long cold winters. Living in a rented room over the general store in Johnston, Jane took in sewing to help make ends meet. She was a woman who possessed a bright outlook through the darkest of times. Later in life, Ella would recall a simple memory of her mother calmly humming while she worked her needle.

Unexpected Casualties

Ten-year-old Ella watched out the window as a blanket of white snow covered the deserted street below. Delicate flakes landed on the glass only to slowly melt away, mesmerizing her young mind. She was expecting her father home at any moment, after spending the day helping a wealthy rancher with some stable work. Ella thought it thrilling that her father was working on a ranch with so many beautiful horses. Needless to say, James was not so enamored, but was grateful for the employment in the dead of winter.

The mantle clock chimed out six times, interrupting its rhythmic ticking. The snow was coming down heavier and the wind had picked up. Ella's mother had a worried look on her face.

"God is in control, Ella,"

she said, convincing herself as much as her daughter that James would arrive home safely.

"We must always be grateful for His love and provision, no matter our current circumstance."

She smiled at Ella as she slipped a woolen shawl over her shoulders. It was getting dark and the wood pile was getting low.

The light snow that had earlier been so entertaining was now a violent blizzard. Visibility became only a few feet as the wind whipped its headstrong fury, creating snow drifts several feet deep. Jane did not know whether James would make it home or if he would wait until the weather broke in the morning. She needed dry wood and she could not wait any longer for James to restack it. The wood pile was only a few yards from the back of the store.

"I'll be back shortly. Remain here,"

she instructed Ella and disappeared through the door and down the back steps. Ella continued to watch out the window, hoping to see her father soon. Sitting alone, the silence only broken by the ticking clock, Ella waited. Then, startled by the chime, she realized that her mother had been gone for too long. Unsure of what she should do, she did as her mother had told her - *"Remain here"* - and so she did, shivering throughout the night.

The next morning Jane's body was discovered only ten feet from the building. Curled up in a tight ball, ice crystals frozen to her colorless cheeks and an arm load of firewood scattered around her. The blinding snow combined with darkness had caused her to lose her sense of direction. Unable to find the door, just a few feet away, she tragically froze to death trying. [7]

Orphaned

Coal was being mined in Trumbull County. The first commercial mine in the county began production in 1843. It was the Curtis (No. 1) drift-entry mine at the state line in Brookfield Township. Only thirty mines at that time were drift-type, meaning entry could be made on the side of a hill rather than the primary entry method which was vertical shaft. James had known many men who worked the mines. These were tough, seasoned men, mostly of Welsh descent who capitalized on their experience and intimate knowledge of the industry.

James didn't know a lot about mining, having worked only a few short hitches years before, but he was willing to learn and the money was good. He hired on with the Brookfield mine in the spring following the tragic death of his wife in 1843. He was paired with a cheery Irishman named Thomas Byrne, who had a propensity for heavy drink and colorful gossip.

> *"Aye, the Welsh are a tricky lot. They apt to lie as it suits their purposes. Yet I has no complaints against them. They like their beer. They get drunk as tinkers and curse worse than the demons of the bottomless pit."*

While appreciating Thomas's jovial outlook on life, James was also thankful for his toughness and judgment inside the mine. Thomas was always on the alert for proper ventilation and clear passageways for emergency exit. He managed to carry his weight and then some. The work was backbreaking as the coal face was undercut to allow blasting it loose. It was then hand shoveled into mine carts. Complete exhaustion ended each day, as the blackened faces of coughing men emerged from the depths of the dark mine.

The Brookfield mine was sixteen miles from Johnston, too far for James to travel daily. Eleven-year-old Ella needed a home, and the townsfolk were sympathetic to the Boyd's plight. It seemed that constant tragedy followed them, and word began to spread for a solution to the circumstances that James and his young daughter, Ella, found themselves in.

The Van Avery's [8] were a respectable family in Fowler. Oscar Van Avery was a carpenter and millwright. Lucinda, Oscar's slim wife, kept their home orderly and clean, which wasn't an easy task with three rambunctious boys, three-year-old Charles being the oldest and an especially boisterous handful. Sitting in church that fateful Sunday while trying to quiet Charles from talking about the spider he saw scampering across the floor, Lucinda, struggled to listen to the sad story of the Boyd's. The minister shared the plight of this unfortunate family, asking the congregants to pray for them. Lucinda quickly turned to Oscar and whispered,

"That poor dear child! Losing her mother like that and now her father having to work the mines!"

Oscar knew what his wife was thinking. Lucinda could not bear to allow a child to suffer. He understood as well that his wife could use some household help. He whispered,

"We'll look into the matter come Monday."

Lucinda smiled at how her husband knew her so well and was pleased to think that they could help the poor dear child, Ella Boyd.

And it came to pass that Ella soon moved into the comfortable home of the VanAvery's in Fowler. James was relieved that his only daughter was being loved and cared for. He simply wasn't capable of giving her what this family could. Ella grieved for her father and over all that he had lost. She missed him. She never saw it as abandonment, but rather a selfless act of love. Learning to approach life in this positive way undoubtedly came from her mother. Ella always found herself grateful in spite of the hardships.

"It isn't so much what happens in your life that dictates your happiness or unhappiness, but your opinion of what happens," her mother once told her.

The scripture verse, Proverbs 23:7, rang like church bells through Ella's thoughts:

"As a man thinketh in his heart, so he is."

For five years Ella enjoyed her life with the VanAvery's. She learned what it meant to be a good housekeeper and cook, how to look after children, and how to read and write. But mostly she learned what it meant to be a family. She would find herself simply watching their interactions and the relationship dynamics that took place. Ella was sixteen years old when the VanAvery's made the decision to move to Kalamazoo, Michigan. She was devastated and worried over what was to become of her future.

Since she had never been officially adopted, she was in a position to make a choice: move to Michigan with the VanAvery's or remain in

Trumbull County. Ella did not want to move; as much as the VanAvery's had become her family, her father still lived and worked in the Brookfield mine. Even as rarely as she saw her father, she did not want to leave him.

At the same time, Henry Perkins [9], of Kinsman, OH, made an inquiry regarding Ella. Hearing that the Van Avery's were moving west, he and his wife wondered if Ella might be available as a live-in servant. The opportunity seemed perfect and Ella, with optimistic hesitation, moved in with the Perkins family. Mrs. Perkins was due any day with a second baby. Ellen, the one-year-old, was a fussy, chubby bundle of energy, and Mrs. Perkins was too exhausted to handle her. Ellen Nicholson, Mrs. Perkins' mother, also lived with them and required assistance, as she had recently taken a bad fall and broken her hip. Ella found herself working from morning to night with very little time for herself.

Mrs. Perkins was attuned to the latest styles and Ella was impressed with the attention that she gave to her personal appearance. Watching Mrs. Perkins dutifully apply powder to her face each morning and carefully place combs in her meticulously styled hair caused Ella to dream of one day having a home of her own and enjoying the same luxuries. She had never been one to pay much attention to her appearance, but suddenly she found herself stopping in front of the mirror in the front parlor more than a few times a day.

The spring of 1877 had quickly transitioned into the heat of summer, and Ella was slowly becoming acclimated to her new home. The Perkins were kind but thought of her less as a family member and more as a servant. Hanging laundry on the line, she tipped her head back to let the hot sun beat down on her sweaty face and prayed,

> *"Lord, I am a sixteen-year-old servant girl with little prospects or advantages. You know my "going out and my coming in,"* [10] *so would you be pleased to 'come in' with a husband, so I may "go out" from here? I do not wish to wash and hang other peoples' clothes for a lifetime. Amen."*

She laughed at her forward and silly conversation with God, yet in her heart she knew the truth behind it.

She had recently met a boy at church. Tall and lanky, he made an impression on Ella. His name was Charles Sheldon. He was from Fowler and had recently been visiting his friend, Jedediah Bidwell, who lived a half mile up the road from the Perkins farm in Kinsman. Charles, at seventeen, was one year older than Ella. He had recently quit school to work the family farm. His thin, muscular, arms were deeply tanned to where his sleeves were rolled up, and the back of his neck was so basted by the sun it looked like dirt. Jedidiah introduced them, something that he later admitted was his mistake, for he himself had eyes for the pretty Ella Boyd.

The Brookfield Mine

As the last rays of the sun were just beginning to set, an unfamiliar wagon pulled up to the house. Mr. Perkins, sitting on the front porch in his favorite rocking chair while casually smoking a cigar, stood to his feet. Walking down the three wooden steps to the dusty ground, he greeted the driver. Ella glanced out the window and then watched as the two engaged in a short conversation. "*Curious*," she thought. The driver climbed down from his seat, tossed the reins over the hitching post and stood nervously next to his horse. Mr. Perkins entered the house and with a sorrowful voice said,

> *"Ella, there is a gentleman here to talk to you. It's concerning your father."*

The headlines in the newspaper screamed the next morning, "*Seven Lives Lost in Brookfield Coal Mine Asphyxiation*". [11] The article went on to describe what had happened. The men had suffocated by gas from the mine locomotive. Thomas Byrne [12] had been correct in his concerns over ventilation, as he and James Boyd both paid the ultimate price.

Ella now found herself truly an orphan. [13] The funeral was a simple ceremony with only a few sympathetic neighbors and friends in attendance. Ella wore a new dress that had been donated to her by the wife of Joseph S. Barb, [14] a well-established and successful family in Fowler. The Perkins had purchased their honey from the Barb farm for years and Mrs. Barb had formed a special fondness for Ella. As much as Ella grieved over her father's death, she couldn't help but also be smitten with the fashionable dress, which possessed a bustle attached to the back.

To have something so in step with the style of the day was as if a dream had come true. It wasn't the customary black dress of mourning, but she had never owned something so beautiful and it did not matter to her. With a belt secured high on her waist and the delicate blue print of the fabric and the added layering effect of the bustle, she felt elegant. It was a feeling she had never experienced before. Securing her flowered bonnet and a shawl, she laced up her leather boots which were too small and pinched her feet. She walked alone to the church. People were kind with their words and sentiments, and it felt surreal as she slowly shuffled along behind the black horse-drawn hearse to the cemetery when the service ended.

A small group of people silently accompanied her as they walked to the cemetery, until Mrs. Foote suddenly began to sing,

> *"I will follow Thee my Savior,*
> *Wheresoe're my lot may be;*
> *Where Thou goest I will follow,*
> *Yes, my Lord I'll follow Thee."* [15]

Others joined in.

> *"Though the road be rough and stormy,*
> *Trackless as the foaming sea,*
> *Thou hast trod this way before me,*
> *And I gladly follow Thee."*

Ella's heart swelled with emotion. It was as if the Lord Himself had wrapped His arms around her sadness to say,

> *"All is well, child."*

Ella's Gentleman Suitor

The clouds were heavy with rain, and brief showers fell throughout the day. Ella's fingers ached, chapped and red after wash boarding the Perkins' laundry. She rubbed them together as she scanned the sky. Debating whether to hang them on the line and risk more rain or carefully hang them about inside the house, she decided to wait a bit. Mrs. Perkins was very fussy about the clothes, and Ella knew that the line would be better if possible.

She sat down in the kitchen, resting her chin on her folded dry hands, staring at the mason jar of daisies on the table. Four-year-old Ellen had picked them from the garden for her mother that morning. Suddenly aware of the familiar echo of footsteps in the hallway, she stood quickly. She wasn't sure why, but she always felt nervous that Mrs. Perkins might find her not diligently at work.

"Ella, you have a gentleman caller," Mrs. Perkins crooned.

Ella's eyes darted past where Mrs. Perkins was standing.

"You shall not find him standing behind me. He is outside, my dear."

Ella always cringed when Mrs. Perkins referred to her as *"my dear"*. It felt demeaning. Ella walked nervously through the kitchen and then through the parlor, unsure of who would be calling on her mid-afternoon on such a dreary day. She turned the glass doorknob, opened the door and there stood Charles Sheldon, his straw hat in his hand with a huge toothy grin spread across his tanned face.

"Good afternoon Miss Boyd, I hope that I haven't interrupted, or what I mean to say is, I hope that it is not an inconvenience that I call on you without notice or advance warning. Not that you should need warning, of course, for my intentions are nothing but honorable."

Charles was rambling out of nervousness. He took a deep breath and started over.

"Miss Boyd, I bring condolences concerning your father's passing."

Ella was confused, but politely replied,

> *"Thank you, Mr. Sheldon. I have grieved during this past year, as grief never truly ends, but now with the passage of time, the grief has eased somewhat, and I find myself in a place of peace."*

Ella smiled at Charles, suspecting that he had not arrived on the doorstep to simply express sympathy over the death of her father, which had occurred almost a year earlier.

> *"I am pleased to hear that,"* he replied.

Looking down at his feet, he continued to the true reason he was there.

> *"If it's not too forward, I was wondering if I could escort you to church this Sunday?"* Ella's smile grew bigger.

> *"Certainly. I would be honored."*

Love and Marriage

It was a sleepy winter morning, and Ella rose early. Butterflies seemed to be doing cartwheels in her stomach. She was nervous but not scared, excited but composed. Standing in her nightdress in front of the large mirror placed over the oak chest of drawers in her room, she rubbed her face vigorously. Examining what she saw in the mirror, she commented under her breath, *"There, that put some color in those cheeks."* She smiled at herself and tipping her head sideways, practiced deep gratitude to those who would be attending her wedding.

> *"Thank you so very much for coming."*
> *"I am so glad you came."*
> *"Oh, thank you, you are too kind."*

Laughing, she spun around and began dressing for her big day...her wedding day.

Slipping her new dress over her petticoat, she carefully secured each button to the high neckline. The brown silk satin sleeves [16] snuggly fit her arms to her elbows where the sleeve then puffed out perfectly to her shoulders in lovely large circular form. The waistline was very becoming, and the fabric flowed to the floor, with a small ruffled hem lightly brushing the floor. After applying the tiniest bit of face powder [17] to smooth any blemishes, she loosely piled her hair into a bun, curled her bangs and ensured that several locks of curls were carelessly falling from the top bun.[18]

Charles was extremely nervous. Not one to seek attention, the thought of being the center of scrutiny was a terrifying one.

> *"I would sooner face the teeth of a ravenous wolf than face this consideration,"*

he told his ten-year-old brother, Leslie, that morning as they climbed into the wagon for the cold ride into town. Leslie shivered, and with an impish smile on his face he questioned his older brother.

> *"Do you refer to your wedding bed tonight or this morning's ceremony?"*

Both Harriet and Chauncey, who were standing directly behind their young son, upon hearing this question, shot each other accusing expressions, each wondering how young Leslie came to know of such things. Charles laughed and said,

> *"That is none of your affair. I'll simply say, don't you worry about me!".*

As Ella walked down the short aisle of the church, all concerns over appearance and impressions faded. Standing in front of her was Charles Robinson Sheldon. In his dark blue jacket, neatly fitted over his white waistcoat and grey trousers, he looked as if he'd stepped from an advertisement in the newspaper. Instead of wearing the grey wool sack suit that she was accustomed to seeing him in, he had purchased a new suit for their wedding day. Tears welled up in her eyes as she realized that he had spent his hard-earned money on what so many would have regarded as frivolous. He had done it for her. [19]

And so, December 12, 1881 began the wedded life of twenty-year-old Charles Sheldon and nineteen-year-old Ella Boyd. Until more permanent arrangements could be made, the young couple moved in with Charles' parents and younger siblings. [20] Charles' older sisters Ella and Eva, having both married and moved away three years earlier, allowed extra room in the house for Charles and Ella to comfortably settle in, albeit, it was still crowded. [21] Thirteen-year-old Warren, the precocious ten-year-old, Leslie, along with the sweet littlest sisters, eight-year-old Louise, and five-year-old, Mary [22], loved Ella and welcomed her easily as the newest member of the family. It was only fitting that Charles and his new bride live with his parents, as Charles continued to carry more and more of the weight of the work on the farm, while his father, Chauncey, continued to decline in health.

The bitter cold of the winter months finally began to subside in early April. [23] The tame temperatures and reduced snowfall made life a little more bearable for those cramped into a small house day after day. The need for chopping wood was reduced greatly, to the joy of the younger boys. Their father had purchased a coal cooking range, piped into the old chimney flue. Now they found themselves shoveling coal rather than chopping wood, and yet many aspects of daily life remained unchanged from previous generations. Candles needed to be made, even though oil lamps now aided in providing light through the dark hours. Soap-making was a necessity, although one could, if extravagant and wealthy, purchase *Ivory*, the famous floating soap bar. Meals required preparation and cooking, cows needed milking, horses needed to be fed, stables needed to be cleaned, water needed to be brought in, clothes needed to be mended and washed, as well as countless other chores.

The harshness of winter had been hard on Chauncey. His strength waned well into spring and it seemed that he was becoming weaker with each passing day. Fever and chills sent him to his bed for weeks at a time. His once strong and viral body had diminished to skin and bone. The children picked up additional daily chores and duties, as their father gradually became totally incapacitated. Harriet was beside herself with anguish over her husband's decline, as she watched him slowly dying before her eyes.

Ella did everything she could to help relieve her mother-in-law of the household chores, providing Harriet the freedom to focus her care and attention on Chauncey. Patty Sheldon, Chauncey's mother, lived less than a mile down the road [24] and visited most every day, being deeply concerned for her son.

Finally, after months of suffering, at fifty-one years of age, on November 10, 1882, Chauncey Sheldon died. His death would spark a series of circumstances to affect the futures of his children and even future generations. But for now, the simple truth was, Chauncey was gone. He was not a complicated man: a hard-working farmer, a faithful and loving husband, a dedicated father to their six children.[25] His faith had carried him through life, and his love for God and commitment to his family shaped who he was.

It did not take long following Chauncey's death for his wife, Harriet, to realize that the stress of maintaining the farm was too great a burden for her to bear. It seemed that life was on a perpetual roller coaster of life and death, as death, again, came so suddenly. One year after Chauncey's death, on November 4, 1883, Martha "Patty" Sheldon died of pneumonia [26] at the age of seventy-six.

"A son should never die before his mother,"

Patty had sadly lamented, just a week before she herself took her last breath. Her son's death had taken its toll on her. For Harriet, the shock of losing her husband and then her mother-in-law in such short order affected her to the core. Fear and worry seemed to overtake her once strong and immovable constitution.

As he sipped his coffee, Charles wondered about the future. Glancing across the room, he smiled as Ella quietly rocked eight-month-old James, their firstborn son. His father's brother, Uncle Henry, had made a tempting offer. Henry and his brother Chauncey had never been especially close, yet Henry felt compassion for the difficult circumstances he now witnessed his widowed sister-in-law to be in. His offer included purchasing the fifty acres of land that now belonged to Harriet after Chauncey's death. But more graciously, it provided that Harriet could remain in the house as long as she lived and that Charles could continue to cultivate the land, earning profits each year.

Fifty acres was not enough land to sustain Charles and his growing family as well as his mother and his younger siblings. Regardless, Harriet believed the offer to be sent from God and she accepted Henry's offer. The money from the sale of the land gave her a sense of security. [27] Charles was skeptical of the arrangement. His mother was a determined woman and in her distraught state, he was afraid that she was possibly not thinking as clearly as she might have otherwise.

The fall of 1883 saw a good harvest, and the spring of 1884 brought renewed hope. Life became ordinary and comfortable, if not habitual. The ebb and flow was generally happy. Ella was of great help to Harriet, and Charles's younger siblings were doting aunts and uncles to baby James. Little sister, nine-year-old, Louisa, was especially enthralled with the baby and spent hours each day holding him.

> *"Louisa, James will never learn to walk if you continue to hold him for hours on end! Stand him on his feet, hold his hands and help him balance. He's one-year-old. He should be walking,"*

Ella chided, though with a smile on her face.

While the children grew and thrived, Harriet began to gradually show symptoms of illness. It began with a loss of appetite. Never one to complain, she went about her daily chores as if nothing was wrong. That is, until the symptoms grew worse and she was soon suffering stomach cramps and vomiting. Bedridden, the doctor was called when her fever spiked to dangerous levels. Prescribing plenty of liquids, including apple cider vinegar and basil to soothe the stomach, he left with words of little comfort.

> *"Gastroenteritis* [27] *is a serious infection. All you can do is wait and pray that it clears from her body."*

It was not to be. At fifty years old, Harriet Sheldon died on May 17, 1884. With Harriet's unexpected early death came a serious upheaval in the Sheldon family. [28] There were questions as to who now had the right to the land, and who was to take charge of the two youngest children, thirteen-year-old Leslie and nine-year-old, Louisa. Warren was sixteen and had already moved out to seek his fortune, initially working the mines. [29] Harriet's two oldest daughters were raising families of their own. Eva lived with her husband, Hugh Hayes in Fowler, and Ellie had moved away with her husband, Adam Resin. [30]

Charles was twenty-three years old and now both of his parents had gone to the grave. He had a wife, young son and a baby on the way. Ella was expecting their second child in three months. The future was indeed uncertain.

> *"Like any bully, I believe that your Uncle Henry has sought his own good fortune over our well-being,"* Ella spouted.

It was out of character for Ella to say such a thing, and Charles was taken aback for a minute. He understood her frustrations and fears. Uncle Henry had informed them that since the agreed upon arrangement had been for the property to remain in Harriet's care until her death, it now, just six months later, must revert back to his estate. Charles and Ella would need to move. But where?

Deep within himself, Charles felt anger and resentment toward his uncle, while knowing that his hands were tied and there was nothing that could be done. The spiral of unfortunate events had culminated in virtually no inheritance except for the small amount of money his mother had saved from the sale of the land to Uncle Henry. That inheritance was rightfully divided among the siblings. It was not nearly enough money to purchase any amount of fertile farmland in Trumbull County.

In an attempt to convince himself as much as his wife, Charles processed his thoughts and feelings aloud.

> *"Ella, I completely understand your resentful feelings toward Uncle Henry. But we must realize that he had no way of knowing that mother would pass away so soon after father and grandmother. I must believe his heart was in the right place with his concerns for the care of Mother, but since she has passed on, he must move ahead with his own business regardless of our current situation. He has graciously given us*

one year to secure other living arrangements. We will get our affairs in order and begin a new future, together, somehow, somewhere, by the grace of God."

With the arrival of summer came the transitions that naturally transpire as the effects of life and death spin a twisted web. The younger children, Leslie and Louisa, went to live with their older sister, Eva, her husband and one-year-old son, Floyd. Eva was bossy, although she loved her young siblings and provided a safe environment. Remaining with family members, rather than being adopted out or functioning as live-in-servants, was important.

On August 22, 1884 Ella gave birth to their first daughter, Alice. Charles desperately thought through and prayed for direction as to their future as a family. There was no longer Sheldon acreage that would ever belong to him. He would need to look toward other opportunities. Times were indeed bleak, but a new beginning was just around the corner.

26

Sheldons in Emmet County

1886-1902

A boundless canopy of forest spread itself above the damp miry ground. Toppled trees, their gnarled roots weakened in the swampy soil, lay across a meandering green river like mossy bridges. Heavy limbs wave overhead, casting deep shadows in the placid current. Charles Sheldon lingered on the riverbank, tossing in small stones, watching the circular ripples expand and disappear under a fallen log. His long legs stretched out before him as he glanced down absentmindedly to notice his worn boots.

The silence was long and profound, only broken by the sapless harmony of chirping birds and the chatter of an angry squirrel. It had been two months since he had ventured to this foreign northern land. An old promotional circular, lauding the attributes of available land, beckoned to its readers, *"Homestead in Emmet County! Where dreams of home seekers are realized!"* Charles believed that this was the opportunity that he and his growing family needed for a new beginning. Packing a small duffle, he boarded the train at Johnston, making the long journey to Northern Michigan. He needed to see it for himself.

The immigration boom of Emmet County had begun in earnest ten years earlier, in August of 1874. At that time most of the land was either given to Civil War veterans, sold to speculators or sold for private farming. Within four years, log cabins were set in scattered openings across the wilderness, as forests were cleared, and crops planted. Nearly all who arrived were poor, if not absolutely destitute. Many came with only enough money to relocate into this northern wilderness, and nothing more. Most had no idea of the trials and hardships pioneer life would require. Dreamers dream big dreams, but without the fortitude to match, they will soon pull up stakes and call it quits.

Even though much of the land had been snatched up a decade before, there remained plenty of smaller 80-acre tracts that were available at prices as cheap as $1.25 per acre. Leaving Ella and the two children behind, in the spring of 1886 [1] Charles traveled as far as unincorporated Petoskey, Michigan. There, he secured a room at a local boarding house before continuing on by train to the small village of Alanson [2], in Maple River Township.

Petoskey, originally known as Bear River when first settled by missionaries and traders in 1855, was a booming town, with an economy supported by mining limestone and lumbering. In the year 1871 lumber was shipped south on Lake Michigan to help rebuild Chicago, after the great fire of that same year which had destroyed much of the city. Growth in Petoskey began in earnest in 1873 when a reporter from Grand Rapids rode the newly connected excursion train to Petoskey. Dubbing it the "Land of the Million Dollar Sunsets", his account of the beauty of this remote area sparked interest and enthusiasm.

By 1875, The Bay View Association had established itself along the high bluffs overlooking Little Traverse Bay and neighborhoods sprang up showcasing gingerbread style Victorian cottages, churches and inns. People came from throughout the Midwest by railroad and steamship to escape the summer heat and soak in the natural, majestic beauty of the area.

Prior to 1873, there were only 150 white people living in Emmet County, with the large majority located along the shoreline communities, with no known white settlers north of Bay View, which included Maple River Township.[3] Development in this section of the county was slow, even though over 5000 acres was already privately owned before 1874. The federal government had been giving land to companies, contractors and private persons as payment for services provided, yet the land itself was not occupied.

It was the government's plan to develop the frontier, and it was financially a good opportunity for the benefactors, but accessibility was exceedingly difficult, and accessibility was the key to future development.

The land to the north was not easily reachable, as the railroad terminated at Petoskey until 1882. Prior to that time, only one road stretched the forty miles from Petoskey to Cheboygan. Old State Road was a solitary ribbon of potholes, stretching as straight as it could, with no other roads extending in any direction. The road was used to transport mail, freight and persons between these two growing communities, with nothing much in between other than deep, wooded wilderness and the stage stop at Maple River/Brutus.

Settlement was also delayed pending the legal rights of previous Indian treaties covering the area. Discrepancy over land rights would continue until The Dawes Act of 1887, when the Federal Government passed a law allowing the President of the United States to break up reservation land (which was held in common by members of a tribe) into small allotments, parcel it out and grant it to individual Native Americans.

After arriving, Charles scouted the area and made an offer to purchase an abandoned eighty acre parcel just north of Alanson.[4] A small three room house sat forgotten and sadly barren in front of ten cleared acres of what was once wheat and beans. And now, as he walked deeper into the remaining seventy acres of uncleared, wooded, partially swampy land, he came upon the river. Lingering for a while, tossing stones and watching the gentle flow, he somehow felt God's pleasure.

Charles was arguably not as outwardly devout in his faith as his father had been, and certainly not as devout as his grandfather. Yet he was a man of quiet faith, and praying that God would guide his steps, he was optimistic that this new land would provide the promising future he dreamed of for himself, Ella and the children.

New Beginnings

Frank M. Joslin [5] greeted the family warmly.

"Welcome to Alanson!"

Mr. Joslin was a high-spirited and boisterous man. Becoming the depot agent and telegrapher in 1883, he had moved his wife and three children into the rugged two room log depot, next to the newly laid tracks. The family occupied one of the rooms until a house was completed that same year, on the steep hill behind the depot.

> *"My wife, Cecelia, will be so pleased to meet a fine family such as yourselves, and our children will be pleased as well to make the acquaintance of your youngsters!"* Mr. Joslin exclaimed.

Ella politely thanked Mr. Joslin.

> *"Your words are a great encouragement to us."*

She smiled, though weakly, while four-year-old James and three-year-old Alice, played a game of jumping back and forth across the rails.

> *"I see that you are expecting another little Sheldon to arrive before too long,"*

Mr. Joslin continued. *"We have no doctor here as of yet, although Petoskey is but a quick train ride away and there you'll find the assistance you may need."*

Ella was initially a little put off by Mr. Joslin's presumption that she was pregnant. Admittedly her slender body was showing quite obviously, but for a stranger to so pointedly mention it seemed too forward. And as far as referring to her possibly needing a doctor, she had already successfully delivered two children at home with no complications. Her pride bristled, yet with no hint of indignation she responded,

> *"I thank you for your gracious concern Mr. Joslin. You have been most helpful."*

To reach their newly acquired land meant crossing the Crooked River. Ella was skeptical of the large logs bound securely together, which acted as a bridge for them to cross, exclaiming,

> *"Oh dear! They haven't the means to build a proper bridge?!"*

She never intended to sound as pompous and haughty as she often did. Collecting herself, she backtracked.

"I apologize, I don't mean to be critical. I suppose my expectations have exceeded the reality of this place."

The family hadn't brought a lot with them, but several steamer trunks and a few pieces of furniture made for an awkward passage over the narrow log bridge. After crossing, the low-lying land was wet and marshy, and their shoes were soaked by the time they reached higher ground.

"Fortunately, this is August, Charles, or we would all catch our death of cold," Ella chided.

Upon reaching the shack that would become their home, Ella was deeply discouraged. Charles had told her that it needed some work, but she was not prepared for the dilapidated condition of the building. Glass was broken out from four small windows and the door swung loosely back and forth on rusted, broken hinges. Taking a deep breath, Ella prayed,

"Lord, let me be a light in this darkness!"

and picking up her corncob broom, she began to vigorously sweep.

Soon, the shack began to feel like a home. One of the first things Charles did was build a new outhouse. He then purchased a wood burning Franklin cast iron stove connected to a flue, which sat free-standing in the middle of the room, warming the family in winter as well as providing grates for cooking or for heating hot water for laundry and candle or soap making year round. Potatoes, a staple for survival, were planted in a small tilled garden close to the house.

Ella, still pretty and petite even after bearing children, possessed a well-balanced and vigorous mind. In many ways she was a proud woman. Her problematic upbringing had trained her to protect herself behind a veil of proper appearance, which gave her an increased level of self-confidence. Cleanliness and order contributed to the presentation of the life she lived. They were resolute values and in them she savored that small taste of vital personal pride. Every day she wore a clean apron and stayed the course set before her with little complaint. Although she was thought of by some who knew her as a "*fussy woman,*" it was an attribute that served her family very well.

Farm life was punishingly hard work. Up before dawn and still at it after dark, the many chores were never ending. There was wood to chop, water to draw, bread to bake, livestock to feed and children to tend. Cows needed milking, eggs needed collecting, chickens needed plucking and gardens needed weeding. For Ella and Charles, if the impulse to give up hovered overhead, the better, stronger instincts prevailed in hope for the future, and a trust in God which always triumphed.

While Ella and the children tended to the household duties, Charles focused on getting the ground ready for the following spring crops. Inclement weather seemed to dog each day, as his young team of newly acquired plow horses slowly adapted to the disking and harrowing with an old one-furrow plow. With the reins tied around his waist, Charles' hands were red and calloused from his tightly held grip on the handles. Keeping the plow the correct depth and direction, his arm strength gradually built up enough to maintain a straight line even when striking a stone, which could throw the plow off course. It was a matter of community pride to plow a perfectly straight furrow.

In the midst of unyielding work, discovering pleasure in the small things of life was always present, and necessary: the calico curtains and bedding that Ella had so loving sown; seeing chickadees on the barn wood bird feeder that Charles had made to surprise Ella; James and Alice chasing each other in a game of tag; and, of course, Ella's growing belly. All helped to make the backbreaking challenges worth it.

As autumn crept around the corner, the anticipation of the new baby grew. Finally, on November 17, 1887, Alma Emily Sheldon came into the world. No doctor was needed for this first Sheldon girl born in Michigan. Winter was fast approaching, and Ella was pleased that baby Alma had arrived before deep snows buried them into their cozy cabin.

The Sheldons and Alanson See Growth

After seven years of firmly establishing themselves in Alanson, Earl E. Sheldon was born to Charles and Ella on December 16, 1894. Four years after Earl came Leslie Lester Sheldon, born on January 11, 1898. Ella was exhausted from all the demands of motherhood. She confided to Charles,

"I should think that thirty-seven years of age is old enough to be finished with giving birth! The good Lord has granted us five healthy children. My heart is satisfied, and your quiver is full!"

Charles laughed.

"Well, it's for God to determine how full my quiver should be! But if He asks for my opinion, yes, I am quite satisfied with five arrows"

Nonetheless, God indeed had other plans. Three years later, Ella gave birth to a beautiful baby girl, born on February 3, 1901. They named her Beatrice. The family was now complete, and the overall future was promising. As challenging as the farm was, it provided enough to meagerly support them and allow for the purchase of the occasional frivolous hat. Charles never begrudged his wife's inclination for purchasing a few pieces of fine clothing or accessories, and he often chuckled at her fondness for hats. Becoming increasingly involved in their community as well as their church, they made friends and enjoyed local festivities where appearances mattered.

James, now seventeen, worked the farm with Charles, but was eager to spread his wings and head back east. Alice helped Ella with household chores, while Leslie whimpered every morning during the school year, as his brother, Earl, and sister, Alma, left him at home. They would wave and holler their goodbyes to him on their way to school, while he inevitably would break down into a puddle of tears.

"You're not old enough for school, Les, but don't worry, you will be soon enough."

Ella would try her best to comfort her active four-year-old son but to no avail. It was not until baby Beatrice was born that Leslie was finally content to be left behind by his older sister and brother. He loved his new baby sister.

Alanson

In the years following the Sheldon's arrival in 1887, Alanson saw significant growth. By 1888 Littlefield Township was created and the population steadily increased. The lumbering industry continued to expand. Charles Ormsby built a sawmill, cutting trees into lumber for houses and barns. J. S. Newberry started a mill in 1886, making shingles, until it burned to the ground just three years later. Shortly thereafter, Mr. McFarland built a new shingle mill. Booms of logs were floated to Alanson and pulled along Crooked River by a tug owned by The Hinckley Company. Lumbering and milling was profitable business [6] and attracted many a man looking for steady work, as well as a fair share of scoundrels.

A store and post office were built right across from the newly constructed depot, with its high steep trusses and spacious waiting area. A long wooden bridge replaced the old "corduroy" log bridge spanning the greenish waters of Crooked River. The rugged pioneer life that once meant a struggle for survival itself was gradually developing into small town life, even as children continued to walk from rural farms several miles to school.

Baby Beatrice

A large bucket of water boiled vigorously on the metal grate of the black iron stove. The morning sun was low in a cloudless sky. As the hard winter slowly crept away, May flowers began to bloom, bringing colorful life again to the once cold, hard ground. Ella had exhausted nearly all her candle supply over the winter, so it was time to make more. As the water boiled, she stepped outside to prepare the sheep tallow, having collected it the previous autumn. She preferred the sheep tallow rather than the pungent odor that came from pig tallow.

Lanterns and candles provided the light needed through the dark evening hours. Dipping them herself was much less expensive than purchasing them, especially when burning through more than three hundred over the course of the year. Ella rather enjoyed candle making. Twisting the cotton and linen wicks and then dipping and re-dipping until the taper was just the right size, granted satisfaction. And today would be a perfect day for this task.

Thirteen-month-old Beatrice had been sleeping inside the house, as seven-year-old Earl and four-year-old Leslie ran around the yard chasing a chicken. Suddenly Ella heard a blood curdling scream coming from the house. Rushing across the yard toward the front steps, her skirts tangled around her ankles. She grabbed her hem, pulling the material up, freeing her legs to run. Bursting through the door, the horror was immediate. Baby Beatrice lay writhing on the floor, the empty bucket of boiling water next to her scalded body. (7)

Falling to her knees beside Beatrice, Ella carefully slid her arms under the baby, her hands burning from the heat, as she lifted the small limp body to the table. Trying to hold back the overwhelming panic, she shrieked to Earl,

"Run! Get your sister!"

Fifteen-year-old Alma was working in the garden not far from the house. Leslie stood back, wide-eyed with fear, watching his mother as she quickly, yet gently, removed Beatrice's hot wet clothing.

Grabbing the flour tin, Ella dusted flour over Beatrice and delicately began to wrap her in cotton wadding.(8) Alma, panting for breath, pushed past the terrified Leslie to get to the house where her baby sister lay screaming in pain. Earl was right behind. Without looking up, Ella, her voice thick with emotion, commanded,

"Get your father. He is plowing the back ten. Hurry!"

Beatrice's breathing was shallow and raspy. Large blisters began forming across her face, and her eyes were swollen shut. Alma felt faint but obeyed her mother and ran from the house toward the field to retrieve her father. Ella glanced at the clock - it was 10 a.m.

It seemed like a lifetime before Ella heard Charles shouting at his team of horses. She recognized the fear in his voice, even at a distance. With his eyes huge with worry, Charles almost broke the door as he rushed into the house.

"Get the doctor!" was all that Ella could voice.

Seeing his baby girls burned and blistered face, chest and arms, Charles spun around as quickly as he had entered. Jumping on the bare back of his plow horse, he kicked her into motion.

Dr. Benjamin P. Pierce [9] had an office just across the Crooked River on Main Street. He was newly graduated from medical school and Alanson was his first position. Charles couldn't get the words out quick enough in explaining what had happened, and Dr. Pierce, grabbing his medical bag, rushed to hitch his horse for the ride to the Sheldon farm. Charles rode ahead, driving his horse as fast as he could to return to his baby daughter's side.

Arriving, the doctor found Beatrice in critical condition. He had seen many burn victims in his few short years in medicine, but none as heartbreaking as this one. As he gently unwrapped the cotton cloth from around her small body, and with emotion in his voice, he said to Charles and Ella,

> *"I will not mince my words. I doubt that she will survive, but I will do my best."*

It didn't take Dr. Pierce long before he realized that he simply did not have the necessary medical equipment and that his efforts would be fruitless.

> *"You must take her to the hospital in Petoskey as quickly as you possibly can. If she has any chance, it will be there."*

The train had already made its return run to Petoskey. It was too late to catch it. Charles hastily hitched the horses to the wagon. Ella gently carried Beatrice from the house, moving ever so carefully, feeling as if she was in a slow-motion nightmare. The agonizing sound of heart-wrenching moans coming from her tiny baby was more than she could bear. Ella climbed into the back of the wagon, her mind a blur of grief and regret. Charles drove the horses hard, yet constantly aware of how the bumps in the road were adding to his little girl's excruciating pain. Silent tears rolled down his thin face, wetting his thick mustache. Ella tenderly clutched her youngest child in her arms, praying for a miracle. The ten miles to Lockwood Hospital felt like an eternity. As they rode through Bay View, along the cliff overlooking Little Traverse Bay, Ella's eyes focused on the watery horizon as she prayed for God to spare her daughter's life. Thin wispy clouds caught streams of sunlight broadcasting oranges and pinks across the darkening blue sky.

Dr. John Reycraft [10] acted swiftly in attempts to save Beatrice's life, but to no avail. The severity of the burns and the shock to her tiny body was more than it could bear, and at five o'clock the following morning, Beatrice died, leaving Charles and Ella with empty arms and grieving hearts.

27

Dodge

1795-1891

Lank Dodge had a reputation as a lady's man. With a strong and well-defined face, the kind of face that made girls stop in their tracks, he easily commanded the attention that he so enjoyed. His icy gray eyes only needed to combine with his playful smile for Lank to pretty much have his way. His subdued cleft chin, cupid's lip [1], and prominent "love charm" (the indentation from just under his nose to the top of his upper lip) only added to his enticing mystique with the girls. These physical characteristics Lank had inherited from his German mother Lucy Anne "Anna", who bore them in a slightly more feminine manner.

Lank was not tall, but carried a stocky muscular build which, although not terribly intimidating, was usually enough to dissuade potential challengers. He was not one to be trifled with, and indeed, he was never one for trite politeness regardless of the company or circumstances. This "*bad boy*" persona became an early concern for his God-fearing parents. [2] His father, Reuben, would often remind his rambunctious son with the exhortation from the Scriptures, "*Bad company ruins good morals.*" Although Rueben often had to ask himself if it was actually Lank who was the "*bad company*".

Yet regardless of the company he kept or any resulting moral lapse, it was the charm and engaging humor of Lank Dodge that invariably carried him through any touchy situation. Even his parents would concede that despite Lank's occasionally corrupted choices, he was very likable.

Melanchthon (Lank) Washington Dodge was born to Reuben and Lucy Anne "Anna" Dodge (b. Shaffer) on July 4, 1871 in Ada, Ohio. He was the ninth born of thirteen children. [3] Lank admired his father, who was known as a man of inflexible conviction and deep patriotism. Reuben [4] was a fun-loving man, preferring to keep the darker side of his life experiences to himself. His Civil War memories ran especially deep and were rarely expressed. As with so many who saw the horrors of battle, the particulars of his experiences were shared in bits and pieces, like a puzzle never fully finished.

In his youth Reuben lived in Savannah, Ashland County, [5] Ohio, where he was born the youngest. His father, Calvin Dodge Sr., [6] died in 1838 when Reuben was just six years old. His mother, Nancy, a strong pioneer woman, continued to diligently raise her nine children alone, until she remarried to Henry Hull, in 1847. Having very few memories of his father, Reuben's childhood recollections centered on his three older brothers and five older sisters. As the baby of the family, his older siblings paid special care to the upbringing of little Reuben, especially his oldest brother, Calvin Jr. "Cal".

The "memories" Reuben held of his father, Calvin, came mostly from the few stories told and retold by his family. Calvin Dodge was born in Canandaigua, NY in 1795. As a teenager, Calvin volunteered in the War of 1812, a war seemingly forgotten other than the dramatic events surrounding the circumstances of a poem written by Francis Scott Key, after witnessing the bombardment of Fort McHenry by British ships in Baltimore Harbor. The poem was called the "Star-Spangled Banner". [7]

Calvin was not a man prone to reminisce or brood over the past. Although his short service in the war (enlisting with the New York 156th Militia) periodically evoked a melancholy of mind or a drunken spree. Reuben's mother, Nancy, once remarked,

> *"Your father was a bravehearted man, who would not shrink from any adversity, except that of his own introspection."*

As an impressionable eighteen-year-old, Calvin had romanticized going into battle against the powerful British empire. America was flexing its muscles with its eye toward expanding its borders westward, as Britain was enforcing new tax restrictions and supporting Indian nations in the

Northwest Territory, [8] hindering American settlers from pushing further west. The New York State Militia was prepared to do its part and young Calvin was there.

The St. Lawrence Campaign

As pale and blistered soldiers marched hundreds of miles north of Canandaigua, the fluctuating greens of dense forest treetops began to slowly transform in blinding brightness as autumn quickly approached. Oranges, yellows and reds flickered like a blazing fire against the rich blue sky. There had been no indication of British presence as the militia worked their way north. All the while, unobserved evidence of Mohawk presence remained all around them. Soldiers walked casually, confidently swapping personal exploits and future ambitions, while their Seneca, Onondaga and Tuscarora allies who travelled with them noiselessly observed the telltale traces of stealth, deadly enemy warriors stalking unseen.

Dawn broke over the bluff of the rivers eastern bank. Having arrived late the previous day, sentries had been quickly posted throughout the night, though struggling to stay awake while their bodies relaxed against sturdy trees. It was easy to become lax, underestimating an enemy they had never seen. As the shift changed, sleepy sentries casually moved back toward the center of camp. Calvin noted how they sauntered in sluggish ease without even giving a glance toward the wall of forest behind them. There were no concerns, no alarms.

The St. Lawrence Campaign was an ambitious plan intended to capture Montreal. Even so, understanding a noble objective did not improve the tedium of the journey. Although stalwart in their dedication to the cause, the weeks of travel had taken the zeal out of their steps and added a lackadaisical attitude toward their duties. It would cost them in the end.

It was November 11, 1813. Lake Ontario and the St. Lawrence River were finally within their sights. Anticipation of something more than the monotony of marching for weeks without a present goal in sight was welcome. The greater mission was closer in reality now and the men understood it.

The morning cold cut like a knife through Calvin's thin wool coat, and a light rain only added to the misery. A foggy mist fringed the riverbank as a shot rang out near their encampment. Someone shouted an alarm and a volley of gunfire followed. By midmorning came the full out assault. The American infantry advanced, driving the British and their Mohawk allies deeper through the woods. The Americans foolishly followed. Suddenly a line of redcoats rose up from behind concealment and opened fire. Calvin quickly threw himself behind an old tree stump to return fire, as a musket ball sent pieces of tree bark flying past his face. By day's end, the American attack had lost all momentum and ammunition was running low. [9] They had no recourse but to retreat.

Screams of wounded and dying men rang in Calvin's ears, adding a sickening sensibility to the mayhem and confusion of the battle. The horror of this conflict would follow him throughout his life, yet he would never verbalize details in totality to anyone, not even to his wife, Nancy. She understood that to press her husband in this matter was pointless. Bits and pieces would, from time to time, find their way to the surface in short, quick comments, allowing her to understand the trauma that her husband had experienced. But for the most part, Calvin would hold his military life in guarded silence, just as his son, Reuben, would do concerning a later war.

When Nancy Williams [10] first met Calvin Dodge in 1819, he was young and full of fire. It was love at first sight for the twenty-two-year-old Nancy, although her parents were much less enamored. Having pioneered across the Appalachians to the Northwest Territory from New Jersey after the War of 1812, Samuel Williams, Nancy's stalwart father, was preparing his family for a more prosperous future. Calvin Dodge did not appear to have the good character or practicing faith that he had hoped for his only daughter.

Samuel, being an upstanding Christian man, was rightly cautious. The frontier was infested with a class of ruffian and criminal who had escaped the clutches of the law in the older settlements. They arrived in the wilds of the west in hopes of melding into their new environment. However, all too often, their past could not be hidden or contained, and their own unseemly behavior, aided by whiskey, ultimately revealed their true nature. Calvin seemed to waver between these two opposing worlds: respected citizen or unruly hooligan.

It was the attractive Nancy Williams who helped Calvin rehabilitate his wayward and whiskey prone ways. He understood that winning the fair maiden required travelling a long road in one decent and moral direction.

Although occasional drunken binges continued to pursue his chaste resolve, Calvin's convictions were true.

"My ability to prevail is not as impressive as my ability to start over," he would say.

At that, Calvin indeed won the hand of Nancy Williams and they married on June 17, 1820, in Milton Township, Ashland County, Ohio.

Fortunately for Calvin, his wife was one possessed of the highest qualities of head and heart. Her patience and love endured until her husband's untimely death after eighteen years of marriage. The life they had built together was hard. Milton Township [11] was untamed and brought with it the usual dangers, such as rattlesnakes and wolves, but on the other hand it also provided a community of fellow pioneers sharing in the trials and triumphs of clearing and farming the clay-covered land.

It was not long before Calvin discovered that farming was not in his blood. As much as he desired to homestead, he found it too tedious. Securing work as a laborer in various mills and becoming somewhat of a jack-of-all-trades, he pieced together enough income to support his growing family. Millwork was more to his liking.

At that time, there were no towns in Milton Township. Rather, there were homesteads and farms scattered across what was once a favorite Indian hunting ground, with towering old oaks, hickory, beech and all manner of hardwood. There were no rivers flowing through the township, but many fine springs of pure water fed several small, picturesque lakes, teeming with fish, creating the ideal home.

The land was broken and hilly, quiet and serene, slowly being transformed from thick, dark forested wilderness into fertile farmland. Civilization, such as it was, could be found thirteen miles southwest, in the town of Mansfield in Richland County, providing retailers, a livery and a tavern. The village of Uniontown [12] was a few short miles from the general population in Milton Township, but it was much smaller and did not offer the variety of supplies needed.

Calvin was an affable man. While speaking with great liberty of mind, he remained liked by most. His good humor assisted his ability to secure consistent work in lumber and grist mills. The downside was relocating his family wherever work led. Richland County alone had over one-hundred eighty grist, lumber, woolen and linseed oil mills. Nearly every road led to a mill. To be sure, the mills were essential to farmers survival, and work was readily available.

Uprooting and moving was a trying event on a family the size of the Dodge family. Although young Reuben, by the time he was three years old, was spared the burden of relocation that his older siblings endured. Once the family settled in Savannah, Ohio, in Ashland County, close to the Richland County border, Calvin commuted to jobs in the nearby area. It was on one of those late-night trips home that Calvin [13] was found dead alongside the road. His horse and wagon were gone. Foul play was never determined for certain; the coroner declared it *"death by accident,"* but there were rumors and suspicions of a more sinister ending to his life. Calvin's belongings were never recovered.

Reuben often felt cheated, losing his father at such a young age. His older siblings recalled stories and would laugh together over things their father had said or done, but Reuben's memories offered only murky images. The one recollection that he owned as his very own involved walking home one cold, wintery Sunday from Hopewell Church. [14]

> *"I must have been no more 'an five years old and my little legs were struggling to keep up. My father scooped me up and set me on his shoulders, sayin', 'Someday those legs of yours will carry you sure as anything. Until then, I got you."*

It was a small thing, a simple gesture from a father who rarely involved himself in the lives of his children, but something that would stay with Reuben all his life.

Reuben's Move

When Reuben's mother, Nancy, ultimately determined *to* remarry nine years after her husband's untimely death, Reuben was not happy.

> *"I don't want to move to Arlington; it's all the way over in Hancock County. It's like living in the boondocks,"* [15]

Reuben declared with a firm stance and folded arms. He wanted his mother to understand how strongly he felt about leaving the only home he had known his entire short life. Nancy tried to encourage him:

> *"Reuben, Mr. Hull* [16] *is a fine and accomplished man. It will do us all well to appreciate the opportunities that a man like him can provide."*

But Reuben continued to resist:

> *"Ma, it's nearly one-hundred miles. I know no one there. I can't begin my life all over!"*

> *"You are just, last month, fifteen years old. You will be fine. Plus, Eleanor, Elizabeth and Fanny will be there to help you settle in, and Henry and Luther will both be working as hired hands. Our family remains together and that is what matters now. And concerning your brother Cal, my prayer is that he will return home after he gets the wandering lust out of his system."* [17]

After several more attempts to convince his mother to let him remain, including an emotional,

> *"I'd rather live in a barn as a squatter than as a field hand for Mr. Hull,"*

Nancy came to a compromise with her disgruntled son:

> *"If, after a year, you discover that you simply cannot continue to live peacefully with your family in Arlington, I will agree to make other arrangements for your accommodations. I do not know what that might look like, but we will cross that bridge if we come to it."*

For the remaining year, Reuben continued to plot how he could escape Arlington. He had hired out doing fieldwork for his brother-in-law Jacob

Tindall, in Seneca County, for two previous summers and was hopeful that Jacob would hire him once again. His sister, Samantha, ten years older, had her hands full with two toddlers and another baby on the way. Considering those added factors, Reuben felt confident that he could talk Jacob into a deal. The Tindall family was well established in Seneca County, and Reuben enjoyed the social connections afforded him. When the letter came from his sister asking him to join them, he whooped with joy. [18]

Reuben happily moved to Seneca County to live with his sister and her family early that spring. He blindly lived the day-to-day, typical of any fifteen-year-old, not concerned with his future and certainly not looking for the love of his life. Girls were not of any great consideration. As a matter of fact, he wasn't even interested in talking to girls. His attentions were elsewhere. While attending the Presbyterian Church in Bloomville, he became acquainted with the family of an extraordinary man named Thomas Blunt. Mr. Blunt had four strapping sons and Reuben was soon enjoying many an early morning fishing Honey Creek with the boisterous Blunt brothers, James, Jesse, Jefferson and Samuel.

Thomas Blunt, [19] a rugged pioneer, had lived in Bloomville as one the earliest settlers, felling tall timbers with his woodsman's axe in the deep wilderness that was to become Seneca County. He was very outspoken and talkative, with his opinions never in question. His thinning white hair, nervous temperament and stoop shoulders may have suggested weakness, but Mr. Blunt was far from weak. He was especially strident on the subject of slavery and was early in the ideals of abolitionism.

Reuben sat at the family dinner table many a night listening to Mr. Blunt expound on the evils of slavery, his fifteen year-old-mind soaking in the principles and solidifying his own stance on the humanity of the black man and the wrongdoing of slave owners. It was a severe shock when Mr. Blunt died suddenly in his sleep that same year, 1847. Reuben was grateful for the time he had spent with this man of strict conviction...a strong father figure. The lessons learned would be carried with him throughout his life and would be the catalyst for his own personal convictions in the war between the states that was brewing under the surface of a soon-to-be-divided nation.

While Reuben was bemused with the Blunt brothers and their father, a young Lucy Anne Shaffer watched from afar. She too attended the Presbyterian

Church in Bloomville. A spunky ten-year-old, Lucy Anne was more of a nuisance than anything. She always wanted to tag along when she heard the boys talking about fishing or exploring the wooded streams feeding into Honey or Silver Creek. The Blunt boys were sometimes cruel in their response. Reuben felt irritated and impatient, yet he was more gentle with his words.

Five years later, Reuben noted that Lucy Anne, who now preferred to be called *"Anna"* was a rather becoming fifteen-year-old girl, with coffee brown hair parted starkly down the middle. Her German heritage displayed itself confidently with a strong, square jaw and a delicate dimple in the center of her chin, which distracted from her thin lips and cupid's bow. Blue/gray eyes conveyed a steely intensity that few would challenge. She was not a classic beauty, although her ample figure combined with her tenacious personality was most desirable. Anna's obvious attributes did not go unnoticed by Reuben, yet the fact remained that he was not looking for love, and besides, she was still too young, and he had other priorities.

> *"We are moving west of the Mississippi, to Iowa,"* Jacob bluntly stated. *"My family has land holdings there, in Tama County.* [20] *We will be selling the farm and packing up to cross country in the spring. If you want to buy up a section of the land here, we can make an arrangement."*

Jacob was not one to mince words and certainly not one to give away the farm. He presumed that Reuben liked living in Bloomville and he was correct. Reuben was now twenty years old and well established within the small community. Being frugal with his earnings, he had saved some money, enough to purchase a small plot of land from his brother-in-law to begin farming.

Reuben and Anna

Thick dark hair was hidden under a loose fitting old felt hat. His deep-set brown eyes presented a weary appearance, with heavy lids that angled starkly downward on the outside corners. He looked melancholy or contemplative even when in joyous spirits. A straight narrow nose and thin features were accentuated by a thick, dark mustache and beard that bristled as uneven as a corncob broom. Somehow, amidst it all, came the face of a handsome and good man. Reuben Dodge was proposing marriage to Lucy "Anna" Shaffer. And as she sat solemnly with her hands in her lap, she wondered why he had kept his hat on.

Down on one knee, Reuben presented his case. Anna was confused. He had been courting her for over a year, since she had turned eighteen, but he had always seemed to hesitate with the idea of marriage. Now he proposed as if entering into a contract, not as one smitten by love.

> *"Anna, as you are aware, I have a small farmhouse and enough land to support myself and a family. You are a fine woman and it is my desire to build a life with you in marriage,"* he nervously sputtered.

> *"Indeed,"* Anna replied, *"and why have you chosen to honor me with this amazing proposal?"*

Reuben heard the sarcasm in her voice and immediately understood that he had not expressed himself in the way that he had intended. Smiling, his eyebrows lifted, and his eyes lit up,

> *"It is my deepest longing and would be my greatest honor to love you and be dedicated only to you for the rest of my life."*

At that, she pushed the hat off his head and a prolonged kiss sealed the deal.

Reuben Dodge (24 yr.) married Lucy Anne "Anna" Shaffer (19 yr.) on July 1, 1856 in Bloomville, Ohio. Ten months later their first child, Charlotte, was born. Over the course of the next four years, three more children arrived, two more girls and then, their first son, Leonard, in October of 1861. Four months before Leonard's birth, the "War Between the States" became a forlorn reality, on April 12, 1861.

The Dodge Brothers

Cal, Reuben's oldest brother, had finally sewn all of his wild oats and settled down. Although, like his father, Calvin Sr., he occasionally slipped back into his old ways. Marrying Nancy Tucker, the widow of one of his good friends, in 1848, had brought a long-needed solemn demeanor to his rowdy living. Prior to his marriage, he had seen some trouble with the law. A fight in a local tavern in 1850 saw him spend some time in prison. [21]

Cal was as passionate concerning the subject of slavery as was Reuben. Following the bombardment and surrender of Fort Sumter in April of 1861, President Lincoln called for 75,000 men to serve in the Union militia for a period of three months. Several northern states, including Ohio, communicated enthusiasm, for what was believed would be a short-lived rebellion by the southern states.

Both Cal and Reuben waited to volunteer. Cal and Nancy's seven children, all under the age of twelve, were still too young to manage the farm without him. Reuben and Anna were expecting their fourth child to arrive sometime during the fall harvest. Corresponding by letter, the two brothers agreed that if the war continued longer than was anticipated, they would do their duty and join the Union cause. As incredibly difficult as it would be for their families, they believed in the greater good and would sacrifice as needed.

When President Lincoln called for more troops, and with Congress sanctioning 500,000 additional volunteers in July, the two brothers knew that they would answer the call. Cal enlisted on Nov. 7, 1861, and Reuben followed suit on December 1st, waiting until after the birth of their baby.

Leonard Colby Dodge, Reuben's first son, was two months old when his father marched off to war. Anna Dodge was naturally very hesitant, but she supported her husband's choice. She was a strong and independent woman, yet also realistic to the suffering that was sure to ensue. She would strive to do her best to maintain the farm and care for their sizable family on her own. The truth of the matter was that the war effort was being fought on many fronts, and it was the banding together of friends, extended family, and a supportive community that gave Anna and so many others the bedrock of their endurance. And Bloomville was just such a community.

The 55th Ohio Infantry

Throughout their lives, [22] there was no one Reuben trusted more than his brother, Cal. Lying quietly with their backs pressed solidly against a small embankment, Reuben concentrated on breathing as evenly as he could. He had seen too many men hyperventilate and panic in dangerous situations. Holding a firm grip on his Henry rifle, he glanced nervously to his right where Cal lay motionless with his eyes closed.

"You sleeping?" Reuben whispered, with a hint of doubt in his voice.

"Praying," came Cal's quick reply. Reuben smiled to himself.

"That makes more sense."

Sweat poured off Reuben's face. He could smell his own pungent body odor, mingled with that of everyone around him. The brooding August heat was unrelenting. [23] He had unbuttoned his dark blue woolen jacket, attempting to get some relief. His light blue trousers were grass stained and dirty. His forage cap hid his dripping hair, while streams of sweat continued to roll over his face into his beard.

Surrounded by the enemy on a hillside near Luray, Virginia [24], Reuben's hands were slippery with perspiration as he readjusted his gun across his chest.

"Cal, do we fight or surrender?" he asked of his brother.

"It's up to the officers," Cal replied in quick, whispered tones. *"But, no sense in a fight. We're outgunned and no place to go."*

The bulk of the 55th Ohio Infantry was spread out across sixteen miles of land between Luray and Sperryville. A battle was shaping up for the next day, one that neither Cal nor Reuben would participate in. [25] They were both captured on August 8, 1862. The two languished in the oppressive summer sun for several hours, along with several dozen other Union prisoners of war. They waited anxiously for their fate to be determined. The Confederate Army was amassing to the west, and with no easy means of dealing with the burden of captured troops, Cal and Reuben were hopeful for paroles and exchange of prisoners.

Parole of Honor was ultimately decided upon, as Confederate troops were on the move eastward toward Cedar Mountain. The two brothers were presented with the exchange agreement which Reuben solemnly read:"

> *"I, the undersigned, Prisoner of War, Private Reuben Dodge, 55th Ohio Infantry, captured near Luray, Virginia hereby give my Parole of Honor not to bear arms against the Confederate States, or perform any military or garrison duty whatever, until regularly exchanged; and further, that I will not divulge anything relative to the position or condition of any of the forces of the Confederate States. This 8th day of August 1862."* (26)

Then, he reluctantly signed his name to the agreement. The two of them were released to return to Camp Chase in Columbus, Ohio. (27)

Some could afford the train fare, but some walked the three hundred miles to their designated garrison. Either way, bitter resentment was created among many of the paroled prisoners. In some cases, there was total dereliction of duty as Union soldiers. What was clear was that *nothing* was clear. Expectations and interpretations of duty varied from one paroled soldier to the next. Extreme heat and weary bodies only aggravated what was already an unpleasant and confusing circumstance. By the time they reached Camp Chase, without officers and with the conflicting opinions of duties proper for them, rebellious spirits insisted that the terms of their parole precluded them from performing any military duties whatsoever. Cal and Reuben, however, remained less agitated, knowing that home was a mere eighty miles to the north.

Conditions at Camp Chase were appalling. Most of the windows were broken out and stuffed with old hats and caps to keep the weather out. What windows remained were stained a rusty black from utter neglect. Plank roofs left gaping crevices to skylight the dismal interior. Rainy days brought wet bedding and damp clothes, while sunny days brought stifling heat and sweat- drenched bodies. With some two thousand disgruntled Union parolees, along with 1,726 Confederate prisoners also being housed at the Camp, conditions could not have been much worse.

The Dodge brothers petitioned to be allowed to return to their homes until a letter of exchange arrived, which would free them at that time to return to active duty. Their petition was granted, and to their joy both men rejoined their families, worked their farms, and returned to "normal" daily life during wartime. Meanwhile, conditions at Camp Chase continued in a state of chaos. Rations were in short supply and many of the men turned to marauding nearby farms, with local farmers complaining of missing fence rails and slaughtered hogs. There was an ever-growing exasperation among the paroled men who were tired of "playing soldier" and fretful of the government's failure to prepare them as Union parolees. Not until the exchange process freed enough Confederate prisoners to lighten the unbearable load did conditions begin to slightly improve.

By the time Reuben received his letter of exchange and rejoined the 55th Ohio Infantry for active duty in April of 1863, [28] Anna was expecting their fifth child. Through tears, she bid him farewell once again, not knowing whether he would return. Her faith sustained her, and she put on a brave face as she stood on the front porch with two-year-old Leonard firmly on her hip, weakly waving until Reuben was out of sight. The older children chased each other around the yard on that warm spring morning, laughing and teasing each other, unaware of the horrors of war their father would soon face. [29]

The Civil War Ends

The war finally ended in April of 1865. On July 11, Reuben was mustered out of service with the Union forces. The previous day, he had packed his belongings, settled up with payroll, and relaxed with some reading before attending a prayer meeting that evening. While rubbing his sore knee, he jokingly said to Cal,

"We may now call ourselves 'Brave Citizens'."

Cal cast a half smile toward Reuben and absentmindedly repeated,

"Brave citizens,"

But in his mind's eye he could only remember the many friends and fellow soldiers who had died or been severely wounded. Gettysburg in particular brought tears to his eyes as the image of thousands of dead lay scattered across the field of battle. It was an image that both he and Reuben would carry with them for a lifetime.

28

Davis and Wingate

1842-1895

Leaning over to kiss Miss Julina Davis, Lank lost his balance and almost embarrassingly fell from his horse. Albeit, it took a lot to embarrass Lank Dodge. Riding side-by-side, the two starry-eyed lovers could barely take their eyes off of each other, as their horses tangled tightly together. The excitement and romance of the previous weeks had a tight hold on them. Julina knew Lank's reputation with the ladies and found tormenting him with teasing flirtations an amusing pastime. While Lank found her voluptuous figure and playful banter to be a vexing complexity of both pleasure and exasperation. Julina was a strong woman.

Lank had known of Julina his entire life. Her father, William Washington Davis, [1] was well respected in the community and her older brother, Anderson, was a good friend to Lank. The Davis family settled in Hardin County, Ohio in 1842, when William was just twelve years old. Prior to that, his family had pioneered through dense forest and rugged land to hack out of the wilderness a new life for themselves and their children. Alvin and Lavina Davis (b. Seeley) built a cabin west of Johnstown (later renamed Ada), Hardin County. [2] They cleared the land and began farming.

However, their son, William, Julina's father, soon found farming was not for him, and that mill work better suited his temperament. After he met and married Sarah "Sadie" Davis (b. Wingate), on December 30, 1852, they took up residence in Orange Township, Hardin County, five miles north of Johnstown where he operated a sawmill for the entirety of his life. The couple raised twelve children in a small two-story colonial house with no dormers. Two single windows flanked a simple front door, which hung in the center of the house. A narrow front porch, large enough for two rockers, provided Sadie many hours of comfort and quiet as she sat snapping beans or peeling potatoes on warm summer days. The railing of the porch served nicely as a hitching post for the horses.

Sadie had journeyed with her family from Tuscarawas County, Ohio, in November of 1844, arriving in Hardin County on Christmas Eve. Sadie was twelve years old, when her father, Samuel Berton Wingate (Julina's grandfather) purchased land on the edge of the Black Swamp area, about one-and-one-half miles north of Johnstown. Several relatives already lived in the surrounding territory when Samuel and Sarah Wingate (b. Tressel), Sadie's parents, arrived with eleven of their children in tow, many of whom were very young.

The Wingate's [3] would go on to have five more children adding to the eleven God had blessed them with. Sadly, forty-five-year-old Sarah died upon the birth of her sixteenth child, Daniel, in 1850. For two years following the death of her mother, Sadie did everything she could to help her father with the baby and her eight younger siblings who still remained at home, until she married William Davis, in December of 1852, at the age of twenty.

Sadie Wingate and William Davis had met each other as teenagers. Sadie's older sister, Elizabeth Ann, married William's older brother, Alvin, in 1848. It was while circling the dance floor at the reception that something sparked, and from that point on Sadie and William had eyes only for each other. They married in Ada, Ohio and went on to have twelve children, six boys and six girls. Julina Priscilla Davis came along, May 6, 1873, eleventh, with her sister Flora being the last born at number twelve, in 1875.

Flirtations

Anderson Davis [4] had convinced Lank Dodge to join him at the county fair that day. It was July and hot, and Lank was not really in the mood.

He had worked with his father, Reuben, on a plastering [5] job all day and was tired. But refusing Anderson was not always the easiest. He had a persuasive way about him.

"Come on! You know there'll be lots of girls there!"

With that, Lank agreed and after splashing his face with cool water and combing Macassar oil [6] into his thick dark hair, carefully smoothing it into place, he was ready.

It was late in the day as Lank waited to meet up with Anderson. He casually strolled along the fairway, his hands thrust deep into his pockets, observing the horses, cattle and hogs on display in their respective categories of competition.

"This is ridiculous,"

he thought to himself, as three rambunctious young boys pushed past him in the crowd. Just as he was about to forget the whole thing and head out to find some excitement, he spotted Anderson and moaned to himself,

"He has his little sisters with him! Unbelievable!"

Before he could duck out of sight, Anderson spotted him and began waving frantically and yelling,

"Lank! Lank! Over here!"

It was unavoidable. He was stuck.

"Lank, you remember my sisters, Julina and Flora, right? Sorry we made you wait."

And then under his breath, Anderson confessed,

"Mother wouldn't let me go without having them tag along. Not the sort of evening I had in mind."

Lank forced a weak smile and then turned to the girls,

"Nice to see you girls again."

Although he had no real recollection of having met them before.
    Julina was a quick study of people. She frowned and responded,

"Really? It's nice to see us again, you say. What's my name?"

She assumed that he would not know it, even though Anderson had just introduced them. But Lank was not one to be pushed so easily into a corner,

"Your name is "I am a child and should be at home with my momma."

Julina, though a little annoyed at his response, laughed. She liked him.

"I am sixteen and more of a grown woman than you will ever know."

And with that, she marched off in the opposite direction, hiding the smile on her face. This girl was fierce. Lank liked what he saw. [7]

Lank and Julina Begin Life Together

A westerly wind swept across the ground, sending dried brown leaves swirling in the air. It was one of those unusually warm autumn days. The sky was clear with but a few high clouds casting the occasional dark shadow across an otherwise sunlit morning. Eighteen-year-old Julina Davis absentmindedly watched from an open window on the north end of the grand Hancock County courthouse [8], as a coal oil wagon stopped across the street.
    Smoothing the front of her dress, she turned to her fifty-nine-year-old mother.

"Well, how do I look?"

Sadie smiled at her daughter,

"Lovely. Absolutely lovely!"

Julina's sixteen-year-old sister, Flora, expounded more enthusiastically.

"It's all so romantic! Your wedding day! I love your dress and your hair!"

Julina's wedding dress was fairly simple. The grey-green silk fabric with silver beading on the lapels, across the bottom of the flowing skirt and along the bottom of the bodice provided an elegance, while at the same time it was meant for use beyond this special day. Julina had removed the small bustle from the back of the dress, laughing,

"I can fill that out all on my own!" [(9)]

As Lank watched his bride walk down the aisle, he noted, with a smile, her full figure and her unruly hair. Julina indeed fit snugly into her dress, while her long, thick dark hair was forever uncooperative. Piling her curls high on her head, as per the fashion of the day, frizzy short bangs, intended to be uniformly crimped, refused to befriend her forehead. Yet, none of that mattered as they stood shoulder-to-shoulder, evenly matched, facing the justice of the peace at the Hancock County courthouse.

The joy of the day replaced a portion of sorrow that held a firm grip on the Dodge family. The unexpected death of Lank's sister, Clara, five months earlier, at just twenty-five, had shaken them to the core with grief. This wedding was a welcome opportunity to celebrate and, in a sense, move on with life. The family was very fond of Julina and they welcomed her gladly.

The Dodge and Davis families would soon see an even greater connection. Two years after Lank and Julina married, Lank's brother, William, married Julina's sister, Catherine. And still later, Lank's sister, Dora Belle, married Julina's brother, George. That was the same year, on June 28, 1893, that Lank and Julina gave birth to a beautiful baby girl. They named her Gladys Louise Dodge and she became the center of their life together.

Both the Dodge and Davis families were known for their musical talents. Lank Dodge played a violin with clear, sharp tones. Fiery, foot stomping rhythms filled a room with infectious energy. His new young wife played the pump organ, and together they would have a grand time playing for parties and dances with vibrant bold melodies. After Gladys was born, Julina's time and energy was taken up with her young daughter. Social activities were set aside for a time and Lank quickly became restless.

Anderson, Julina's brother, although two years older than Lank, preferred to play the field as a single man. His lifestyle afforded him a freedom that he relished, and as was his custom he often invited Lank along to embellish in a night of drunkenness, which always made Julina mad. Her anger was fueled by the knowledge that it wasn't always her brother who dangled the proverbial carrot in front of Lank, but all too often it was the other way around. She understood very well that her husband had a wild, wandering streak in him.

While on one hand Lank was prone to occasional drunkenness and partying, he could also at times seem to be a very God-fearing man, walking the straight and narrow and becoming quite religious. He was always straddling the fence of two opposing lives. He would promise Julina that he could change, that he could be a man to walk the good and moral path. But it never took long for him to revert back to his old, roaming ways. God was not personal for Lank. God was a religion with lots of do's and don'ts. Religion brought boredom.

"Babe", as they called Gladys, was twenty months old when her father and Uncle Anderson decided to make a raid on a rich farmer's meat house. It was stocked with pork, and in a moment of devilishness, the two broke in and helped themselves.[10] The next day, law enforcement was hot on their trail, as the farmer was angry and wanted to see justice, suspecting that Lank and Anderson were the culprits.

On the Run

"Julina, I'm on the run from the law. Anderson and I are going to jump a freight train tonight, heading north, to Michigan. Once I am safely out of the state, I'll contact you to join me."

Lank was speaking fast and his breathing was labored as he hurried to pack a small duffle bag. Julina was furious.

> *"How could you do this!? I have Babe to care for and a baby on the way! You expect me to leave the only home I've ever known and move to some God-forsaken land I've never set eyes on?"*

Lank understood her anger.

> *"It'll be fine. It'll all blow over. It was just a prank."*

He tried to calm her, but she was beyond any reasoning that he had to offer.

> *"A prank! Is that what you call it? You have upset our family, risked your own future and brought chaos into our lives, all for a prank?"*

The lonesome whistle echoed through the dark night. A light snow dusted the ground as the two men ran alongside the slowly moving train. Anderson, taller and faster, quickly jumped through the open door and into the boxcar. Swinging his long legs around, he threw himself onto his belly and reached for Lank. The train was picking up speed as Lank clutched Anderson's outstretched hand. With one awkward leap, he was on. Both men fell back laughing.

A cold March wind whipped through the boxcar as the noisy freight train clicked its rhythm across long stretches of isolation. Pulling into the depots of small towns along the way, Lank and Anderson carefully avoided detection and scavenged for food. Their exact destination was unsure, but they had heard stories of work available in the logging camps of northern Michigan.

29

Lank and Julina
Dodge in Michigan

1895-1909

"You have a son!" the doctor pronounced.

Julina's mother, Sadie, had sent for the doctor when contractions had extended for far too long. In the end, baby Freddy was delivered safely at home, a strong healthy boy. Julina was elated.

> *"Babe, you have a baby brother!"*, she weakly called over to
> Gladys, who was not yet two years old. [1]

An irritated sadness swept over Julina, as she sat up in bed nursing her newborn son. Lank was working in a place called Oden, Michigan. He had found a little house for them to settle into, sending a letter for her to join him. They would begin a new life together. Julina was lonely and she missed her fugitive husband but traveling with a newborn and a young child would have to wait several months. Despite her frustrations over Lank's foolish behavior, the love she had for her husband pulled her to reunite with him.

By August Freddy was thriving. Boarding the train at the Ada depot, Julina was overwhelmed with grief. As she sat down on the hard bench, she pressed her face against the window and weakly waved to her parents and siblings who had gathered to see her off. Gladys excitedly ran up and down the train aisle squealing with joy as the train jerked to a start. [2] Julina held four-month-old Freddy firmly in her lap, anticipating a difficult journey alone with a rambunctious two-year-old and an infant.

After several days of exhausting travel, they finally arrived at the Petoskey depot. Scanning the crowd, Julina spotted Lank, and her heart leaped in her chest. There he stood, in his rumpled suit with his felt slouch hat firmly set on his head. His handsome face was suntanned dark. He looked fit and trim, as his eyes darted from one window to the next trying to find her. Gathering her belongings and corralling Gladys toward the door, she was anxiously pushing past other passengers to disembark and reach the platform.

Lank sprinted toward them, as Gladys ran ahead yelling, *"Papa!"* Swooping up his little girl in his arms, he joyously swung her around. Julina, not one prone to crying, laughed as tears of joy and relief rolled down her cheeks. They hugged and kissed, with Freddy squished between them. Apologizing for her womanly emotions, she said,

> *"I swear, I've cried more in the past month than all my life combined. I'm just a mess! I never wanted to be one of those silly over-wrought types, but here I am behaving like a giddy schoolgirl."*

Collecting their baggage, they loaded into a wagon that Lank had rented and headed north from the Petoskey depot, toward Oden, a distance of about eight miles.

As they rode north through Bay View along the high bluffs overlooking Lake Michigan, Julina marveled at the beauty.

> *"There is so much water! It looks like an ocean,"* she exclaimed.

Lank laughed,

> *"Yes, it surely does. I knew you'd be surprised."*

They continued on until they came to a large lake. The water glistened in the sun and Julina could see shadowed, wooded hills on the far side.

"What's this one called?" she asked.
"Crooked Lake. Not much further now and we'll be home."

She gently jostled Freddy in her arms to settle him down, while Gladys sat snuggly between them on the seat, intrigued with the team of horses diligently pulling the wagon, her eyes heavy with sleep. It was late afternoon, well past nap time.

Tragedy Strikes

Lank had found work in the lumbering camp around Oden and was eager to help his young family settle into their new world. The small house he had secured was very meager, but it had a solid cook stove and a stone fireplace. It would do just fine until they found something better. Julina quickly adapted and settled in for the approaching winter.

As autumn gave way unexpectedly early, a crisp blanket of white snow covered the ground. It was a Sunday morning and Lank had a surprise for the family. A friend at the Haskins Livery in Alanson had offered the use of his sleigh. Lank knew that both Julina and Gladys would love nothing more than to be outside enjoying the fresh air and the thrill of a sleigh ride. Gladys squealed with excitement when she saw the horses. They climbed on and covered themselves in blankets.

"Hang on Babe! Here we go!" Lank shouted, and off they went.

Snow crystals glistened. The sun felt warm against the cold afternoon breeze. After an hour of gleefully singing random songs, Lank pulled back on the reins and the horse obediently made a tight turn around. As they looked in the distance, they could see black smoke billowing over the treetops. Julina's heart sank, fearing the worst. Lank whipped the horse to a fast trot to get to the house as quickly as possible. The house was engulfed in flames. Everything they owned was lost.

Lank found temporary shelter for the family in an abandoned railway boxcar which was quickly converted into a makeshift house. Needless to say, it would not serve as a satisfactory dwelling. Fortunately, after a few days,

Lank was able to secure some space over the top of a dancehall in Alanson. [3] Little Freddy had developed a cold during their stay in the boxcar. Every night Julina paced the floor over the noise of the dancehall, with him in her arms, as he struggled to breathe. However, he was not improving. He had been desperate for air throughout the night, his breathing raspy and labored. Finally, he settled into a deep sleep, and Julina, exhausted, slept as well. Gladys climbed out of bed early.

"Mama. Mama", she said, tapping her mother's arm.

Julina woke with a start and quickly realized that Freddy was not breathing. [4]
After desperate attempts to revive him, Lank and Julina's precious six-month-old son was gone.

"I feel as if God himself has cursed us,"

Julina said, her mind numb with sorrow.

"We have lived here only a few months and have lost all of our worldly possessions in a fire, and now we have lost our Freddy. If it wasn't for Babe, I would be completely undone."

Lank also grieved deeply and felt tremendous guilt for the calamities that he felt he had brought upon his family, a guilt that would haunt him for many years. [5]

Squatters

Lank's personality was one that made him never afraid to take a risk. When he heard of eighty acres and a decent house that could be homesteaded across Crooked Lake in the "town" of Epsilon, which amounted to a store and a post office, he quickly acted.

"Julina, pack your bags, we're moving."

Julina didn't need any convincing. For two years they had lived over the dance hall. As much as she enjoyed music, playing the pump organ with Lank on the violin, she was becoming impatient with Lank's many friends who kept all hours of the night playing music and drinking. And then there was little Gladys who was now four years old and was growing up over a dance hall. Julina wanted a more stable life for "*Babe*", who was already chording on the organ and playing for dances with her parents. She had a natural ear for music. A true gift.

A few days after moving into the house in Epsilon, a gentleman came knocking at the door. His face red with anger, he demanded,

> "*Who are you?*"

Lank confidently responded that he was Melanchthon "Lank" Washington Dodge and he was homesteading this property with his family. [6]

> "*This is my property! You are trespassing, and I'll have the law after you if you aren't out of here by tomorrow!*" the man continued to shout. "*I don't know who you are, but I am within my legal rights,*" Lank retorted, slamming the door shut.

The next day, an officer from Petoskey rode up on a brown, jittery gelding. Lank had gone to work at the mill in Alanson, and Julina was serving coffee to a house guest, Orpha Headley, [7] a new acquaintance from the lumbering community.

> "*Good afternoon ma'am. I am an officer of the law, and I am here to inform you that you and your family are trespassing and will need to vacate these premises immediately.*"

Stepping resolutely in front of him, Julina stated firmly,

> "*I certainly will not.*"

Pushing his way into the house, he demanded,

"You will remove yourself!"

"I will not!" she responded a second time, raising her voice.

The officer abruptly picked up a chair and began to carry it out toward the door. *"I will even help you!"* he arrogantly stated. At that, Julina had enough. She grabbed him by the shoulders, for he was a small man and she was a sizable woman and hoisted him through the door. He stumbled, lost his balance and fell onto the ground. Flustered and angry, he cursed and exclaimed,

> *"I'll have you arrested for laying your hands on an officer of the law!"*

Orpha, who had stepped out onto the porch, calmly reached into her handbag and boldly pulled out a Smith & Wesson revolver. Pointing it in his direction, she didn't say a word but glared intently, and as quickly as his short legs allowed, he mounted his horse, kicked into a trot and was down the road sputtering threats all the way.

Julina stood in the doorway, stunned by the developments, as Orpha laughed.

> *"You danced that little man right out of the house!"*
>
> *"Orpha! I didn't know you had a gun!"*
>
> *"Well I do,"* Orpha boasted, *"and I'm not afraid to use it if I have to."*

When Lank came home, Julina excitedly recounted to him what had happened. He chuckled to himself.

> *"Orpha is one tough character and no bluff. So far, she apparently hasn't killed anyone, but she supposedly shot a girl she was jealous of."*

From that point on, Julina stayed clear of Orpha Headley.

With all of Lank's faults, he was well liked and had many friends. A plan was hastily created to solve the problem with the law and successfully homestead the property. The entire work crew from the lumber mill arrived one night and built a shanty right next to the house that was finished by mid-morning and served as temporary housing and allowed them to claim the land as homesteaders while the house remained empty. That ended the legal battle, and they were soon able to move back in and make the house a home, which it would be for over eight years. Clearing the land of timber and selling it was profitable, and they did well enough that Julina was able to hire live-in help around the house.

Lank: Prone to Wander

The spirit of a restless vagabond lingered deeply in Lank, and a rambling lust took hold of his heart. Life was comfortable for him and his family, and they were enjoying their friendships and life in the community. However, the mundane could not hold him. The timber was gone, and the money had been good, allowing Lank a means to, as he said, *"see the world."* At the same time, Julina was lonely for her family back in Ada, Ohio. Lank thought it the opportune time to make his argument.

> *"Julina, I want to travel. I need some adventure, and you want to see your family. We have the money, so let's both get what we want."*

Convincing Julina that it was a reasonable idea, Lank sold the property, unfortunately for next to nothing, took his thirty-year-old wife and ten-year-old daughter back to Ada, and set off to explore the country. [8]

Julina's parents, William and Sadie Davis, happily welcomed their daughter and granddaughter into their home, but had serious reservations over Lank's irresponsible behavior.

> *"A man should look after the welfare of his family before his own selfish desires,"* said Julina's father, William Davis.

She knew that he was right, but she also knew that Lank always found a way.

Living back in Ada with her parents, enjoyable memories of her childhood washed over Julina. And while Lank was off *"seeing the world"*, she did not hesitate to have some fun herself, exploring old haunts, reuniting with old friends and spending time laughing and playing music with her family. Young Gladys became a special center of attention when she would sit down at a piano and without any sheet music, pound out any tune given her, and in any key. Gladys's musical abilities brought Julina a great sense of motherly pride.

Letters from Lank came sporadically and from various parts of the country, from the Dakotas to the Carolinas. After a little over a year, a letter arrived from Lank requesting money, telling Julina that he was ready to come home. Arriving back in Ada, Lank told stories of all he had experienced. He had seen the Appalachian Mountains and the Atlantic Ocean, the wheat fields of North Dakota and the plains of Kansas. Julina's father was not impressed.

> *"Self-absorption distorts the big picture and destroys the deeper, sweeter, simpler things that matter, replacing them with an empty meaningless life."*

His words sounded harsh unless you knew his heart. William loved his daughter, but he also loved his son-in-law. His words came from a place of great tenderness and concern.

Lank was not interested in remaining in Ada. He saw his future back in Northern Michigan where he knew he could find work again in the lumber camps. His father, Reuben, had a good horse and an old buggy.

> *"Father, I'll pay you double the worth of that ancient buggy and nag you have in that rundown barn."*

Reuben laughed,

> *"Son, you do have a way with words. Tell me the worth and we'll talk."*

Lank and Reuben came to an agreement, and within the week Lank was off again. This time, he was headed back to Northern Michigan. [9]
The lumbering business in and around Alanson, Brutus and Pellston was booming. Lank found work in a lumber camp near Alanson and sent for Julina and Babe to join him. However, this time there was no house.

Living and moving from one lumber camp to the next, they were in the truest sense vagabonds. As a result, schooling for Babe was occasional and random. Education was an afterthought and a luxury, but not a priority.

Gladys as a Teenager

Finally, in the winter of 1907, at the age of fourteen, Gladys began to regularly attend the Alanson School. She was behind her own age group academically, and the school determined to put her in the sixth grade. Being physically mature for her age, she could easily pass for a girl of seventeen or eighteen. Of course, she attracted a lot of attention, some of it flattering and some hurtful. She felt self-conscious and out of place.

While the boys were especially enamored with her long black hair, full figure, quick wit and feisty personality, the girls were quite jealous and mean spirited. Gladys made few friends and was eager to quit. Eleven-year-old Leslie Sheldon was one of the boys in her class who was enamored with this new girl and fell smitten. But the fact remained, she was much older and had no interest in a skinny, pale schoolboy four years younger. It was simply a juvenile crush. Later, they would laugh together over their youthful encounter, but for now Leslie was just a boy to be ignored.

Gladys continued to rebel against attending school. She was intelligent, talented and creative, but every day it was a struggle for her to go. Comparing herself to other girls, even though a striking beauty, she always came up short. In the spring the family followed the lumber camp to Indian River and her parents allowed her to quit school altogether. She had made it through the eighth grade.

Men were beginning to notice Gladys. One young man in particular had aimed his attention in her direction. His name was Dale Flick. [10] He was a handsome, educated twenty-year-old Alanson boy who had secured a job in Chicago as a bookkeeper. Gladys had met Dale the prior summer when she was fifteen, and her girlish heart was stricken. He was very shy and unassuming; she was young, naive and a bit flirtatious, and used her feminine ways to draw Dale's attention.

Lumber Camp

By autumn of that year, the Dodge family had moved yet again. This time, they followed the lumber camp to Brutus, three miles north of Alanson. Twice a week, Gladys would walk the dusty road, cutting across fields of harvested wheat, to the Brutus post office, hoping for another love letter from Dale. Their long-distance love affair was growing serious.

Evenings in the lumber camp brought people together. Fires blazed as violins, banjoes, trumpets, drums and various instruments played loud, lively tunes. Clapping, stomping, singing and making general merriment was just the ticket after long hard days of camp life. Men, exhausted from a long day's work, leaned back drinking and telling stories, as shadows cast by dancing children played in the tall dark forest behind them. Women relaxed from their heavy chores and recounted the day's events, knowing that tomorrow would be more of the same.

This particular autumn night was no exception. As the fires were doused, everyone settled into their tents to sleep. During the night, a strong north wind picked up, reigniting some small embers, swirling them into the air, with some of them landing in the tops of tall dry trees a short distance from the camp. Suddenly everyone was awakened by the yell, *"Fire!"*. Men quickly sprang into action, but their desperate attempts to stop it proved fruitless, as the wind shifted its course and would not die down. It was a lost cause and it soon became apparent that it was heading directly toward the camp. Abandoning their efforts, the men came running, exhorting their wives and children,

> *"We've got to go now! It's moving this way fast and we don't have much time!"*

Julina began furiously packing their supplies. Bedding was quickly stripped off the bunks, and food and dishes were thrown into any baskets and boxes they could find. Gladys helped her mother while keeping a sharp eye on the fires raging and getting closer by the minute. The crackling and roaring of the inferno was only interrupted by shouts of panicked men and women, crying children and falling trees.

Lank swiftly harnessed the team of horses to the wagon. Pulling his red handkerchief over his mouth and nose, he called to Julina,

"Load up now! There's no more time! Where's Gladys?!"
"I'm here!" Gladys yelled as she jumped onto the back of
the wagon.
"Let's go!"

With the reins gripped in each hand, Lank gave them a quick jerk.

"Get up!"

And with that, the team of horses started with a jolt, already wild-eyed
and nervous. But a few yards down the road, the horses suddenly spooked,
tossing their heads in fear as a tall pine came crashing down across the road
in front of them, ablaze with flames. Lank stood up and slapped the reins.

"Get up, Bess! Get up!" [11]

Taking off at a dead run, they jumped the tree at its narrowest point,
wagon and all.

"Lank! Stop! Gladys fell off!" Julina shouted in a panic.

Looking back, Lank saw Gladys jumping to her feet, laughing as she ran
to catch the wagon.

"I guess she's fine," Lank replied. *"She just bounced right up
off the ground!"*

The moment of levity brought a much-needed laugh and Gladys thought
it great fun.

Pulling into a large open field a good safe distance from where the
fire persisted, they laid out their bedding to spend the night. Others from
the camp joined them. All had stories to share of close calls and narrow
escapes, and Gladys, loving the adventure, enjoyed every bit of it. To be
thrown from a wagon in the middle of a raging forest fire would be a story
she would be able to tell for years to come.

Gladys Marries Dale

While Gladys was experiencing the wilds of camp life, Dale Flick had accepted an offer for work in Detroit. Arriving back in Alanson for a short visit to see his parents late in the summer of 1909, Dale's greater motive was to gain Lank's approval to marry Gladys. In the meantime, his mother smugly remarked,

> *"You'll be sorry if you marry that girl. She'll most likely turn out just like her mother, brazen and flirtatious."*

Mary Louise Flick was a bitter and unhappy woman who was accustomed to getting her own way. Nonetheless, Dale ignored her pretentious warning and after asking Lank for Gladys's hand in marriage, he traveled back to Detroit to wait for an answer.

Gladys, though only sixteen years old, was eager to accept Dale's proposal. Convincing her parents that this was the life she dreamed of, Gladys was soon on her way, with her parents, to the big city and to the man with whom she anticipated spending the rest of her life. It was all very romantic and exciting!

Gladys Louise Dodge married Dale Martin Flick on November 6, 1909. It was a simple ceremony in the county courthouse. [12] Moving into a small house, the couple began their life together, with her parents living with them. Gladys was especially happy to have her mother close at hand, since Dale worked long hours. As a young wife, Gladys would need all the encouragement and advice that Julina could give her. They were as much friends as they were mother and daughter and they spent hours talking and laughing together.

Married life agreed with Gladys and she was quickly learning how to keep house, something she had never done before. Her mother helped her with cooking skills, and as the bleakness of winter arrived, she was becoming adept at baking pies. Life was happy and Gladys felt safe and content.

But Dale held a deep, dark secret. And that secret was about to change everything.

30

Difficult Choices

Lank did not care for city living. When word came from Ada that his mother was ailing, he and Julina made the difficult decision to move back to help with her care. Julina was torn. She did not want to leave Gladys, yet her own father, William Davis, was also aging quickly and she believed that if she waited too long, she may not have the chance to see him again.

Standing at the train depot on a warm August morning, Gladys sadly watched as the train pulled away. Dale stood with his arm around her, but a coughing spell overtook him, and he had to step away to spit the phlegm from his throat. Gladys worried about him, for it seemed that his cough was getting worse.

> *"Dale, you need to see a doctor,"* she said.
> *"I have already seen a doctor,"* he replied.

Then, wiping some blood from the corner of his mouth, Dale took a deep breath and began.

> *"Gladys, I have to tell you something. I am sorry that I have not told you Sooner, but I was afraid to. I have contracted tuberculosis."*

Gladys was stunned.

"But how long have you known this?"

"I suspected it over a year ago, but I feared that you would not marry me if you knew. I spoke with my parents and they thought it best that I wait to tell you."

Her mind was swirling with a mixture of thoughts and emotions - confusion, betrayal, fear, anger, worry.

"What about this baby?" Gladys asked. *"We can't expose a baby to TB!"*

"I know. With the baby coming, I knew that I could not keep this from you any longer. I am so sorry," his voice weak and contrite.

Over the next few weeks, they discussed the options. Unsure of what to do, it was finally decided that they would join her parents back in Ada. [1] Dale had suggested that they return to Alanson where his parents could be of assistance, but Gladys had no real use for John and Mary Flick, especially after realizing that they had kept the news of Dale's illness from her. And now, she was not about to give up her firstborn child to them. She would willingly risk her own life to be a wife to Dale, but not that of her child, and the only other person she would trust was her mother. So they packed up their belongings and moved to Ada.

Blaine Martin Flick was born September 3, 1910 in Ada, Ohio. [2] Gladys was seventeen years old and practically a baby herself when thrust into the role of motherhood, as well as caregiver to her ailing husband. Dale suffered with weight loss and a persistent cough, while his immune system continued to weaken. Chronic fatigue plagued him. His parents begged them to return to Alanson and it was ultimately decided that for Dale's well-being they would move back. Packing their bags once again, in early spring of 1913 they boarded the train heading north. Gladys was now expecting her second baby.

Considering the situation, there was really no question that Lank and Julina would also relocate back to Michigan. Gladys was their only child and she needed them. Furthermore, there was no way that Julina would allow Mary Flick the opportunity to get her hands-on Blaine and the new baby to come. Julina was as possessive as a mother hen and always felt that Gladys's babies were her own, and in one sense, they were. Blaine had lived with his grandparents since he was born, and now this new baby would as well. In Julina's mind and heart, it was not even up for discussion; they would move back to Alanson, or the ends of the earth for that matter. And besides, any opportunity to twist the proverbial knife into Mary Flick's heart was relished. Julina held a deep hatred toward this woman who had permitted their daughter to marry Dale, all the while knowing of his illness.

The timing for a return to Alanson for Lank and Julina was ideal, although not without its heartache. Julina's father, William Washington Davis, had passed away on October 19, 1911 and Lank's mother, Lucy Ann "Anna" Dodge, sadly succumbed to death's door one year later, on October 11, 1912. As painful as it was saying a final goodbye to their beloved parents, the even greater sadness was leaving their surviving parents. Julina's eighty-one-year-old mother, Sadie, as well as Lank's father, Reuben, now eighty, were both healthy, but age was naturally taking its toll.

Sadie Davis deeply grieved for her husband, William. They had been married for fifty-nine years, and now she suddenly found herself alone. Even the myriad of twelve children and fifty-plus grandchildren could not fill the void. She was as frail as a twig, [3] yet she chose to live independently in the home that she and William had shared. The two-story house located just east of Ada gave her comfort and security. Julina admired her mother's emotional strength and stalwart resolve.

Reuben Dodge [4] also refused to leave his home. He would continue to work for as long as he had any energy left in him. Ignoring the aches and pains that come with age, he was as stubborn as the day was long. Through the horrors of war, the challenges of pioneering a new land, the birth of thirteen children and having lost two of them, and now the death of his beloved wife after fifty-six years of marriage, Reuben had become a strong and self-reliant man.

Lank fondly recalled in later years a conversation with his father on the day of his mother's funeral. As they walked away from Anna's gravesite, Lank listened attentively as Reuben reminisced,

"My time on this earth has been filled with poverty and plenty, joy and sorrow, hardship and comfort. I cannot complain. God has given me more than I deserve. Anna was a good and faithful wife, and I am thankful for the years we were blessed to have together."

Lank understood that his father's memories provided him great comfort. The same was true for Lank himself, for it was almost a certainty that leaving Ada would mean that he would never see his father again and memories would be all he had.

While loading the old buggy that Lank had purchased from his father so many years before, Julina gently squeezed her mother in a long, lingering hug, pressing the moment into her heart and mind. Sadie's lips quivered as she held back tears. A huge chasm of three hundred and seventy miles from Ada to Alanson would separate them, most likely forever.

By spring of 1913, the Flick and the Dodge families found themselves once again back in Emmet County, Michigan. Dale, too sick to work, remained housebound, as Gladys faithfully kept house in Alanson, took in laundry for other people and waited for the birth of their second child. Lank found a rundown house located on several acres of fertile land in Brutus and began to farm. Julina was happy as she raised her grandson, Blaine, while patiently waiting for the birth of her second grandchild.

Gale Flick was born on December 5, 1913. The hard choices Gladys made to protect her children combined with the exhausting caregiving that she provided for her husband came at a cost. She felt trapped and alone. She was twenty years old and the future only promised heartache with more daunting decisions on the near horizon. In the meantime, Dale continued to decline.

Two years later a third boy arrived. On October 4, 1915, Doug Flick was born. With each birth, Julina, in effect, became their surrogate mother, as Gladys remained faithful to the care of her invalid husband. Everyone knew how it would end. Dale would eventually succumb to the unrelenting tuberculosis, leaving Gladys alone with three small children.

Finally, the inevitable arrived. On November 17, 1916, Dale Martin Flick died in Alanson, Michigan. He was twenty-nine years old. Gladys buried her husband, grieving her loss yet also experiencing a twinge of guilt at feeling relieved that this prolonged season of hardship was finally over. She was now a widow at the age of twenty-three. Dale had been sick most of the seven years they had been married. It had been an extremely hard life. She would later comment concerning Dale's death,

"I wouldn't have cried at all, except that my mother did."

Gladys was a woman of great passion. She was filled with energy, fun, music and laughter. All of that had been put on hold for so long, but now she was free to have and express these feelings for the first time since she was sixteen years old.

"Dale was a good man. He was the father of my three boys. I remained faithful to him through all of the suffering, and for that I can hold my head high. I was never tempted to stray,"

she recounted to her mother, who understood her daughter very well. Lank and Julina soon approached Gladys with a bold request.

"The boys have lived with us since they were babies. They should rightfully have the name Dodge, not Flick."

Gladys knew how much her mother hated the name Flick. She also understood how much her mother loved the boys. Both Lank and Julina had always wanted to have more children after the death of baby Freddy, and now they had three grandsons who considered them to be their Momma and Papa.

Believing that she was making the wisest choice, Gladys granted the adoptive rights of all three boys to her parents. They were seven, four and two years old. Julina was thrilled, while Mary Flick seethed with anger. Julina's bold and flirtatious ways proved to be a thorn in Mary's flesh and Julina savored it. Mary, a church-going woman, unfortunately owned a heart of bitterness and was well-known for her cold and judgmental ways. Julina relished changing the boys' names to *"Dodge"* and felt a great sense of satisfaction with Mary Flick's misery. Lank was pleased with the decision as well, but at the same time the recent prohibition on alcohol had him distraught. [5]

Gladys worked several jobs after Dale passed on. During the day she folded sheets in a laundry, and on late afternoons and evenings she played piano for the Palace and Temple Theaters, both in Petoskey. Watching the silent screen carefully, she would play the appropriate music to match whatever was happening on the screen. One evening she was accompanied by a drummer, and the two of them were rambunctiously pounding out a fast paced, toe-tapping rendition appropriate for the film's chase scene. They were having such a good time that they forgot about the film, and when Gladys eventually looked up at the screen, she realized that the scene had changed to a mournful funeral. They quickly transitioned into a dirge.

An Old Acquaintance

Gladys was often asked to "tickle the ivories" for dances, high school programs, PTA affairs, weddings and funerals. At one of these gatherings, she by chance bumped into Leslie Sheldon. He remembered her from the sixth grade and was aware of the current gossip buzzing around their small town. She said she remembered him as well. The two of them talked and laughed for hours. Gladys found Leslie to be very charming and quite funny. Plus, he was over six feet tall, strong and handsome, and always had a twinkle in his eye. Even his slightly receding dark hair she found to be intoxicating. He was quite different from the scrawny boy she remembered from sixth grade. Here was a man's man, so distinctly contrary to who Dale had been, even when Dale had been healthy. Gladys felt safe when she was with Leslie, and he made her laugh. He swept her off her feet, and when they kissed, she thought her heart would beat right out of her chest. (6)

As a young widow, Gladys found that she was being watched by people in the community at every turn. Gossip was a means of entertainment in a small town like Alanson, and rumors began to fly like bees on honey:

> "Her husband is barely in the grave and she's running around."

> "I heard that she had an eye for that Sheldon boy long before Dale even died."

*"Can you believe it? I saw that widow Flick walking hand
in hand with Leslie Sheldon!"*

*"She sure doesn't behave much like a grieving widow, if you
ask me."*

On and on the gossip mongers of Alanson would chatter. Gladys was very
aware of the busy-body chitchat, and when asked how she was handling it
all, she simply smiled and commented, *"The least said, the easiest mended,"*
refusing to engage in defending herself in the face of the lies that were
being spread.

*"The truth will bear itself out in the end. Besides, those old
biddies have nothin' better to do. I guess at least I give them
a little excitement,"* she laughed.

31

Gladys Dodge and Leslie Sheldon

1918-1919

Today was different from any other day she had ever experienced; this day was magical. Her pale green dress felt glamorous, with a soft layered ruffle laying neatly across the front of the square neckline and a dainty chiffon collar occasionally caught the breeze, brushing the side of her face. A simple gold necklace provided the perfect accent. Her dark hair was pulled loosely up at the back of her head, as heavy bangs swept across her forehead in wavy softness.

The warm summer air felt fresh and clean, as a soft breeze brushed lightly across the bay. Gladys could not stop smiling. The horse plodded along, passing the prestigious cottages of Bay View overlooking the sparkling blue water, which extended all the way to the horizon.

Today was her wedding day and she would become Mrs. Leslie Sheldon. It almost seemed like a dream. After all the pain and difficulties of her first marriage, she was embarking on a new life with a man she absolutely adored! The only dilemma she faced was the painful fact that Leslie did not want her boys, and her heart ached because of it. [1] At the same time, her mind was assured that they would always live nearby and that she would be deeply involved in their lives, as her parents lovingly raised them.

She sat between her parents in the old buggy, with three-year-old Doug sitting on her lap. Blaine and Gale sat behind with the suitcases, and with strict instructions to sit very still. Ages eight and six, they were energetic, rowdy boys, readily prone to accidents. Julina was especially concerned that they could easily fall off the back of the buggy if it were to hit a bump. Gladys was mostly concerned that her new dress not become terribly wrinkled, while persistently chiding the youngest,

"Stop squirming around Dougie!"

Even so, the big smile on her face could not be diminished, as she glanced down at her new gray cloth ankle boots neatly laced.

The marriage ceremony was simple and short at the Petoskey courthouse, [2] Gladys barely heard the words spoken by the Justice of Peace, until he pronounced them man and wife, and they kissed for the first time as husband and wife. She felt that she could never be happier than she was at that moment. Her parents congratulated them, as the boys ran up and down the halls of the courthouse chasing each other.

"Quit your running now and come say goodbye to your momma," Lank admonished.

Spending their wedding night in Petoskey before boarding the train the next morning for Toledo, they talked of the future. His parents, Charles and Ella Sheldon, had recently sold their Alanson farm and moved to Toledo, after their son, Leslie's brother Earl, had found a job as a brakeman with Willys-Overland Motors. [3] *"Willys"* was ramping up its production of jeeps in support of the Great War [4]. The U.S. had finally entered the war on April 6, 1917, joining with its European Allies to defeat German aggression. As a result, factories across the nation were hiring to meet the increased demands.

For Charles, farming had provided only a meager livelihood, and his health required a change of pace. Earl had written to inform his dad that jobs were readily available in Toledo. Upon their arrival, Charles quickly secured a position with Champion Spark Plug. He also encouraged Leslie and Gladys, upon their marriage, to move to Toledo as well, since there was a guaranteed position for him as an extractor at the plant.

So, having moved up their wedding date from September to June, the newlyweds were on their way. His parents lived at 805 Hanover Street in

Toledo, with plenty of room for Leslie and his bride to move in with them. Leslie's sister Alma and her husband, Orrie Webster, also lived nearby, having moved to Toledo eight years earlier. Leslies' oldest sister, Alice, also decided to make the move to Toledo with her two young children. Her husband, Merton Smith, [5] had died unexpectedly at the age of thirty-four, and she needed a new beginning, as well as the love and support of her family. After arriving in Toledo, Alice soon met and married a widower named George Harrington, who worked at the Champion plant alongside Charles.

James, Charles and Ella's oldest son, had moved to Lancaster, New York, near Buffalo, many years before. He was married with two children. They were happy that James was making a good living as a machine operator but saddened that they had not seen him in many long years. Gladys had never met James. Leslie, who was fifteen years younger than his oldest brother, had very few memories of him while growing up as James had left home shortly after baby Beatrice died.

As for the rest of the Sheldon family, Ella was pleased that they were settled so nearby, all with good paying jobs. The house was quite crowded but filled with love and laughter. Ella was very fond of her new daughter-in-law, and Gladys found Ella to be gentle and kind, although hard of hearing, which meant, out of consideration, everyone yelled. But the noise and activity of a crowded household charmed Gladys. Being an only child, she had always missed not having the company of brothers and sisters. The Sheldons welcomed her as one of their own and they filled a spot in her heart that had felt so empty for her entire life.

In 1918, when Leslie and Gladys arrived, Toledo was bustling with activity. Industry was growing and job opportunities were abundant. Factories began recruiting women to fill jobs now vacated due to so many men now fighting in Europe. Even though the women were paid lower wages, Gladys was thrilled to find work at the Champion factory and was proud that she was able to do her part to help out the family.

By mid-summer, she was ready to have her parents and her three boys join them in Toledo. Returning to Petoskey, she and Leslie helped her parents pack their bags, and they too moved to the bustling city. Life now felt more complete. She had her boys and her parents close and everything seemed to be falling into place. Summer soon turned to autumn. Leslie registered for the draft in September, but thankfully the Great War (WWI) ended in November. After getting through the cold winter months, the approaching arrival of spring was much anticipated. Little did they know that very soon, life would never be the same.

Death Brings Grief and Dilemma

Julina had complained earlier in the week of a loss of appetite, along with some nausea and a dull stomachache. Making light of it, she believed it to be a simple influenza. However, three days later her symptoms worsened, and she writhed in pain with chills and a high fever. Lank tried to convince her to go to the hospital, but she refused, arguing,

"I'll be fine. I hate hospitals. Just give it time."

A few more days passed, and it became apparent that Julina was seriously ill. Lank finally made the decision to take her to Robinwood Hospital on May 4th. Surgery was performed on May 5th. But just five days later, on May 10th at 2pm, Julina Percilla Dodge died, two days after her 46th birthday. [(6)]

Gladys was beside herself with shock and grief. Never had she experienced such a devastating loss. Her mother had been the pillar of her life. She was not only her best friend and confidant, but a significant source of emotional support, as well as the most responsible person in the raising of her three boys. Julina's sudden and unexpected death cast life into grievous turmoil. It was clear that Lank was not prepared to raise the boys by himself, nor was Leslie ready to accept the boys as his own. On top of it all, Gladys suspected that she may be pregnant.

Julina was buried on May 12th in Forest Cemetery in Toledo. Gladys stood over the grave, her mind whirling with confusion and her heart filled with sorrow. Leslie slipped his arm around her. His love and closeness gave her great comfort. Without Leslie she was not sure how she would have ever managed.

When John and Mary Flick heard the news of Julina's untimely death, they rightly assumed that Lank would be unable to continue to raise the three boys. After their son, Dale, died, they had feared that they would lose contact with his young sons forever. Julina had been the driving force behind their adoption, and now that she was gone, it appeared as if a door had been opened for them to come back into the boys' lives. Julina's death was not a matter of celebration, yet the Flicks could not help but feel as if the tide might turn in their favor.

Mary Flick confidently confided her hope to her ladies sewing circle.

"Knowing Leslie Sheldon, he will never consent to raising those boys!"

It was widely known that she had no use for Leslie, or any of the Sheldons for that matter. The "bad blood" carried over from an incident years earlier concerning her daughter, Fanabel, who was the same age as Leslie. [7] They grew up together in the Alanson school and their mothers attended the same Pentecostal church. Whatever it was that happened, young Fanabel was somehow slighted, and the sting still lingered.

Gladys was surprised when she received a heartfelt letter from the Flicks, expressing their condolences and at the same time offering to help. *"We would like to offer to keep the boys through this time of grief and uncertainty,"* Mary carefully wrote. Gladys thought it a very kind and Christian offer, but Ella wasn't so sure. She did not trust Mary Flick for a minute, but at the same time, the dilemma over where the boys were going to live was very real. In the end, expediency would win the day. Lank quickly took the boys back to Alanson.

Soon and with little difficulty, Mary convinced Lank that it was in the boys' best interest to live with them permanently. Lank was forty-eight years old, and his free spirit was beginning to feel crimped by the demands of taking care of the family. He loved his grandsons, but without Julina to help carry the load, he wasn't prepared or mentally ready to settle down as a doting father figure. Without the consent of Gladys, he hastily signed the papers giving the Flicks full legal adoptive custody of all three boys. Once again, the boys' names were "Flick".

When Gladys heard what her father had done, she found herself in a state of shock, overwhelmed with heartbreak and concern. At the same time, she could understand why her father had consented to the idea and wanted to believe that maybe it was all for the best. She had no doubt that the Flicks loved the boys. But she also knew that she could not continue to live in Toledo while her three sons were living in Alanson. Leslie was sympathetic and supportive and agreed that they would return to northern Michigan. He would find work and Gladys could be close to her boys. So, in July they moved into rented rooms in Petoskey where Leslie quickly found a job, working at The Michigan Block Factory. [8]

32

Joy and Heartache

1919-1936

With her shopping basket hooked over her arm Gladys casually strolled up one aisle and down the other. Money was tight and she was careful to buy only what she and Leslie needed. It was an especially hot day, even for August. The paper fan that she had constructed from an old newspaper served to cool her down a bit. At three months pregnant, she felt as if she had a perpetual heater running inside of her, and the excessive outside temperatures didn't help. The owner of the store was a woman with a jovial and friendly manner who had once lived in Alanson. Her name was Minnie Ramsby [1] and she was friendly with the Flicks. Minnie noticed Gladys struggling to lift a large bag of flour.

"Let me help you with that!"

she said, reaching in to lend a strong hand.

"I'll just carry this up to the front for you, so you won't have to lug it around the store."

Gladys smiled and thanked her.

"You must be feeling pretty lonely this morning," Minnie continued.

"Why no, not at all. Why should I?" Gladys asked, somewhat confused.

"Well, the Flicks, they sold everything and moved out. Lock, stock and barrel. Word is they were heading to Kalamazoo."

Stunned, Gladys fumbled with her purse, quickly shoving her paper fan inside and snapping it shut. Eyes blurred with tears, she mumbled an apology and left her groceries on the counter. In a daze, she walked out of the store crying. Once back to their rented room, she fell across the bed and sobbed uncontrollably until finally, exhausted, she drifted off into a fitful sleep.

Late in the afternoon when Leslie got home from work, Gladys fell into his arms and cried out in despair,

> *"They are gone! I was just with them yesterday! I took the sewing that I had done for Doug and then I walked part way to school with Blaine and Gale before taking the train back here in the afternoon. No one told me! No one said a word! Mary and John sat at their kitchen table smiling and talking to me just like it was any other day. And now they are gone! My boys are gone!"* [2]

The only comfort Gladys had was her love for Leslie and the love and tenderness that he gave her. She had experienced so much mourning over so few months. First her mother's unexpected passing and then the choices she had made in giving up her three boys. And now the boys were gone. She hadn't really thought much about God until this point in her life, yet now she couldn't help but wonder how He fit into the scheme of the tragedies she was facing. She knew she couldn't blame Him. Afterall, what had she ever done to deserve God's favor? Guilt plagued her mind, but her resilient heart picked itself up and she forced herself to refocus toward the future. Forgetting the past as best she could, she thought she would work harder to be a better person and maybe God would see fit make life a bit easier. Her unborn child would provide a source of hope and joy, as well as a chance to start over as a mother.

Naomi Louise Sheldon was born six months later, on February 8, 1920. Gladys couldn't help but think of her mother. Julina had desperately wanted a granddaughter.

"Maybe now we'll get our girl!" her mother had said.

Gladys smiled to herself at the thought of how happy her mother would have been to hold this precious baby. Naomi was the first real sunlight Gladys had had since the death of her mother. Finally, life provided a gift. But that happiness was not to last for long.

The telegram coldly read, *"Blaine Was Killed at 7 This Morning."* Gladys had taken the morning train into Petoskey with three-month-old Naomi to visit a cousin of hers. After a fun day, they returned to the Alanson depot at 4:00 pm, tired but happy, as the depot agent solemnly handed her the telegram. Those few short words struck her heart like a knife. Blaine was ten years old. He had been driving a team of horses pulling a land roller, [3] and he had fallen between the team and the roller and was crushed.

A few short weeks after Blaine's death, a job opportunity became available for Leslie in Brevort, in Michigan's Upper Peninsula. Excited about the prospect, Leslie explained the situation to his still grieving wife.

"Your dad has some old lumbering connections and he pulled some strings and got me on with him for a three-month stint."

"I feel doomed," Gladys exclaimed. *"Just when I was beginning to pick myself up with new hope, you and my dad are flittin' off to work in a logging camp, in the U.P, leaving me here alone with a baby and my sorrows."*

It was true. Nothing was easy. Life was hard. They were dirt poor. And on top of it all, they had experienced deep loss. But in the end Gladys knew that they had to do whatever was necessary to get by. The wages were good, and it made sense for Leslie to take it, leaving her home alone with little Naomi, along with her thoughts and her grief.

Several lonely weeks passed until Leslie finally sent for Gladys and Naomi to join him in Brevort. She was so happy to see him and for the three of them to be reunited. Throughout that summer, camp life brought back happy memories of her childhood. But with the memories came a deep loneliness. A melancholy haunted her day and night. By autumn, 1920, they were back in Alanson and she was pregnant again. The anguish increased with a vengeance. Adding to what felt like an endless cycle, her grandfather, Reuben Dodge, died in November. Although he had lived a long life of eighty-eight years, it seemed as though death was relentlessly circling for the final blow. Her fragile nerves had found their end and she had a complete nervous breakdown.

Leslie tried his best to bring her out of her despair, but it would take time to remove the dark cloud of depression and unrelenting fear that had swept over her. She felt without hope, as though she would die. There was no therapy available and no drugs to ease the mental and emotional pain. Leslie's faithful and loving affection was the only thing that held her up, and together they pressed on, gradually finding some remnants of contentment and happiness over the course of time. While there would still be some difficult roads ahead and rifts of that dark depression would at times raise its ugly head, she would look back on that year of her life, 1920-21, as the worst she'd ever experienced.

At the end of the summer in 1921, Evelyn Pearl Sheldon was born on August 24th. The name came from a surprising conversation she had had with her mother years before in Ada. While lifting a rug to sweep under it, Gladys found a letter addressed to *"Evelyn"*. She asked her mom,

"Who is Evelyn?"

Julina scratched her head and thought for a minute and then laughed,

"Oh my goodness! I almost forgot about that! I stepped out with a train conductor to get back at your dad for his wanderings. I told him my name was Evelyn. I always liked that name."

And thus, Gladys named her second daughter, *"Evelyn"*.

The decade of the 1920's proved to be a blur of birth and death for Leslie and Gladys. Another daughter, Cleah "Jane" Sheldon, was born on April 1, 1923. A year later, June 12, 1924, Charles Robinson Sheldon, Leslie's father, died at the age of sixty-three in Toledo, leaving behind his grieving widow, Ella. Paul Hugo Sheldon, a son, was born on November 20th of that same year. A year later, Alice Ida Harrington (Leslie's sister) died on October 11, 1925, at forty-one years of age. Two years after that, in 1927, Lorna Lou Sheldon was born on August 11th.

The United States economy was booming after World War I had ended, with industry and innovation reaching new heights. But for the Sheldons, with five children to feed, clothe and shelter, life was never easy, yet it was always fun. The resilience, humor and love that Gladys brought to everyday life that would keep them a happy family in the face of a poverty that they would never truly recognize or define as such.

> *"We haven't two nickels to rub together,"* Gladys would say,
> *"but I'll take my poor little flock over anything else, today
> and twice on Sunday."*

When work was scarce, Leslie would head for the woods. He was a skilled trapper, and selling pelts brought in extra money. Tramping through the quiet woods, setting traps and hoping for a good day's catch was not only necessary for supporting his growing family, but it satisfied that part of his nature. Leslie was a man of action. Never one to sit glumly brooding over life's circumstances, he found fulfillment in tangible results. He could sling a beaver, muskrat or raccoon pelt over his shoulder and feel success for a day. And he had the gift of always being able to make Gladys laugh.

The 1920's were truly "roaring." It was a new, racy culture, with women wearing short skirts, smoking cigarettes, drinking alcohol and bobbing their hair. With these newly gained cultural freedoms including the right to vote, Gladys knew that she could help supplement Leslie's meager income. She played piano for social events and local dances, along with her father Lank on violin. Prohibition was still in place, [4] but moonshine liquor was readily available.

Leslie didn't drink alcohol, but he did enjoy smoking. Although it was neither of these that were of any concern to Gladys. It was her own jealousy that hung over her heart and mind like a black cloud. Leslie enjoyed going with her to the dances where she would provide the rambunctious, ragtime music at the piano. But while she was busy pounding the keys, she was never quite confident in Leslie's good judgment. She watched as pretty young women danced and flirted with the men and couldn't help but compare herself to them. She felt guilt and shame over her jealous feelings and fears.

She also felt guilt over playing for these dances, which she believed only encouraged bad behavior of drunkenness, infidelity, brawling, crude language and lewd conduct. She wasn't particularly faithful in her Christian beliefs at this time, but a strict moral code had been instilled in her at an early age through the godly example and lessons of her grandparents, especially her Grandpa Davis. One particular verse from I Peter 2:11 in the Bible kept coming to her mind: "*...abstain from fleshly lusts, which wage war against your soul.*" While she was not participating in any debauchery or licentious behavior herself, she also knew that she wasn't fully trusting God, and was allowing her heart to be consumed with jealousy, fear and guilt.

On the other hand, her father, Lank Dodge, especially enjoyed these social events with the added pleasure of the attention given him by admiring ladies. One such young woman caught his eye. Mabel Ferguson Emans [5] was twenty-seven years old and very recently divorced, with three young children. It had been five years since Julina had passed away and soon after meeting Mabel the fifty-seven-year-old Lank Dodge remarried.

Lank had been a lumberman for most of his life, with spurts of farming as well as a stint operating a dairy farm. His extroverted personality and charisma carried him a long way throughout his life. Alanson was experiencing some success in tourism, and Lank hired on as the captain of the canal boat "Buckeye Belle". [6] Lank had actually never piloted a riverboat before but learned quickly. Particularly known for his skill in piloting around "Devil's Elbow" on the river, Lank relished the applause and accolades coming from entertained guests. After a time, his new wife, Mabel, encouraged a move and they packed their bags for Cadillac, Michigan, about a hundred miles south of Alanson.

A Matter of Faith

Gladys and Leslie hadn't given faith too much consideration or serious thought throughout their nine years of marriage. Gladys had been told the story of Jesus in her younger years, and Leslie had been raised reading the Bible and attending church. But neither one had found much interest in spiritual things until Lorna was a baby, in 1927. Their friends in Alanson, the Fairburnes, invited them to a tent meeting. At that time God's powerful hand of conviction fell upon them both, and they saw their need for a personal Savior.

As Gladys sat in the cold folding chair in the tent that eventful evening, listening to the Good News of Jesus Christ, that he had died for her sins, tears flowed freely, as her mind whirled with the events of her life and the dark heaviness of her own sinful heart.

> *"I didn't think that God could ever love me or forgive me for so many wrongs in my life,"* she thought. *"And why should He? I am undeserving of such love. But can it be true? I don't have to be 'good enough'? I don't have to earn God's love? That Jesus, who was without sin, took all my sins upon himself when he died on the cross, and I can be forgiven! All of this grieving and guilt that I have carried can be lifted from my shoulders! What incredible love! Such amazing grace! Thank you, Jesus!"*

Leslie, too, accepted the free gift of God's mercy and grace, as he and Gladys together publicly walked hand-in-hand down the aisle at that revival meeting that night.

After that day, life took on a whole new outlook. No matter what they faced, they knew that God's love was real, and they lived with thankfulness in their hearts for his mercy and grace.

Leaning on the Everlasting Arms

Paul had complained that his stomach hurt all morning. By the next day, his fever spiked, and he lay doubled over in excruciating pain, his six-year-old body drenched in sweat. Leslie wired his mother in Toledo, asking her to pray. Several years had passed since giving his life to Christ and his faith had gradually been set on a back burner, so to speak. But now, his only son was sick and not recovering, and he felt desperate. Reaching out to his mother seemed the logical thing to do, especially since he had long forgotten how to pray himself.

Leslie had gradually neglected God and church attendance. Gladys, as well, had allowed the busyness of the everyday to creep in and take hold of her time, thoughts and her love for God. Over time, Leslie's heart had grown cold to the things of God, and the whole family "backslid", drifting away from God altogether. Now, with Paul's life hanging in the balance, Leslie turned to the only hope he knew. Prayer.

Ella attended a Pentecostal church, and upon hearing the news of Paul's condition she immediately fell to her knees in prayer for her young grandson. The next day she secured a prayer cloth, believing that it had some inherent power, and promptly mailed it north. By the time it reached Leslie and Gladys, Paul was hospitalized with what was ultimately diagnosed as a ruptured appendix. It was unlikely that he would survive. But miraculously, he did. Paul's young life was spared, and everyone knew without a doubt that God had intervened and answered their prayers.

The circumstances of life can either harden a heart to the things of God or soften it. Leslie and Gladys saw the healing of Paul as the miracle that it was, and it quickened their hearts to rekindle their faith and recommit themselves to loving and serving the Lord. It was also the first motivation for them to consider attending the Pentecostal Church in Alanson. But not quite yet; that would be a decision made later. And it would be a decision that would ultimately have devastating ripple effects for generations to follow.

The Depression

A fat robin landed on the edge of the old wicker laundry basket. Gladys quickly shooed it away, bending down to check on the baby. Beatie was sound asleep. Gladys adjusted the faded blue blanket, tucking it tightly around her three-month-old and turned back to the cleanup work. The crumbling old shack looked beyond inhabitable. With trash and broken-down cars strewn across the yard, it appeared to be more of a junkyard than a possible home.

Thirteen-year-old Naomi directed the younger children in collecting the smaller bits of debris into a pile that could later be burned, while carrying her two-year-old sister Martha [7] on her hip. Gladys leaned heavily on Naomi's strong personality and motherly instincts. Gladys's recovery after Beatie's [8] breech birth had been slow. Both came close to dying before Gladys was ultimately rushed to the Petoskey hospital on that cold February day.

When spring finally arrived in 1933, it had been all too apparent that living above the Post Office in Alanson was no longer an option. Complaints were constant from the patrons below concerning the thumping and noise coming from overhead. With six rambunctious children and a newborn baby, Leslie and Gladys knew that they needed to move. A rundown shack north of town, close to the railroad tracks, was the only place they could find.

Gladys cried when she first saw it. Yet just when she was beginning to feel overwhelmed and completely doomed, she heard God's voice. It wasn't audible, but it was as clear as anything she'd ever experienced. Standing amid the junk surrounding her, holding Beatie in her arms, God spoke.

"I didn't even have this much. I had no place to lay my head. This is the place I have chosen for you. Take it and I will bless you."

Her heart was cheered, and she felt an unreasonable joy with this new decrepit shack they would call home. She began humming one of her favorite hymns, *"What a Friend We Have in Jesus"*.

With two more daughters added to their little flock since the time of their salvation six years before, and with the Great Depression [9] pushing hard on the whole nation, life was a struggle for survival itself. In January 1933, Franklin Delano Roosevelt (FDR) had been sworn into office as the thirty-second President of the United States and wasted no time implementing his New Deal programs. A hope began to stir as people hung on every word their President offered over the radio in his popular "Fireside Chats". [10]

For the Sheldons, after back breaking work and homey touches, the old shack was nicely transformed into a home, with two rooms on the first floor and a large open loft upstairs. The stove pipe went up from the first floor through the center of the house, passing through the loft and then up through the roof. There was enough space upstairs to crowd the children in for sleeping, and the stove pipe provided warmth during cold winter nights.

Gladys bought fabric for ten cents a yard and made curtains, while

Leslie built a new outhouse. Sipping her coffee on a cold afternoon soon after they had settled in, Gladys couldn't help but admire the transformation.

"Mercy, Mercy!" she sighed to herself, *"We did ourselves proud."*

She especially admired the beautiful straight fence that Leslie had lined along a large section of grazing pasture. Watching the five milk cows, each with a baby born that spring, Gladys had to chuckle as the mommas mindlessly chewed their way from grass to grass and the newborns ran across the small pasture on wobbly legs, enjoying the cold spring air. It wasn't really the calves that tickled her fancy so much as it was the feeling that God was going to bless them with better times. She patted her growing abdomen and wondered if this time it was a boy or another girl.

"Lord, you know that Paul wants a brother. Six sisters are a lot, being the only boy. I'll leave it in your hands, but a boy would sure be nice."

Leslie burst through the front door, the way he always did, always in a hurry. He'd been trapping all day and had a nice batch of pelts to sell. Fifteen-year-old Evelyn had gone with him. He enjoyed Evelyn's company and often invited her to join him tramping through the woods to check or set traps. Evelyn, the only girl in the family who couldn't sing, was a colorful personality and often referred to herself as her dad's favorite. There was some truth to it. Fun-loving, impatient and straight-forward, she was the free-spirit that Naomi was not.

Being the oldest, Naomi asserted herself with proper confidence, while taking on a lot of responsibility in helping her mother with the younger children. Jane, the third born, was the pleasant and adaptable daughter. With so many girls, it was natural to try and judge who was the prettiest, and Jane certainly was in the running for the top of the order.

Then came Paul, the only boy. Leslie wasn't quite sure how to be a father to him. Paul was not the jokester or the robust outdoorsman that Leslie was. He was more leisurely, logical and caring. Lorna Lou (named by her grandfather Lank) and girl number four, was musical, expressive, resourceful and possibly the most prone to dramatics.

Martha was smart, quiet and classy. Her tendency for remaining private made her harder to get to know, but she was definitely worth knowing and became her younger sister's best friend. Beatie, the daughter who almost died at birth, was two years younger than Martha. Gladys was forty when Beatie was born. The breach birth had almost killed her, so she had hoped that it would be her last pregnancy.

For years after the difficult birth, Beatie's nose appeared squashed. Gladys would say,

> *"You hasn't got any nose,"* and little Beatie would respond,
> *"Has to, 'ittle bit."*

Ultimately her nose recovered from the difficult birth and Beatie grew into a beauty with ringlets of dark curls. She was a combination of many of the same attributes her older siblings owned. She was smart, musical, fun-loving and strong-willed. Later in her life she would refer to herself in her teen years as, *"an ornery little bugger"*.

The Train Whistle Blows

As Leslie sat down for lunch one day, Gladys shared a premonition that she had earlier that morning.

> *"I have a feeling that God has better times in store for us. I just feel it. All we need to do is reach around the corner and grab it. 1936 will see good times for us."*

That very night the much-anticipated arrival of spring seemed to retreat as a cold north wind whipped up snow and ice. They woke to a blanket of white stretching across the frozen ground. With a chill in the air, Gladys lit the stove. She began her daily routine early, mixing flour, yeast and the ingredients needed for three loaves of bread.

The older children scarfed down the warm buttered bread with a big glass of milk and, grabbing their knapsacks, jackets and scarves, hollered goodbye over their shoulders and raced off to meet the sleigh bus. They waited next to the icy road, throwing snowballs and playing chasing games until the sleigh came up over the hill to take them to school. It was pulled by two strong work horses and provided an enclosed "bus" with a wood stove in the corner for warmth. Leslie had already left to check his minnow traps, and Gladys breathed a sigh of relief as she buttered the warm crust and handed it to three-year-old Beatie. Martha had already eaten.

It was late morning when the train whistle began to blow.

"Isn't that strange? That train must be in some kind of trouble to be carrying on like that,"

Gladys absentmindedly commented to Beatie as she sat on the floor playing tug-of-war with their dog, Brownie. [11] The whistle continued in a frantic rhythm.

"Well for land's sake, what is going on with that train?" Stepping outside, she smelled the smoke.

The roof of their house was engulfed in flames and the train's engineer had been trying to alert the family. It did not take long for the house to quickly burn to the ground. One neighbor commented,

"That poor Sheldon family lost everything, but at least they didn't have much of anything to begin with."

Beatie and Martha sat wrapped in a blanket in the yard as men from the community doused the smoldering ruins with buckets of water.

A spark fluttered in the air, landing on the blanket, and the two girls watched it slowly burn a hole before it extinguished itself out. By the time the older children arrived home from school, volunteers from town were working to extinguish the remaining flames, consuming the last remnants of the Sheldon's worldly possessions. It was determined that the fire had been caused by a blanket that had ignited. Jane, who struggled with bedwetting, had washed out some personal items and hung them along with the wet blanket too close to the stove pipe upstairs. With the cold morning, the stove had been stoked red hot and the pipe was the culprit in setting the blanket on fire.

> *"I feel so ridiculous now,"* Gladys lamented to Leslie. *"Seems my big prophecy about better times is nothing but a big joke."*

Leslie scratched his bald head and commented with a smile,

> *"Well, at least we have our health,"* giving her a wink.

He was always ready to make Gladys laugh, even in the darkest of times. His ability to make a joke and bring a smile in the worst of situations, perhaps even at times appearing a little crazy, often carried the family through. There was no *"woe is me, for I am spent!"* They picked themselves up in faith and practiced humor. Gladys smiled as she recalled their laughter two days before the fire. Having a meager dinner of black beans and bread, she yelled across the yard like she was calling the pigs,

> *"Pooey-pooey!"*

and Leslie came running out of the barn, grunting and squealing, just like he was one. They sat down to dinner laughing as a family and feeling as good as if it was a steak dinner.

Good things often spring from tragedy. The fire brought forth a generosity from the townsfolk of Alanson, who provided temporary assistance and housing for the destitute family.

> *"Chet Rabinald says we can move into his farmhouse and he'll guarantee us three years there until we can get back on our feet,"* Leslie told Gladys.

She clapped her hands in celebration,

> *"Well, thank the Lord! Otherwise this baby is gonna be born alongside the road somewhere."*

And so, with nothing to their name other than five cows, five calves and a dog named Brownie, they moved into the ramshackle Rabinald farmhouse and waited for the birth of their eighth child, expected to arrive mid-summer.

Two Final Blessings

Leslie took out his hanky and wiped the sweat from his brow. He'd been with the work crew responsible for breaking up old potholed pavement for most of the week along W. Levering Road east of Cross Village. The paving crew was on their heels with fresh tar, and the foreman was pushing them to work faster. Leslie commented to the short, chubby man working next to him,

> *"This may be a paying government job, but sometimes it feels like forced labor,"* [12]

> *"Yeah, I'm too old for this,"* came the man's reply, stopping for a moment to lean on his shovel. He then added,

> *"But it puts money in my hand and food on the table."*

Leslie nodded in agreement, and said,

> *"Yes sir, a man's gotta do what a man's gotta do. I guess we should just be thankful for the WPA, even if it kills us!"*

The two laughed together and went back to work repairing the pothole, muscles glazed in dirt and sweat as the August sun beat down.

It was already dark by the time Leslie drove home to the little, dilapidated farmhouse. A lantern flickered in the window. He threw the old Model-A Ford [13] gear shift into neutral and cut the engine. Locking the brake, he breathed a deep sigh of exhaustion. Another day, another dollar. He was hungry and his thirty-eight-year-old body was weary and sore. Gladys had a plate of food waiting for him on the table. Quickly washing his hands and splashing his face he sat down to eat. It was unusually quiet in the house.

As he scraped up the final remnants of potatoes and peas with his fork, sixteen-year-old Naomi walked through the front door. Leslie smiled at his daughter and asked,

"How's Sam doing tonight?"

"Oh, he's fine. We went for a drive and then met some friends at Stear's Cafe. Jack was there and gave us all a free slice of pie. I don't think his daddy was too happy with him!"

Leslie laughed.

"Jack's dad is a skinflint, tightwad, penny-pincher."

Naomi smiled back at her father and gave a knowing laugh. Glancing around the small room, she asked,

"Where's ma?"

"Hmmm...I don't know. I was just so tired and hungry I didn't even think."

Opening the bedroom door, Naomi stuck her head in to see her mother laying on top of the bed. Gladys weakly lifted her head and grimaced.

"The baby is coming. I've been timing contractions. Won't be too long now."

"Mom! Why are you laying in here all alone!?"

"I wanted your dad to have his dinner before telling him. He's always so exhausted from that back-breaking road work."

Naomi shook her head with exasperation and commented under her breath,

"Well that's just the craziest thing I've ever heard!"

Two hours later Leslie sent Evelyn for the doctor. Pon-She-Wa-ing was only a few miles from the farmhouse and Dr. Mitchell [14] had been anticipating a call from the Sheldons. The children, except for Naomi and Evelyn, slept through the night as their mother suffered through contraction after contraction. At the break of dawn, the baby had still not arrived. By midmorning, exhausted from an ordeal that she was well acquainted with, Gladys finally gave birth to a beautiful baby girl who came into the world with a full head of black hair. Even in her weakened state, Gladys marveled at the fact that she had given birth to her seventh girl, and eleventh child.

Naomi and Evelyn stood next to their mother admiring their new baby sister when, after examining Gladys further, Dr. Mitchell made a shocking discovery.

"There is another baby still on its way!"

Slumping back in complete weariness, Gladys turned toward the girls in disbelief and uttered,

"Evelyn! Why did you wish this on me?!"

Weeks earlier, Evelyn had commented that she hoped her mother would have twins so that she and Naomi would each have one to hold. It now came back to haunt her, and she rushed from the room in tears. [15]

A few minutes later, yet another baby girl was born. Identical twins. Upon hearing the news, twelve-year-old Paul was distraught.

"Two more stupid girls!" he cried.

33

Leslie and Gladys - The Grievous Years

1939-1947

With a twin on each hip, Gladys stood back and admired the stone house.

> *"Praise the Lord! I've always said that I'd be happy in a tar paper shack, if it was mine, but here we are now with forty acres and a house to boot. So, what do you think?"*

She was looking down at Joie and Judy as if asking for their approval, laughing as she set the toddlers down on the grassy ground.

> *"You two are getting heavy!"* she exclaimed. *"Now watch where you're stepping. I don't want those little bare feet catching a nail or a splinter."*

The two-year-old, black-haired look-alikes happily ran off to play with their big sister, Beatie. Gladys loved all of her children, but she had to admit that she was especially proud of those twin girls and had fun dressing them in matching outfits every day.

The property had come to them through circumstances that had the hand of God written all over it. Chet Rabinalt had reneged on his promise of a three-year lease on the rundown farmhouse that the family had moved into after the fire. And Gladys marveled,

"What looked like the worst news possible for us, being kicked around again and again, God used it for good."

A well-to-do lady from Petoskey had approached them with an offer. The lady told Leslie that if he could give her fifty dollars, she would give him a clear deed to forty-acres of prime farmland, northeast of Alanson. The bank was skeptical to provide the loan, for it was at the tail end of the depression and loans were hard to come by. But with enough cattle as security, the approval came. Things were looking up for Leslie and Gladys and their nine children.

Naomi graduated from high school and was anticipating marrying her high school sweetheart, Sam Haines. But for now, it was all hands-on deck to build and settle into a story-and-a-half stone house and get the farm running. The house wasn't glamorous, but it was built with their own hands, and it was theirs. After a lifetime of living in poverty, it felt like a mansion, even though the children slept in an unfinished upstairs where roofing nails were covered with frost on cold winter mornings and they could hardly move under the weight of heavy blankets as they snuggled together in shared beds. Yet life was good and within two years they were up to twenty-two head of cattle, several fat pigs and an untold number of laying chickens.

The younger children loved country life. Having so many siblings meant that there was always someone to play with, and the open, rolling hills provided space and freedom to explore. Animals were always a part of life as well and they even adopted a pig as a pet, naming him *"Georgie."* Gladys refused to allow him in the house even though he was as much like a dog as any pig could be.

That being said, it was their dog, Buck, who was by far everyone's favorite. He was smart and could play hide and seek, round up the cattle for the night, and was devotedly protective. When the sheriff pulled up the driveway on a warm summer day to say that Buck had been spotted running with a pack of dogs, killing the neighbor's livestock and would have to be put down, the children cried for days. The family never believed that it was Buck, but the law believed it, and that was that.

As pleased as Gladys was with the farm, and the way God had provided the means for them to own their own place, she missed having trees. She had always loved trees and surmised that it probably stemmed from her many years of living in lumber camps and being surrounded by ancient oaks, pine and maple trees. But whatever the reason, the land around the stone house felt barren, because it was. There was not a single tree on their forty acres.

As America struggled to fully recover from the Great Depression, life continued to look up for the Sheldon's. They had a home of their own, forty acres of good land, a couple dozen head of cattle, and a flowing well. [1] The well was just outside the back door, making it easy to pump fresh spring water each morning and throughout the day, even in the dead of winter. Leslie built a stellar outhouse located several yards and, wisely, downwind from the house. Electricity wasn't available on country roads, but they did not miss something they had never had. The house felt more than adequate and even though the children would continue to wake on winter mornings with their noses cold from the frosty air, laughter was always heard coming from the Sheldon household.

> *"Get my gun Gladys! I'm gonna shoot that old bull this time!"*
> Leslie shouted.

Gladys laughed. She knew that he would never shoot a neighbor's bull even if it was staked on their property. Leslie had purchased the adjoining forty acres that spring, adding to the original forty. Here it was late summer and Ol' Man Kidder continued to use the land like it was his property. Leslie blustered,

> *"That old coot just won't give up. I've told him three times that we bought that land fair and square, and he still sets his cattle to graze and stakes that stupid old bull right in the middle of our property."*

Mr. Kidder had never owned the land but had used it for so long that most folks believed it was his. And adding fuel to the fire he commented to another neighbor,

> *"Where could Les Sheldon get the money to buy a cat, to say nothing of buying forty acres that I've been using for years!"*

It wasn't until Leslie actually showed Kidder the bill of sale that he finally conceded that the property belonged to the Sheldons. Even so, Les put up a good fence to keep that bull and meandering cattle from wandering onto their property.

Just as it seemed that the country as a whole was on track for better times, the unthinkable happened. On December 7, 1941, the Japanese bombed Pearl Harbor. *"A day that will live in infamy,"* came the words of President Roosevelt. America was outraged and boldly united in a common unifying cause. Men eagerly volunteered to enlist, ready to do their part. Leslie was forty-three years old with seven remaining children at home, as both Naomi and Evelyn were married. His age and family excluded him from service. Naomi and Evelyn's husbands, Sam Haines and Al Wilde respectively, were rejected from service with medical deferments. It was especially hard on Al, who was a big, strong man and felt that he was being unfairly judged as cowardly for not serving.

As Americans were giving rapt attention to the news coming in from naval engagements in the Pacific and from the battles being waged in Europe, they were all pitching in to do their part on the home front. Patriotism consumed the hearts of young and old alike. People were glued to their radios for the latest reports, while posters and newspaper advertisements encouraged everyone to find ways to help. *"When you ride alone, you ride with Hitler. Join a car-sharing club today!"* *"Help put the lid on Hitler, save your old metal and paper."* *"Dig for victory! Grow your own vegetables."* *"Buy war bonds!"* American pride filled hearts and minds, and there was a very real awareness that the fate of the world was at stake. It was good versus evil.

Out of this turmoil came a declaration. Leslie came home and announced,

"Gladys it's time we get back to church."

After Paul's brush with death, almost ten years earlier, encouraging a recommitment to a life of faith at that time, the whole family had sporadically attended the Littlefield Mission Church, so it was a wonderful surprise for Gladys when Leslie decided that it was time to dedicate themselves back to regular church attendance. Tears of joy came unexpectedly as Gladys looked away to hide them.

"We've backslid long enough," she silently thought.

Gladys didn't question why Leslie was ready and eager to begin church attendance. She thought maybe he needed the solace of his faith to bring perspective and hope, balancing the grim news of the war they read about each day in the newspaper. Or maybe it was the children. Or maybe it was God's conviction on his heart. Regardless, she was more than ready to make her faith real and to put God back in the center of her life and that of her family. They soon decided that the Alanson Pentecostal Church would be their new church home. Jane was in a serious relationship with Merlin Hughey and Merlin's mother, Rev. Bertha Turk, was the pastor of the small congregation. Bertha was a warm and charismatic personality, and both Leslie and Gladys liked her very much.

Rekindling a love for God and His Word while serving people in a church family sparked a spiritual growth in Gladys that had laid dormant for years. She found herself immersed in God's Word and discovered the joy of the Lord to be rich. Using her God-given gift of music, she began playing her ragtime style piano in church to the familiar hymns of the faith, with a teenage drummer pounding out the strong beats, bringing life and energy to the worship each Sunday. Sister Turk would bring the spoken word and people were getting saved...finding Jesus as their Savior. Leslie served as the Sunday School Superintendent.

However, this charismatic and free worship style was new to the children. Eight-year-old Beatie was especially affected and often wide-eyed scared by the spontaneity of the leading of the Holy Spirit manifested in song, dancing and speaking in tongues. On one typical Sunday she began to cry out of fear. It was misunderstood by some of the parishioners as a work of the Holy Spirit, leading them to surround her, hovering over her with loud shouts of praise, only creating within her tender soul an even greater sense of terror, as she had become the center of attention for the entire church. (2)

Leslie, along with Gladys, was caught up in the high-powered energy of the worship. But even more so he was enamored with the allure and magnetism of Sister Turk. He had always been faithful to Gladys, focusing all his time and energy on providing for his growing family. That is not to say that he had never been tempted because he had been, but he never pursued those inclinations, believing that a man's character was better kept than recovered. Yet now, week after week, he attended church and found himself privately thinking of Bertha with impure and lustful thoughts. Gladys confided to her friend, Ruby:

> *"I am so ashamed of my sinful and jealous heart. Bertha is not only my pastor, she is my friend, and I find myself comparing her stylish ways to my house dress and apron, with these chicken legs of mine. Jealousy just raises its ugly head!"*

Ruby did not attend the Pentecostal Church and so was less careful with her words.

> *"Stylish is one thing. Flirty is another. I see her when she bats her eyes at the men, with her hips swaying in those sling-back shoes. She is not foolin' me!"*

Gladys cringed at Ruby's harsh, but probably accurate, assessment.

> *"Well, I can't judge. All I know is that I find myself feeling mighty inadequate in her presence."*

Bertha did indeed have a magnetic personality, with a sensual appeal for most men, an appeal that she was well aware of. Bertha came from a ministry background, her mother, Sister Alma Nelson, also a minister in the Pentecostal movement. Bertha was divorced from her first husband, Chester Hughey, with whom she had her son Merlin. Merlin graduated from Petoskey High School in 1941 and met Jane Sheldon the summer he came back from California after his first year in school. Jane was quickly swept off her feet by this good looking and charming young man. They married a year later, both at the age of nineteen. Merlin enlisted in the Navy when WWII broke out and was soon deployed, leaving his wife, who had quickly become pregnant with their first child. Baby Doug was born in May of 1943.

Bertha and Gladys were casual friends but became even closer with the common bond of a grandchild. Even so, Gladys continued to struggle with feelings of jealousy which gradually evolved into suspicion, which she chose to brush off as her own "silly insecurities". She chastised herself for these hidden feelings, while at the same time sensing some subtle, and some not-so- subtle, changes in Leslie. He was becoming more distant with her. His usual fun-loving personality had converted into moody impatience, which led to more frequent arguments between the two of them, especially after Gladys finally expressed to him her fears and suspicions. He was not the loving father that he had once been, but rather had become detached from and harsh with the children.

Gladys thought maybe it was the stress of his job at the Oden State Fish Hatchery [3], and the burden of keeping the farm running. He had begun full-time work at the hatchery in 1940, a year before WWII, which left most of the farm work to the children. Most of that work fell on Paul's young shoulders, as the only boy. But it was Lorna, along with Paul, who took the brunt of the workload, along with their father's wrath when the work wasn't done to his satisfaction. Lorna idolized Paul, and because of the way Paul was unfairly treated, Lorna would harbor a deep resentment toward their father that would eventually border on hatred, lasting for years.

Leslie and Paul did the milking in the morning before Leslie left for work at the hatchery. Then it was Paul and Lorna who filled the fifty-gallon barrel with water for the 24 head of cattle, cleaned the barn and gutters, and forked in clean hay, all of this needing to be done each morning before school. Gladys would lovingly tease Lorna, calling her *"John"*, her "other boy." By the time Paul was sixteen, he had had enough. He was not cut out to be a cattle farmer, and rather than continue to endure the thankless daily chores of farm life, he quit school and moved to Hart, Michigan with his sister Evelyn and her husband, Al Wilde.

The next four years became an increasing struggle for Leslie to keep up with the farm along with work at the Oden State Fish Hatchery. It was clear that the farm would need to be sold. That same year, 1944, a telegram came. Leslie's mother, Ella Viola Sheldon, had died in Toledo. She had lived a long life of eighty-two years. Charles, Leslie's father, had been gone for almost twenty years before Ella took her last breath. Her faithfulness to God and love for her family would be her lasting legacy long after she was gone.

In quiet grief, Leslie mourned his mother's passing. Gladys tried to get him to talk, asking him how he was feeling, but he would only mumble indiscernible words and then walk away, ignoring her attempts to comfort him, almost with antipathy. Hard questions are not usually prone to easy answers, and it was clear that Leslie was unwilling to entertain either, at least with Gladys. He continued to push her away, becoming more and more removed, emotionally as well as physically.

Gladys remained optimistic that the future would bring brighter, happier days. She never lost her joyful spirit or her creative wit. She began to anonymously write an editorial/gossip page called *"Alanson Side-Track News"*, for The Emmet County Graphis, the newspaper out of Harbor Spring. Disguising herself as an uneducated, simple-minded busybody, she purposely wrote with misspelled words and improper English:

> *"Miss Margie Coors jest ups and gets married tother day. They got married in Detroit then they comes back to Alanson by plane and her folks jest gat her the sweelst exception. I got a Invite. They served Ice Cream and angel food cake and Devils food. The men most all et the devils food cake and jest oddles of gum and candy. Oh ever thing just went grand, only poor Mrs. Bob Hairy fell down - it hurt her too a little, right in the middle of the back porch."*

She also included herself and Leslie in her column:

> *"Mrs. Sheldon done a right smart business a doin' laundry work this summer. I was there one day, poor sole, the sweat was runnin down her cheeks. Her husband resorts at the Oden Fish Hatchery."*

After a lot of local speculation, someone discovered who was writing these columns.

> *"I sort of got my dander up about my other news. It was them there (East Alanson Farmers) well the reason was why I got mad someone went and found out who I was, but by gorsh I got ye fooled this time cause it ain't me a tall."*

Gladys didn't continue much longer once her identity was revealed. As it turned out, Leslie's boss, at the Oden State Fish Hatchery, didn't think it was very funny.

As word spread that the Sheldon's were looking to sell, Zelma Ferguson stopped by the house. She said that she was interested in expanding her property holdings and offered $2000 for the stone house and eighty acres.

> *"Praise God!"* Gladys hollered right after Zelma walked out the door. *"We are being blessed again, even if we have no idea where we are going to live now! It's in the Lord's hands and I'm not gonna worry one speck. All things come to those who wait."*

Fortunately, *Zelma* was a patient and kind woman, giving the Sheldons ample time to figure out what to do next.

Standing on the Pentecostal church's front steps in Alanson, a light breeze brushed across Gladys's face. Loose strands of slightly greying hair tickled her cheek, and she carefully pushed them back in place with the palm of her hand, then moving it up to shield her eyes from the brightness of the afternoon sun. There was a sign in the yard across the road.

> *"What does that sign say?"* she quietly asked herself.

Squinting, she read, *"For Sale"*. Looking into the property, they discovered that the small house came with seven acres and could be purchased for $2000. On top of that, the house was surrounded with big beautiful trees and came with a flowing well. Gladys saw God's loving provision for the family once again. Leslie readily agreed, and they struck a deal to purchase the house and land. Work began immediately to add the necessary rooms required to accommodate their still large family. After almost a year of renovation, they moved into their new house in 1945. "I think I've died and gone to heaven!" Gladys exclaimed. This was the first time that she had ever had an indoor bathroom and running water. Lorna, Martha, Beatie, Judy and Joie excitedly picked out their new rooms and soon their dad would arrange for electricity. Things were looking up indeed.

Beatie was now twelve years old. The upstairs had four bedrooms, and she had chosen the smallest one at the top of the stairs on the left. She was indeed a *"lazy little bugger,"* as her mother would tease. The girls were to keep their rooms clean, and Beatie figured the smaller the room the less the work. She spent hours alone in that room, reading by lantern light and allowing her imagination to take her far away, with the *"Girl of the Limberlost"*, her favorite book. A year later they finally had electric power, and no more having to read by lanterns.

All too often, in the still quiet of evening, the girls would lay in bed and hear their parents arguing through the heat crate in the floor. Beatie would try to cover her ears and hum to drown out the voices, but it was no use. The issue was almost always the same; her mother expressing her suspicions, and her father angrily defensive.

> *"Gladys, you are being ridiculous. I work too hard to be running around with another woman,"* he would emphatically exclaim.

Deceit, Lies and Betrayal

Bertha's phone rang again. It was her lunch hour and she was just getting ready to meet some friends. At first hesitating, she finally decided to answer. It was Les. He'd been calling her at her work at the bank [4] almost every day during his lunch hour at the hatchery.

> *"Do you have time to meet?"* came the familiar request.
> *"I can't today. I'm meeting friends at Stear's Cafe around the corner. Let's plan on tomorrow."*

Bertha fanned her face with her free hand. It was hot for September. Disappointed, Les hung up.

> *"He's going to get me fired calling me every day like this,"* she thought to herself, as she stepped around her desk and picked up her purse.

Bertha had taken the office job to help supplement the meager income she received from the church. She needed the money in order to feed her expensive tastes, and she did not want to risk losing her job. Frank Armstrong, the bank manager, was a stickler for protocol. Too many personal phone calls and she could lose her job, although Mr. Armstrong did seem to like her. Everyone did.

The next day Bertha was waiting in the alley behind the bank as Les pulled up. Looking around to be sure no one was watching, she quickly hopped in. Slouching down into the front seat of the black Chevy Coupe, she tucked a loose strand of hair behind her ear and gave Les a smile and a wink.

> *"We only have an hour,"* she said. *"I told Mr. Armstrong that I needed an extra half hour for lunch today. He didn't even ask why."*

Les smiled, but also felt a twinge of jealous suspicion. Was Frank Armstrong having eyes for Bertha? Shrugging off the thought, he nodded and turned the car onto Hwy 68, and then right onto Banwell Road. Finally, pulling a short distance down an isolated two track, Les put the car in park.

> *"You look beautiful today,"* he smiled, turning to face her.

Bertha scooted over close to him and with the tip of her finger traced the curve of his neck.

> *"We don't have much time. Let's not waste it talking."*

She was surprised at the seductiveness of her own voice. A chill of excitement ran down Les's spine and he pulled her closer, wrapping her tightly in his arms. An hour later, Bertha pulled a mirror from her purse and reapplied her lipstick.

> *"Drop me off at the corner of West and River Streets, to be sure we're not spotted. There's an empty lot there. If anyone happens to see us, we'll say that you were giving me a ride back to work because I was having car trouble."*

Les reached over and gave her elbow a squeeze. Smiling, she hurriedly opened the door and slid out.

Discovered

Recognizing the 1940 Chevy, Paul was confused.

"Why is Dad's car parked way out here in the middle of nowhere in the middle of the day?" he wondered.

Paul drove for Parker Motor Freight. His route didn't usually take him down Banwell Rd, but a detour had rerouted him. As he slowed down, questioning whether his dad was having car trouble, he saw two heads, close together. Squinting he recognized the woman. Shocked by what he saw, he was unsure of what to do, so he kept driving.

Arriving home in Petoskey just before dinner time, he angrily explained to his wife, Lucille, what he had seen.

"Are you positive it was your dad and Bertha?" Lucille questioned, taking another bite of meatloaf.

"Yes! It was his car and I recognized Bertha from her hairstyle. It was definitely her."

"Do you think they saw you?" she asked.

"No, they seemed pretty preoccupied with each other," Paul answered, with disgust and bitterness in his voice.

"Are you going to tell your Mom?" Lucille asked with concern.

Paul paused for a moment. *"She should know, but I can't tell her. I just can't.*

It'd break her heart."

The next day Paul broke the news to his sisters, and they were equally shocked and angered.

"He's our father, and the Sunday School Superintendent! What a hypocrite!

How could he do this to Ma?!" Lorna furiously exclaimed.

Naomi broke down in tears.

"This is unbelievable!" she sobbed.

Paul had already called Evelyn the day before. She and her family still lived in Hart, a four-hour drive south of Alanson. Now, Paul sat with Lorna and Naomi, debating whether or not to tell Jane. It had been quickly decided not to tell Martha, Beatie and the twins. [5] They were still so young and living at home. But Jane was another story.

Jane had been through so much heartbreak already. Merlin Hughey had divorced her, leaving her alone with two young children. Doug was now four and Cindy was two. Bertha had comforted and supported Jane through the devastating agony of the break-up, taking Jane's side against her son's actions. To now inform Jane of this wretched betrayal was an uncertain decision. One the one hand, Jane had a right to know that her loving ex-mother-in-law was having an affair with her father. On the other hand, Jane had moved home with her two small children. Living in the same house with her parents while knowing such a dark secret would be an added burden to her already broken heart. As they weighed the decision, it was soon taken out of their hands.

34

Sin Confessed

1947

Gladys, accompanied by the young drummer, finished pounding out *"Onward Christian Soldiers"* with a flair and energy that inspired the congregants in their heartfelt worship. Voices soared, hands were raised, and feet were tapping.

> *"Amen!"* came the shouts. *"Praise the Lord!"*

Sister Bertha then stood to give her sermon.

> *"Today we look at James 1:14,"* she began. *"Reading from the Good Book, it says, "But every man is tempted, when he is drawn away of his own lust, and enticed,"* [1]

Leslie squirmed in his seat as Bertha went on with the morning message, railing against fornication and adultery.

> *"Amen sister! Amen!"* came the enthusiastic responses.

After twenty minutes of passionate preaching, Sister Turk ended, with her outstretched arms reaching toward heaven. She fervently prayed,

> *"Lord! We beseech you to convict our hearts! O God, lead us to repent of our sinfulness! For we cannot restore our souls if*

our bodies are corrupt with sin. Let your Holy Spirit fall upon us with conviction! Make us clean, O God!"

Cries of heartfelt agreement came from those sitting in the pews:

"O yes, Lord, yes! Convict us, Lord. Praise Jesus!"

At that, Leslie could not contain himself any longer. He stood to his feet and bound onto the platform, his long legs taking only three quick strides. Bertha was visibly confused, but benignly stepped to the side, with a nervous smile on her red lips, wondering what was coming. Les glanced at her quickly, and then turned to face the congregation. He cleared his throat and then began.

"For six years I have been engaged in a sinful, adulterous affair..."

The entire room fell silent. He continued:

"...with Sister Bertha Turk."

An audible, collective gasp came from the entire church. Bertha's mouth gaped in shock, yet she remained composed. Leslie continued, intent on giving as much detail as he could, both to ease his own guilty conscience and to expose Bertha's hypocrisy.

Gladys collapsed in shock as Leslie pressed on with his confession, seemingly oblivious to his devastated family sitting and taking it all in, in front of the entire church. Beatie, Martha and the eleven-year-old twins quickly surrounded their mother in confusion and tears. Stunned by the revelation, the congregants sat in silence, unsure of what to do or how to react. Some simply shook their heads in anger and disgust while others cried. And still Leslie continued.

"I was tempted and lured to give in to the lust of my mind and heart. God has convicted me of my sin and I confess before you all today the adulterous affair that I have conducted with this woman," pointing toward Bertha.

Sister Bertha stood motionless, silently contemplating how to respond to the accusations being put forth against her. Her mind was spinning. On the one hand, she fully understood the gravity of her own sin. But true repentance requires more than a knowledge of one's sin. In her case, it would require that she too publicly confess, due to her position as pastor, and then turn away from this sinful behavior, and toward God seeking His forgiveness. She wasn't sure what to do or say; she knew she was caught; there was no sense in trying to deny it. Her thoughts were reeling:

> *"Surely this is God's way of exposing and delivering me from my adultery and lies. But what of my reputation? How will I ever recover from this?"*

She meekly began to speak:

> *"I am relieved and thankful for Brother Sheldon's confession and I do not deny it. God has worked in his heart to bring him broken before you and make his way straight with God again, and I must do the same. Before God and all of you, I confess my sin. I have betrayed my calling as a minister of the gospel. I was led astray by temptation and by the deceitfulness of my own heart."*

Choking back tears, and having great difficulty looking into the eyes of those sitting before her, she continued.

> *"I have sinned against Gladys and the children. I have sinned against all of you. And most importantly I have sinned against God."*

As she spoke, the weight of her own immorality and the emotion of the whole situation appeared to completely overwhelm her, and she broke down sobbing with her face in her hands.

Leslie continued to stand off to the side, his arms hanging listless and his teeth clenched. Only then did he notice his wife and children. The girls helped their distraught mother exit down the aisle, then down the church steps. Leslie walked behind them. Crossing the road and walking into the house, no one spoke a word. The girls ran up to their rooms, and Gladys slumped down in a chair in the living room, still dazed and muddled from the morning.

"Gladys, I'm sorry. Please forgive me," Leslie pleaded.
"I can't talk right now. Please, just leave me alone. I need time. I can't even think straight,"

she said, nervously twisting her hanky in her hands. She stood abruptly with,

"I'll get lunch on the table,"

as if desperately needing something to do. She marched through the dining room and out into the kitchen. The smell of a pot roast with potatoes and carrots that she had put in the oven before church permeated the house. The girls came down and set the table, then they all sat down to eat. Some ate as quickly as they could, while others poked at their food with no appetite. After getting the food on the table, Gladys had gone into the bathroom and hadn't come out. No one spoke a word, not knowing what to say. Finishing their meal, the girls hurriedly cleared the table, washed and dried the dishes and scurried back upstairs. Leslie remained sitting at the table, unsure of what to do next.

Gladys never felt so plain. She looked in the mirror and saw a fifty-four-year-old mother of twelve. Tears came frequently. A weighty sadness and gloom penetrated her heart, and she feared that she would never recover. Questions surged through her mind like rolling waves on a stormy sea, with no safe harbor in sight. Should she feel sorry for herself, or was she somehow to blame for her husband's waywardness? Would have he remained faithful if she had been "enough"? Did Bertha lure Leslie into adultery, or was he the pursuer? Did Leslie even really know God or was it all a facade of hypocrisy, pretending to be one thing to hide the truth of who he really was? Would she ever be able to overcome the anger, pain and sense of betrayal that she felt in her heart? Could she possibly find a way to forgive him? So many questions that, at least for now, had no answers.

Smoothing her apron, she finally came out of the bathroom and slowly sat down at the dining room table. Leslie sat staring out the window. His face was stony and cold. Gladys contemplated how to proceed. She felt numb inside. At the same time, the excruciating events of the morning had been so eye-opening for understanding the emotional and physical distance that he had put between the two of them for so long. His impatience and seeming contempt for her made sense. It all made sense now. She decided that she would neither put on a brave front nor blame herself. She would find answers. There were so many questions.

Though he sounded contrite, she sensed that he wasn't as concerned about her pain and humiliation as he was about the ending of the affair itself.

> *"Do you love her?"* Gladys firmly asked, afraid of what his answer may be.

Leslie hesitated, clearing his throat and shifting in the chair. Folding his hands on the table he finally looked at her.

> *"I don't know what to tell you, Gladys. I mean, obviously I was drawn to her. But no, I wouldn't call it love. I don't love her, Gladys, I just gave into my temptations. And besides, it doesn't matter much anymore, she has her eye on a new man."*

Taking a deep breath, Gladys asked a probing question:

> *"So, did you confess just to hurt her? Are you truly repentant before the Lord and me, or are you just angry that she dumped you for someone else?"*

Les replied with a jerk, continuing to stare out the window.

> *"I don't know. I don't know! I didn't plan on confessing. My anger and guilt just overwhelmed me and I had to tell everyone who she was and what she'd done. Please, forgive me, I love you. Please believe me. And we have the children to consider."*

Gladys was a smart woman, and very discerning. She knew that Leslie was aiming for love in his response to her, but it was falling short. Shooting for love he only hit sorry sentimentality.

> *"Les, you didn't care about the kids or about me for six years! How can I believe you now? I know that you loved me once, and I want to believe that you can again. But love isn't always enough. It's an act of the will, and somehow along the way you gave yourself permission to turn your back on me, and the kids, and especially on the Lord, to go and have an affair with a Jezebel."*

Her voice rising. Leslie winced at her words but said nothing.

> *"Forgiveness is one thing, but trust is another. Right now, I can't really muster either one."*

Her voice was shaky, and she felt her face flush with anger. A light breeze rustled the trees outside the window as Gladys went on:

> *"Make no mistake Leslie, adultery takes two people. You cannot wiggle out of blame. A woman enticed you and you succumbed like a brainless bull."*

Leslie was anxious to end the conversation.

> *"I know I have hurt you and you have every reason to be angry."*

But Gladys wasn't done, in fact she was just getting warmed up:

> *"And why, in the name of God Himself, would you choose to confess in front of the whole church without first confessing to me?! You say it wasn't planned, but I find that hard to believe. This makes me doubt the sincerity of your repentance. It felt like you were simply angry with her, more than heartfelt grief over your own sinful actions. I can only take your word for why you did it, but make no mistake, God knows your heart!"*

Leslie nodded.

"You're right. I am sorry. I should have talked to you first. It was an awful shock, I know."

Gladys continued:

"It was and it wasn't. Do you think I haven't seen the discontent and animosity in you? Do you think I haven't felt the distance and even the disdain that you've had for me? Do you know how long it's been since you've shown any desire for me? Let me tell you something. I tried to make you happy and failed because no woman is going to fill the void that you have in your life. You will not find any rest or peace until you satisfy the deepest hunger of your heart. You have tried to satisfy it your way, in the arms of another woman. But Leslie, your life will be lived in vain if you don't find your way good with God."

He nodded, his eyes looking down at the floor. She continued, now softening her voice,

"Leslie, I love you. I have always loved you. You are my husband and I will eventually choose to forgive you. I will give myself permission to forgive you, as you gave yourself permission to cheat and lie to me, and I will choose to do it every day. But I do have a requirement. I don't want to ever hear that woman's name mentioned in this house again. Moving on from this will not be easy. But it will be impossible if she is a part of our lives in any way. Hearing her name will be like ripping a bandage off the wound and I can't bear it. Do you understand what I am saying?"

Leslie nodded. Now, the conversation was over.

JENNIFER BROOKS

Ramifications

Time has a way of settling certain memories deep within the heart, which can easily turn opinions into truths, even if those opinions are distorted or false. Over the following years, Bertha became the epitome of the evil seductress and Leslie the victim, though a very willing victim, of her wiles. Yet certainly, a six-year affair could never be laid on the shoulders of only one of the guilty parties. Both were equally to blame. Regardless, in the family's eyes, Bertha became a most despicable person, a true Jezebel. Gladys held true to her stance that Bertha's name would never be mentioned. When it was required for some reason that her name be used, the family would simply refer to her as "Ole B.T."

The affair was swept under the proverbial rug, never to be fully discussed again, allowing time to do its work. And work it did. In a myriad of ways, feelings of unspoken anger, bitterness and hurt would, for years to come, affect the lives of Leslie and Gladys' family, some more than others. Sin has a long memory. Leslie's transgressions of deception, lies and adultery had far-reaching consequences, bringing with it undying suspicions among the children and grand-children. Stories would quietly emerge of Leslie having attempted to harm Gladys during the years of the affair. Whether true or not, these tales added to the underlying feelings of betrayal by a supposed Christian man. Did Leslie remove screws from the hinges on the passenger side of the car? Were the boards on the porch steps loosened by accident? Speculations quietly abounded.

Faith itself became suspect and misunderstood among many of the children and subsequent grandchildren, with only the love and grace of God's redeeming power able to correct. Leslie's choices would do more long-reaching damage than could have ever been conceived. Beatie was fourteen years old when her father confessed in front of the church in 1947. She would not set foot in church again for almost ten years. Her heart became cold and indifferent to the things of God.

Several of the siblings would doubt the truth of Biblical faith altogether, while others, regardless, continued to commit themselves deeply to loving Christ. The Sheldon's became divided along a mute fence line of faith and worldviews. These two "sides" placed a schism of veiled antagonism in the family, yet all the while they remained uniquely and staunchly devoted to each other. Life is a complicated matter. While blame cannot be cast in total on Leslie and his failings as a husband and a father, his decisions undoubtedly carried a most significant impact.

Despite the growing differences in opinions and beliefs, which seemed to grow broader as the years went by, the family, for the most part, avoided confrontational conversations that could only cause further hurt and pain. Rather they chose to move forward with an abiding and deep love for each other, regardless of their differences. Gladys, the one who had been most hurt through the choices her husband made, was the unifying factor of family stability. Her love, joy and undying faith served as the glue. She had a unique ability to see only the good in all her children. Her love was strong and formidable, and devil beware if anyone came around to hurt or damage one of her kids...or her husband.

A Fresh Beginning

A new Pastor, Brother Keeler, soon arrived at the Alanson Pentecostal Church, following the confession and removal of Sister Turk. Fully aware of the situation, he befriended the Sheldons and did his best to help them salvage the vestiges of their marriage and their faith, speaking often on forgiveness - what it is and what it isn't, and what it looks like.

> *"Gladys, I know that you are hurting, and I know that you love Leslie and want your marriage to survive. Forgiveness is the only way that will happen. As believers we are called to forgive others as God has forgiven us. While you were dead in your sins Christ died for you. You and I don't deserve to be forgiven any more than Leslie does. That's why it is such an amazing and gracious gift from God, and now it will be a gift that you, with God's help, can offer to your husband. Gladys, forgiveness is something that you will struggle with from this point on. Holding onto bitterness and resentment is a heavy burden not easily cast off. Jesus wants to lighten your load. And understand, for us humans, forgiveness isn't a onetime accomplishment. Only Jesus accomplished that, once*

and for all, on the cross. But for us, it is much harder. It's going to be a 'one-day-at-a-time' effort on your part. But God will help you if you let Him. And when you get discouraged, never forget what Psalm 23:6 promises, "Surely goodness and mercy shall follow me all the days of my life...." Goodness and mercy, you can't beat that!" [2]

Brother Keeler turned to Leslie,

"Leslie, this is your responsibility. You have betrayed your wife in the most horrific way. You have cheated and lied. It is one thing for you to receive forgiveness, but make no mistake, there are consequences for you. You are not to remain passive. You need to spend the rest of your life devoted to your wife and her care. You have placed a terrible hardship on Gladys. Easing her pain is now your job. Building her trust is your purpose. Selfless love is your goal."

Over the years Leslie followed Brother Keeler's advice in as much as he was able as a conflicted man of shallow faith. Gladys recognized his efforts and felt his love for her returning. Although feelings of anger, resentment and insecurity were the easiest and most natural to give in to, she knew in her heart that those feelings could never bring her peace. To the contrary, they only served to stir up her negative emotions and insecurities even more, bringing back the pain and humiliation. The only thing that calmed her spirit was turning it over to Jesus, realizing goodness and mercy, which allowed her to apply her energy and love into forgiving her husband and moving forward, which is what she did.

The Legacy of Lank

On March 31, 1948, Lank Dodge died. Some live well and see their children rise up to call them blessed, while others die with bitterness, sorrow, dissatisfaction and a legacy of regret. Many, perhaps most, leave this world with a combination of both. Such was the case for Lank. He was loving, adventurous, curious, talented, free-spirited and resourceful.

He understood his place in the universe before an almighty God, and even at times in his life became very "religious". Yet he was also conniving, adulterous, dishonest and selfish. He understood an almighty God, but he never fully surrendered to God's love, choosing rather to go his own way. As a result, he was an extremely complicated, confusing, interesting, and in many ways difficult man to know and to live with. Gladys knew all of this about her father and she loved him deeply.

She admired how her father cultivated laughter, song and dance into their lives, while she also understood that his life was messy and hurtful to others. Throughout his seventy-six years, despite some of his painful choices, there was never any doubt of his love for his daughter, his "Babe", or for his wife Julina before her untimely death. His second wife, Mabel, did not have the patience or sense of humor to handle Lank for the long haul. After eighteen turbulent years of marriage, she chose to divorce him in 1944, four years before his death.

35

The Final Years

1947-1967

Looking to build a privately-owned fish hatchery, a wealthy investor from Harbor Springs named Mr. Holiday enlisted Leslie's help to find the best location. After combing the area carefully, Leslie soon realized that the natural flowing springs on the acreage next door to his own property was the most ideal. Holiday was agreeable to this.

> *"Good. This is fine. You speak to Mr. Skeel and find out if he will sell and his price, and then let me know."*

Mr. Skeel agreed to sell, and Holiday was happy with the price. Mr. Holiday quickly hired Leslie to develop and manage the endeavor. With his twenty years of experience as a culturalist and foreman with the Oden State Hatchery, Leslie was the perfect man for the job, bringing all the skills and knowledge of the fishing industry that he had acquired over the years.

The acreage was low-lying marsh grass and weeds, which backed up to the Crooked River, just south of and bordering the Sheldon property. Leslie supervised the digging of twelve ponds, and the construction of a building needed for hatching trout. He put up a high chain-link fence around the entire property to keep animals and children from wandering in.

> *"Les, put a gate and build a path leading to your house. This will probably all be yours someday anyway,"* Holiday told Les.

The following year Mr. Holiday died. His three grown children were not interested in the hatchery. Prior to his passing, Holiday had given Leslie an interest in the trout business, and with that and seven-thousand dollars, Leslie bought the entire property...ponds, building and all. Soon, working at the Oden Hatchery and operating his own trout business became too much. So in 1952, Les took his retirement eligibility and left the Oden State Fish Hatchery, devoting all his time to running his own business. [1]

The business grew and the income was exceptionally good. After so many years of financial struggle, at last they had money in their pockets. Leslie remained frugal. At the same time, he never wavered on the tithe to the church. Tithing was something he believed in. Honoring the Lord with the first 10% was his way of helping to keep his life in proper perspective. He had hardened his heart through so many years of deception, softening it was a long process and tithing was but one small piece.

For the first time in their lives, they were finally out from under the heavy hand of poverty. With the children grown and the new business providing so well, they could afford luxuries that they had never dreamed of before. Leslie bought two new cars, and a new truck boasting the business's logo, *"Have Fish Will Travel"* [2] inscribed on the back. In the ensuing years, the two of them would enjoy a trip to California by train, as well as four trips to Canada for some moose hunting. Life was good and Gladys thanked the Lord for His blessings and for the return of her loving husband.

Sitting at the dining room table, watching Leslie saunter along the path toward the house, Gladys noticed a slowness to his usually fast paced gate. Later that evening she asked him about it.

"Are you feeling Ok."

"I'm not sure what's going on, but I'm in a whole lot of pain. It's my stomach, and it's been going on for a while now. I guess I'd better see the doctor, even though I don't want to. You know how much I hate going," Les confided to Gladys.

"Ha! I know you hate going, but I think you should...before he runs out of patients," she said with a smile.

Gladys added a little corny humor to soften her own worries as much as Leslie's obvious concerns. He smiled back at her though weakly and returned to reading his newspaper.

"Would a heating pad help?" she asked.
"Maybe," he replied, not looking up.

The next day Gladys made the phone call, taking Naomi's suggestion of which doctor to see. The appointment was set for the following week. Leslie's symptoms were not getting better and Gladys was fearful of the worst. The waiting seemed like forever, but finally the day came. Traveling the ten miles into Petoskey, Gladys felt a knot in her stomach as Leslie, thin and gaunt, winced at every bump in the road. The drive would be forever etched into Gladys's mind, as the events of the day would change everything, like a perpetual bad dream.

After several tests, the diagnosis was confirmed: colon cancer. It had been metastasizing for some time and had already invaded the liver. The prognosis was fatal; Leslie had only a few months, maybe a year, to live. His 6'2" body began to quickly shrivel away. His face yellowed from jaundice and his cheeks became sunken as he continued to lose weight. His once robust and energetic physique and personality both faded into fragility, succumbing to the disease.

It had been fifteen years since buying the hatchery. Now seventy years old and dying of cancer, he was unable to continue working the ponds. Judy, the older twin, stepped in. Having moved to California soon after graduating from high school, Judy was concerned for her parent's wellbeing and readily agreed that if she could help alleviate some of the stress from them, she would buy the hatchery. The decision was finalized, and Judy, who was not married, moved back to Alanson to take over her father's business.

Damaged Relationships

On December 30, 1967 God took Leslie Lester Sheldon home. Leslie and Gladys had twenty additional years together, from the time of his devastating confession to his death. By all outward appearances, they were good years. Gladys stated,

Leslie was the love of her life and she never regretted her marriage or her
life with him, even through the sting of his betrayal. Her grief was deep
and lasting when he died.

Leslie's children felt grief along with their mother, but their
relationships with their dad differed from one to the other. The older
children had a much different relationship with their father than the
younger. Naomi, Evelyn and Jane remembered their dad as hard working,
fun-loving...a jokester. Paul and Lorna, being in the middle, remembered
him as impatient, mean and a taskmaster who didn't really connect with
them other than to bark gruff orders. These were the years that their
father, unbeknownst to them, was having the affair. They hated him. The
younger children - Martha, Beatie and the twins - remembered their dad
as someone they never really knew very well. He was there, but not really
too interested in them or involved with them as individuals. He wasn't
good or bad, just disengaged.

This is not to oversimplify complex relationships, but rather to give a
broader perspective on how life choices affect the bond between children
and a parent. For example, Beatie felt distant from her father, while at the
same time, she shared anecdotal positive stories, which expressed a sense
of pride in who her father was. She remembered the whole family piling
into the car to race down two track roads looking for deer and elk. Or
following her dad through the woods, *"his walk was a dead run,"* to check
traps and having to duck quickly before branches would swing back and
knock her over as he barreled through. There was a tone of admiration in
her voice for her father.

Gladys Louise Sheldon (b. Dodge) lived for twenty-nine more years
after Leslie's passing. At the age of one-hundred and three on July 28,
1996, she took her last breath and stepped from this life into the next.
Those twenty-nine years provided a rich inheritance of memories for
those who knew her. Her ragtime piano still rings in the ears of long-ago
listeners, and toes cannot help but tap while faces light up in joy. The
strong voices of sisters, Naomi, Jane, Lorna, Martha, Beatie, Joie and Judy
(Evelyn wasn't a singer) gathered around their mother's piano, all singing

in loud harmony, still echo from those days gone by. Grandsons Doug, playing trumpet, and Sonny, playing saxophone, alternating with his Aunt Beatie on the alto-sax as well. The rest of the family merrily joined in the mayhem of music. The energy and happiness was profound!

When the family was not gathered, Gladys suffered a natural loneliness, sitting hour after hour in a silent house that was once filled with noise and activity. She would anxiously wait for one of her kids to call her on the phone and would anticipate expectantly from the large picture window for a familiar car to pull in the driveway. Sunset brought on a weighty melancholy. She looked forward to Sundays when most, if not all, of her children would arrive to visit, coming and going throughout the day. In between, her little dog Suzette and *The Lawrence Welk Show* gave her some company while she waited. But it was her Bible and time alone with God that brought the most peace to her heart and mind through the lonesome times. She never lost her sense of humor, her creativity, her talent, her immovable faith, or the joy she found in life. Upon entering the nursing home in her late nineties, where she would spend her final years, she hollered over to an old man sleeping in a wheelchair *"Wake up and live!"* A life lesson we should all take to heart.

Final Thoughts

Although I have attempted to portray each ancestor with as much accuracy and factual detail as research would allow, the fact remains there is much that can never be known about the past. Much is constituted fiction. In their book, *The Lessons of History*, Will and Ariel Durant write,

> *"Our knowledge of any past event is always incomplete, probably inaccurate, beclouded by ambivalent evidence and biased historians, and perhaps distorted by our own political or religious partisanship."* [1]

This quote attests to the fact that much of my narrative includes a necessary amount of guesswork and speculation, although hopefully in as candid and educated a way as possible, notwithstanding my own prejudices and beliefs.

I have attempted to paint a portrait of specific people, my people, each one having lived in the context of where and when they were born, and the historical, political, sociological and economic conditions of the times in which they lived. My desire was to present a historically accurate portrait of each person as a way of honoring their life - these were real people, living in real places, with real hopes and fears, aspirations and disappointments, joys and sorrows. Unfortunately, historical records of ordinary, non-famous people are most often simply that - records: birth, marriage, death. What they invariably lack is much in the way of description concerning personality, vocation, physical or personal characteristics, let alone relationships they shared and conversations they had with others, or what they enjoyed doing, or how they died.

I discovered that writing a "historical novel/narrative" such as this was much like putting a jigsaw puzzle together, whereupon you quickly realize that you are missing a fair number of pieces. My attempt was to use the known "pieces" of individual lives, and then fill in the ones that are missing by using a combination of various elements: 1) the tendencies of human nature and how people are apt to react in certain life situations; 2) a fair amount of "common sense imagination" as I tried to put myself in their shoes, so to speak, with the circumstances of the day influencing their lives; and 3) some creative license on the part of the author - that's me! - pertaining to individual personalities and appearance.

While I was as careful as I could possibly be in gathering as much factual detail as I could through hundreds and hundreds of hours of study and research (all of which I found to be most intriguing, while at times frustrating), I am certain, without a doubt, that there will be details, data, and speculations on my part that may prove disagreeable or flat out wrong. Please understand my heart and my desire in writing this was to attempt to both preserve and honor the past, while at the same time hopefully encouraging those of us still living to remember that we all leave a legacy for those who come behind us.

Like the puzzle I referenced earlier, each of our lives is intrinsically connected to each other, especially within a family. One generation passes on to the next generation the good along with the bad. Some that is ugly along with some that is gloriously beautiful. Such is the case with my ancestry. It is only by God's grace that the "bad" and "ugly" in our lives can be transformed into that which is good and beautiful. For me, I believe just as so many of my ancestors, that God sent his Son, Jesus, into the world to make that possible.

One of the most interesting and significant threads that seemed to weave its way through my family history was the constant presence of the Bible itself. From one generation to the next, there it was, again and again, bringing with it a living faith that was birthed across the ocean, carried into the wilderness of the New World, planted and bearing fruit in small towns in Massachusetts, Rhode Island, then on to The Northwest Territory (Ohio), and lastly carried north into the lumber camps of northern Michigan. From the Greenwoods to the Sheldons, God's faithful and providential hand of blessing is undeniably seen, and I am humbled and very honored to be a part of it.

Endnotes

(All underlined names indicate direct line ancestry)

Chapter 1 - John Greenwood and Isabella Lea
1550's

1 "_Isabella Lea_" is the name sighted from Family Research as the name of John Greenwood's wife, b. ABT. 1555, d. unknown. John Greenwood b. 1556 or 1560, in Heptonstall, Halifax, West Riding, Yorkshire, England. He died in Tyburn, Blatherwycke, Northampton, England. It is not known where Isabella and Abel lived in 1593, when John Greenwood was hanged. Abel was born in Heptonstall. Family Research records Isabella's birth in Halifax, West Riding, Yorkshire, England. Other records indicate more children born to John and Isabella.

2 When John was in prison, he was interrogated by the Bishop of London and asked if he did not have a son who was unbaptized. John replied that, yes, he did have a son, 1½ years old, unbaptized, but that he had been in prison and was unable to take his son to a reformed church where he could be baptized according to God's ordinance. _Greenwood Genealogies, 1154-1914, Chapter 5, The Execution of John Greenwood,_ by Frederick Greenwood, East Templeton, MA, 1914.

3 Speculation.

4 Speculation based on research of Heptonstall.

5 The English Reformation did not begin in earnest until 1534, with Henry VIII rebelliously divorced his first wife, Catherine of Aragon, and thus appointed himself the Supreme Head of the Church of England.

6 Not John Greenwood's words. Thoughts compiled from, _The Puritans, Their Origins and Successors,_ by D.M. Lloyd Jones.

Chapter 2 - Growing Discontent
Mid-1570's

1 Tyndale's version from the Epistle of Romans. The text is from the edition of 1534.

Chapter 3 - Separatists
1577-1586

1   From: Wikipedia, *John Greenwood* (Divine)

2   It is not known when or where John and Isabella married.

3   There is no physical description on record of John Greenwood. Although, there is a stained-glass window with his image at Emmanuel United Reformed Church, Cambridge, England.

        NOTE: Painting Puritans with a broad brush, so to speak, as stiff-necked and somber would be a misconception. As David McCullough writes in his book, *"Pioneers"*, pg. 5, *"Puritans were as capable as any people of exuding an affable enjoyment of life. Many a Puritan loved good food, good wine, a good story and good cheer."*

4   Conjecture.

5   Robert Browne (1550-1563) was one of the first to popularize the movement of Separatism, in his publication of 1582, *"A Treatise of Reformation Without Tarrying for Anie"*. Browne graduated from Corpus Christi College, Cambridge, in 1572, eight years before John Greenwood. He found no redeeming features in the Church of England and formed the Separatist church meeting in private houses. Browne was a harsh controversialist, unduly censorious and judgmental and a known wife-beater. Later he withdrew from the movement, submitted to ecclesiastical authority and lived in relative comfort, while his brethren suffered persecution. In approximately 1585, John Greenwood (with Henry Barrow) carried on Browne's Congregational Separatism in London.

6   A message was presented at Cambridge around graduation that roused strong interest in Separatist thought. The presenter of the speech is unknown.

7   <u>John Greenwood</u> propagated many seditious opinions, such as: the Church of England is no true church; it's worship is idolatry; it's ministers have no lawful calling; the government is ungodly; and the use of set forms of prayer as ungodly.

8   Lord Robert Rich, of Rochford, Essex County, was the grandson of Richard Rich, 1st Baron Rich and Lord Chancellor during the reign of King Edward VI of England. Richard tortured those who opposed the Established Church of England. He secured the operation of King Henry VIII's Act of Supremacy.

9   Speculation.

10   Portions of prayer taken from *The Puritans*, by D. M. Lloyd Jones, pg. 52

11   The Clink was a prison in Southwark (central London), England. It operated from the 12th century until 1780. By the 16th century it became mostly a prison for heretics who held views contrary to those of the Established Church of England.

Chapter 4 - Sedition
1586-1592

1   Fleet Prison was a notorious London prison by the side of the River Fleet. Built in 1197 and rebuilt several times, it remained in use until 1844 and was demolished in 1846. (Wikipedia)

2   Data taken from *Greenwood Genealogies*, 1154-1914, Chapter 5, The Execution of John Greenwood, by Frederick Greenwood, East Templeton, MA, 1914.

3   John Aylmer was consecrated as Bishop of London in 1577. He once stated, "*God is English*", attempting to fill his parishioners with piety and patriotism. While in the position of Bishop of London he made himself notorious by his harsh treatment of all who differed from him on ecclesiastical questions, whether Puritan or Roman Catholic.

4   Quote taken from *Greenwood Genealogies*, 1154-1914, Chapter 5, The Execution of John Greenwood, by Frederick Greenwood, East Templeton, MA, 1914.

5   Quote from John Greenwood from "*An answer to George Gifford's pretended defense of read prayers and devised liturgies with ungodly calls and wicked slanderers.*" comprised in the first part of the book entitled, "*A Short Treatise Against the Donatists of England*".

6   Speculation.

Chapter 5 - Tyburn
1592-1593

1   *Greenwood Genealogies*, 1154-1914, Chapter 5, The Execution of John Greenwood, by Frederick Greenwood, East Templeton, MA, 1914.

2   Conjectured thoughts inspired from random passages in "The Valley of Vision", a collection of Puritan Prayers and Devotions.

Chapter 6 - Abel
Early 1660's

1   Abel Greenwood, b. 2-26-1585 or 1587, Heptonstall, England, d. 8-14-1623, Heptonstall, England. Buried 10-14-1623 at St. Thomas a Beckett. (38 yrs.). Speculation that he died in a location other than Heptonstall based on the date of death vs. his burial date.

2   There is no specific information regarding Isabella after John Greenwood was hanged.

3   John Mitchell is the name listed in Family Search for Elizabeth Greenwood's (b. Mitchell) father. He is placed in Halifax because Elizabeth was born in Halifax.

4   There is no known connection between John Greenwood and John Mitchell.

5   There was a plague in London in 1603 during the elaborate festivities at the coronation of James I, which restricted activities, although the streets were *"paved with men."*

Chapter 7 - Abel and Elizabeth
Mid 1660's-1610

1   No other specifics are known regarding Elizabeth Greenwood (b. Mitchell) b. 1-7-1588, Halifax, England, d. unknown.
2   Nothing is known of John Mitchell's occupation or personal life.
3   The year and location of the marriage between Abel and Elizabeth is uncertain.
4   Conjecture.
5   Queen Elizabeth died, after 44 years of rule, in 1603, at 69 years of age, after falling into a state of severe melancholy and depression.
6   John Knox: (1513-1572) Scottish minister, theologian and leader of the country's reformation. Founder of the Presbyterian Church of Scotland.
7   Abel and Elizabeth had at least one daughter (possibly three) and one son. The dates of birth are in question: Ellen (1600-1622), Maria (1601-1602), Ann (1606-1657), Thomas b. 2-26-1610 or ABT. 1617, Heptonstall, d. Unknown. NOTE: There appear to be several "Thomas Greenwoods" born throughout Heptonstall over a period of several years.

Chapter 8 - Thomas
1623

1   There is no record of Abel Greenwood's death other than he died 8-8-1623, at age 38 yr. Thomas, Abel's son, would have been approximately 13 years old. Abel was buried in October of 1623. One source notes, *"revolutionary patriot"*, but no specific records back that up currently.

Chapter 9 - King Charles I and The English Civil War
1625-1651

1   William Bradford (1590-1657) was a Puritan Separatist from West Riding, Yorkshire, living in the same area that the Greenwoods were living and would have been approximately the same age as Abel. William Bradford was also a weaver. Bradford joined reform-minded believers and began to worship with them. Experiencing severe persecution, at age 18, Bradford and these believers, in 1608, escaped to Leiden, Holland where it was free to practice their faith. Bradford married in 1613. By 1617, the congregation in Holland began plans

for the establishment of a colony of their own in America. In September 1620, this group of Puritan Separatists sailed for America...leaving from Plymouth, England, on the Mayflower.

2   Records appear conflicting concerning Thomas Greenwood's birth in 1610 or 1617 and his wife's name is under question. Elizabeth Hurd supposedly married Thomas Greenwood in MA. Records are conflicting, but Elizabeth is unlikely Thomas Greenwood's wife. He did not immigrate to the colonies.

Greenwood Family Genealogies lists three women who married Thomas Greenwood (s) in Heptonstall in the mid 1640's and only Elizabeth in MA. Bay Colony. Heptonstall seems the likely option according to corresponding records. OPTIONS:

Thomas Greenwood married Sarah Crossle, 7-15-1641
Thomas Greenwood married Ellen Wood, 10-15-1642
Thomas Greenwood married Sarah Sutcliffe, 4-30-1642
Thomas Greenwood married Elizabeth Hurd in MA, 1642.
I have randomly chosen "Sarah Crossle" as our Thomas's wife.

3   There is no record of Thomas's involvement in this battle, but it is certainly likely.

4   Unsubstantiated. The grammar school was built that year and was rather centralized, but whether it was a fortress for the protection of women and children is speculation.

5   The Buttress is the old packhorse trail leading to Heptonstall.

6   Conjecture.

7   January 1644.

8   There is no record of Elizabeth's life regarding remarriage or time and place of death.

9   Reasonable conjecture. Thomas would have been approx. 34 years old at the time, and Heptonstall had been embroiled in significant conflict.

10 Cromwell was wounded at the Battle of Marston Moor, July,1644. There is no record of Thomas Greenwood as a cavalry soldier in Cromwell's army or of his death in that battle. Speculation based on possibility, due to the dates of events.

11 Early 17th Century hymn. This particular "hymn, was found on a handwritten document and deciphered with difficulty.

12 Henry Brooks is a direct ancestor of Gary Brooks (husband to the author). Records indicate that Henry served in Cromwell's army as a "shoer of horses" or farrier.

Chapter 10 - Thomas II Immigrates
1665

1   Thomas Greenwood II, b.1643 in Heptonstall, England. Baptized 6-4-1643 in Heptonstall. He immigrated to Boston in 1665 or 1666. He died in Newton (Cambridge) Massachusetts in 1693.

2   No records concerning cause of death for <u>Elizabeth Greenwood</u>, <u>Thomas's</u> grandmother.

3   <u>James Maxwell's</u> 4x-great granddaughter, <u>Martha "Patty" Shipman</u>, would marry Thomas Greenwood's 4x-great grandson, <u>Jonathan Sheldon</u> in 1830. <u>James Maxwell</u>, b. ABT.1638, Dumfries, Dumfriesshire, Scotland, d.1720, Boston, MA, a direct descendant to the author. He immigrated to Boston approximately the same time as <u>Thomas Greenwood</u>, sometime prior to 1666. <u>James</u> married <u>Margery Maxwell (b. Crump)</u> after 1624, who gave birth to ABT. 21 children. <u>James</u> had between 21 and 30 children between his first wife, <u>Margery</u> and his second wife.

    * He was a member of the Scots Charitable Society and a door keeper for the General Court of Boston.

    *<u>James</u> was admitted to the First Church of Boston. Sept 6, 1666.

    *On Feb 27, 1697, he was admonished and suspended from the Lord's Table for "notorious drunkenness".

    *Restored to communion April 24, 1698.

    *On Dec 29, 1706, with the consent of the church, again admonished publicly for drunkenness.

    *Restored to communion upon "his public repenting his repentance for his sin of drunkenness".

    *He was ultimately excommunicated, Feb 14, 1714 (79 yrs old), for the sin of drunkenness, before the church, with a lifting of hands.

    *April 24,1715, James, on a solemn and serious confession read before the church, was again admitted to the church with a solemn warning against the sin of drunkenness.

    There is no record of <u>Thomas</u> and <u>James</u> meeting in Boston, a town of over 3,000 people by this date, but they most likely overlapped in living there for at least a few years.

Chapter 11- Thomas II and Hannah "Anna" Ward
Late 1660's-1670

1   Rev. John Wilson (1588 -1667), Puritan clergyman and minister at First Church of Boston from (1630-1667). No records of <u>Thomas Greenwood</u> being a member of this church.

2   Increase Mather (1639-1723) preached John Wilson's funeral sermon in 1667. Mather was a Puritan minister at North Church, Boston. He was connected to the Salem Witch trials in 1692.

3   On the establishment of Harvard University, in 1638, it was ordered by the General Court that Newtown should be called Cambridge in complement to the place where so many of the clerical fathers of New England had been educated.

The large territory obtained on the south side of the Charles River, comprising nearly the whole of what is now Brighten and Newton, was at first called "*the south side of the Charles River*", and sometimes "*Nonantum*", the Indian name. After religious services were held regularly on the south side of the river, it was called "*Cambridge Village*", until 1679, and then by authority of the General Court, after December 1691, Newtown. Later, it changed to what is today, *Newton*.

4   Hannah Greenwood (born Ward): (we are calling her "Anna" here to help avoid confusion)

      b. ABT. 1651, Cambridge Village (Newton), Middlesex Co, MA.

      d. ABT. 1686, Newtown (Newton), Middlesex Co, MA.

      m. Thomas Greenwood Jr, 6-8-1670.

5   John Ward, b. ABT. 1626, England, d. 6-1-1708, m. Hannah Ward (born Jackson), 1650, Cambridge Village (Newton), MA. They had 13 children.

6   "Turner": maker of objects of wood, metal or bone by turning on the lath.

7   William Ward, b. ABT. 1613, in England, d. 8-10-1687, Marlborough, MA. Buried in Spring Hill Cemetery. Immigrated 1638, with his second wife, Elizabeth and five children, settled in Sudbury, MA, where he was granted land in 1640. William and his family settled on a sight with a good spring and built their house. In 1643, Sudbury built its first meeting house. William was chosen as one of six to represent the town in the meeting house contract. May 10, 1643, William became a freeman and the following spring he was elected deputy representative to the General Court. In 1645 and 46 he was appointed commissioner to "*end all small causes*" in Sudbury. He also represented Sudbury on the Grand Jury of the county court at Charlestown and Cambridge. William's holdings were two to three hundred acres. In 1655, cattle increased and so did the number of his children, who were becoming adults and feeling the space restriction. It was decided to form another plantation about 8 miles west of Sudbury. William was awarded one of three fifty-acre allotments of land, showing that his wealth had increased considerably. Most of Williams' children joined him in Marlborough. In 1660 the General Court confirmed the plantation and named it Marlborough. William continued to be active politically and was a deacon in his church. However, settling in Marlborough was not as smooth as Sudbury and there were many conflicts and dissensions. In the town records, William and several of his sons and sons-in-law were involved in multiple years of lawsuits with others in the town of Marlborough--- a series of events cut short by King Philip's War in 1675. The Indian raids leading up to and during King Philip's War were a constant source of concern. Several houses were fortified as garrisons. Williams' house and his daughters, Deborah and Joanna, were among them. On March 26, 1675, the Indians approached. The Indians did not attack these houses, but burned the meeting house and thirteen

houses, eleven barns and mutilated cattle. The following night, Lt Jacobs with some soldiers attacked an Indian camp, killing and wounding several them. Many Marlborough residents fled. <u>William</u> at 73 years old remained. On April 18, the Indians suddenly returned, destroying every remaining unfortified house and structure. They hung around for a few days hoping to get at some of the settlers in the fortified houses, but on April 21, they went on to attack Sudbury. <u>Williams</u>' daughter, Elizabeth, lost her husband, John Howe, and William's youngest son, Eleazer, was shot. The Indians did not return to Marlborough.

8   <u>Hannah Ward (born Jackson)</u>, b. 1634, Stepney, London, England, d. 4-24-1703, New Town (Newton), MA. m. <u>John Ward</u>. Her parents were <u>Edward and Frances Jackson</u>.

9   <u>Edward Jackson and Frances Jackson (born Taft)</u>. <u>Edward</u>: b. ABT. 1602, in Stepney, Whitechapel, London, England. Edward m. <u>Frances Taft</u>, 12-7-1629, London, England, (Frances died 10-5-1648) m. Elizabeth Oliver (b. Newgate), 3-16-1649, Cambridge Village, MA. Baptized at St Dunstan's Church, Stepney, London, England. Immigrated 1643, as a "nailor" (a person who makes nails). A relatively wealthy man. Purchased a house from a Samuel Holte (Holt) in Cambridge Village with six acres. Over the years he accumulated more houses through purchase and grants, including 500 acres purchased. <u>Edward Jackson</u> took the freeman's path in May 1645. He was deputy to the General Court of MA eighteen times between May 1648-Aug 1676. He was appointed part of a committee to revise the articles of confederation of the United Colonies. <u>Edward</u> was a distinguished citizen. He was a townsman of Cambridge in 1665 and served on the town's commission to end small cases under 40 shillings. On Oct 6, 1663, he was released from ordinary military training. He was to pay eight shillings per year to the military company for the privilege of being released. He was easily 60 at the time. In May 1678, he and 51 residents (including his grand-son-in law <u>Thomas Greenwood</u>) of Cambridge Village, living on the south side of the Charles River, petitioned to be separated from Cambridge and become a new town, asking that the court choose a name. He was the author and first signer of this petition. Cambridge protested vigorously, which delayed the split until Jan. 11, 1687 (9 years). <u>Edward Jackson</u> died in 1681 and never saw the results of the years of petitioning to be a separate town. It was given the name New Town in 1691 and later became "Newton". <u>Edward</u> left a huge estate, with a will. He left bequests to his wife, Elizabeth, 9 children, three stepchildren; 6 sons-in-law; numerous grandchildren and great grandchildren and his friend; Capt. Thomas Prentice. <u>Edward</u> was a land surveyor and surveyed his own lands, making divisions to his children. He was also a large proprietor of the Billerica lands and in the division of 1652, he had four hundred acres which by his will he gave to Harvard College together with other bequests. He organized the coming of the first church of Cambridge Village in 1664 (although they

had several ministers before this point). Edward was a deacon in 1654. In 1668, Elder Wiswall, Edward and John Jackson (Edwards brother) were appointed to catechize the children of the new church at the village. (Wiswall is another ancestor as well; he presented a case to the General Court with a plea to build a bridge across the Charles River, 1661). Edward was probably the first slave owner in Newton. His will included "two men servants".

Chapter 12 - Cambridge Village and King Philip's War
1673-1675

1   Birthdate of Thomas "Tom" Greenwood is uncertain. There is little doubt that he had a brother, John, and they were possibly the only surviving children born to Thomas and Hannah "Anna" Greenwood. Some researchers list the brothers as having the same birth date. There are at least two sources claiming 7-15-1673 for both men, but there are also some researchers listing Thomas's birth as 1-22-1671. "Anna" and Thomas possibly had a son, named Thomas, born January 22, 1671, who died in infancy. He was either premature, born only seven and a half months after the marriage or he was conceived before the marriage.

    NOTE: The author leans slightly against the twin theory, believing that Thomas "Tom". and John were brothers, born two years apart. Thomas on 1-22-1671 and then John, born 7-15-1673, although for the purposes of this writing, the twin option was used. Thomas graduated from Harvard in 1690; ordained 1693 and moved to Rehoboth as the pastor.

2   Swansea, MA, 47 miles south of Boston, was the first Indian attack of King Philip's War after the hanging and had 70 settlers confined to their stockade on June 20, 1675. By June 25th, the entire town had been burned. Before it was finished, over half of the 90-110 existing towns and villages in the middle colonies were attacked and destroyed to one degree or another. Over 1000 colonists lost their lives and hundreds captured. Countless Indians died

3   John Howe Jr, b. 8-24-1640, d. in Marlborough, MA, m. Elizabeth, 4-21-1676. Most likely, this was Elizabeth Kerley (b. Ward), daughter of William Ward. Elizabeth remarried to "Kerley" after John Howe's death. William Ward, John Howe's father-in-law, lived in Sudbury, but removed to Marlborough, building his house there in 1659, being also one of the first settlers.

4   A 60-man militia was ambushed on the road between Sudbury and Marlborough on April 21, 1676, after Marlborough was destroyed on the 18th. They were reinforcements from nearby towns and drawn into an ambush by the Algonquians. Marlborough Captain Samuel Wadsworth was killed along with half the militia, including John Howe and William Ward's youngest son, Eleazer Ward, shot.

5   Metacom or Metacomet (King Philip), (1638-1676) became chief of the Wampanoag People in 1662. At the beginning he sought to live in harmony with the colonists, adopting a European name and wearing clothes he bought in Boston. But as colonists continued to expand, Metacom was forced into major concessions. In 1671, he surrendered much of his tribe's armament and ammunition and agreed that they were subject to English law. The encroachment continued until hostilities broke in 1675, with the goal of stopping Puritan expansion.

6   Speculation that Thomas was involved that day with Anna's family in Marlborough or Sudbury.

7   Rev. Nehemiah Hobart m. Sarah Jackson, sister to Hannah Ward (b. Jackson) on 3-21-1675. He served as minister in Cambridge Village / New Town from 1674-1712.

8   First Church of Cambridge Village (later Newton) remained the only church until 1780 1st minister, John Eliot, 1664-1668, 2nd minister Nehemiah Hobart, 1674-1712.

Chapter 13 - War and Death
1686-1690

1   There is no documentation regarding how Hannah "Anna" Greenwood died. / Ps 37:3.

2   Capt. Noah Wiswall, b.1638 in Dorchester, Suffolk County, MA, d. 7-6-1690. He was the father of Elizabeth Greenwood (born Wiswall), who married Rev. Thomas "Tom" Greenwood. Capt. Wiswall was killed in the battle at Wheelwright Pond, Lee, NH, during the King William War between Britain and France and their respective Indian allies. His father, Thomas Wiswall (1601-1683) was one of the first settlers at Cambridge Village (later Newton, MA), in 1654, with Edward Jackson, John Jackson (Edward's brother and literally the first settler in the area) and John Ward. Thomas Wiswall and his wife, Elizabeth Berbage (1601-?) had ten children. Noah Wiswall was born forth.

3   New France was an autonomous Catholic French colony, located from eastern Canada, across the Great Lakes, all the way to the Gulf of Mexico. Land disputes were often, and they were violent. Acadia (present day Maine) was claimed by the Massachusetts Colony and by New France. King William's War was over the rights to settle this land. The war was also an extension of the Nine Years War taking place in Europe at the same time. Catholic King James II was deposed from England in 1688. Protestant King William joined a war against France, where James had fled. Neither Britain or France sent troops to assist with New France or the British Colonies. Indian allies on both sides were heavily involved.

4   Five principle Indian nations.

5   Present day, Portland, Maine.
6   Newington, NH.
7   Exeter, NH, located 13 miles from Wheelwright Pond, was attacked on July 4, 1690.
8   Lt. Gershom Flagg and Ensign Edward Walker were both killed at the battle of Wheelwright Pond.
9   Captain Noah Wiswall died at Wheelwright Pond in that battle, July 6, 1690. The exact circumstances or details of his death are pure speculation.
10 Interesting trivia: Exeter was founded by John Wheelwright (died 1679), brother of Anne Hutchinson, after being banished from Boston.

Chapter 14 - Rev. Thomas "Tom" Greenwood and Elizabeth Wiswall
1670's-1720's

1   Thomas "Tom" graduated from Harvard in 1690. The same year that Elizabeth's father, Noah Wiswall was killed in battle.
2   Theodocia Wiswall (b. Jackson) was the daughter of John Jackson (b. 1600) and Margaret Jackson (b. Taft). John Jackson immigrated from England on 7-13-1635 on "The Blessing". Buried East Parish Burying Ground, Newton, MA. He was the brother of Edward Jackson, making Theodocia Wiswall a cousin to Hannah Ward (b. Jackson). Later, Theodocia's daughter, Elizabeth Greenwood (b. Wiswall) would marry Hannah Ward (b. Jackson)'s grandson, Thomas "Tom" Greenwood.
3   John Greenwood (Tom's brother) would remain in New Town as a weaver, farmer and a well-respected, accomplished member of the community and church. He was selectman from 1711-1728, representative to the general court for three years and justice of the peace for many years. Practically all marriages were performed by him.
4   John Greenwood m. Hannah Trowbridge in 1695, two years after Rev Thomas "Tom" and Elizabeth Wiswall married.
5   A phrase inspired from the book, "The Valley of Vision".
6   Thomas Greenwood Jr was a weaver and the town clerk. He became a freeholder in 1679. In 1681 Thomas purchased Isaac Parker's homestead, house, barn and 24 acres; he also bought additional 40 acres. He was a member of the church, justice of the peace and a constable. Hannah "Anna" Ward, Thomas's first wife, who died in 1686 is presumed buried there as well. Nothing is now standing to mark her grave. The grave of her father, John Ward and others of the Ward family are yet in place. Thomas Greenwood re-married in 1687, approximately one year after the death of his wife, Hannah "Anna" Greenwood (b. Ward). Abigail Spring was twenty years younger than Thomas. She was twenty-two

when they married, and he was forty-three. They had at least two sons, James b. 1687 and William b. 1689. <u>Thomas</u> died of unknown causes, 9-1-1693, at fifty years of age, one month before his son, <u>Thomas "Tom"</u> was ordained at Rehoboth, MA.

7   The grave of <u>Thomas Greenwood</u> is still standing in Newton well preserved in the old cemetery on Center St. <u>Rev. Thomas "Tom" Greenwood</u> was ordained in this church, October 1693. Sometimes referred to as "Church of Christ", not to be confused with the denomination.

8   Quote based on John Calvin's, *"Let us not despair of the smallness of our accomplishments. But go forward in the utmost of the Lord.*

9   <u>Rev. Thomas "Tom" Greenwood and Elizabeth Greenwood (b. Wiswall)</u> married on this date, 1693, in New Town, MA (formerly Cambridge Village and later, Newton, MA). They were married on Monday and documents state that they moved to Rehoboth on Tuesday.

10   <u>Theodocia Wiswall</u>, Elizabeth's mother, re-married to Rev. Samuel Newton of Rehoboth, sometime after the death of his second wife on 9-29-1693. Rev Newton was 17 years older than <u>Theodocia</u>. She was 51 yr. and he was 68 yr. when they married. He died in 1711. <u>Theodocia</u> d. 11-27-1725.

11   "Half-hanged Mary Webster".

12   Judge Samuel Sewall (1652–1730) was a judge, businessman and printer in the Province of Massachusetts Bay, best known for his involvement in the Salem witch trials, for which he later apologized, and his essay *The Selling of Joseph* (1700), which criticized slavery. He served for many years as the chief justice of the Massachusetts Superior Court of Judicature, the province's high court. Judge Sewall references <u>Rev. Thomas "Tom" Greenwood</u> several times in his diary.

13   Old South Church, where young <u>Thomas Greenwood</u> likely first attended after landing in Boston from England in 1665.

14   Conjectured conversations between <u>Thomas "Tom" Greenwood</u> and Samuel Sewall. Quotes inspired from Valley of Vision.

15   <u>Rev. Thomas "Tom" Greenwood and Elizabeth Greenwood (b. Wiswall)</u> had six or seven children: Hannah: b. 2-5-1694, m. Adam Cushing. <u>John</u>: b. 5-20-1697, m. <u>Lydia Greenwood (b. Holmes)</u>, b. May 1721, d. 12-1766. Noah: b. 4-20-1699, d. 3-26-1703 (4 yr. old. Unknown reason for death. Smallpox epidemic 1702).
    Esther: b. 8-20-1701, d. 9-14-1701 (3 wks. Unknown reason for death).
    Elizabeth: b. 4-5-1704, m. 1723, in Rehoboth, *Ezra Carpenter (1698-1785).
    Esther: b. 6-25-1709, d. 8-29-1731 (22 yr.). Ichabod: ?
    John Greenwood (<u>Tom's</u> brother) remained in Newton, d. 8-29-1737)
    *Rev. Ezra Carpenter minister to the churches in Keene and Swanzey(?), NH 1753-1760. Chaplain at Crown Point during French and Indian War 1757

16   Sept 30, 1709, Sewall found <u>*"Mr. Greenwood"*</u>, *"dangerously ill of a malignant fever. At parting Mrs. Greenwood, with tears, desired prayers for her husband and*

that word be left Caleb Stedman at Roxbury to acquaint (make aware) her husband's brother, John at Newtown."

Caleb Stedman, b. 1671, d. 1748. m. Hannah Wiswall (<u>Elizabeth Greenwoods</u> sister). Roxbury and Newton - 8 miles apart.

17   Inspired by a Puritan writings.

18   It should be noted here that in the years immediately preceding the 1st great revival, which occurred in New England in the 1730's-1740's, the Puritan church had become weakened. Here is a quote taken from the book, The Puritans, Their Origins and Successors", by D.M. Lloyd Jones, as given by Rev W. Cooper, a minister at that time, *"But what a dead and barren time has it now been, for a great while, with all the churches of the reformation. The golden showers have been restrained; the influences of the spirit suspended; and the consequence has been that the gospel has not had eminent success. Conversions have been rare and dubious, few sons and daughters have been born to God and the hearts of Christians not so quickened, warmed and refreshed under the ordinances, as they had been. That this has been the sad state of religion among us in the land, for many years (except one or two distinguished places) has been lamented by faithful ministers and serious Christians."*

Chapter 15 - Rev. John Greenwood and Lydia Holmes
1720-1743
The First Great Awakening

1   Judge Sewall continued his friendship with <u>Tom</u> over the years. <u>Tom</u> died 9-1-1720. On 8-31-1720. Sewall writes of <u>Rev. Mr. Thomas Greenwood</u> *"falls sick, apprehending he should die"* and in September writes, *"<u>Mr. Greenwood</u> dies much lamented"*

2   Quoted from Judge Samuel Sewall's diary

3   Although we do not know how exactly <u>Rev. Thomas "Tom" Greenwood</u> died, we do know that it was an illness.

4   <u>Rev. John Greenwood</u> b. 5-20-1697, d.12-1-1766. Graduated from Harvard in 1717. He preached in Seekonk, 3-12-1720, and he agreed with the selectman of Rehoboth to teach school for 6 months at 12 (assume pounds) the first quarter and the second quarter rate of 45 per year. Five months after his father's death. 2-13-1721, the town voted him as their new minister.

NOTE: Rev. David Turner was ordained minister of the Palmer River Church in Nov., 1721. He and <u>John Greenwood</u> petitioned the town of Rehoboth on several occasions seeking salary increases. It can be assumed that if they were not friends, they at least close allies in ministry. The fact that Rev. Turner officiated the marriage of <u>Benjamin Sheldon</u> to <u>John's</u> daughter, <u>Sarah Greenwood</u>, speaks to that.

5 Bandy-wicket: A *bandy* is an L-shaped or J-shaped wooden bat. Bandy-wicket was an 18th century form of cricket.

6 Source taken from town records.

7 Lydia Greenwood (b. Holmes), b. 11-19-1696, Boston, MA, d. 1743, Rehoboth. Her parents: Nathaniel Holmes b.1670, England- 7-1-1711, Boston, m. 10-1-1691 to Sarah Holmes (b. Thaxter) b. 9-26-1671, Hingham, Plymouth, MA. d. 1718 or 1726, Boston.

   They had seven children. Lydia was born second or third. Her mother remarried between 1711-1714, to Hon. Judge John Cushing and had two children, Josiah Cushing b. 1715 and Mary Cushing b. 1716. Elizabeth Holmes, Sarah's daughter and Lydia's older sister, married Judge John Cushing's son, John Cushing III.

   Sarah Holmes (b. Thaxter) parents: John Thaxter, b. 1626, Morley St Peter, Norfolk, England, died at Hingham, Plymouth Colony, 3-14-1686, m. Elizabeth Thaxter (b. Jacob)

   b. 12-4-1648. Elizabeth was born in England, 1632, died at 93 yrs. in 1725 in Hingham, MA. They lived on North Street in Hingham and their property later became the location of St. Paul's Catholic Church. Beginning in 1662, John served as selectman for the town for eight years. John was a representative to the General Court in 1666. In 1664, while serving against the Dutch in New York, he was made Lieutenant. He was afterwards a captain and was in command of the town's cavalry troop in 1680. After his death Elizabeth remarried, in 1691, to Daniel Cushing (uncle to Judge John Cushing III) the father of her sons-in-law, Daniel and Theophilus.

   John Thaxter's father was Thomas Thaxter, b. 2-1-1595, Hingham Norfolk, England, d. 2-4-1654 Hingham, MA. Buried in the Hingham cemetery. Deacon Thomas Thaxter, of St Andrews Church was a linen weaver. He came from England ABT.1635 and settled in Hingham, MA. Thomas married Elizabeth Thaxter (b. Coffin), b. 1604, d. 7-17-1660, Dedham, MA. She survived Thomas, remarried twice, and committed suicide by drowning in the Dedham well.

   Elizabeth Thaxter's (b. Jacob) father was Nicholas Jacob, b.1597, Hingham, Norfolk, England, d. Hingham, Plymouth, MA. He arrived on the ship Elizabeth Bonaventure from Yarmouth, England, June 15, 1633. He traveled with his wife, two children and their "cosen" Thomas Lincoln, the weaver. Puritans. Forced to flee Norfolk when they fell afoul of the strict doctrines of The Church of England. Nicolas became an innkeeper with Samuel Lincoln (Abraham Lincoln's first ancestor and a cousin to Nicholas Jacob) in Hingham, MA. He was Deputy of Hingham to the General Court. Married Mary Jacob (b. Gilman), b. 1600, d. 6-15-1681, Hingham, Plymouth, MA. Married before 1629.

8 Lt. Nathaniel Holmes, of South Boston, a large landowner, brickmaker and joiner (joyner), son of Joseph Holmes of Roxbury, was baptized 7-10-1664. His

parents moved to Boston about 1660. His mother, <u>Elizabeth Clap</u>, daughter of <u>Capt. Roger Clap</u>. Nathaniel married <u>Sarah Thaxter</u>, 10-1-1691. In January 1705, he was granted liberty to burn brick and lime, for the space of one year, over against the land of Joseph Allen, at the South end of Boston. In 1706, he was a tithing man of Boston. *"At a meeting of selectmen, January 23rd, Sarah, ye wife of Capt. Nathaniel Holmes, her petition to sell strong drink as a retailer at her present dwelling house at ye south end of ye town is allowed by ye selectmen."* In 1711, the same license was granted to *"<u>Sarah Holmes, Widow.</u>"*. <u>Lt. Holmes</u> was a sergeant of the artillery Company in 1695. He was interested in military affairs and took part in the expedition to Port Royal in Canada, 5-12-1707. While on this expedition he became ill. Two years later he passed away after a voyage to the Leeward Islands which he had taken to improve his health. <u>Lydia</u> was nine years old when her father died. Three years later <u>Lydia's</u> mother, <u>Sarah Holmes (b. Thaxter)</u> married Judge John Cushing of Scituate and Hingham.

9   As recorded in historic records from Rehoboth, MA. in approximately 1756 Mr. Jenkins, who was troubled with infirmities, sent for Rev Robert Rogerson, who followed <u>John Greenwood</u> as minister at the first Congregational Church and provided this bit of advice. The quote is verbatim.

10 George Whitfield: In 1740, twenty-six-year-old evangelist who had stirred emotions throughout England, toured the Connecticut Valley and amplified the spirit of the awakening. His sermons, many of which were printed by his good friend, Benjamin Franklin, emphasized grace and advocated justification by faith, arousing sinners and instilling a concern for salvation.

11 Quotes from "Valley of Vision", Puritan prayers, pg.128, 129

12 "The Great Awakening" began in the colonies in 1740 and lasted for several years. It began with evangelist George Whitfield, who toured the colonies on three separate occasions and Jonathan Edwards, who was a minister in Northampton, MA. It is credited as a spiritual awakening that also provided the impetus for the American Revolution. It built up inner-colonial character, to increase opposition to the Anglican Church and the royal officials who supported it and to encourage a democratic spirit. This was the first movement of importance against slavery and various other humanitarian endeavors. It also led to the founding of Princeton, Brown, Rutgers and Dartmouth.

13 Benjamin Franklin was good friends with George Whitefield, although, as a deist, he did not share Whitefield's faith in the gospel of Christ.

14 Lydia "Liddy" Greenwood b. 2-4-1724, d. 5-1-1804, was the oldest child of <u>John andLydia Greenwood</u>, after they experienced the death of two earlier babies.

    <u>John and Lydia Greenwood's</u> children: Lydia: 12-24-1721- 1722 (7 weeks). Thomas: 1723. Lydia "Liddy": 2-28-1724-1804- m. Joseph Reynolds Sr, 1744, Moved to Bristol, RI.

Sarah: 3-26-1725, d. 1763. m. 1745 to Benjamin Sheldon (1720-1781), Rehoboth. Elizabeth (1ˢᵗ): (1726 -1728). Molly: 1729-1795, m. William Cole, 1747. Elizabeth: called "Betty" (2ⁿᵈ), (1732-1759), Rehoboth, m. 1749 Solomon Bradford. Esther: (1733-1814) m. Elisha Carpenter. Nathaniel: (1735-1780), Rehoboth, m. 1755 Freelove Crawford Carpenter. John: (1738-?), m.1756 Rebecca Hunt and 1775 Anne Peck.

15   Yellow Fever caused thousands of deaths.

Chapter 16 - Sarah Greenwood and (Rev.) Benjamin Sheldon 1740-1757

1   Benajah Sheldon, b. 12-12-1720, Providence, RI, d. 11-19-1743, Suriname, West Indies. Unknown occupation or cause of death, but assuming that he was a sailor on a trade ship. Twin brother to Rev. Benjamin Sheldon.

2   Providence, RI, founded by Roger Williams in 1636, after being banished from the Massachusetts Colony for religious views. In 1643 he obtained a charter for Rhode Island. Rhode Island became a haven for refugees from bigotry.

3   Sloop: *The Mediator,* Built in Virginia 1741. The first slave ship to ever sail from Providence was the *Mary,* owned by James Brown, which sailed for Africa in 1736. The Brown brothers were spirited in their defense of slavery, eventually running one of the biggest slave trading enterprises in New England. Their donations to Rhode Island College were so significant that it changed its name to Brown University.

4   The cargo ship *"Brookes"* could accommodate 454 slaves and reportedly carried as many as 609 people. There is no record that the Brookes docked in Newport.

5   Rhode Island was among the most active northern colonies importing slaves. Between 1709-1807, merchants sponsored at least 934 slaving voyages to the coast of Africa and carried over 100,000 slaves to the New World.

6   Rev. Benjamin Sheldon, b. 2-12-1720, Providence, RI, d. 12-31-1781, Pawtuxet (Providence), RI. or Tiverton (Newport), RI. Married Sarah Greenwood, 6-7-1745, Rehoboth, MA, by Rev. David Turner. According to Wikitree, "Rev Benjamin" is the pastor of a church in Pawtuxet, RI. In the list of colonial ministers, he is listed as *"sett. Tiverton, RI, 1752-1775; Baptist; Died Tiverton, RI, Dec 31, 1781.* (Rehoboth to Tiverton = 21 miles) He possibly remarried after Sarah's death (1763), to Hannah Lindley on 12-1-1768, in Rehoboth, by Rev. Ephraim Hyde. All children born in Rehoboth, MA. (Rehoboth to Pawtuxet = 13 mi/Tiverton to Pawtuxet = 27 mi) Children born to Sarah Greenwood and Benjamin Sheldon: Benajah: (1745-1830). Sarah: (1746-?). Lydia: (1747-?). Capt. Jonathan Sheldon: b. 2-16-1749, Rehoboth, MA d. 8-8-1835, Trumbull, OH. Rebecca: (1750-1828). Betsey: (1754-?). Molley: (1754-1846). Esther: (1756-1836). Benjamin: (1758-?). Daniel: (1761-1789). Died in Suriname, West Indies. Same as his Uncle Benajah.

7   William Carpenter (1710-1685), brother of <u>Fridgewith Vincent (b. Carpenter)</u> (1609-1671). Fridgewith never immigrated to the New World, but her daughter <u>Joan Sheldon (b. Vincent)</u> immigrated (date unknown). She married <u>John Sheldon (of Providence)</u> at the age of 28 years, in 1660, in Providence. Speculatively, Joan's Uncle William could have been the reason she immigrated alone, without her parents. Possibly to help care for William and Elizabeth's eight children? Speculation.

8   It is not known how Benajah died in Suriname. The Maroons were fugitives from slavery who continually raided plantations from the forest, for food and women. Governor Joan Jacob Mauricius, in 1741, tried in vain to come to terms with the rebellious Maroons, to no avail. Subsequent governors were just as unsuccessful. Suriname was known for exceptional cruelty with slave-masters using whips to enforce long hours of work. By 1791, there were 5,000 Europeans and 53,000 slaves.

9   Speculation as to where <u>Benjamin</u> received his education. Yale University is 100 miles from Providence. Harvard is 55 miles from Providence. Rhode Island College (later renamed Brown University) was established when <u>Benjamin</u> was already forty-four years old, therefore, not an educational option in <u>Benjamin's</u> youth.

10 Seemingly conflicting research provides information regarding <u>Benjamin</u> as the minister in Tiverton, RI and the minister at First Baptist Church, Pawtuxet, RI. Combined with the fact that all of his children were born in Rehoboth.

11 On December 2, 1757, <u>Rev John Greenwood</u> composed this letter to his congregation at Rehoboth, (during the time of the French and Indian War): *"Brethren; Whereas by Divine Providence I am rendered unable through bodily infirmity to carry on the work of the ministry any longer, after 30 odd years labor, and whereas you presented me to the town's resolutions not to grant any support for another minister here except I release my salary, ye ministering lands and quit my pastoral office; altho I think it not reasonable in the town to defer it; yet for peace's sake and that the gospel not be hindered, I release my salary from the eleventh day of March next as a forsaid and by the advice of some ministers and brethren called to advise in the affair, and at the desire of this church, I do likewise promise to ask and to receive of this church a dismissal from my pastorate over them as soon as a council of churches can conveniently sit for the orderly doing of it, provided the church, particular persons, or the town, or any or all of them, will come under obligation for my support and maintenance during my natural life to give me 20 (pounds) annually to be paid one half money and the other half in specie equal to money, the first yea to be paid the 11th day of March, A.D, 1759, and so from year to year by the 11th of March successively during my natural life as aforesaid, and that I and my estate be not taxed toward public charges. - John Greenwood"*.

12 Sarah Sheldon (b. Greenwood) d. 5-24-1763, in Rehoboth. Cause of death is unknown, although she apparently died the same year her last baby was born and therefore it may be assumed that she died in childbirth.

13 Rehoboth ministers years served: Rev Noah Newman (1668-1678) - (10 yr.), Rev Thomas Greenwood (1693-1720) - (27 yr.), Rev John Greenwood (1721-1757) - (36 yr.), Rev John Carnes (1759-1764) - (5 yr.), Rev Ephraim Hyde (1766-1783) - (17 yr.) Rev John Ellis (1785-1796) -(11 yr.), Rev John Hill (1802-1816) - (14 yr.)

14 Rev John Greenwood d. 12-1-1766, Rehoboth; unknown cause.

15 Rev Benjamin Sheldon. There is conflicting research concerning re-marriage. Hannah Lindley is referenced in some research as a second wife to Benjamin, marrying in 1768 and having three children. In other research Benjamin and Sarah's son, Benajah, is listed as marrying Hannah Lindley in 1768 and having three children (one girl, Lucynda, living to adulthood). For the purposes of this account. Benajah married Hannah Lindley.

- 1st - Sarah Greenwood married for 18 years (approximately 10-14 children several dying in infancy) until her death at age 38 yr.
- 2nd - Possible marriage to Phoebe Church.
- 3rd - Possible marriage, at age 58 yr., 12-1-1768 to Hannah Lindley, 20 yr old, Had three children: Benjamin 1770, Lucynda 1772 and Betsey 1778.

Note: Hannah Lindley's brother, Capt. Joshua Lindley (1748-1822) married Benjamin Sheldon's daughter, Sarah (1746 -?)

16 Daniel: (1761-1789) - Died in Suriname, West Indies.

Chapter 17 - Jonathon Sheldon and Mary Durfey
1754-1769

1 Later to be known in America as the French and Indian War. It pitted the Colonies of British America against those of New France. The outnumbered French depended on Indian allies. Notes taken from *"Killing England, by Bill O'Reilly."*

2 Benjamin Franklin, b. January 17, 1706, Boston, MA, d. April 17, 1790

3 Current Pittsburgh, PA

4 George Washington, b. Feb 22, 1732 in Colony of Virginia, d. December 12, 1799

5 The British captives were paraded back to Fort Duquesne, the men burned alive for amusement, the women raped. Female members of the British caravan were either wives accompanying their husbands or "necessary women", whose duties were associated with being maids. There were thirteen of these women taken captive by the Indians, one was clubbed to death for walking too slow.

6   Capt. Jonathan Sheldon, b. 2-16-1748 or 49 in Rehoboth, Bristol, Massachusetts Bay, British Colony America, d. 8-8-1835, Vernon Twp., Trumbull County, Ohio. Buried in Sheldon Cemetery, Fowler, Trumbull, Ohio. Married twice: #1. Mary Durfey or Durfee (1752-1790) in Tiverton, RI, m. 1771. Jonathan had 7 surviving children with Mary. #2. Priscilla Manchester b. 6-13-1760 in Little Compton, Newport, RI, d. 8-19-1847, Fowler, Trumbull, Ohio, married, ABT. 1791. Buried Sheldon Cemetery, Fowler, Ohio. Children with Priscilla: Daniel: (1793-1857). Chloe: (1794-?). Lois: (1795-1832). Jonathan:(1795-1871). Joan (1797-?). Lucina (1799-?). Sarah (1800-?). Rhoda (1803-?). Benjamin: (1805-1868). Priscilla's parents: William Manchester, b. 1734 in Newport, RI, d.1797 in Newport, RI, m. Mary Irish, b 1734, Little Compton, RI.

7   Conjecture. Benjamin Sheldon was 34 yrs. old when the French and Indian War began. It is unknown as to why he did or did not serve. His uncle by marriage, the Rev Ezra Carpenter married Elizabeth Greenwood, Rev John Greenwood's sister, served as chaplain at Crown Point, in NH at age fifty-nine. See note, Chapter 14, #17.

8   Actual location of the house is unknown.

9   Historical records from Tiverton record that Rev Benjamin Sheldon petitioned the town for permission to garden in order to supplement income.

10   James Durfey was Mary Durfey's older brother. He was born the same year as Jonathan Sheldon, 1748. Conjecture concerning friendship.

Chapter 18 - Captain Jonathon Sheldon
1770-1775

1   Lot Shearman m. (1764) to Susannah Shearman (b. Durfey), Mary Sheldon's (b. Durfey) sister, in Tiverton. No records of him, other than his name.

2   Patrick Henry (1736-1799) was a fiery attorney, orator and planter from Virginia. Most well-known for *"Give me liberty or give me death"*.

3   Gaspee Affair, June 9-10, 1772. The two-masted schooner, HMS Gaspee, with eight cannon and 26 crew, commanded by Lt. Duddington was under orders and financial incentives to stamp out illegal smuggling, beginning in 1768. (Info from "Gaspee History and Washington's General; Nathanael Greene and the Triumph of the American", by Terry Golway and ushistory.org) Christopher Sheldon and Pardon Sheldon participated as raiders of the Gaspee. There is no documentation that Jonathan Sheldon was involved.

4   Revised quote from Samuel Adams, regarding the Gaspee insurrection.

5   Delegates from thirteen colonies, except for Georgia, which was fighting a native-American uprising and was dependent on British military supplies.

6   Parliament's Coercive Acts: a series of punitive laws passed in 1774 after the Boston Tea Party. Also called the Intolerable Acts by American patriots.

7   The Battle of Lexington and Concord drew thousands of militia forces from throughout New England.

8   Jonathan Sheldon (27 yr.): Master on sloop Tryall, RI sloop, 25 tons, owner John Cooke (46 yr.), bonded Feb 17, 1776, for trip to CT. Master on the privateer, Tryall. Privateering was common practice. "Master" is the historic rank for a naval officer trained in and responsible for the navigation of the sailing vessel. They were professional seamen, rather than military commanders. The colonies had no navy to protect the seacoast towns or shipping. Tender to a ship = a boat used to service and support other larger ships.

9   About 55,000 American seamen served as Privateers, accounting for over 300 British ships seized during the war. A *"Privateer"* = an armed private vessel, licensed to seize commercial, lightly armed vessels of the enemy, confiscating "prizes". This activity was sanctioned, carried out and enforced by law.

10 *"Richard Cooke"* is listed in the 2nd Regiment, Newport Co, Tiverton, 17 years old.

11 The *Katy*, a Frigate owned by John Brown, built in Providence, RI. Commissioned in 1775, by the RI General Assembly, to defend the coast. Abraham Whipple (of the Gaspee Affair) commanded the *Katy*. Later, the Katy was re-commissioned by Congress as the *Providence*, a sloop-of-war. Some of R.I. most prominent families were owners of "private ships of war" (Privateers). The Browne family in particular, along with the names Green, Russell, Cooke, Corlis, Casey and DeWolf.

12 Oil was in demand for lamps and whaling was a highly lucrative industry. British targeted whaling vessels as legitimate prizes and in turn many whalers fitted out as privateers against the British. A whaling ship had Tryworks = furnace attached to the deck with iron braces. Two cast iron pots heat and then store the blubber in barrels (thus, the need for a cooper). Cooper= a maker and repairer of casts and barrels

13 The British evacuated Boston in March 1776.

14 Each man who formally signed the Declaration of Independence on August 2, 1776, committed an act of high treason against the crown. After the final wording of the Declaration was complete, the vote for independence took place on July 4th.

Chapter 19 - Revolution and New Beginnings
1776-1790

1   This incident occurred between "Witch", "Betsey", "Guadeloupe" and Tryall (a schooner out of Philadelphia). Occurred in November 1779. No records found of engagements involving the Tryall out of Providence. No records of her other than that she existed as a 25-ton (small) sloop and that Jonathan Sheldon was master of the sloop.

2   *Two Brothers*, a ship commissioned out of Providence, RI. No records of engagement.

3   Samuel Spencer was the captain of "*Witch*".

4   May 29, 1776, *The Spy*, *Providence* and *Gamecock* sailed together on patrol between Montauk Point and Block Island. They were sighted by *HMS Frigate Cerberus*. *Cerberus* focused attention on *The Spy* and the other two ships slipped away. *Cerberus* chased *The Spy*. In the pursuit, *The Spy* lost her topmast, but escaped safely into New London, CT.

5   Newport on the Island of Aquidneck (also known as Rhode Island) incorporated in 1639. Many of Newport's first colonists came as (or became) Baptists. Cotton Mather, called Rhode Island, "*A cesspool of religious practice.*" Quakers (Society of Friends) also found refuge in Rhode Island (they were banned from Massachusetts Colony) and settled in and around Newport. RI was recognized for its religious tolerance and freedom of worship. Jews, fleeing from the Spanish inquisition in Portugal and Spain, settled there. They brought commercial experience, capital and a spirit of enterprise. Sperm oil became a leading industry. Slave trade, ships, barrels, rum, candles, textiles, shoes, hats and bottles were also engaged in. Rum was carried to Africa, traded for slaves who were then traded in the West Indies and the Caribbean for sugar and molasses. State law in 1787 made the trafficking of slaves illegal. The 1807 Congressional Act made trans-Atlantic slave trade illegal.

6   December 8, 1776, British arrived and occupied Newport.

7   The Colony Meeting house was built in 1732 to hold government meetings.

8   From the Germanic state of Hesse. Highly trained mercenary soldiers. Reputation for cruelty and abuse.

9   Population went from 9,000 to 4,000 residents.

10 Mary Gould Almy, a notable Loyalist, ran a boarding house, on Thames Street. Mary's husband fought for the rebel cause, but she stated, "*I am for English government and the English fleet.*"

11 Col. John Cook's 2nd Regiment (Newport Co, Tiverton) had been commissioned in September 1776 by the Council of War. Men served three months in the state militia. Or occasionally called up for brief periods of service to meet specific needs. There is no record of Jonathan's service here, but he was living in Tiverton at this time. John Cook, who was the owner of "Tryall" and had commissioned Jonathan as master on that vessel, commanded the 2nd regiment out of Tiverton.

    Contradiction: The Sheldon genealogy lists a Jonathan Sheldon as a private in the Revolutionary War from Granville, MA, as documented by the Veteran Graves Registration Card on file in the Trumbull County courthouse, in Warren Ohio. It states that he was an Army Pvt. in Capt. Amasa Sheldon's Company, Col. Elisha Porter's Regiment. The problem with this is that Jonathan Sheldon did move to Granville, MA, before 1790, well after the war was completed.

Records show that his wife, Mary Sheldon (b. Durfee), d. in 1790, in Tiverton, RI. He remarried in ABT. 1791, to <u>Priscilla Sheldon (b. Manchester)</u> who was born in Little Compton, RI, a town adjoining Tiverton. It appears that all of <u>Jonathan and Priscilla's</u> children were born in Granville/Tolland, MA and surrounding area, beginning in 1793, with Daniel, but definitely by 1797, when <u>Jonathan Jr</u> was born in Tolland, MA. Due to these indicators, for the purposes of this record, the recorded registry from The *Daughters of the American Revolution* appears to be more reasonable.

    Sheldon, Jonathan Ancestor #: A102625
Service: Rhode Island Rank: Staff Officer
Birth: 2-16-1748 Rehoboth Bristol Co, Massachusetts
Death: 8-8-1835 Fowler Trumbull Co Ohio
Service Source: RI Arch, Maritime Papers, Bonds - Master of Vessels, Vol 2, p 26
Service Description: 1) Master on Sloop "Tryall"

12   General John Sullivan: transferred to the post of Rhode Island where he led the Continental and militia troops in 1778, intending to work together with the French. Disagreement over battle approaches led to an international incident between the two allies, after Sullivan issued a letter accusing the French commander D'Estaing of treachery and cowardice. While it is recorded that Samuel Durfee *"quartered and provided firewoo*d" for the Continental and militia troops which flooded into Tiverton, there is no record of where Sullivan lodged when preparing to besiege British troops in Newport, although he did direct operations from Tiverton.

13   Battle of Freetown, May 25, 1776

14   *Cockalorum*: a small man with a big opinion of himself. A self-important little man.

15   Valley Forge, 77-78. The following winter, 1778-79 one of the worst in recorded history

16   Ephesians 6:10,14, KJV.

17   British abandon Newport in Oct. 1779

18   On July 10, 1780, French fleet arrived in Newport.

19   It appears from records that the child named Oliver, as well as Jonathan along with an unnamed infant did not live to adulthood. Research conflicts, but it most likely <u>Jonathan</u> and Mary Sheldon (b. Durfey) had 6 children survive to adulthood: All surviving children pioneered to the Connecticut Western Reserve (Ohio). Parry: (1772-?) m. Rhoda Sutlief, Hartford, Ct in 1794. Occupation unknown. He named his youngest daughter after his mother and his stepmother, "Mary Priscilla". Pioneered to Vernon, OH. Prudence: (1774-1863) m. Timothy Hall, b. In Granville, removed to Charlestown, OH. She married at 19 yr and had 11 children. (Rev) Joseph: (1776-1821) m. OH. Pioneered to Vernon,

OH. Jonathan: (1783-1788) Died at 5 yr. Mercy: (1785-1867) b. Granville, m. Archibald Black, pioneered to Vernon, OH. Infant: (1787). Mary: b. 4-9-1789-d. 10-3-1869, m. Osmond Williams in 1812. Pioneered to OH, possibly prior to 1813, but more likely 1815, although one source records their first child born in Vernon in 1813. Mary died in Vernon. They had 13 children. Six or seven lived to adulthood. Osmonds parents, Isaac Williams, also immigrated.

20   The British surrendered at Yorktown. Although King George remained defiant, British Parliament had enough and was not willing to spend any more money on a war in America that had already extended for over six years. On Feb 27, 1782, Parliament voted against further war in America. In January 1783 negotiations began to end the war with Benjamin Franklin in Paris. Feb 14, 1783: King George finally admits defeat, bowing to public pressure. In April 1783 Congress responds to news from Europe and issues resolution to end "*hostility against His Britannic Majesty and his subjects*"

21   Christmas trees were not yet a part of decoration.

22   Benjamin Sheldon died Dec. 1781 (cause of death unknown) Minister of the Baptist Church in Tiverton as well as serving at Pawtuxet. He died in Tiverton, 12-31-1781.

23   Mary Sheldon (b. Durfee), d.1790, Tiverton, RI (38yr) Cause: unknown.

24   High infant mortality rate. Often did not name a child until two, prior to that they would call the baby, "it", "the little angel", or "the little visitor."

Chapter 20 - Jonathan Sheldon and Priscilla Manchester
1792-1815

1   Priscilla Manchester, b. 2-13-1760, Little Compton, RI d. 8-19-1846, Fowler, OH (86 yr). No marriage records were found for Jonathan and Priscilla in RI, but it is likely that they married in RI and moved to Granville, MA together. Capt. Jonathan Sheldon, b. Feb 16, 1749, Rehoboth, MA, d. August 8,1835, Trumbull, OH. Jonathan married Mary Durfey in 1771 at age twenty-two. Mary d. 1790. John married Priscilla Manchester in 1791 at age forty-two.

2   William Manchester (Priscilla's father). b.11-18-1734, Little Compton, RI, d.1797, Little Compton, RI, m. Mary Irish, Newport, RI. Lois Manchester (Priscilla's sister), b.1759, Little Compton, RI, d. after 1810, unmarried. Priscilla named a daughter after her sister, Lois. William Manchester's father: Edward Manchester, b. 1697, Portsmouth, Newport, RI, d. 1-5-1793, Little Compton, RI. m. Anna Williston (Newport, 1720), b. 9-16-1697, d.1778, Little Compton, RI. Edward Manchester was born sixth of nine. His father, Thomas Manchester, (1650-1722), Portsmouth, RI, m. Mary Browning, 1-6-1677, Portsmouth, RI. Thomas was born first of eight. His father: John Manchester b. 1656, Will, Yorkshire, England, d. 1691, Portsmouth, Newport, RI. Before moving to

Portsmouth, he lived in New Haven, CT. By 1642, he resided in Portsmouth. Married 1650 to <u>Margaret Wood</u>, Portsmouth, RI.

3   <u>Mary Manchester (b. Irish)</u>, <u>(Priscilla's mother)</u> b. 1734, Little Compton, RI, d. 1790 (same year as Mary Sheldon (b. Durfey). <u>Mary Manchester (b. Irish)</u> was born fifth of six children. Her father: <u>John Jedidiah Irish III</u>, b. 5-1-1699, Little Compton, RI, d. July 1773, Little Compton, RI, m. <u>Thankful Wilbore</u>, 5-10-1720, Little Compton, RI. <u>John Irish III's</u> father: <u>John Irish II</u>, b 1641, Duxbury, MA, d. 1717, Little Compton, RI. Buried in Friends Meeting House Cemetery, Little Compton, Newport Co, RI, in the Irish lot. Quaker. <u>John II</u> was a carpenter by trade, moving from Duxbury to Little Compton, RI about 1673. As a youth he was listed as a servant to Captain Myles Standish and is mentioned in the Standish will. <u>John II</u> was appointed as constable of Little Compton on 7-5-1678, with the oath of office being administered by Captain Benjamin Church. He was a surveyor of highways in Little Compton in 1683. <u>John Irish II's</u> father: <u>John Irish</u>, b.1609/11, Cleveron, England, d. March 5, 1677, Duxbury, Plymouth, Massachusetts Bay. John Irish came to America in 1629 and is considered the founder of the IRISH family here in the United States. He came to Plymouth with John Bradford, son of Governor William Bradford of Plymouth Colony. He became noted as a surveyor of lands. At his death he left much property in Seaconnet, RI (Little Compton). He was a volunteer during the Pequot War in 1633-37. The first settlers in "Little Compton '' were Englishman from Duxbury, MA, seeking to expand land holdings, beginning in 1674. *For more information search "John Irish, Little Compton"

4   John Manchester, b 1756, Tiverton/Little Compton d. 1838, Colebrook, CT was the brother of <u>Priscilla Sheldon (b. Manchester)</u>. He served in the Revolutionary War. Either before or after the war he moved to West Granville, MA (incorporated in 1754) Census has him living there in 1800. Records indicate that John Manchester was one of the founders of Granville/Tolland. <u>Jonathan Sheldon</u> is not mentioned that early in limited town records, although his first child with <u>Priscilla</u> was most likely born in Granville in 1792. No cemetery records found for Manchester or Sheldon in Tolland or Granville. But a large portion of the history of Tolland was lost in the destruction of town records in Northampton, covering 1810-1849. When <u>Jonathan Sheldon</u> pioneered in Fowler, Ohio, he traded 70 acres of land in CT (not Massachusetts) for 700 acres of Ohio land. Tolland is in MA, but on the border with Connecticut and family members lived in Colebrook, CT, which is only 14 miles from Tolland, so it is assumed that John Sheldon, with his family, owned 70 acres of land as far west and south of Tolland as possible....dipping over into CT.

5   This is an approximate date. Records indicate that <u>Jonathan and Priscilla's</u> first child, Daniel, was born in Granville, in 1793. Although records are conflicting concerning the location of births. <u>Jonathan and Priscilla</u> married in 1791.

6	Lois Manchester, according to census, lived in Little Compton in 1800, unmarried. 41 yr. old. It is assumed that she was a beloved sister. Both John Manchester and Priscilla Sheldon (b. Manchester) named daughters after their sister, Lois.

7	William Manchester, (64 yr.) Cause of death unknown

8	The Congregational Church of West Granville: established in 1778. Tolland (West Granville) was formerly a part of Granville and was set off and incorporated June 4,1810. No Sheldon's or Manchester's seem to be buried in the Tolland Cemetery. There is a marriage record for *Mercy Sheldon (Jonathan's daughter with Mary Durfey) and Archibald Black*, Feb 18, 1810. So, we can assume that possibly Jonathan and Priscilla remained in Tolland/Granville at least until that date. One researcher has the date of the move to Ohio as 1816. Jonathan would have been 67 years old. At some point Jonathan converted to Methodism, becoming a preacher. There were many Methodist itinerant preachers throughout the wild and untamed land over the Appalachians, preaching to people, for the most part, who knew nothing of stable churchgoing life, only relying on the circuit preacher. They had moonshine on their breath, tobacco in their cheeks and their hands were hardened by long hours toiling in the fields, building a better life for themselves and their families. It is unknown to the degree that Jonathan preached, but it is mentioned in historical documents that he was a preacher.

9	Daniel Sheldon: (1761-1789, 28 yr.). Died in Suriname, West Indies. Priscillas brother, Shadrack, b. 12-18-1766, is listed as "a sailor" in records. The date or circumstance of his death is unknown.

10	Jonathan (1749-1835, 86 yr.) and Priscilla's (1760-1847, 87 yr) children all born in MA. Daniel: (1793-1857). Chloe: (1794-?). Lois: (1795-1832), m. Zaphna Stone,1813, NY (37 yr). Joan: (1797-?) Speculation: Jonathan Jr and Joan were possibly twins and she died at birth. Jonathan Jr: b. 6-6-1797, d. 6-1-1871 (84 yr.), m. Martha "Patty" Shipman 1830, Fowler, OH. Loucina: (1799 -?). Sarah: (1800-?). Rhonda: (1803-?). Benjamin: (1805-1868), m. Ada Ames, 3-22-1835, Fowler, OH.

11	Sally Sherman and Josiah Remington were real people, who married each other in Granville on Feb 14, 1807. Whether she was a teacher is extremely doubtful. Whether he was a man of extreme stature is purely conjecture.

12	John Manchester is listed as one of the original settlers in the area, although he was born in 1757. Granville was established in 1754, so he cannot have been an original settler. Tolland was officially separated from Granville (West Granville) in 1810, so possibly that reference is regarding settling in that portion of Granville, becoming Tolland. It is certain that he lived there before 1779.

13	John Manchester served in the Revolutionary War. His rank and duration is unknown at this time.

14 The Methodist Episcopal Church of Colebrook CT held its first services in 1816, with Rev. Moses Potter in a log schoolhouse. "Episcopal" was dropped from the name in 1939.

15 Actual names and places

Chapter 21 - The Connecticut Western Reserve
1783-1815

1 Revolutionary War: April 19, 1775-September 3, 1783. At the Paris Treaty of 1786, British commissioners pushed vehemently to make the Ohio River the westernmost boundary for the new United States. John Adams and John Jay insisted that the British relinquish all the lands west of the Allegheny Mountains and Northwest of the Ohio River. After John Adams threatened to *"take up arms again"*, the British concede.

2 The Legion of the United States was a reorganization and extension of the Continental Army from 1792-1796 under the command of Major General Anthony Wayne.

3 Battle of Fallen Timbers: Final battle of the northwest Indian war. Native tribes affiliated with the British against the United States for control of the Northwest territory. Battle took place near present day Toledo, Ohio.

4 Current day Oswego, New York

5 Titus Fowler was an early founder of Granville/Tolland, 1750. Possible relation to Samuel Fowler, of Westfield, MA. Westfield is only 15 miles from Tolland. Titus Fowler did not pioneer to Ohio, but died in Tolland in 1821, at 88 yr.

6 Located in current day northeastern Ohio. This immense unsettled territory was often spoken of as "the vast interior" or "the howling wilderness".

7 There is a slight possibility that Jonathan and his family pioneered to the Connecticut Western Reserve in or around 1805, rather than 1815. In a quote from the *"History of Trumbull County (pg. 366)"* it says, *"In 1805 the grandfather of Henry O. Sheldon (Jonathan Sr) traded 80 acres of Connecticut land for 700 acres of timber land in the wilderness of Fowler township."* This is where it is also stated that Jonathan Sr, *"...later became known as an earnest Methodist preacher"*. For the purposes of this writing, 1815 is used. In other documentation it is stated that on November 20, 1815 Samuel Fowler deeded to Jonathon Sheldon "seven hundred and ten acres in township No. Five in the second range of towns in the Connecticut Western Reserve so called in the state of Ohio county of "Trumble". (Interesting spelling of Trumbull). The original handwritten deed was received and recorded February 8, 1817 and June 24, 1817. It is more likely that Jonathan and family pioneered to Ohio in 1816.

8 Based on information gathered, it appears that all of Jonathan's children, including his children born with Mary Durfey, immigrated across the mountains

to *The Reserve* at approximately the same time. <u>Jonathan and Priscilla</u> settled in Fowler with their children. <u>Jonathan</u> and Mary Durfee's children, Parry, Ruth, Mercy and Mary with their spouses settled in Vernon (nine miles from Fowler). Prudence and her husband located in Charlestown, Ohio (30 miles from Fowler).

9   Also known as the *"National Road"* and *"Braddock's Road"*. The contract for reconstruction on the road was awarded on May 8, 1811, with the road reaching Wheeling, West Virginia on August 1, 1818. It took seven years to construct 140 miles.

10   The Cumberland Narrows acted as the western gateway from Cumberland, Maryland to the Appalachian Plateau and the Ohio Valley beyond. It was the "road" cut through by British General Braddock during the French and Indian War.

Chapter 22 - Fowler
1815-1820

1   Actual quote taken from a letter Margaret Dwight wrote to a friend in 1810 on her way across the mountains to the Reserve.

2   On January 2, 1812, Henry Clay related this true story in the United States House of Representatives, concerning the ship "Western Trader". Although this account states that the Sheldon family journey took them to Pittsburg, it is also likely that the National Road took them to Wheeling, West Virginia where they followed the Ohio River north to Wellsville, Ohio and then followed the newly created (1814) "turnpike" to Lisbon, Ohio. Known as New Lisbon until the name changed in 1895 to Lisbon. Originally known for iron and whiskey.

3   George Parsons, Clerk of County (Trumbull County), (1806-1838). Alexander Sotherland, County Recorder, (1813-1821).

4   James Hillman was a brave, judicious and useful character whose life was an often-told story of "the early days". Hard sense and "rife knowledge" of Indian character is attributed to him. A hero of frontier legend. A trader with "sterling qualities".

5   Speculation.

6   Actual names of early settlers in Fowler. Information found online in *"Fowler Township"* under *"Pioneer History"*, pg. 411-417.

7   True story, taken from *"History of Trumbull & Mahoning Counties"*, archive.org.

8   When William Henry Harrison ran for President of the United States, he ran the slogan *"Tippecanoe and Tyler Too"*, to remind people of his heroism during the Battle of Tippecanoe.

9   Alfred Bronson settled in Tyrrell Hill in 1812. He was the first Methodist minister in Fowler Township, and he was on the muster list for serving in The War of 1812. Newman did move into Alfred's house while he was away to war. *"Fowler Township"*, under *"Pioneer History"*, pg. 411-417.

10   Girdling: ringbarking is the complete removal of a strip of bark, resulting in the death of the area above the girdle. The entire tree will die.

11   Cabin building description and furnishings information taken from, *"Fowler Township"* under *"Pioneer History"*, pg. 411-417.

12   Aaron Burr was the third vice-president of the United States, under President Thomas Jefferson. Burr fatally shot his rival Alexander Hamilton in a duel in 1804.

13   True story taken from, *"Fowler Township"* under *"Pioneer History"*, pg. 411-417.

14   David Shipman was the brother of Martha "Patty" Shipman, who married Jonathan "Jon Sheldon". Jon was Lois Stone's (b. Sheldon) brother. Patty's parents: David Shipman Sr., b.1762 and his wife, Abigail Shipman (b. Meachem or Fox), b.1765, pioneered from Hartford CT sometime after 1809. Abigail died 10-8-1833. David Sr died 10-6-1835. Both died in Gustavus, Ohio. Their children were: David: b 1792, m. Lydia, buried in Gustavus 1875. Joel: 1794, died at 4yrs old, 1798 (Hartford). Tabitha: (1796-1880), m. 1815, Curtis Coe. William: (1798-1869), m. Lovina Wakefield, 1823. Desdemona: 1804-1886, m. Elijah Wakefield, she was thirty-one when she married on Feb 15, 1843. She was his second wife, His first wife died in 1838. Patty?: (1807- deceased). Martha Patricia "Patty", (1807-1883), m. 1830 to Jonathan Sheldon, 1797-1871.

15   First church services in Gustavus were held in Jesse Pelton's cabin. The Pelton's (Methodists) were early settlers, before 1807. A log house was erected by the Methodists, sometime before 1840.

16   Written by Charles Wesley, 1741.

17   Lois Stone (b. Sheldon), b. 1795, in Tolland, MA, d. 1832. She was the third child born to Jonathan and Priscilla Sheldon. She married Zaphna Stone, b. 1794, Lee, MA, d. 1877, Gustavus, Ohio, in 1813. They had three boys: Philemon b.1815, William, 1820, and Cyrus, 1819. On May 14, 1890, Lois drowned all three boys, *"while her husband was attending Sunday service. All three children were under the age of five. Lois had had a recent religious conversion and thought she had committed the unforgivable sin. In her confusion she thought she could avoid punishment for this sin by sending her children to heaven while they were still innocent. The coroner ruled that the children were murdered by drowning in the local spring by their mother, and that she was insane. It is not known if Lois was punished, but the couple remained together until her death in 1832 (37 yr.), the same year that she gave birth to George Stone."* - "Family Search" unidentified source. John Kingsley was the first Justice of the Peace. He died in 1856 at age 73, being thirty-seven in 1820, when Lois murdered her children. The log jail was built in 1815. David Abbott was the sheriff and John Hart Adgate was the coroner.

18   It is factual that in the early days most corn and rye was turned into corn whiskey and sold in Pittsburg or the lakeshore. Whether Jon sold whiskey is speculative.

Chapter 23 - Jonathan "Jon" Sheldon
and Martha "Patty" Shipman
1830-1876

1   In a documented description of Jonathan Sheldon Sr, it states, *"A man who has great liberty in talking and used many curious similes. His conversation was very instructive."*

2   No documented history proving that friendships were established between the Shipman's and the Sheldons. Pure speculation and certainly possibility.

3   Jonathan "Jon" Sheldon Jr and Martha "Patty" Shipman were married on 7-4-1830 or 4-4-1830. Patty Shipman b. 4-23-1807, d. 11-4-1883. Jon was thirty-three years old and Patty was twenty-three years old when they married. Corn whiskey: Temperance societies began to form around the same year, 1830.

4   Corn whiskey was as free as water in the harvest fields or public gatherings. Most men were temperament, but every community has its inebriants.

5   Information provided by research in "History of Trumbull County", written sometime after 1907.

6   Information found online. Later, fifty-four acres of property (only 2 acres of which was cultivated) was evidently passed down to Jonathan "Jon" Jr. and Patty's fourth born Henry O. Sheldon, who in 1883, added another 50 acres, *"Which is now an attractive and productive piece of property"*. Here are the children born to Jonathan "Jon" Jr. and Patty Sheldon: Chauncy: (1831-1882), m. Harriet Trumbull, (1834-1884) in Trumbull Co. 10-19-1854. Edith: (1833-1911), m. "Shearer". Mariah: b. 1835, m. Atlas Ingman. Sheldon: 1836 (2 months). Henry O: 1837-1915, m. Orpha Smith. Desdemona: (1840-1857) named after Patty's sister. Dustin :(1840-?). Newton J.: (1841-1917). Newel David: 1841-1890. Wealthy: (1844-1910), m. William H Headley in 1866. Curtis S: (1846 - 1936), m. Laura Alice More. Died in DeSoto, KS. Martha Adelaide (1848-1930), m. Charles S. Caldwell. Died in Fowler. Laura: (1850-1923).

7   No record of how Tabitha Shipman died but there was a cholera outbreak in 1832 and so it is possible that she died due to it. Martha "Patty" Sheldon (b. Shipman) lineage: Patty Sheldon's father: David Shipman, b.10-5-1762, Glastonbury, Hartford, CT d. 10-6-1835, Gustavus, Ohio. m. 1-6-1791, Congregational Church, East Hartford, Ct. Tabitha Sheldon (b. Meachem), b. Abt. 1765, Glastonbury, Hartford, CT, d. 10-8-1833, Gustavus, Trumbull Co, OH David Shipman's father: Pvt. Jonathan Shipman b. 7-28-1723, Glastonbury, Hartford, CT, d. 12-3-1806, Hartford, CT, m. 12-5-1748, Hartford, CT, Abigail Fox, b. ABT. 1729, d. 11-28-1821

Daughters of the American Revolution
Shipman, Jonathan Ancestor #A103910

Service: Connecticut
Rank: Private
Service Description: 1) 6th Co, 7th Reg, Capt. Edward Shipman
2) Col. Charles Webb, CONT line
Revolutionary War Service: General Horatio Gates Regiment

Pvt. Jonathan Shipman's father: Stephen Shipman, b. 1699, Colchester, New London, CT, d. 1-28-1747, Glastonbury, Hartford, CT. m. 11-1-1720, Glastonbury, CT, Mary Pellet, b 1-14-1691, Saybrook, Middlesex, CT, d. Jan 14, 1747, Glastonbury, CT Stephen Shipman's father: William Shipman, b 6-6-1656, Saybrook, CT, d. 9-9-1725, Saybrook, New Haven, m. 1690, Guilford, New Haven, Alice Hand, b. 1-2-1670, Hartford, Hartford, CT, d. ABT. 1741, Hebron, Tolland, CT Mary Pellet's father: Thomas Pellet, b. April 18, 1666, Concord, MA, d.?, m. 1688, Concord, MA, Phelice Maxwell, b. 9-22-1667, Concord, MA, d. 1-1-1730, CT Phelice Maxwell's father: James Maxwell, b. 1635, Dumfries, Dumfriesshire, Scotland, d. 1720, Boston, MA, m. 1667, Margery Crump, b. After 1624, d.? *Information on James Maxwell in Footnotes: *Chapter 10, Thomas Jr Sails to America- 1665*, point #3. William Shipman's father: Edward Shipman, b. 1620, Hull, England, d. 9-16-1697, Saybrook, Middlesex, CT, m. 1651, Saybrook, CT. Elizabeth Comstock, b. Before 1631, Uxbridge, Middlesex, England, d. July 1659, Saybrook, Middlesex, CT.

8   Jonathan Sheldon Sr died on August 8, 1835. 86 years. No record as to how he died.

9   At one-point Tyrell Hill (Fowler) was bigger than Youngstown. However, by the 1830's industry began to relocate or be replaced by industry in Warren and Youngstown.

10 Not the actual eulogy. No record of a eulogy is found.

11 David Shipman, b. 10-5-1762, d. 10-6-1835. No record as to cause of death.

12 Historical events of the 1830's:
      1830s – Second Great Awakening - religious revival movement
      1830s – Oregon Trail which comes into use by settlers migrating to the Pacific Northwest
      1830 – Indian Removal Act
      1831 – Cyrus McCormick invents the mechanical reaper
      1832 – *Worcester v. State of Georgia* the Supreme Court rules in favor of Cherokees
      1832 – Black Hawk War, Department of Indian Affairs established
      1832 – United States presidential election, 1832: Andrew Jackson re-elected president;
      1832 – John C. Calhoun resigns as vice president
      1835 – Texas War for Independence begins

1835 – Second Seminole War begins in Florida as Seminole tribe resist relocation

1836 – Battle of the Alamo; Battle of San Jacinto (Feb 23-March 6)

1836 – Creek War of 1836, Samuel Colt invented the revolver, Arkansas becomes a state.

1836 – U.S. presidential election, 1836: Martin Van Buren elected president,

1837 – U.S. recognizes the Republic of Texas, Michigan becomes a state

1838 – Forced removal of the Cherokee Nation from the southeastern U.S. leads to over 4,000 deaths in the Trail of Tears

13   Henry Olcott Sheldon was the son of Joseph Sheldon. Joseph was the son of Jonathan Sheldon Sr and Mary Durfee, making Joseph a half-brother to Jonathan Jr and Henry a nephew. Henry Olcott. Sheldon was a Methodist circuit preacher. He traveled on horseback three to four thousand miles a year covering the Wayne circuit of Michigan and the North Ohio Conference. Married three times. His second marriage in 1860 to Eleanor Robinson was unhappy. Chauncey named his son Charles Robinson Sheldon, born in 1861, possibly after his cousin's wife? It is also possible that Jonathan and Patty Sheldon named their 6th child, Henry O Sheldon (Chauncey's brother) after Jonathan's nephew. Roswell Abel's father moved from CT to Ohio when Roswell was 17 years old, in 1817, making him approximately the age of Jon. Friendship is purely speculation.

14   Democratic Party: Formed in 1828. During the late 1820's and early 1830's the party formed the foundation of the party until the 20th century, believing that states should retain as much power as possible. The federal government should only have power when absolutely necessary for the nation to function. They emphasized the rights of the individual. This message was especially well received by small farmers and factory workers. Slave owners also favored this message, fearing the federal government might try to end slavery. Jonathan Sheldon Jr was an active member. The major leader of the party at this time was Andrew Jackson. Most Ohioans were not abolitionists, but they did not want to see slavery expand, principally because they did not want to compete economically with slave owners. The Republican Party stated that slavery was morally wrong, but its platform only called for preventing the expansion of slavery into new territories where it did not already exist.

15   Dr. Chauncey Fowler: Chauncey was a conductor on the Underground Railroad in Mahoning Co, Ohio, which was still Trumbull Co. He actively assisted slaves in attaining their freedom, providing runaways with his care, clothing and food. He found himself in jeopardy in 1845 and the story concerning that is true in this narrative, although whether Jon Sheldon knew Chauncey Fowler personally is not known.

NOTE: Priscilla Sheldon, (b. Manchester), b. 7-13-1760, d. 8-19-1847 (87 yrs.) Cause of death is unknown. Her husband Jonathan is described in some detail in accounts of his life, but we must never forget that beside him was a strong and capable woman. These following words are taken from the Sheldon Magazine, written by Rev. Henry O Sheldon in the mid 1800's: *"Chauncy Sheldon was born at Fowler, April 11, 1831, son of Jonathan Jr. and Patty Sheldon (b. Shipman). The father being a native of Tolland, MA and the mother of CT. The grandparents were Jonathan Sr and Priscilla Sheldon (Manchester). The former (Jonathan Sr.) being several years a cooper on a whaling ship, but later became known as an earnest Methodist preacher. In 1805 this grandfather of Chauncy's traded eighty acres of CT land for seven hundred acres of timber land in the wilderness of Fowler Twp. Jonathan Sr. gave his son Jonathan Jr. 285 acres of homestead, in return for the care of himself and his wife. Jonathan Sr. died in 1835, age 83. 30 years spent on the old homestead (Fowler). Jonathan Jr. continued cultivation and improvement, residing for some years in the original log house, but afterward erecting a residence more in keeping with his comfortable circumstances. An active Democrat - often called to participate in the conduct involving local offices. Jonathan Jr. died in 1871, age 73 yrs. Patty died 11-4-1883, 12 children. Jonathan Jr. gave 54 acres of land to his son Henry O. Sheldon. At that time, there were only two acres under the plow. In 1883 Henry added 50 acres."* Although Priscilla is mentioned only in passing, her story interwoven and is worth pondering.

Chapter 24 - Chauncey Sheldon and Harriet Trumbull
1854-1884

1   Records confirm that <u>Chauncey</u> registered for the mandatory draft for the Civil War in 1863. The draft was not popular. No record is found confirming that he actually served. It is possible that his service was deferred through payment, but again, no records are available. Two *"Chauncey Sheldon's* appear to have served, but both lived in Illinois.

2   Speculation since they were Democrats.

3   It is not known what year <u>Jon and Patty</u> moved from the original log cabin built. The Sheldon Magazine states, *"The grandfather (<u>Jonathan Sr</u>) and founder of the family fortunes in Trumbull County died in 1835.......<u>Jonathan Jr (Jon)</u> continued the good work of cultivation and improvement, residing for some years in the original log house, but afterward erecting a residence more in keeping with his comfortable circumstances"*

4   The Democratic Party doubted the wisdom of the war and generally hated President Lincoln.

5   <u>Chauncey Sheldon and Harriet Trumbull</u>: Chauncey, b. 4-11-1831, d. 11-10-1831. Harriet, b. 9-6-1834, d. 5-17-1884. Married 10-19-1854. They had six children, all born in Fowler, Ohio. <u>Harriet's</u> parentage is uncertain. The 1880 Census states that <u>Harriet</u> was born in Massachusetts in 1835, although another

record source states she was born in CT and that both of her parents were born in Massachusetts. <u>Chauncey and Harriet's</u> Children: Eva A: (1856-?), m. 1878, Hugh Hubert Hayes. Ellie: b. 1858, m. Resin ABT. 1878. <u>Charles Robinson Sheldon</u>: b. 03-15-1861, d. 1924 in Toledo, OH, m. 12-25-1881, Ella Viola Boyd. Warren G: (1868-?), lived in Fowler 1880). Leslie: (1871-1926), m. 1900, Florence M. Tidd. Louise or Louisa: b. 06-26-1873, m. 1919 -Silas Ordell Thompson in Knox, ILL. d.? (1880 Fowler)

6   No records available indicating Harriet's beliefs or opinions concerning the war.

7   In the Sheldon Magazine it is recorded that <u>Jonathan Jr</u> gave his son Henry O, b. !837, 54 acres. <u>Jonathan Sr</u> originally acquired 700 acres of timber, in approx. 1815. If <u>Jonathan Jr (Jon)</u>, then, as he aged, gave his children acreage and he gave Henry O. 54 acres, it can possibly be assumed that he gave his other sons acreage as well. If splitting fairly, his oldest son, Chauncy, b. 1831, would have received approximately 50 acres. At <u>Chauncey's</u> marriage to <u>Harriet</u> in 1854, his father, <u>Jonathan "Jon" Jr,</u> was fifty-seven. <u>Jon</u> died in 1871. <u>Chauncey's</u> mother, <u>Jon's</u> wife, Patty, died in 1883, and at that time Henry O. added another 50 acres. <u>Chauncey</u> had already died in 1882 and his wife, <u>Harriet,</u> died two years later in 1884. Assumption here is that <u>Chauncey's</u> son, <u>Charles</u> (34 yrs. old) and siblings, sold 50 acres to their uncle, Henry O. Land can only be divided so many times before it can no longer support a family. Upon their father <u>Chauncey's</u> death in 1882, their grandmother <u>Patty's</u> death 1883 and then their mother <u>Harriet's</u> death 1884, the inheritance for <u>Charles</u> would have been nothing or next to nothing. It was time to sell and move to where there was more opportunity. This may account for <u>Charles's</u> relocation to northern Michigan.

8   No record of military service found. There is a large gap in the birth of his children 1861-1868, which caused pause as to whether he did serve, but there is no proof.

9   <u>Jonathan Sheldon Jr</u> d. 6-1-1871. Cause unknown.

10   Squabbling is purely conjecture here, based on human nature.

11   5th cholera pandemic (1881-1896), cost at least 50,000 deaths in the Americas.

12   Fowler, Ohio: 1864- brick general store built and first teaching of higher grades.

13   The schooling <u>Charles</u> completed is unknown. <u>Chauncey</u> would not have had the opportunity for education in the higher grades, but <u>Charles</u> had the option. It was common for young men who planned on a life of farming to forgo the upper grades to begin their work on the farm.

Chapter 25- Charles Robinson Sheldon and Ella Viola Boyd
1861-1885

1   <u>Ella Viola Boyd</u> - Family tradition states that <u>Ella</u> was adopted and therefore no record of her family background. Yet, there do seem to be records suggesting that <u>Ella's</u> father was <u>James Boyd.</u> Two James Boyds lived near Johnston, Trumbull

County at the time of Ella's birth. Two possibilities: James #2 married a "Janet" early in life and then remarried a "Jane Howe", who was twelve years younger and she was the mother of Ella, or Jane was actually on older half-sister to Ella, with James #1 as the father of Ella and Jane. Ella's Life Events:

- #1 James Boyd on 1850 census for Johnston, Trumbull Co, OH, b. Scotland in 1816.
- #2 James Boyd on 1850 Census, 22 yr. old in Johnston, Trumbull County, OH, b. 1828.
- m. Jane Howe, b. 2-18-1840. m. in April 1861.
- 1862, Ella born in Ohio, to James Boyd
- 1870 (8 yrs. old) (Census) Ella lived in Johnston with father James. Ella's father is listed as being born in New York and Ella's mother, Jane, in Ohio.
- 1880 (18 yrs. old) Ella lived in Kinsman, Ohio1881, December 12 (license issued) married Charles (19 years old)
- 1882 Chauncey Sheldon dies, November (Charles father)
- 1883, March, James (1st son) born in Ohio (named after Ella's father?)
- 1883 Henry O Sheldon (Charles uncle) adds 50 acres
- 1883 Patty Sheldon dies, November (Charles grandmother)
- 1884 Harriet Sheldon dies (Charles mother)

2   It is estimated that about a third of the population of the western Scottish Highlands (about 90,000) immigrated between 1841-1861.

3   Five Points was a 19th century neighborhood in lower Manhattan, New York. It developed as a disease-ridden slum absorbing large numbers of immigrant poor.

4   "The Old Brewery" was the name given to the Coulthard's Brewery built in 1792. Following the economic depression of 1837, it became a tenement rookery.

5   Janet's last name is uncertain, if indeed she even truly existed. The Johnston district of Trumbull County became almost exclusively Scotch. Mostly Presbyterian.

6   The 1870 Census indicated that Ella (8 yrs. old) lived with James Boyd, and Jane Boyd in Johnston, Ohio (5 miles from Fowler). A census is not always accurate. In piecing together a story, the facts are supplemented with assumptions and imagination.

7   The year and cause of death are unknown for Jane Boyd. It is assumed that she died between 1870-1880. Assumed poor. Ella married Charles Sheldon in 1881.

8   While family tradition mentions the name Van Avery. No one seems to know the connection between Ella and the name. In researching, there seemed to be no Van Avery's living in Johnston Township or Trumbull County at the time.

9   1880 Census: Ella Boyd (18 yr. old) lived in Kinsman, OH. Servant to Henry (34 yr.) and Priscilla (24 yr) Perkins, Ellen (4 yr.), Anna (2 yr.) and Ellen Nicholson, (53 yr.).

10 Psalm 128:8

11 There is no record indicating that <u>James Boyd</u> ever worked in the Brookfield mine or was one of the seven victims of this July 11, 1877 disaster. Ella named her first son "James", therefore, it is surmised that he died an honorable man. For this narrative, the fact of the Brookfield mine disaster was randomly chosen. Coal was discovered in the 1830's and flourished until the 1930's. Trumbull Co led the state in coal production in the mid-1870's.

12 Fictional character

13 If <u>Ella</u> was "adopted", at some point she was either orphaned or given up. This narrative chooses for both of her parents to die, leaving her alone in the world.

14 Recorded in the History of Fowler, OH, Joseph S. Barb resided on the old homestead on which he was born in Fowler. "As *a keeper of honeybees, he has achieved note, having forty stands, from which he secured over one thousand pounds of surplus honeycomb during the season of 1908.*"

15 "I Will Follow Thee", published 1871

16 Wedding dresses in the 1880's had high necklines and long sleeves. Socially prominent brides wore white while the working-class wore a new best dress which was a more practical color, such as a brown or blue silk satin. After the 1860's, a veil was worn over the face.

17 Between 1880-1900, the mark of a true lady was her natural, untouched appearance.

18 The more carefree look of the 1870's carried over into the 1880's. Bangs were frequently worn, and curly, frizzy locks were quite popular.

19 Men wore a morning coat or cutaway of dark blue or black was worn with grey trousers and a tie and a white waistcoat. The "sack" suit was casual attire for the upper class but considered best-dress for rural classes.

20 Speculation.

21 Speculation.

22 <u>Charles</u> would name a son, born 1898, after his brother, Leslie, while his brother, Leslie, also named a son, Charles, born 1905, after his brother.

23 The Meteorological Summary: 1882, "*the warmest winter months upon our 15 yr record*".

24 The 1856 map of Trumbull Co. locates "J. Sheldon" north of the town of Fowler.

25 <u>Chauncy and Harriet</u> had six children. Charles was born third.

26 It is not known how Martha "Patty" Sheldon died. She was 76 years old.

27 Gastroenteritis is a bacterial infection that can result from poor hygiene. It can also occur after close contact with animals or consuming water contaminated with bacteria. It was a common cause of death in the 19th century. <u>Harriet</u>'s cause of death is unknown.

28 The Sheldon's had lived in Fowler, Ohio for over 90 yrs. at this point. There were evidently significant ramifications of <u>Chauncey</u>'s death (1882), <u>Patty</u>'s death (1883), Henry adding 50 acres (1883) and <u>Harriet</u>'s death (1884).

29 Warren Sheldon: 1880 Census has him living in Fowler. He was 12 yrs old. He later married Mamie Sheldon, 5-31-1888, in Trumbull County.

30 No information regarding Ellie or her husband, whose last name was possible "Resin".

Chapter 26 - Emmet County
1886-1902

1   Based on the births of <u>Charles and Ella</u>'s children, we know that they moved to Alanson (Maple River Twp., Emmet County) between 1884-1887. Alice was born in Fowler in August of 1884 and Alma was born in Michigan in November of 1887. Speculation that Charles traveled to the area alone prior to moving his young family to an unknown land.

2   Alanson was established in 1875. Originally named "*Hinman*", until the name changed on June 22, 1882. As Alanson became larger, Littlefield Twp. was created. The railway system extended to Alanson and on to Mackinaw City and Cheboygan in 1882.

3   First white child, Cora Pearl, born in Maple River Twp. to Frank Powell, 9-25-1876.

4   It is not known where <u>Charles Sheldon</u> purchased land or how large it may have been.

5   Frank Melville Joslin, 1848-1909, was the first depot agent and telegrapher in Alanson. When he moved his wife and three children to Alanson in 1883, there was no school, church or store. Only a few shacks and a two-room log depot.

6   From the mid 1880's and well into the 1920's Alanson was the home of several sawmills. The Hinckley Mill (1885-1924), The Bowl Mill (1883-1889), Shingle Mill (1890-1912). Merchant Mill (1894-95). Hemlock bark was shipped to the Kegomic Tannery located along the southeastern shore of Little Traverse Bay. It shut down in 1952. The water in this area was so polluted that swimmers refused to swim there for many years. Current location of Petoskey State Park.

7   <u>Charles and Ella Sheldon's</u> six children: James Chauncey: b. March 20, 1883, Fowler, d.-?. In the 1910 Census James was a boarder in Lancaster, NY. In the 1920 Census James married Laura and they had four children, 8, 6, 4 and 0, in Lancaster, NY. James registered for the Draft (WWI) in Genesee County, NY, 1918. He worked as a Machine Operator, "Batavia Steel Products". Brown eyes, black hair. Alice Ida: b. 8-22-1884, Fowler, OH, d. 10-11-1925, m. Merton Smith & George Harrington. Alma Emily: b. 11-17-1887, Alanson, MI. Married 3x.- Webster, Crane and Sargent. She smoked and had a reputation as being "man crazy". Earl Edward: 12-16-1894-11-29-1951, m. Esther Pickering & Emma Green Rumpp, m. 1924. <u>Leslie Lester</u>: b. 1-11-1898, d. 12-30-1967, m. Gladys Dodge, 6-27-1918. Beatrice Sheldon: b. 2-3-1901, d. 5-23-1902.

Tradition and records state that baby Beatrice was scalded to death. The details of how that occurred are not known.

8   *"Cassell's Household Guide: Being a Complete Encyclopedia of Domestic and Social Economy and Forming a Guide to Every Department of Practical Life, Vol 2"* was commonly referred to during the Victorian Era. Whether <u>Ella</u> owned and/or referred to this book in her immediate treatment of baby Beatrice is unknown. The book promotes the use of flour and cotton wadding for the treatment of burns. Dr Benjamin P. Pierce was the attending physician who signed Beatrice's death certificate. She died 19 hours after her scalding. The death certificate states that Dr Pierce had last seen her on the 22nd of May, and she died on May 23rd, 5am, "immediate cause of death" listed as "Shock". There is no record that states they went to the hospital in Petoskey.

9   According to historical accounts, this first hospital, Lockwood Hospital, opened in 1902. It began with Dr John Reycraft and Dr A.G. Oven. In 1909, these two doctors had an altercation and Reycraft, with his brother George, and another physician moved to start a new hospital, The Petoskey Hospital. Later to become Little Traverse Hospital.

Chapter 27 - Dodge
1795-1891

1   Cleft chins (cleft dimples) cause a dimple in the center of the chin. It is an inherited trait and more common in European populations such as Germany. The Cupids bow is where the curve of the upper lip is said to resemble the bow of cupid, the Roman god of erotic love. The peaks of the bow coincide with the philtral columns (or "love charm"), giving a vertical indentation connecting from just under the nose to the top of the upper lip.

2   <u>Lucy's (called "Anna")</u> maiden name was "Shaffer", from Pennsylvania, which could imply German Protestant. <u>Lucy Anne "Anna" Shaffer</u>, b.7-17-1837, Bloomville (near Tiffin) in Seneca Co, OH. Bloomville was established in 1824. Incorporated in 1871. There is a "Samuel Shaffer" listed as an early settler in Bloomville, although Lucy Anne's father was "<u>George Shaffer</u>", b. Reading, PA, 1801. <u>Lucy's</u> mother, <u>Hannah Stout</u>, b. PA in 1811, d. 1857, Bloomville, Seneca Co. In Seneca County white settlement grew slowly due to the Great Black Swamp occupying large sections of northwest OH, lower MI. and northeast IN. <u>Lucy's</u> mother, <u>Hannah Stout</u>: There is a "Bartholomew Stout" listed in "History of Bloom Township OH" as an early settler. Speculation that <u>George Shaffer</u> met his wife <u>Hannah Stout</u> in Bloomville.

3   13 Children: Charlotte Alvina: (1857-1947). Nancy E: (1858-1937) (Reuben's mother's name was "Nancy"). Elizabeth: (1860-1943). Leonard Colby: (1861-1952). Minnie Jane: (1863-1952). Calvin: (1866-1877) (Reuben's father was

also named "Calvin"). Clara: (1866-1891). John Richardson: (1868-1957). Melanchthon (Lank) Washington: (1871-1948). William Millard: (1873-1964). Dora Belle: (1876-1960). Mary Arminta: (1879- ?). Charles Lee: (1884-1969) Anna was 47 yrs. when her last child, Charles, was born.

4   Reuben Dodge b. 7-15-1832, d. Savannah, Ashland, OH, d. 11-27-1920, Ada, Hardin, OH. Married Lucy Anne ("Anna") Dodge (b Shaffer, 1856, near Tiffin, Ohio (Bloomville).; Buried, Woodlawn Cemetery, Ada, OH.

5   Savannah, in Ashland County, OH, was a part of Clear Creek Twp. Ashland County formed in 1846, eight years after Reuben was born (1832). Savannah was established in 1818, shortly after the War of 1812. Clear Creek Twp. lies on the border with Richland County (with Huron County just north). It wasn't until 1846, when the counties defined themselves, that definitive locations of birth/death could be determined. This was a heavily wooded wilderness. The first church was built in 1830. Before that people would walk to attend church (in a home), carrying torches of hickory bark through the woods.

6   Reuben's parents: Calvin Dodge, b.1795, Canandaigua, NY, d. 1838, Richland County, Ohio and Nancy Dodge Hull, b. Williams, b. April 1, 1797, Monmouth, NJ, or PA, d. Feb 1, 1884, Hancock County, Ohio. Married, June 17, 1820, Milton Twp., Richland, Ohio. Milton Township was organized in 1816. The population in 1820 was 544 people. Milton Twp. was under the jurisdiction of Mifflin, Richland County. When Ashland County was created in 1846, the township of Mifflin was divided. Today, Milton Twp. is in Ashland County, Ohio. Nancy re-married 9 yrs. after Calvin died, on Aug 17, 1847, to Henry Hull. Calvin and Nancy Dodge: 9 Children (order of birth is in question): Margaret: (1820-1877), b. Richland, OH d. Defiance, Ohio. Calvin Jr "Cal": (1822-1898) b. Richland, OH d. Sandusky, OH, Ohio Veterans Home, m. Nancy Tucker, 1-20-1848, Richland County, OH. Samantha: (1822-1899) b. OH, d. Iowa, m. John Tindall, Seneca Co, OH, 1841. Henry: (1826-1916) b. Hardin Co, OH, d. Ada, Hardin Co, OH, m. Nancy Simmons, 1852, Crawford, OH. Frances "Fanny": (1827- 1862), b. OH, d. Hancock Co, m. 1849, James Henry. Elizabeth: (1829- 1931), Union Co, OH, m. 1855, Thomas Latimer. Eleanor: (1831-1925), no details. Reuben: (1832- 1920), b. Savannah, Ashland Co, OH, d. Ada, Hardin Co, OH, m. 7-1-1856, Lucy Anne (Anna) Dodge (b. Shaffer), Bloomville, Seneca Co, OH.

    (NOTE: Savannah was originally named Vermillion. It was changed in 1837.) It appears that Reuben was extremely close to his brother Calvin Jr. (we will call him "Cal" to avoid confusion with his father "Calvin"). Cal was ten years older than Reuben. They served in the Civil War together with the 55th Ohio Infantry, Company K and after the war Reuben moved his family from Bloomville, Seneca County to Liberty Twp. (Ada), Hardin County (55 miles). Cal and his family lived in Liberty Twp., Hardin County, as all of Calvin's seven children (from 1848 to 1860) were born there. Although there is a discrepancy as to the 1850 Census putting Calvin's family in Liberty Twp., Crawford Co, OH, the 1880 Census has them in Liberty Twp., Hardin, OH. Calvin's oldest son, Richard was born in Hardin County in 1848 and his youngest daughter, Fanny, born 1857 in Hardin County as well. Cal's residence was Ada, Ohio when he died in 1897.

Calvin Dodge (Reuben's father): The only consistent record regarding Calvin is that he was born in Canandaigua, Ontario County, NY, Feb. 26, either in 1795 or 1799 and that he died in Richland County, 1838. Tracing the Dodge ancestry becomes problematic.

The name "Calvin Dodge" is listed two times as serving in the War of 1812. Once with the 157th Detachment and with the 131st Reg, New York Volunteer in the War of 1812. Whether either of these is "our" Calvin is uncertain, although, "our" Calvin lived in the heart of the area of conflict (eastern NY) and he is the appropriate age, if born in 1795, as a 17-year-old.

Who is Calvin's father?

Reuben Dodge is one possibility. Reuben was born in 1756, in Brookfield, MA. and died in Bloomfield, NY in 1813. Calvin would have been 17 or 18 yrs. old. Bloomfield is eight miles from Canandaigua, NY, where Calvin was born. Did Reuben live in that area or was he enlisted in the War of 1812 and simply died in Bloomfield? Possible clue: Calvin named one of his sons, "Reuben". *Problems*: Reuben is found on the Oxford, NY Census in 1800 (150 miles from Canandaigua). Only two children are recorded for Reuben and wife Elizabeth "Betsey". Their daughter, Asenath, b. in Brookfield, MA in 1785. Interestingly, Asenath is recorded as living in Canandaigua in 1846. Reuben's son, Hori, b. 1800, Oxford in Ontario County. No indication that Reuben and Elizabeth ever lived in Canandaigua. If Reuben is Calvin's father, the Dodge family ancestry line follows William "Farmer" Dodge, not Tristram Dodge.

Abimael, **Amos Jr** or **Stephen Dodge** were three brothers and one of them is likely the father to Calvin. They are descended from the Tristram Dodge line in Rhode Island. **Abimael Dodge**: There is documentation of at least two" Abimael" Dodge men, just as there are two "Calvin" Dodge men born approximately at the same time in New York. "Our" Abimael (1) was born in 1760 and served in the Revolutionary War. He died in 1817 in Canandaigua, NY. A tree fell on him. The other Abimael (2) was born in 1784 and cannot have been Calvin's father, but could have been a brother. This young Abimael (2) married in Canandaigua in 1808. In 1810, "Abimael" (1 or 2?) appeared on the Census for and on land records in Oneida, NY, along with Amos Dodge. A most intriguing "coincidence" concerning Abimael occurs over a series of land transactions. In 1814 a Stephen Dodge (no one knows who he is) buys 4 1/2 acres in Canandaigua. In 1816 Abimael (1 or 2?) sold 10 acres in Canandaigua.

In 1817 Abimael (1 or 2?) sold 10 acres in Canandaigua. In 1817 Stephen R Dodge died in Richland County, OH. In 1818 Abimael (2) voted in Jefferson, Twp., Richland, OH. In 1820 Calvin married Nancy Williams in Milton Twp., Richland County, OH. In the 1830's Abimael (2) was administrator for a Samuel Dodge estate, Cuyahoga County, OH. In 1830 Calvin appeared on the Census for Richland County, OH. This trail puts Abimael (2) and Calvin. in the same county in Ohio at the same time, indicating that they were possibly related. Potentially brothers, which could reasonably make Abimael (1) their father.

Amos Dodge, b.1758 and resided in Oneida County, NY. Amos is a younger brother to Abimael Dodge (1), by two years. There is not a lot of evidence that Amos is the father of Calvin. Some researchers suspect that Abimael (2), b. 1784, is the son of Amos, which could indicate that Calvin is also a son or simply a cousin. Amos married Huldah Dodge. He was a carpenter. In 1816 he moved to Chenango County, NY, where he appeared on the 1820 and 1830 Census. *Problems:* We have no documentation of his children. We cannot put Amos in Canandaigua. **Stephen Henry Dodge**, b. January 1775 in Shelburne Falls, Franklin, MA. Several researchers assign Stephen as Calvin's father. Stephen is the youngest brother of Abimael (1) and Amos Dodge. If he is Calvin's father, he was about 20 years old when Calvin was born in 1795. Stephen m. Mehitable in 1796, so, either Calvin was illegitimate, or his birth date is 1799, rather than 1795, as some sources claim and therefore was most likely too young to serve in the War of 1812. A son was born to Stephen/Mehitable, Stephen Henry Jr, in 1797 and a daughter, Mary, in 1800. It is possible that Calvin could have squeezed in there in 1799. Another son was born to Stephen named Reuben. *Problems:* All of Stephen/Mehitable children are listed as being born in Cazenovia, Madison, NY, except Mary who was born in Conway, Franklin, MA (Mehitable's family home). If Calvin is a son, why is he not listed with his siblings? If Calvin is a son, why is he born 100 miles north of where his siblings were born? We cannot put Stephen/Mehitable in Canandaigua.

7   The Star-Spangled Banner, written Sep.14, 1814, was recognized for official use by the United States Navy in 1889 and was made the National Anthem in 1931.

8   The Northwest Territory included the area north of the Ohio River and west of the Appalachian Mountains. Present day: Ohio, Indiana, Illinois, Michigan. Wisconsin and part of Minnesota.

9   The Battle of Chrysler's Farm took place on November 11, 1813. Unknown whether the 157th N.Y. Militia was involved, although the St Lawrence Campaign was ambitious.

10 There is little information regarding Nancy Williams prior to her marriage. Parentage is speculation regarding Richland County's early settlers. The name Samuel Williams appears as a treasurer in the county sometime after 1813 and before 1823. Possibly Samuel was Nancy's father? Calvin and Nancy m. June

1820. <u>Nancy Williams</u> was born 4-1-1797 in Monmouth, NJ and she died (86 yrs.), 2-17-1884, in Hancock County, Ohio.

11 Milton Twp. is located today in Ashland County, Ohio. The people who settled there were well behaved and orderly. Robert Nelson signed the marriage certificate for <u>Calvin and Nancy Dodge</u>. The name "Robert Nelson" is listed as an early settler in the history of Milton Township. Birth records indicate that the couple's first two children were born in Milton Twp., 1820 and 1822. <u>Calvin</u> evidently did not farm his own land.

12 Until 1846, the city of Ashland in Ashland County was named Unionville.

13 There is no documentation as to how <u>Calvin</u> died at the age of 39 or 43 years.

14 The early settlers of Milton County worshiped at Old Hopewell Church, which stood near the line between Milton Twp. and Montgomery Twp.

15 Henry Hull lived in Arlington, Hancock County, OH. His second wife, Catherine, died there in 1846. Arlington was located in the southern end of Hancock county, just a few miles north of the Hardin County border. In 1848, it was a small farming community.

16 Henry Hull, b. 1800, PA, d. 1852, Hancock County, OH, Henry was forty-seven years old when he married his third wife, <u>Nancy Dodge</u>, in 1847. Nancy had been widowed, since her husband, <u>Calvin Dodge</u>, died nine years before. Henry was a widower twice over. Henry served as Justice of the Peace, a mill builder, juror and farmer. He spoke German and English. It would seem that he was a successful and influential man. Henry died five years after his marriage to <u>Nancy Dodge</u>. <u>Reuben</u> was fifteen when his mother married Henry and twenty when Henry died. The 1840 Census has Nancy living in in Richland County, after Calvin's death. No additional census is available, but she died in Hancock County in 1884. <u>Nancy Dodge Hull</u> was buried in the Hasson Cemetery in Jenera, Hancock County.

17 Samantha Dodge, <u>Calvin and Nancy's</u> second-oldest daughter was the only one of <u>Reuben's</u> siblings to be married at the date their mother married Henry Hull. Samantha married Jacob Tindall in Seneca County, Ohio, in 1841. Cal, the oldest son, would marry Nancy Devinbaugh (b. Tucker) (her 2nd marriage) five months later, in 1848 and settled in Liberty Twp., Hardin County.

18 Somehow <u>Reuben</u> found himself in Seneca Co. where he met and married <u>Lucy Anne Shaffer</u>. Samantha, Reubens' sister, lived in Seneca County (1841) and <u>Lucy</u>, with her family, also lived in Seneca Co. Speculation that Reuben either visited or moved to Seneca County with his sister and brother-in-law. Reuben and Lucy married in Seneca Co. in 1856.

19 Thomas Blunt, whose real name was Thomas Boyd, settled in Bloomville in 1822. A respected and revered citizen. An outspoken abolitionist. There is no record that <u>Reuben</u> ever met Thomas Boyd.

20 Jacob Tindall and Samantha (b. Dodge) pioneered into Tama Co. IA. after 1849.

21 Research discovered a Calvin Dodge in Auburn Prison, Cayuga, New York, in 1850. There is no confirmation that this Calvin Dodge is "our" Cal Dodge, brother to Reuben Dodge, although his age does correspond appropriately. On the other hand, Adam Dodge, b. 1860, from Hancock County was found in prison in OH in 1899 (39 yr). Some probability that this is Calvin's youngest son. His offense is not noted.

22 Military records show that Calvin "Cal" Dodge enlisted Nov 7, 1861 and Reuben Dodge enlisted Dec 1, 1861. Both served with the 55th Ohio Infantry. Both were captured near Luray, VA on Aug 8, 1862 and released in a prisoner exchange. The 55th Infantry participated in the Battle of Cedar Mountain on August 9, 1862, 45 miles from Luray. 231 Union soldiers killed and 1,106 wounded.

23 A severe heat wave was recorded for August 1861.

24 The New-Market-Luray Virginia area was at the crossroads of the Shenandoah Valley's wartime campaigns. May of 1862 had seen Confederate Gen. Stonewall Jackson take advantage of this mountainous landscape throughout his Valley Campaign.

25 August 9, 1862, the 55th Ohio Infantry would engage in the Battle of Cedar Mountain. 1,336 Union casualties: 231 killed, 1,106 wounded. Neither Calvin or Reuben would have engaged in that battle, as their capture was the previous day.

26 This quote was taken word for word, apart from including the name Reuben Dodge, from a sample Parole of Honor form used by the Confederate States.

27 From campaigns in the east, paroled soldiers began arriving at Camp Chase in August 1862, the very month and year that Reuben and his brother Cal were captured. By September 9th maintaining discipline was becoming extremely difficult. Major General Lewis "Lew" Wallace arrived on September 17th to take charge of the parolees and organize them for the Minnesota Campaign. There is no indication from current records that Reuben and/or Cal participated in that campaign. Many other paroled soldiers opted for "French leave", risking being charged with desertion. There were some instances where soldiers could wait at home for their letter of exchange. Camp Chase was a mere eighty miles from Bloomville, Ohio. Both Reuben and Cal served three years and mustered out July 11, 1865, so it is assumed that they received their letter of exchange and returned to active duty sometime in 1863.

28 Reuben must have been at home waiting for his exchange letter in Bloomville at least until March of 1863. Daughter Minnie was born in December 1863.

29 The Ohio 55th Infantry participated at Chancellorsville, VA, May 1863, Gettysburg, PA, July 1863 and Mission Ridge, TN, November 1863. In 1864, they saw eight significant engagements with the enemy, including Atlanta, GA, (siege of) July-September. 1865 took them to North Carolina, with the final engagement, Bentonville, March 19-21

Chapter 28 - Davis and Wingate
1842-1891

1   Information provided here was taken from <u>William Washington Davis's</u> obituary.

    <u>William Washington Davis</u> was the youngest child of four brothers and a sister born to <u>Alvin and Lavina Davis (b. Seeley)</u>. Alvin and Lavina m. 10-10-1820, in Cuyahoga Co, OH. Alvin was killed by a cannon 11-4-1836 in Bedford City, Cuyahoga Co, OH. Their fourth son was <u>William Washington Davis</u> b. 3-31-1830, in Cuyahoga Co, OH, d. Thursday, 10-19-1911 in Orange Twp., Hardin Co, OH, after a brief illness from paralysis, his illness not extending over a week. His parents came to Hardin Co about 1842 and located on a farm west of town. Two years later this son, <u>William</u>, walked from their former home to join his parents (ABT. 14 yr. old). Most of his overland journey made through dense forest that covered most of the region at the time. <u>Mr. Davis</u> was married to <u>Sarah "Sadie" Wingate</u> in 1852 in Ada, Hardin Co, OH and late in the 1860's they took up residence in Orange Twp. at the corners five miles north of Ada where he operated a sawmill almost all the remainder of his life and which is known all over that region as Davis Corners. To this worthy couple were born twelve children - six sons and six daughters. (the obituary states, "Nine sons and three daughters", (records seem to contradict those numbers) Their names in order of their ages are: Almeda, who married Rufus Evick. Lucy, who married Zack Parrish. Samuel, who lives in the area. William; of Petoskey, Michigan. Elahi, who died in childhood. Wesley, who drowned at Fort Wayne when a young man. Anderson and Catherine (twins). Catherine; married William Dodge and lives near Chandler Cemetery. Anderson; lives in Toledo. Ebenezer, who lives in Ada. Jane, who married William Robolt and lives in Petoskey, Michigan. <u>Julina</u>, who married <u>Melanchthon "Lank" Dodge</u> and lives east of Ada (in 1911). Flora, who married Newton Snyder and lives in Lima, Ohio.

    <u>Mr. Davis</u> never cared for public office. When his parents were still living, he was elected constable of Liberty Twp., but he refused to serve. Many years ago, he became a member of the Disciple Church. During the war of the rebellion he enlisted with the 135th Ohio Regiment and served with Company I. (William was 34 years old when he mustered in at Camp Chase, May 11, 1864. He was married for 12 years, with six children at the time.) He was a strong, rugged man as fine a neighbor as any man could desire as there was nothing too great for him to do when a neighbor needed his aid in any way. A quote from the obituary printed in The Record (newspaper): "The Record had learned to know him quite well and to appreciate his worth. A mutual friend related a circumstance that shows the character of the man. In his earlier years he made use of alcoholic drinks and sometimes to excess. In those days a disease

known as "milk-sickness" (a kind of poisoning characterized by trembling, vomiting, and severe intestinal pain that affects individuals who ingest milk, other dairy products or meat from a cow that has fed on white, snakeroot plant, which contains poison.) The disease was very serious and dangerous, and many fatalities followed it. A well-known physician, practicing here at the time, was called to treat Mr. Davis and advised that the only thing that would save him was whiskey. "Then", said the patient, "let me die; I am through with that stuff."

The funeral was held at his late home on Sunday, October 22, Rev Noah Blosser conducting the service followed by internment in the Chandler Cemetery. William Davis was a member of the Disciples Church. Mr. Davis was also a member of the IOOF lodge (Independent Order of Odd Fellows. A non-political, non-sectarian international fraternity founded in 1819, with a motto of "Friendship, Love and Truth")

2   Located in the northwestern corner of Hardin County, Ada, OH was originally called Johnstown and under that name was platted in 1853, when the railroad was extended to that point. Ada became the name of the community's post office, after the postmaster's daughter, Ada. A post office called "Ada" has been in operation since 1854.

3   The Wingate ancestry story: Henry Wingate (1768-1817) and Mary Wingate (b. Biddle/Beddles) (1773-1818) both were born in Sussex County, DE. They married in 1788 and had 15 children. Among those was born Samuel Burton Wingate b. 3-14-1799, d. 8-15-1882. Sometime between 1800-1810 Henry and Mary Wingate moved to Tuscarawas County, OH. Henry lived to be 66 years old, dying approximately 1816. Samuel Burton Wingate married Sarah Wingate (b. Tressel) 8-25-1824 in Tuscarawas Co, OH. Sarah was the daughter of George Franklin Tressel (1781-1861) and Catherine Tressel (b. Shuster) (1782-1854). Sarah was born in Washington Co, PA. She moved with her family to Tuscarawas County sometime before 1820.

Samuel and Sarah Wingate had sixteen children. Two sets of twins were included. Sarah Wingate (b. Tressel) (1805-1850) died giving birth to her sixteenth child in March of 1850. Sadie Davis (b. Wingate) was born fifth in 1832. Just after Thanksgiving in 1844, Samuel and Sarah Wingate packed up and pioneered to Liberty Township, Hardin Co, OH, where Sarah's brother, John Tressel, was well established with his family. They arrived on Christmas Eve, after a long and difficult journey in the middle of winter, with several small children. Other relatives also lived in the area: Samuel's sister, Elizabeth, as well as an uncle to Sarah, John Shuster. By 1861, men throughout the county were getting ready for war. The Wingate family was well represented in the War Between the States with three sons and four sons-in-law.

Samuel and Sarah's son, Adam, died of Typhus Pneumonia while enlisted during the war. Their daughter Mary's husband was killed in action. William

Washington Davis, the husband of their daughter, Sadie, served in the 135th Ohio Infantry. In 1866, Sadie's father, Samuel Wingate, moved to Benton Co, MO, along with several other sons and daughters. The move was most likely to get away from the Black Swamp and the diseases that accompanied living there. Samuel purchased land and lived in Missouri for twenty years, until showing signs of dementia. He was moved back to Ada, Ohio to be cared for by his son Ebenezer. Interesting NOTE: Samuel Wingate's land in Missouri was later sold to the government to make way for the Truman Lake and Damn.

4   Oliver Anderson Davis was 4 ½ years older than his sister, Julina. He was 2 ½ years older than Lank Dodge.

5   The 1880 Census, Reuben Dodge's occupation was a plasterer. It also records his father born in NY and his mother in PA.

6   Macassar oil was by far the most popular hair conditioning product of the time.

7   In Gladys Sheldon (b. Dodge) memoire, "Smiling Through the Tears", she states that her parents, Lank and Julina met at the county fair. No other details were explained.

8   Although Julina lived in Ada, Hardin Co, OH, Lank and Julina's marriage certificate states that they married in Hancock Co, OH. Lank's grandmother, Nancy, died in Hancock County and all indications point to the family residing there. The county seat for Hancock County was 24 miles north of Ada in Findlay. In 1885, when natural gas and oil was discovered the Ohio Legislature authorized construction on a new courthouse in Findlay. It consisted of unique architectural and eclectic stylings, with ornately tiled floors, floral motif stained glass and imposing early Victorian original woodwork.

9   Lank Dodge and Julina Davis m.10-29-1891, in Hancock Co, OH. Julina's wedding dress is an unknown detail.

10 In Gladys Sheldon (b. Dodge), "Smiling Through the Tears" she recounts how her father and Uncle were "*quite stinkers*" and broke into a rich farmers meat house to steal pork. Whether it was a prank on their part, or an actual robbery is unclear. Gladys writes about it in a lighthearted way, but on the other hand, the law was after them and they fled.

Chapter 29 - Lank and Julina Dodge
1895-1909

1   In Gladys Sheldon (b. Dodge) memoir, "Smiling Through the Tears", she says that she was 21 months older than her baby brother. She was born June 28, 1893. Her baby brother was most likely born in March or April 1895.

2   The means by which Julina Dodge and two young children traveled to northern Michigan is unknown. Gladys Sheldon mentions in her book that her father

"*sent for us*". Since Lank was running from the law, he would not have returned to Ohio to accompany his family.

3   We do not know whether the dancehall was in Alanson, Oden or elsewhere.

4   The 1895 Oden house that <u>Lank and Julina</u> burned to the ground, taking everything, they owned. They lived in a boxcar for a while with their two small children, until moving over a dance hall, where their baby son died. The cause of death regarding baby Freddy is unknown, as is the date. <u>Gladys</u> states in her book that her baby brother lived six months, twenty-one days. Calculations indicate that he died in late autumn 1895.

5   Speculation as to Lank's feelings of responsibility.

6   The Union Congress passed the Homestead Act, allowing an adult over the age of twenty-one, male or female, to claim up to 160 acres of land from public domain. Eligible persons had to cultivate the land and improve it by building a barn or a house and live on the claim for five years, at which time the land became theirs. With a $10 filing fee. In this case the property was not occupied and evidently there was no legal claim on the land, making it eligible for homesteading, even though there was a house on the property.

7   The actual name of this tough "lumbering lady" is unknown.

8   1903.

9   1905.

10   How <u>Gladys</u> met Dale Flick is unknown, but his family lived in Alanson.

11   This horse's actual name was "Babe", but since Lank and Julina referred to Gladys as "Babe", the name "Bess" was chosen here.

12   The location of the marriage is unknown other than it was in Detroit. The 1910 Census has Dale Flick, 22, head of household, living in "Detroit Ward 17, Wayne, Michigan", with <u>Gladys Flick (Sheldon, b. Dodge)</u>, 16 yrs. old. It also lists <u>Melanchthon</u>, 37, and <u>Julina P. Dodge</u>, 35, as in-laws living at the same address. Two lodgers (married couple) are also included; Wales W., 24, and Helen B Aldrich, 21, both born from Ohio.

Chapter 30- Gladys faces Difficult Choices
1910-1918

1   It is almost a certainty that <u>Lank and Julina</u> moved to Ada around the time <u>Gladys</u> had her first child, Blaine, b. 9-3-1910. In her memoir, <u>Gladys</u> states, "*My folks moved to Ohio and I was married at this time with one baby.*" The timeline here is confusing. Census and death records indicate that all three Flick babies were born in Ohio. Family tradition has always believed the boys were born in Alanson, Michigan. The 1920 Census states that they were born in Ohio, although John and Mary Flick would have provided that information and speculation holds that they may have lied in a misguided attempt to keep <u>Gladys</u>

from claiming the boys in the future. Blaine's death certificate also states that he was born in Ohio. The 1913 U.S. City Directories have <u>Gladys Flick</u> living in Petoskey, Michigan. Gale, b.1913 and Doug, b.1915. <u>Gladys</u> maintained that each baby boy lived with <u>Lank and Julina</u> after birth, to protect them from being exposed to TB. Dale was buried in the Littlefield Twp. Cemetery Alanson, MI, November 1916.

2   Blaine's middle name in some records is listed as "Morton", but since Dale's middle name was "Martin", it can be assumed that the middle name is indeed "Martin". He died in a farming accident on May 28, 1920 at 9 years old, in Richland Twp., Kalamazoo, MI. Buried in Littlefield Cemetery, Alanson, MI.

3   <u>Sarah "Sadie" Davis (b. Wingate)</u> d. 8-28-1917, (85 yrs.). She died from pneumonia with contributing factors: sprained hip. She lived six years after the passing of her husband <u>William Washington Davis</u>. <u>William</u> died of a stroke (81 yrs.).

4   <u>Reuben Dodge</u> d. 11-30-1920, (88 yrs.). He lived eight years after the passing of his wife <u>Lucy Ann "Anna" Dodge (b. Shaffer)</u>.

5   Prohibition began in 1916 and lasted until 1933.

6   <u>Gladys</u> describes her *"love affair with the Sheldon boy"*. *"I fairly worshipped <u>Leslie</u>."*

Chapter 31 - Gladys and Leslie
1918-1919

1   <u>Gladys</u> states in her memoir, "Smiling Through the Tears", that, *"[<u>Leslie</u>] wasn't too crazy about children. He wasn't even crazy about having his own."*

2   Speculation that they were married in the courthouse and not in a church.

3   According to Earl Sheldon's June 5, 1917 Draft Registration he was single and worked as a brakeman at "Overland Auto Co". Brand name was "Willys" (Willys-Overland Motor Company), known for its design and production of military jeeps. 1912-1918 it was the 2nd-largest producer of automobiles in the country.

4   Although The Great War (later known as World War I) had begun in Europe in 1914, it wasn't until April 6, 1917 that the United States joined its British, French and Russian allies. The level of confusion was high in the first twelve months, with the systematic mobilization of the entire population and the economy to produce soldiers, food supplies, munitions and money. More than two million U.S. soldiers fought on battlefields in France and western Europe. Some 50,000 lost their lives. Germany ultimately surrendered, November 11, 1918.

5   Merton (or Martin) Smith, b. 1881, m. Alice Sheldon (<u>Leslie</u>'s sister) 4-17-1902. He was the son of <u>Frank Smith</u> and Frank's first wife, Eveline Panghorn. NOTE: Frank, 42 years old, re-married to Nina Smith (b. Croff), 15 yr. Frank

and Nina Smith's first child was a daughter, <u>Sylvia Augusta Smith</u> (half-sister to Merton Smith). <u>Sylvia</u> was the mother of <u>Herman Casper "Jerry" Smeltzer</u>. <u>Jerry</u> married <u>Beatrice Lavonne Sheldon</u>, Leslie and Gladys's seventh child (sixth girl). Seth Smith (<u>Sylvia's</u> brother, Jerry's uncle and Merton's half-brother) was good friends with Earl Sheldon. They grew up together in Alanson and when Seth died, alone, in Toledo, Earl signed as the "informant" on Seth's death certificate.

6   According to <u>Julina's</u> death certificate, <u>Julina</u> died from "subluxation" (dislocation of a joint or organ) "peritonitis", (serious infection in the abdomen) tinnitus from pustule...infection in the abdomen. "Cause unknown". Peritonitis can be caused by any number of reasons, ruptured stomach ulcer or appendix, as well as Crohn's disease, pancreatitis or diverticulitis. She died at Robinwood Hospital in Toledo, Ohio on May 10, 1919, at 2pm. <u>Julina</u> was 46 yrs. and 4 days.

7   While Dale Flicks younger sister, Fanabel, was <u>Leslie's</u> age, born the same year, it is conjecture that there was any trouble between them. The fact that the Flicks had a special dislike of Leslie, led to the speculation of a slight of some type.

8   <u>Gladys</u> states in her memoir, "Smiling Through the Tears" that her dad, <u>Lank</u>, moved back to Alanson *"right away"* after her mother died in May and she and <u>Leslie</u> moved back in June or July. She also states that Leslie got a job at the Michigan Block Factory. They made maple blocks. They moved into *"rented light housekeeping rooms"* in Petoskey. The 1920 Census has them living in Alanson, so they must have moved back to Alanson after the summer of 1919.

Chapter 32 - Joy and Heartache
1919-1936

1   The actual name of the store owner is unknown.

2   That afternoon was the last time <u>Gladys</u> would see her boys until Gale was seventeen years old when he visited her in 1930, eleven years later.

3   The roller is an agricultural tool used to flatten land or break up large chunks of soil, especially after plowing or harrowing. Prior to mechanism, rollers were pulled by a team of animals such as oxen or horses.

4   The 18th Amendment and the Volstead Act did not make it illegal to drink alcohol, only to manufacture and sell it. Many people stockpiled liquor before the ban went into effect on 1-20-1920. The federal Volstead Act closed every bar, tavern and saloon in the United States, driving the liquor trade underground until the 21st Amendment was adopted in 1933.

5   Lank re-married to Mabel Emans the same year that she divorced her husband, Stephen Emans. Mabel and <u>Lank</u> (54 yr.) m. 11-30-1925 in Painesville, Ohio.

They moved to Cadillac, Michigan according to the Census. By 1940, they were back in Alanson. They divorced 5-12-1944. <u>Lank</u> died in 1948 (76 yrs.).

6   The timeline as to when <u>Lank</u> was a river boat captain is unknown. In a photo taken of the Buckeye Belle, it mentions Lank as captain, husband of <u>Julina P. Davis</u>. This job was earlier in his life than portrayed in this narrative.

7   Martha Belle Sheldon was born January 30, 1931 in Alanson, Michigan.

8   <u>Beatrice LaVonne Sheldon</u> was born February 3, 1933 in Petoskey, Michigan. She was originally named some long-forgotten name, until Leslie realized that she was born on his baby sister Beatrice's birthday. He rushed down to the courthouse and changed her name in honor of his sister.

9   The 1929 crash was caused by an excessively bullish, overvalued and overbought market coupled with an imbalance of supply and demand. The October 29, 1929, "Black Tuesday" crash bottomed out in 1932. FDR's New Deal programs and America's involvement in WWII would help bring the U.S. out of the Great Depression, that would take more than a decade.

10   The fireside chats were a series of evening radio addresses given by the U.S. President Franklin D. Roosevelt ("FDR") between 1933 and 1944. FDR spoke with familiarity to millions of Americans about the Emergency Banking Act in response to the banking crisis, the recession, New Deal initiatives, and the course of World War II. On radio, he was able to quell rumors and explain his policies. His tone and demeanor communicated self-assurance during times of despair and uncertainty. (Wikipedia)

11   <u>Beatie</u>, in a book of her memories, mentions the first dog she remembers was named Brownie. Later, Buck was a favorite dog of the entire family. A smart dog, who would play hide and seek with the children. It was a horrible day when the sheriff came to the door and said that Buck had been killing sheep with a pack of dogs and they were ordered to put him down.

12   <u>Leslie</u> worked for the WPA (Works Progress Administration; renamed the Works Projects Administration in 1939). It was an American New Deal agency established on May 6, 1935, employing millions of jobseekers to carry out public works projects, including construction of public buildings, parks and roads. It dissolved on June 30, 1943, after the country recovered satisfactorily from the Great Depression.

13   By the mid-1920's the Model-T dropped in sales, as competition arose, giving consumers more choices. It quickly became considered old-fashioned and the butt of jokes. Ford announced in 1927 that Model-T's discontinued and the Model-A debuted in December 1927. Production ended in 1932.

14   In all likelihood Dr. Edward Mitchell was not the attending physician, although possible. "Pocket Directory & Yearbook of Alanson & Vicinity 1938".

15   Story conveyed by Josephine Gladys (Joie) Deits (b. Sheldon). Joie was born after her twin Julina Lee (Judy) Sheldon. She was covered in a film, which meant that

she was gifted, according to old time tradition. Indeed, of the eight girls and one boy born to <u>Gladys and Leslie</u>, Joie, the last child born, was the only one to inherit <u>Gladys's</u> gift of music. She could play the piano by ear in the same style as her mother.

Chapter 33 - Leslie and Gladys, The Grievous Years
1937-1947

1   The Sheldons bought 40 acres for $50 in approximately 1938 and built the stone house. Two years later they added 40 acres adjoining their property for $80.

2   This was recounted by <u>Beatie</u> to her daughter.

3   Records and personal notes indicate that <u>Leslie</u> retired from the Oden State Fish Hatchery after twenty years. Best guess is that he began between 1940-1945, if he retired at age sixty-five. He built his own hatchery with a benefactor named "Holiday" from Harbor Springs in 1959/60. A year later the man died, and his children sold their shares to <u>Leslie</u>. Judy bought the fish hatchery from her dad, <u>Leslie</u>, in 1965, when <u>Leslie</u> was diagnosed with colon cancer, which spread to his liver.

4   Oral tradition has it that Bertha worked in an office and Leslie called her so much that she feared that she might lose her job. It is not known what kind of office. Stear's Cafe is taken from the "Directory and Yearbook of Alanson, Michigan, 1938", From the same source, Frank Armstrong is named as manager of the Citizen's Finance Company of that same year. There is no intention to implicate Mr. Armstrong as having any interest in Bertha. The comment is only meant to identify <u>Leslie's</u> jealousy.

5   The details and timing of Paul's disclosure of what he witnessed (his father and Bertha parked alongside the road) to his sisters is unknown. Conjecture is used to explain the progression of events as far as informing the sisters. It is known that Paul told his married sisters, and he did not tell his mother. It is also known that the older sisters did not tell their mother or the younger sisters.

Chapter 34 - Betrayal
1947

1   The progression of the events that took place on this Sunday and the sermon are complete conjecture.

2   After the confession, which occurred sometime between 1947-1950, <u>Gladys and Leslie</u> began attending the Pentecostal church in Petoskey, until 1953, when Brother Keeler finally convinced them to return to the Alanson church. Any quotes attributed to Brother Keeler are strictly conjecture.

Chapter 35 - Final Years
1947-1967

1   Information here is based on oral tradition from Joie Deits (b. Sheldon), who stated that she was still in high School when her father retired. She graduated in 1953.
2   In 1957 the television show "Have Gun Will Travel" aired on CBS.
3   Quote from Gladys's memoir "Smiling Through the Tears", paragraph titled "Our Little Church"

Final Thoughts
1   The Lessons of History, Will & Ariel Durant, Simon Schuster Paperbacks, pg. 11-12